Keith Baker is a former ~~~~~ News and Current Affairs, BBC Northern Ireland. He lives in County Down.

Also by Keith Baker

Inheritance

Reckoning

Keith Baker

First published in Great Britain in 1998
by HEADLINE BOOK PUBLISHING

First published in paperback in 1998
by HEADLINE BOOK PUBLISHING

A HEADLINE FEATURE paperback

10 9 8 7 6 5 4 3 2 1

ISBN 0 7472 5553 9

Typeset by
Letterpart Limited, Reigate, Surrey

Printed and bound in Great Britain by
Mackays of Chatham PLC, Chatham, Kent

HEADLINE BOOK PUBLISHING
A division of Hodder Headline PLC
338 Euston Road
London NW1 3BH

For Jo, Louise, Rose and Simon

Several people were gracious enough to allow me to pester them during the writing of this book. I would like to thank Patrick Culligan, the former Commissioner of the Irish police; Chief Superintendent Fachtna Murphy of the Criminal Assets Bureau in Dublin; and John Gallagher of the public relations department at Dublin Airport. I am also indebted to my good friend Dr. Johnty Calvert, the psychiatrist; to Marty Johnston, of BBC Northern Ireland, who helped me with computer problems, real and imaginary, and to Sheila Reynolds who gave me the freedom of her comfortable home on the County Antrim coast while I started to plot the story line. Finally, the wise observations of my agents, Carole Blake and Julian Friedmann, and my editor, Bill Massey at Headline, have made all the difference to the book you are about to read.

Chapter One

For a heart-stopping second Sean Donovan thought he had been shot.

Again.

In that moment instinct took over and he sprang back into the hall, slamming the door shut.

But where the hell was Vinnie? 'Come down to the front,' he had said on the mobile. 'I'll have the car there in five minutes.'

Although the door was solid and secure, Donovan leaned against it anyway, as if doing so would stop someone pushing it in. Recovering himself quickly, he realised it was the bright light that had freaked him, a sudden, searing assault on the eyes, just like the last time. He felt the side of his head, remembering, but there was no blood. No one had been shooting at him at all. He was okay.

At least two years ago, he had carried out a big warehouse robbery in a part of south Dublin where the criminal known as the Lorryman liked to operate. Except the Lorryman had decided that nobody pulled strokes on his patch without paying tribute, providing him with a cut of the proceeds. And since the rule had not been obeyed on that occasion he had sent someone to Donovan's house to kill him.

Damn near managed it, too. Caught him off guard. Far too careless he had been, before he had put the burglar alarm system in and the lights and the security cameras at the front and back doors.

The bastard had just rung the doorbell and Donovan had gone to answer it. Normally, his wife would have done that only she had left him about a month before.

Not that he wasn't glad to see the back of her, but he still missed the boy. Fintan. His wee son.

Someone was poking the letterbox open and shouting through it.

Donovan stepped away and walked backwards into the hall, putting distance between him and the voice outside.

It was all still vivid in his mind, right up until the moment when the blackness obliterated everything. There had been a flash, like now, except it had been painfully hot as the bullet scorched his temple and he went down. The gunman had fired twice more while he lay unconscious, but they were careless shots which hit him in the shoulder and the thigh and did little damage. This was not a professional, just a boy sent to do a man's job and leaving it half-done before running off into the night.

Vinnie Dwyer caught up with him a couple of months later when the Lorryman was starting a twelve-year stretch for being in possession of half the contents of a whiskey warehouse. Donovan did not know what Vinnie had done to the boy, nor had he ever asked, but Vinnie would certainly have taken his time about it, somewhere where the sounds would not have been heard, away out in the sticks.

He did know, because Vinnie had told him this much, that in the end he had bound the lad into a refuse sack, stuck him into the back of a van and driven in the blackness of the early hours to County Kildare where he had buried him in a lime pit.

But it was never entirely clear whether the boy was actually dead at the time.

The voice outside was calling his name.

'Sean Donovan. We want to talk to you.'

And where was Vinnie now? Gone to get something done to the car while he was in here under siege. He looked at his watch. Some fucking five minutes.

He knew who was outside. It was that bastard Kelly again, following him everywhere like a shadow. He realised, as well, what the flash had been: a television camera light being switched on so that they could get clearer shots of him in the gloom of the hallway.

How the hell did they know he would be here? It would make him look like a coward, diving back inside like that.

'Mr Donovan,' the voice called again, strong and assured, a broadcaster's tones. 'This is Marcus Kelly. We're from a television programme called *The Kelly Inquiry*.'

You don't say.

'We know you're there. We've already seen you opening the door. We've tried several times to make appointments with you for an interview and now we're trying to get to talk to you by other means. There are some questions we want to ask you about this property. We understand you're the owner of these premises, Mr Donovan, and that you rent it out in flats but we're also given to understand that you've not listed any income from this building in your most recent tax returns. Is that the case?'

Jesus, where the hell's he getting this stuff?

It was becoming ridiculous. Only a couple of months ago, Kelly had made a programme about him, as a result of which he was now labelled in the media as public enemy number fucking one, thank you very much. The documentary had traced his rise from robbing warehouses and selling stolen goods to becoming the leading figure in Dublin's underworld of drugs and vice.

For all of about a minute, Donovan had preened himself at the thought that he was becoming famous but reality set in very quickly. He could hardly turn a corner without a policeman stopping him on some pretext or other, always pretty slim, for in spite of his growing infamy they had not managed to come up with any charges that might stick.

But worse, the public knew his face. His heart sank every time he saw long lens shots of himself staring furtively out of the front pages whenever there was any kind of a story about crime.

After the documentary, his solicitor had written to Kelly and to the Director General of RTE, the Irish national broadcasting service, demanding immediate apologies and an indication of what sort of sum they were prepared to pay to repair the damage to his client's reputation. RTE's lawyers had written back in polite terms but the message was none the less clear: get stuffed.

The only weapon Donovan had left, short of blowing up the whole fucking television station and by Christ he felt like it sometimes, was to issue a writ for libel, which his solicitor had done on his instructions. That, at least, had kept at bay those faint-hearted newspapers who had merely been hanging on to Marcus Kelly's coat-tails, reporting at second-hand, but it had not dissuaded Kelly himself, who kept on coming in spite of this hail of protective legal fire from the trenches.

Donovan took in his surroundings. His property.

It was a late eighteenth-century Georgian terraced house with a dignified façade but through neglect and a history of dubious ownership, like its current one, it had fallen into disrepair and decay. He looked at the wallpaper, a stained and greasy yellowish brown, clinging stubbornly to the damp surface. Mould spread like an extra-terrestrial growth across the ceiling and dank odours no longer recognisable as food smells hung in the air.

It was a shit hole but it paid its way.

There were twelve flats in it, some of them no bigger than a single room, delivering him rent money every week. He had no idea how many people were crammed in here, illegal immigrants some of them, but no doubt Marcus Kelly planned to find out and tell the world.

One young woman had fallen behind with her payments, which was why Donovan had chosen to visit her this morning, although now he wished he had not bothered. Vinnie usually took care of this sort of thing but he had asked Donovan if he would handle it while he went and got the car looked at. Something to do with the ignition.

On the infrequent occasions when he came in person, Donovan always wore a well-tailored suit and expensive shoes so that these people could see how far beneath him they were. He liked the feeling of control, too, the fear on their faces when he clicked his fingers and held his hand out.

This woman owed him three weeks' rent and, apart from that, where was the money she got from the johns she brought back here or who stood her up against the wall in the alleyways nearby? She claimed she had been too sick to go out on the street and she looked like death, that was true. He had thrown her a little packet of something to straighten her out and then he had roughed her up a bit, nothing too severe, just a few slaps in the face that bled her lip a little and would not deter the customers.

He did not like it when he felt sorry for them. Pity led to weakness and Sean Donovan was not weak. He had proved that.

He had once been a user himself but he had gone cold turkey in prison when he was serving eighteen months for burglary. Sometimes it came to him in the night, the sweats and the shivering and the vomiting. The taunts of the screws, those bastards. When he came out, his sentence reduced to a year for good behaviour, he was clean and he had stayed that way ever since.

Vinnie would be back for the money tomorrow. If she did not have it, Vinnie would not be so gentle.

Marcus Kelly was not going to go away.

'Mr Donovan,' he said, 'we have information that you flew to Zurich via Amsterdam on two separate occasions in the past few months – on the fifteenth of December and on the sixth of February – and that on both occasions you had with you approximately £100,000 in cash. I'd like to ask you first if this information is correct and, second, how this money was obtained and where you were taking it.'

He had to stop this. Right now.

Hearing what Kelly was saying, the truth of it, ignited his anger and he flung the door open again. The reporter and his cameraman were caught unawares and they stepped back sharply.

There was a second while Donovan took in the scene. Kelly stood there, tall and slim in a perfect grey suit. His fair hair was sculpted in waves and it appeared to be immune to the light spring breeze. The cameraman had lifted the Sony to his shoulder once more and was focusing on his quarry. No need for the extra light now.

Passers-by paused to see what was going on. Elderly women. A man with a cap and a muzzled greyhound. Three young men with ear-rings.

Kelly began to speak, although not with the same confidence that the barricade of the door had provided. There was something about Donovan's appearance that discouraged people instantly: the stocky frame, the contradictory combination of soft rosebud lips and eyes of winter.

'Mr Donovan,' Kelly started.

Donovan lunged at him, grasping his lapels and pulling him sharply so that he fell forward with the bridge of his nose in perfect alignment when Donovan butted it hard with his head.

A blue Mazda that needed a wash was pulling up to the kerb in a hurry.

Kelly reeled back, blood pouring from his nostrils and dappling the grey suit, which was not nearly so perfect now. Donovan came at him again with a sweeping kick towards the groin. Kelly swung his body sideways and the elegant shoe hit him hard on the thigh instead. He lost his balance and fell.

There were gasps from some of the on-lookers, who had grown in number, but the lads with the ear-rings laughed and cheered. They liked a good fight, although this one looked a bit one-sided. No one did anything to help.

Kelly held his arms over his face and tried to slither out of the way across the pavement as Donovan kicked him. Anywhere his foot made contact. On the shoulder, hard in the lower back. Once, twice, three times.

He could be heard all over the street.

'I'll kill you, you bastard. You hear me? I'll fucking kill you.'

He lifted his foot again just as Vinnie Dwyer grabbed him by the shoulders and pulled him backwards. Donovan struggled but Vinnie was bigger and stronger and hauled him easily to the open passenger door of the Mazda.

'We'd better get you out of here,' he muttered.

Donovan had the window open and was shouting obscenities from it as Vinnie screeched into the traffic, forcing several other drivers to swerve out of the way.

The cameraman helped Kelly up while holding on to the Sony with one hand because he was afraid that if he put it down it would not be there when he turned round. It was that kind of street.

Kelly got to his feet and stood there swaying slightly, feeling his nose with cautious fingertips. It was broken; no doubt about it. He was a mess. His hair hung around his bloody face in lank strands and he pushed some of it back out of the way.

But in spite of everything, he wore a triumphant smile.

This would not just make it on to his own programme, it would be all over the evening news, with stills of the action being given to the daily papers who were sure to come calling when they saw the bulletin. He would have to make sure that the pictures they distributed did not make him look too undignified, although it was difficult to appear heroic when you were crawling on the ground, being kicked.

'Did you get all that?' He turned towards the cameraman and the movement hurt. Maybe a cracked rib, too.

'Certainly did.'

'Great. Now I'll do a piece to camera.'

In the car, Donovan's blood was still up and he thumped the dashboard with his fist.

'Where were you? You said you'd be here in five minutes.'

'Sorry,' Vinnie said. 'Fucking traffic.'

Donovan fell silent as his rage began to subside and then he sighed as if he had been punctured.

'Oh Christ,' he groaned. 'How the hell do I get myself out of this mess now?'

Vinnie shrugged but kept his eyes on the road.

'I don't know,' he said, although he knew for certain there was no way Donovan could.

Chapter Two

'Oh, Tom, you'll have to go,' Kate Forrest said and gripped his hand tighter as they walked. 'It's just what you need. It'll be good for you.'

They had driven a little way along the coast south of Dublin. Gallagher saw her brown eyes imploring him. He turned from her to look at the golden curve of the strand and the sparkling sea beyond.

'I'm not sure,' he said. 'It's a long time since I stood up in front of a bunch of students.'

'They'll love you. How often do these new recruits get to hear from an FBI man?'

'A has-been,' he corrected. 'All the time, for all I know.'

She ignored the self-deprecation. 'Don't be silly – they never see an FBI man at all. Even if they did, how often would they get to meet someone like you? Born and bred right here in Dublin? A distinguished career fighting crime in the United States?'

'Roll up, roll up,' he mocked. He was not having one of his better days.

Kate tugged his hand and stopped, looking up at him. There were still traces of the boy she had known and had

10

not seen for so many years. Until six months ago.

His build was the same, lanky and thin, and the lean face was not unduly lined. But she saw the younger Tom Gallagher most of all in the soft hazel eyes and in that brush of sandy hair, with its tendency to stray towards disobedience.

He looked his fifty years, she conceded, just about.

'You've got to try, Tom' she said. 'You can't hide away from the world. Okay, so you've been ill. It happens. It's not a crime, it's not your fault. You'll have to stop blaming yourself for being human like the rest of us.'

'Your brother has a lot to answer for, you know,' he grumbled, as they resumed their Sunday-morning stroll. 'If he hadn't persuaded me to write something for his damn paper, none of this would have happened.'

Alan Warnock, the features editor of *Dublin Sunday*, was the same age as Gallagher and he was Kate's older brother by six years. The three of them had grown up in a Dublin suburb together.

She gave a secret smile. He was relenting.

'So you'll do it then?'

'Yeah,' he sighed, 'I suppose so.'

She stretched up and kissed him on the cheek. 'Good for you.'

A week later, as he felt the sweat on the palms of his hands and the dryness in his throat, he was not so sure. Maybe it was normal nervousness but he never used to get like this.

He adjusted the driving seat in his Renault in order to give his legs a bit more room. He was on his way to the college at Templemore in County Tipperary where they trained recruits to the Irish police force, *an Garda Siochana* in the mother tongue, guardians of the peace. He wondered what the kids would be expecting from him. What did they think an FBI-man looked like?

If they thought they were going to get sunglasses, a dark suit and a dazzling white shirt, they were in for a disappointment. He had not worn that sort of thing for years and even then he had always managed to look slightly rumpled, which had never pleased his superiors, with their eye for neatness and uniformity and suspicion of anything that did not correspond.

They would get the accent, though. After thirty years in the United States, all trace of Dublin was gone and most people who met him simply assumed he was an American. They read it in his voice and in his clothes, wheat-coloured jackets and slacks with that Abercrombie & Fitch look about them.

He knew what they wanted to hear: tales of scams and stings and great capers we have known.

'A few anecdotes, that sort of thing,' Chief Superintendent Niall Phelan had said on the phone from Templemore. 'Some of the recruits are finishing their training and we like to have a guest to give a little talk to them, something a bit different, you know? I read the article you wrote in the paper, the one about the dangers of criminals becoming more professional and advanced if police forces didn't make the effort to stay ahead of the game. I thought it was most interesting and it struck me that you might be just the man.'

'How did you get my number?' Gallagher had asked him.

'Mr Warnock at the paper was very helpful. Said you wouldn't mind me having it.'

'I see. Look, I'll need to think about it. Check a few things in the diary. Why don't I call you in a day or so?'

Alan, damn it. Trying to rehabilitate him.

Gallagher was aware that crime was a big issue in Dublin and he had been happy enough to write an article about law enforcement. He knew that in part this was Alan's way of bringing him out of his mental hibernation and so he had gone along with it.

It was also a bit of extra cash and that would be very useful. Living in Dublin was stretching his FBI pension to the limits. As well, he had thought naïvely, print on a page had a kind of anonymity. But that perception was dispelled when he saw the by-line Warnock had given him: a former Deputy Assistant Director for New York, dealing with organised crime, law degree from Harvard, books on racketeering and money-laundering – the works.

But writing was one thing, standing up on your hind legs was another. There was certainly no anonymity there.

Kate was right; he knew that. He had to get his confidence back.

Reactive depression, the doctors in America had called it. He was coping better now and the black moods were fewer. Yet he was wary that between them Alan and Kate might be rushing him into something for which he was not quite ready.

They knew he had had a breakdown. He had made no secret of that although he had not revealed to them the depths of the guilt he suffered on sleepless nights and why he felt that way.

He had come back home to Dublin to search for the warmth of times long past but it had been hard to find. There were few acquaintances still around from the old days but he had always kept in touch with Alan Warnock. Theirs was a friendship which each man took for granted. It could be picked up and put down at any time and it was not remotely affected by long periods in which there was no contact between them at all.

Meeting Kate after a lifetime had given him an unexpected boost. It had done more for him than all the tablets and the counselling and the group therapy sessions he had gone through in New York. She had been a revelation. Gone was the shy fourteen-year-old he had remembered. In her place was a confident, attractive woman with chocolate eyes and a smile that was an embrace and as he had learned more about her, the tragedy in her own life and the battles she had fought, his admiration for her had grown.

Admiration? Not much of a word, that. You admire a painting, a view, Abraham Lincoln. You look at them from a distance, marvel briefly at the act of creation and then you move on to something else.

He had reached the plains of Kildare, the home of the Irish national stud, flat and even and almost golden. It was not yet nine am and the sun had been reluctant to brighten but it was beginning to do so at last. A veil of mist slipped slowly away, revealing a landscape that appeared almost empty, but as he looked to his right he saw two riders away in the distance taking a pair of colts for a liberated morning gallop.

He did not view Kate from afar but altogether closer.

They had met at a dinner party at her brother's house and they had begun seeing each other shortly afterwards. In the months since then their relationship and his feelings towards her had grown.

She was an exceptional woman.

She was in her forties and she had already been a widow for ten years.

One warm May evening, her husband had driven his car off a pier and into the Irish Sea. No explanation, a complete mystery. Such a nice man, everyone said, shocked when they heard, kind neighbour, great company, ran a travel agency which had three or four branches. A lovely wife and a young son, Paul, aged about seven.

At the inquest, there had been an open verdict. It was not foul play; it might have been an accident. Suicide was the most likely conclusion. But why?

Kate found the answer, not long after, when she uncovered the layers of debt shoring up the business, debts which she had known nothing about and which he had managed to conceal behind a façade of prosperity which had cost him a fortune to maintain: a BMW each, expensive clothes, exclusive golf club membership and frequent fabulous holidays.

When the shock and the pain had eased, she felt angry at being duped and she became consumed with guilt at having taken part in his charade, even though hers had been an unwitting contribution. But gradually she had buried these feelings under a layer of resolve and she had taken charge of her life, determined not to let everything go down.

There had to be sacrifices, of course, hard decisions to

be faced. She had to close all the branches of the company except one, paying off the staff, and then she had sold the extravagant family home in Dalkey. She found a smaller place at Ranelagh for her and Paul and bit by bit, year by year, making slow but firm progress, she had got to grips with the problem.

At the same time, she had developed the business out of the one remaining branch to a level beyond anything her husband had ever achieved with several. Budget Irish-American holiday deals became her speciality, there was an alliance with a French group specialising in visits to *l'Ile d'Emeraude* and she ran guided cultural tours of Dublin which had been over-subscribed ever since a glossy magazine with an international circulation had run a feature on them.

Gallagher marvelled at how she had done it. But there had been a cost, perhaps inevitably. So much pressure. So many emotions not released. A tragic loss that she had not had time to cope with properly.

When the horizons were brightening, the drinking started. Not just social drinking, but the eye-opening kind in the mornings after the trade fair the night before. But that was in the past now. She had beaten that, too.

And what of his own scars, the things he concealed, even from this woman in whom he had found he could confide so much else?

Perhaps not today.

An orange sign in a hedge told him there were major road works ahead. It was a familiar message. It seemed as if every road in Ireland was being dug up by Caterpillar excavators and men in yellow hard-hats. A fortune in

European Union money was being spent in a hurry before the EU reviewed Ireland's grant status and decided that the country's economy was strong enough for it to find the funds from within.

He hit another round of ruts and potholes, negotiating a chicane of traffic cones, until finally the road was blocked altogether and there was an incomprehensible detour that seemed to be taking him back the way he had come. He followed it anyway until eventually, as he saw from the map unfolded on the passenger seat beside him, it led to a virtually parallel road that would take him in roughly the right direction.

This was even narrower and more winding than the one before. It reminded him of roads along the coast in northern Maine, up near the Canadian border.

There was a tractor and trailer ahead and neither room to pass it nor visibility beyond. He would just have to be patient. He turned the radio on, avoiding the talkative egos which occupied RTE's morning schedule, and searched for something else.

On one local station, a reporter was interviewing homeless people in Dublin. There was a girl, barely articulate, describing being thrown out of her flat on a housing estate by vigilantes who accused her of dealing in drugs, which, of course, was a lie, she said. Gallagher thought she sounded stoned but he continued to listen.

It was one of those programmes without artifice, with a presenter who did not impose but let the voices speak for themselves. Gradually he became immersed in it.

There were interviews with people who slept each night on the floor of a derelict building which had once been a mental hospital. One of them was a young man with a baby.

'*No, I'm on nothing at the moment. I was on the heroin, like, but I'm trying to stay away from it. It's hard, though; so many people offering you gear all the time. But I've got the baby to look after.*'

'*And the mother?*'

'*Don't know where she is now. Disappeared, you know? I just carry the wee fella around with me. Nothing else for it. There's no money for a pram or anything like that. Begging in O'Connell Street. That's what I do. Try to scrape a few bob together to feed him.*'

The programme finished and a commercial slot came on.

There was a woman's voice, warm and comforting. '*Wake up each day to Ireland's number one breakfast cereal . . .*'

A man sounding trustworthy. '*Need a mortgage? Then all you have to do is pick up the phone and call . . .*'

The tractor had gone and Gallagher had reached a village. An old man with a pipe and a stick sat outside a pub with window boxes full of spring flowers and gave him a cheery wave as he passed.

It was hard to believe that all of this was the same country.

Half an hour later he arrived at Templemore. The town was one main street that looked two hundred yards wide. Cattle would have been herded up and down it once upon a time but these days they came through in high-sided trucks, protesting loudly about their cramped circumstances. The middle of the street was used as a parking zone but there was no order to it and the vehicles had been abandoned at crazy angles.

An old stone building stood in the centre, the Urban District Council offices, Gallagher saw as he approached. His eye was drawn to two engraved stones set into the wall of the building. One commemorated the men from the area who had died in the 1914-18 war.

It's a long way to Tipperary.

There it was, a reminder of what the old song was all about: the sorrow of young men who might never come home.

Others had taken part in a different struggle. The second memorial was to those who had died in the years to 1922 when they had fought the British and then their fellow countrymen in the bloody conflict which had led to the founding of the Irish Free State.

The police college itself was a historical footnote. A well-maintained former British Army barracks with bleached stone walls and a clock tower, it stood at the end of a long residential avenue. The trees which lined each side had undergone extensive surgery recently and the stumps of amputated branches were still white and unweathered.

He thought of the roads in the woods around Quantico, in Virginia, where the FBI and other agencies trained, the high security which protected its secrets. Here things were simpler. There were open iron gates and just beyond them a slim, wooden barrier being attended by a young woman in a police overcoat and cap.

She directed him to where he could park. As he got out and stretched to ease the stiffness of the journey, three young men in green tracksuits passed him carrying sports bags. They were like recruits everywhere, short-haired, eager and pink with health.

'You're very welcome,' a hearty voice said.

He turned to see Chief Superintendent Phelan striding towards him. The college was under the command of an Assistant Commissioner but it was Phelan's job to run it. He had the weathered features of a man who preferred to spend his time out of doors. He was heavier and younger than Gallagher but they were eye to eye as they shook hands.

'We're so grateful you've taken the trouble to come and see us,' he said as he led the way to his office in the main building.

A secretary was waiting to pour coffee.

'I hope it won't be too much of an ordeal for you,' Phelan said.

'Maybe just a glass of water?' Gallagher asked, aware of a faint fluttering in his stomach. He forced a smile and looked at Phelan. 'No, I'm looking forward to it.'

He sat down in an armchair and the secretary left the room.

'It was my idea,' Phelan said when she had closed the door. He lowered his voice to share a confidence. 'My boss – well, he's a bit unadventurous, you might say. He wasn't exactly sold on the idea of having you here but I told him we needed to expose our young people to the reality of the wider world, how international gangs operate, how experiences in law enforcement beyond these shores might have a bearing on them and, well, maybe to hear a few stories from someone who's been there and seen it and done it all.'

'And got the tee-shirt,' Gallagher added.

'The very thing. The people you'll meet are coming to the end of their training so this is a bit of a wind-down for them, a little bonus. Now – I should tell you there'll be a few officers from other patches here as well, Dublin, Cork and Limerick. They're around today to see how the recruits are getting on. I hope you don't mind if they sit in?'

'No problem,' Gallagher said. This was a nightmare.

Phelan suggested a short walk round the college before the session started. He was on his feet before Gallagher put his empty glass down.

The tour helped Gallagher's nerves because he found himself in surroundings that were reassuringly familiar. The centre had been refurbished at the end of the eighties and although it had nothing like the acreage or the budget of Quantico it was nevertheless a pretty well-constructed facility. He told Phelan so.

By way of returning the compliment as well as reinforcing it, Phelan took him first to the specialist library where Gallagher was flattered to find on the shelves a tome dealing with the subject of the economics of organised crime, a textbook to which he had contributed a section himself.

Next they looked in on the teaching areas which included a mock courtroom and a scene-of-the-crime room, fully furnished, with chalk marks still on the floor from the last exercise held there. They meandered on into the television studio, the language laboratory, the computer room, the printing unit and then the gym, until they were outdoors again.

Gallagher could hear gunfire dampened by sound-proofing. In places like this it punctuated every activity. At the entrance to the indoor range they donned ear protectors. Inside, half a dozen recruits were practising with hand-guns. These, Phelan explained when they emerged again, were the raw material just starting their training. He knew his guest would have observed the scattergun groupings and the need for improvement.

He had organised the main lecture room for Gallagher's talk and they went there at last. About eighty trainees, young men and women in blue shirts, chattered to each other and doodled on the pads in front of them while they waited. They stood as Gallagher and Phelan entered but Phelan waved to them to sit again.

The front row had not stood at all and Gallagher saw that it was occupied by half a dozen men in suits. The visiting firemen in the VIP seats. No women, he noted, although there were about twenty among the recruits.

He felt his nervousness returning. His brow was a little clammy but he did not want to be seen wiping it.

As Phelan introduced him, he tried to take his mind off his anxiety by scanning the faces of the youngsters and attempting to guess their background. Which of them, he wondered, came from a long line of policemen, running back to the foundation of the State and maybe beyond? Was there a future Commissioner in this room? Who of their number would get into detective work?

One or two might drop out, leave the force altogether. Some might get killed in the line of duty.

It had been known to happen.

A fingernail tapped on the windowpane of remembrance.

22

There was courteous applause as Phelan finished his introduction and then Gallagher got up to speak, taking his notes from an inside pocket and praying that the pages would not tremble when he turned them.

But at the last moment, looking at his opening words, he made a detour he had not expected. Just like his journey.

He began to tell them about the radio programme he had heard in the car.

'I guess it was meant to be about poverty and homelessness but it really wasn't about that at all. Drugs – that's what it was about. And what kind of shocked me was the fact that there was an underlying theme that was almost taken for granted. It's as if rampant drug addiction is just one of those problems we've given up on, that we can't do much about. Like – I don't know – the weather, maybe.'

He looked around the room. His inner fears had begun to disperse and as he continued he felt at ease and in control.

'Behind every nickel and dime bag being sold on a street corner, there's somebody who cut the stuff and put it in those bags. And then there's the guy who supplied it to him. And behind that supplier there's the importer who got it loaded off a ship somewhere. And behind him again, there's somebody in Spain or Amsterdam who's operating the export network.

'And how did he establish that network? With the help of the big cartels in Colombia or the Far East and their associates, and believe me, these guys are in bed with people of cut-glass respectability. Big business chains, large corporations of success and reputation, boards of directors and share-holders, the majority of whom know

23

nothing of the billions of pounds and dollars of dirty money which flow in all directions through vast and complex banking systems, into one account and out again, all the time being washed and dried and laundered impeccably so that the origins are completely obscured.

'And those origins are the small sums of money, multiplied over and over again, which have been paid for a bag of what do they call it here – *gear?*' – he saw some nods – 'mixed with aspirin, flour, God knows what else, and sold by a dealer with a mobile phone standing on O'Connell Bridge.'

He paused, hearing the slight echo of his own raised voice dying away in the big room. This was not exactly what they had been expecting to hear but if these young people were to be any good, they had to know what they were up against. Still, he did not want to sound like some hell-and-damnation preacher.

He came back on course, finding that he did not need his notes to chart the way. He gave them a thumbnail sketch of the FBI, what its role was, what it could and could not do, how it was not to be confused with the CIA or the DEA or the Secret Service or any of the other agencies. Then he told them stories about famous FBI operations in history, from Dillinger via the Cold War to the present day, including some of the cases in which he himself had been involved, particularly in the area of money-laundering schemes and organised crime.

'Laundering's not new. It's been around at least since Al Capone. He had a string of car washes which did the job for him. What are known as service fronts are still an effective cover. Restaurants, jewellery stores, bars – they all deal in cash and they make substantial deposits in the banks each day. If you have your own service front you can hide drugs money very easily. The Colombian cartels are a stage further on, of course. They've got commercial real estate, restaurants, TV and radio stations. They own manufacturing and retail businesses, some of them world wide.'

He told them about the great secrecy havens – Switzerland, the Netherlands Antilles, the Cayman Islands, Liechtenstein – about dummy corporations and the byzantine loan-back systems which criminals had devised to cover their tracks.

'Suppose you're a launderer living in Dublin with a million dollars of drugs profits stashed away in a bank in Zurich. It would be nice to get your hands on some of it but you can't because the authorities in Ireland would kind of wonder where all this wealth came from, wouldn't they?

'However, you've also taken the trouble to register a couple of companies in Switzerland. One of them has a bank account with the drugs cash in it and the other company is a fake finance outfit. You arrange for the bank holding your million bucks in the name of the drugs company to lend your phoney finance outfit a million dollars, using the million in the drugs account as collateral for the loan. With me so far?'

There were nods although he was not entirely sure that all of them were.

'Our launderer here in Dublin is an apparently respectable figure and the phoney finance outfit lends him a million dollars to purchase a legitimate business. The business gives him a legitimate source of income and he uses the profits from this to repay the loan to the fake finance company – which, in fact, is himself.'

He paused to let them work it all out.

'And that's one of the simple ones.'

They smiled. He went on, into wire transfers, currency exchanges, stocks and bonds. Even the internet could be used. There was not much he did not know about the subject and with each area he came up with a real illustration.

The one that tickled them most was the case in which the FBI had uncovered a ring of twenty elderly women travelling regularly to big cities where there were hundreds of banks. Each woman had a shopping bag of cash and each bought money orders and drafts for under $10,000.

'Enormous amounts of drugs money were successfully dropped this way. They also each made three deposits a week of $8,000 at six different banks and at the end of a year they had laundered $150 million.'

He told them of undercover operations, stake-outs, delicate surveillance operations which went on for weeks and sometimes months, wire taps on houses and business premises, and he observed the wide-eyed eagerness that he had seen in the faces of many of their kind before, a barely restrainable enthusiasm to be in the thick of it.

He came to the end and threw the proceedings open. Nothing had changed over the years. As ever, the questions were of the most basic kind, including the inevitable – Did you ever meet J. Edgar Hoover? To which the answer was no, not formally, although he had once been at a meeting Hoover had held in Washington near the end of his career, when Gallagher had been a very junior agent just starting out.

'I think I was just somebody's bag carrier that day,' he said.

Somebody asked about the *X-Files* on TV and no, there was no special unit involved in investigating paranormal activity, as far as he was aware.

'Although if there was, I guess I'd have to deny it, wouldn't I?'

But there was a question, too, from one of the visitors in the front row. Gallagher had noticed him already, a grey-faced man with sceptical eyes and hair like corn stubble. He had been shifting restlessly in his seat throughout Gallagher's talk.

'We've heard a lot about the FBI's great successes,' he said, 'and especially your own. But did nothing ever go wrong? Is there anything you would do differently if you got another chance?'

There was a sneer there. Everybody heard it.

Gallagher looked at the hard face. Although the man could not know it, he had hit close to home.

He smiled the thought away. 'Maybe I'd ask for a note of the questions in advance.'

There was a ripple of amusement but his questioner did not join in.

'Of course, there are things you'd do differently,' Gallagher said. 'Of course, not everything's a success. And yes – things do go wrong and sometimes people get killed. If I had a free hand to change things, I'd do more about the major players who are operating now on an almost unimaginable scale. The world of organised crime is becoming even more organised while we stand here talking about it. We do our best within the limits of the law but maybe those limits don't extend far enough.'

'What does that mean?' the man said.

Gallagher stretched his arms out to his audience as if appealing to them for assistance.

'The sort of people I'm talking about aren't the little old ladies with their shopping bags of cash but the organisations behind them. Some of these people control more funds than the entire Irish national economy. You can't get to grips with them with the kind of laws we have now.

'The best way to combat them is to disrupt them. These people depend on the flow of money. If you can interfere with that flow somehow, then you begin to cause them big problems, you start them getting paranoid about each other. Use sabotage tactics, guerrilla warfare, if you like, start wars among them.'

'Covert activity?' the man said. 'I thought the CIA had the franchise on that.'

'Can you think of a better way? If you're going to wait for them to make a mistake, then you'll wait forever. These guys don't even pick up traffic violations. They can navigate their way around every law that's ever been devised.'

He looked at his opponent and waited for a rejoinder but it did not come. There were a few additional questions and then Phelan drew matters to a close.

'Sorry about that,' he said, as he led the way to lunch. 'A hot-shot from Dublin.'

'Don't worry,' Gallagher told him. He felt uplifted by the exchange, a bit of cut-and-thrust. It had refreshed him.

They were interrupted in the corridor by a couple of trainees. That was a familiar part of the routine, too: lousy questions at first and then they came to you afterwards with things that would take a month's research to answer.

The lunch itself was a finger buffet in a hospitality room adorned with plaques and trophies as well as photographs of presidents and prime ministers visiting the college. A group of the students had been invited and one of them took him off round the room, introducing him to some of the instructors.

As Gallagher's elation subsided, he looked for the inquisitor from the front row and realised that the man was the only guest not there. He felt a hint of regret. The incident had begun to leave a sour taste.

When he drove away an hour later, with Phelan standing at the gate waving him goodbye, it struck him that he did not even know the man's name.

Chapter Three

Jerome had worked the night shift and part of the morning and now he was on his way back to the depot.

He sat waiting for the lights to change, his bare elbow resting on the open cab window-frame. Next to him there was another taxi and he looked at its driver, a wild-eyed Ethiopian in a funky woollen hat. A picture of Haile Selassie hung from his mirror. By contrast, Jerome wore wrap-around shades and a black DKNY tee-shirt of the finest cotton because if he was going to sit in this taxi all day he might as well look cool and feel cool.

He had become a part-time cab-driver to help put himself through medical school, after which he would go back home and become the best surgeon Kingston had ever seen. Jerome was part of no herd. He was Jamaican but he was not into all that lion from Zion shit. As if to proclaim this to the world, he stuck a tape into the dashboard deck and turned the volume up high.

Vivaldi's 'Four Seasons' burst out joyously on to Fifth Avenue and swirled around the opposing armies of pedestrians crossing in front of him. The music caught the ear of one or two and they turned to look at the yellow vehicle with its dented front fender and the driver nodding his head in time.

He saw a frown of confusion drift across the face of one white woman as she took in the conflicting image being presented to her but he just smiled a broad Jamaican smile as she passed.

'Have a nice day,' he called after her.

The last stragglers reached the kerb as the lights changed and the 'Don't walk' sign came on. Jerome turned the player down and slipped the car into gear.

He was gunning the accelerator when a man stepped off the pavement in front of him. He braked with a screech. Behind, horns blared their indignation.

The offender stepped back into safety. Jerome thrust his head out the window and glowered at him. An old guy, deaf maybe.

'Hey man,' he shouted, waving angrily. 'You wanna get yourself killed?'

The pedestrian turned his head slowly and looked at him and there was something about the way he stared, the steadiness of the gaze, that spooked Jerome a little so that as he drove on he was more subdued and what he had to say he delivered almost as advice, rather than as a warning.

'You want to be careful where you walk, you know?'

The man's eyes followed the progress of the vehicle, watching it merge into the traffic and disappear among the stream of yellow cabs. Then he resumed his journey. He would cross further on up.

Gilbert Leslie was on his way to a meeting. He could have taken a taxi from Grand Central but he preferred to walk since it was not all that far to where he was going and anyway it might have meant getting a cab and a driver like that one.

These people. Their smell. The dregs of the earth lived in the city now and he was glad he did not do so any more. He had lived on the lower east side when he first came to this country but now his home was in the altogether more pleasant environment of Westchester county.

His real name was Gabor Laszlo. He had been born in Hungary in 1937 but he had anglicised himself with a kind of alphabetical cosmetic surgery not long after arriving from Budapest in the brutal winter of 1956. His English was fluent, although perhaps a touch formal in its construction, and his accent was still inlaid with traces of Europe which people found hard to place precisely.

Some thought Italian, perhaps Greek. Leslie did nothing to enlighten them.

To the outside world he was a retired investor living on a private pension and the secure but modest income which his prudent investments had provided. His finances would stand up to any scrutiny, as indeed they had done at various times in the past when the Internal Revenue Service, encouraged by the FBI, had turned its attention to him.

But no IRS examination could reveal the true extent of his wealth, nor would it ever expose the funds held securely in bank accounts in the Netherlands Antilles and on the island of Gibraltar and totalling approximately $17 million.

The man walking along Fifth Avenue this morning did not look like a multi-millionaire, nor did he really think of himself as one. His clothes were of good quality but were not extravagant in appearance. In fact, they fitted him in more senses than one. They were unremarkable.

You passed Gilbert Leslie on the street but there was nothing about him that drew your eye his way, nothing distinctive about his presence that you would note and store in your memory, and that was how he preferred it. Only when you had reason to stop and stare, as Jerome the cab-driver had found himself doing just a few minutes ago, did you see the ice that sometimes formed in the pale grey eyes.

There were some women, on the other hand, who had had occasion to spend time in his company over the years and had found those eyes fascinating, not intimidating at all. But perhaps it was that very thing, the veiled suggestion of some inner power, which had drawn them.

He felt warm in the overcoat he had put on just in case it got chilly in the city. It was still only early March. But this morning Manhattan seemed to have decided that spring had arrived. The sky was an outrageous blue and a golden sun flashed its dazzling reflection from the glass towers.

Two years ago, when he last met all these people together, it had been winter . . .

They came out of the darkness and into the discreet and elegant little mid-town hotel, stubbing the snow from their shoes before making their way up to the room which had been arranged.

There were six of them, all men of power and influence. They controlled banks and business conglomerates but they each had wealth greater than anything their legitimate enterprises could provide.

Leslie's plan would make them even richer.

Their leader, Michael Grant, arrived first. Not yet forty, he was the head of a major Wall Street investment firm. Playing squash kept him supple and fit and he did not allow alcohol to dim the sparkle in his blue eyes. With his careful clothes and his dignified manner, he was a symbol of east coast establishment ways. But more than Yale and Wall Street had forged him. The blood of his mother flowed in his veins.

And his mother had the blood of Sicily.

Leslie shook hands with the members of the group, renewing acquaintances, knowing some of them felt uncomfortable in his presence. He embodied something from which they were far removed, hermetically sealed in their fine offices, but they were nevertheless content to receive the enormous proceeds that came their way.

They gathered round a table and Grant called the meeting to order.

'Gentlemen, thank you for coming,' he said when they were seated, ashtrays located and glasses refilled. 'For some time we've been pondering new ways to expand our operations world-wide, particularly in relation to Europe, and how we might devise new methods of laundering. As you know, I asked our consultant, Mr Leslie here, to explore the opportunities and I'm pleased to say that he's come up with a strategy which I think you will find very exciting indeed. Gilbert – if you would?'

Leslie got up and placed a folder in front of each of them. Inside was a copy of a glossy annual report and several sheets outlining the proposal and what it would yield. He let them read for a few minutes before he said anything.

What he had to tell them next could not be written down.

This was a business plan that involved murder.

As he spoke, he watched for a reaction but if any of his listeners were the slightest bit alarmed by what he was proposing, distressed by the thought of the blood that would have to be spilled, they did not show it.

When he finished and sat down they talked among themselves, their eyes gleaming as they registered the enormous potential of what was on the table.

Grant took over. 'Thank you, Gilbert. There you have it, gentlemen. I think you'll agree – a proposal that's both adventurous and a very sound business project that will open all sorts of doors for us in the future. It will not be achieved easily; there are several years' careful preparation work involved here and we'll have to establish a number of associates on the ground, as it were, to see it through to its final stages. But –' he sat back '– enough from me. There are bound to be things you want to ask Gilbert.'

There was little Leslie had not made clear but there were plenty of questions, all the same. These were men who liked to dot the *i*'s and cross the *t*'s.

Half an hour later they seemed satisfied.

'So,' Grant said, 'I think it's time to put it to the vote. First, though, I should tell you I've already discussed a fee with Gilbert and we must approve that, too.'

He gestured to Leslie.

'My fee will be four million dollars – half to be paid now and half when the initiative is concluded. If at any stage you decide to abandon the project, then that will also constitute a conclusion and payment of the remaining two million dollars would then be appropriate.'

He waited for a response.

'Four million. I think that's a bit excessive.'

The speaker was Heywood Corbett, the President of the Foundation Bank of Richmond, Virginia. A florid man with a cigar, he sat directly across the table from Leslie.

There was silence except for the sound of Grant tapping a pencil on a pad.

Leslie looked at Corbett with a smile but his eyes had hardened.

'I see that times have not changed,' he said.

'What does that mean?'

'It has always been the same,' Leslie said. 'No one ever quibbles about the killing that has to be done. But spending money? – ah, that's a different matter.'

'But a fee of that size—' Corbett started.

'Just look at us,' another voice said.

Their eyes turned towards Roger Hurll, the CEO of a computer giant, who had recently been featured in *Forbes* magazine. When he had their attention, he continued.

'The six of us round this table, plus the organisations run by our associates in Colombia and elsewhere, control what is virtually an alternative world economy. We are all extremely wealthy men, we create a steady stream of profit running into billions each year, yet we're going to sit here bickering over a paltry four million?'

He shook his head in disbelief. 'The fee seems fine to me. Let Mr Leslie have his money.'

Leslie nodded his head in a gesture of appreciation.

'I agree,' Grant said. 'Let's all remember how much has been achieved. Thirty or forty years ago, the equivalent of

this meeting, if there was one, would have been a bunch of
boys sitting in the back of a restaurant in Mulberry Street
or somewhere with a couple of goons at the door. It was
Gilbert Leslie, more than anyone, who saw the writing on
the wall for those of the old families who did not move
into a new age, who allowed themselves to languish under
the inadequate leadership of inferior men, like John Gotti,
for example.'

He put his hand on his heart. 'The influence of
Gilbert Leslie on my grandfather meant the development
of my own family's activities in the world of legitimate
business. You could say that he's directly responsible for
me being in my current position and, as a consequence
of that, for the links I have created with all of you. For
that I am grateful to him. Damn it, we should *all* be
grateful to him. His loyalty to our interests is immense
and it's evident every single day in the profits he's made
for us.'

'And for himself,' Corbett muttered.

'Oh come on, for Christ's sake,' Grant said. He opened
his arms wide. 'Roger's right. Look at what we represent –
the cream of the crop. Corporate America at its finest.
What we're being presented with is a plan to provide a
clean stream of revenue that's undetectable from other
sources of income and with it a whole new network of
distribution. In the circumstances, I find Gilbert's fee
entirely reasonable.'

He looked round them all. 'Anyone else got anything to
say?'

No one spoke.

'So are we agreed?'

They each nodded, although Corbett's affirmation was a little reluctant.

'And the main proposal – are we agreed on that?'

To their surprise, Leslie interrupted before they could decide. 'There's one thing. I've left it to the last because I think it needs separate consideration. With all that's involved in this project, with the high public profile it will have, it is quite possible that you may face a challenge at the last hurdle. In that case, the – the *opposition* – will have to be neutralised in some way to prevent that happening. I have been studying the personalities involved and I have some thoughts.'

For the next few minutes he outlined the problem and his solution to it.

His words were measured and calm but they brought a chill to the room.

Corbett threw his chair back and stood up.

'This is monstrous!' he shouted.

'Heywood, please,' Grant said.

'It is savagery,' Corbett continued. 'I know we have sanctioned the – the elimination of certain individuals and that that will be necessary if the plan is to succeed but this – this is not necessary. It is simply barbaric. Sickening.'

He glared at Leslie. 'What kind of man are you?'

Leslie stared at the surface of the table for a moment and when he looked up again his eyes were like glass, drained of feeling.

'I am a man who has no false illusions about what is acceptable and what is not,' he said. 'There can be no cries of outraged morality here. Blood and money – both are our currency and always will be. That is the business we are in, no matter how sophisticated the veneer.' He gestured round the room to illustrate what he meant. 'If you all find this unpalatable, then fine – you can say no. But I warn you of the risks of leaving anything to chance and I remind you that I will not be the one dealing with the consequences.'

His thoughts hung over the room. The men were silent for what seemed like minutes until Hurll spoke at last.

'Let's go for it,' he said . . .

Now they had sent for Gilbert Leslie again and with a little trepidation he wondered why.

Since that winter night he had not been involved; others had been selected to see the operation through. The first two million dollars had gone into one of his off-shore accounts and it would soon be time for the second payment. If there was a problem, if that was why they had sent for him, it was not a fault of the concept. Of that he was certain.

He saw his destination ahead of him.

The Plaza Hotel, eighteen storeys and 800 rooms of elaborately re-created French Renaissance, stood at the south-east corner of Central Park. The flags over its entrance swayed in a gentle breeze. Alongside the building, a row of carriages with gleaming brasses waited to carry sight-seers round the park. One or two of the horses were restless between the shafts, feeling spring's renewal in their blood.

Leslie walked up the steps and through the revolving door. He did not pause to take his bearings, to study the ornate surroundings or to gaze at all the people flowing through the vast lobby. Instead he walked straight through to the bank of lifts.

Several people were already waiting. Nearest to him was a young woman. She was in her early twenties, dark hair in waves, a dress that required her exquisite shape.

She turned towards him. Just the kind he had always liked. Black eyes, brooding.

A quickening of the pulse.

He smiled at her and nodded, a slight, courtly inclination of the head which almost constituted a bow. She smiled back, a response which was both instinctive and appreciative, and he saw that she was in no hurry to look away again immediately or to resume her study of the closed elevator doors.

It was gratifying to Leslie to confirm that although he was over sixty he could still touch something in women on occasion, even the young ones.

Unlike many of those from the old days, he had never let himself go, never allowed himself to deteriorate and become fat through too much food and wine. He had remained a slight figure, light on his feet, unburdened so far with stiffness or with arthritis opening its creaking door to him. His skin was unravaged by excess and the neatly trimmed hair was still full although it was now a gun-metal silver instead of deepest black.

But when it came to a young woman like this, with the softness of her dark eyes, with her gypsy hair, deeply scented, as he could now sense, well then, there was a day when Gilbert Leslie would have been as weak and wanton as any man.

And unfaithful? Yes, unfaithful.

Still, that had not been an issue for a long time. For five years he had led a rather austere existence. Physical pleasures had not occupied his mind much since his wife had died but he was surprised and a little excited to find the old feelings returning in the presence of this delightful creature.

The elevator arrived and they got in. At the ninth floor, where Leslie got off, they parted, she travelling further on up. To where, he wondered wistfully as he walked along the corridor. Alas, he would probably never know.

He knocked on a door and it was opened by a tall man he did not recognise, a man with glasses and cautious eyes. He helped Leslie out of his coat and hung it away in a closet.

Leslie took in his surroundings. He was in the sitting-room of a small suite and Michael Grant was walking towards him to shake his hand. Behind Grant, he could see the other members of the group sitting at a table, observing his arrival.

The man with the glasses took up a position on a settee which sat beside the fireplace and would give him a clear view of the door.

Grant saw Leslie's look and responded with a smile that was a little pained.

'This is Mr Parrish,' he explained and the man nodded a greeting. 'Unfortunately we had word today that some of our Colombian friends are experiencing a little local difficulty among themselves. There will be one or two people, I imagine, with whom we will not be doing business again. It will settle down, of course, but until it does one can never be too careful.'

He gestured to the room with its expensive soft furnishings. 'That is the business we are all in, no matter how sophisticated the veneer.' He looked at Leslie. 'I think I quote you correctly, if memory serves me.'

'It serves you very well,' Leslie said and glanced towards Heywood Corbett. He had put on weight and he was redder in the face.

Grant pointed towards an empty chair and Leslie sat down.

'Now – to matters in hand,' Grant said. 'I'm afraid there's not a lot of time and I'm grateful to Gilbert for coming all this way. Downstairs there's a seminar being run by my firm and a few others on the subject of investment opportunities in the emerging eastern European countries. I'm hosting a lunch for the Mayor which my colleagues here will also be attending so I thought we might handle some additional investment business while we're all on the premises.'

He grinned. 'Maybe I should get the Mayor up here. See what he thinks of all this.' They chuckled.

To Leslie they sounded a little smug.

Grant opened a buff folder that sat in front of him. He looked at Leslie. 'We're reviewing various operational matters and your European plan is part of that. It is all pretty much on course, everything in place, but I wanted to bring you up to date.'

Leslie frowned slightly. This was a bit unusual. Why bring him all the way into the city for this?

From the file Grant took a sheet of paper and passed it across the table. 'This will give you a progress report. As you'll see, one of our associates has become kind of greedy, looking for more money for his part in all of this, making what I assume we are to take as threats' – he smiled as if the notion were ridiculous – 'that he'll expose us in some way if we don't comply.'

Leslie read the paper, shrugged and slid it back.

'So you dispense with his services,' he said. 'That was always part of the plan. Now you've got another good reason to do so. I don't really see what the problem is. Or, if I may say so, how this involves me.'

Grant smiled and Leslie thought he saw a mischievous glint in his eye.

'Gilbert, let me explain. The operation's at a crucial stage. We can't afford for anything to go wrong. We have good people handling it over there but at this time it needs a superior navigator to get it safely into harbour. In other words, my old friend, it needs the special touch which you can give it.'

'Me? Don't be ridiculous.' He was irritated. 'This is a job for a functionary.'

Corbett spoke for the first time. 'You think this is beneath you, do you?'

Grant ignored him. 'Perhaps this will change your mind.' He passed Leslie the whole folder. 'In there, among the cast list, you will find someone who might interest you.'

Leslie did not understand. He frowned, then began to read. After a few moments, he stopped and looked up abruptly. His face was pale.

'Is this— surely it can't be true?'

Grant nodded slowly. 'Oh, it's true, Gilbert, believe me.'

Leslie looked at the folder again. 'This is – this is—' He swallowed.

'*Fortuitous* is probably the word you want. Fate lending a hand. It took me by surprise, I have to say. I thought it might appeal to your sense of – natural justice, I guess you could call it.'

He leaned forward. 'Look, take this operation on for us. See it through. It's been your baby from the start, anyway. Once it's wrapped up and you're tidying the loose ends ' – he pointed across the table to the file – 'well, then you can take care of this personal business.'

He looked towards the man on the settee. 'Mr Parrish will be happy to assist you. He's been involved with a lot of the preparatory work on this project already.'

Leslie got up from his chair and walked to the window with a thousand excited thoughts going through his mind. He looked down on to the open greenery of the park. It was here, at the southern tip, that it was at its most beautiful. From such a high vantage point, you could gaze right over its placid lakes and graceful boulevards. He had a sudden urge to be down there, to feel the sun on his face, smell the freshness of the new season and give thanks for what had just been presented to him.

He turned back to the room.

'Who will make my arrangements?'

Chapter Four

Gallagher could see it in her face as soon as he opened the kitchen door and found her sitting there. Something was wrong.

'What is it?'

She pointed to the table in front of her. 'I found this in a pocket of his jeans when I was about to stick them in the wash.'

She was staring at a small white tablet. He picked it up to look more closely. A tiny picture of a dove was outlined on the surface.

'What the hell's this thing?'

She gave him a dry look. 'Where have you been? Or don't they have this stuff in the States?'

'Shit,' he said, catching on. 'This is Ecstasy, right?'

'At a guess. I read something about how they decorate these things. This fits the bill.'

He sat down with a sigh. 'Paul? Doing stuff like this? I can't believe it. He doesn't – you know – seem the type.'

'What type? Is there a type?'

Gallagher looked at her. She was right. Who knew what

went on inside young people's heads. He didn't. That was for sure.

He set the tablet back down delicately on the table and they both stared at it in silence, as if expecting it to do something.

He did not know what to say.

Since the day of his visit to the police college at Templemore, he had begun to feel his self-confidence returning. He was even sleeping better at nights. So when Kate's brother, Alan, called and asked him to write another article for *Dublin Sunday*, this time about the furore caused by Marcus Kelly, the television reporter, being attacked by the infamous Sean Donovan, he had accepted eagerly.

The entire local media were consumed with pious indignation over the incident. Pictures of the assault had been all over television screens and newspapers for days and people were harking back to Veronica Guerin, the crime reporter who had been murdered just a couple of years ago.

Gallagher had his own views on the episode. He had just finished the piece and handed it in.

It was Wednesday. Kate rarely went into the office on Wednesdays since she often had to work on Saturdays, usually on one of her cultural tours of the city. This way she was more or less guaranteed a day off but she spent it catching up on housework, the penalty of being a working mother. There were two girls to look after the office and if there was anything urgent, then she could be contacted at home where she had a fax and a computer and a modem to link her with the outside world.

Knowing she would be here, he had driven out from

the city, hoping she would share his sense of accomplishment, but now his mood turned to one of concern and confusion.

'What are you going to do?' he asked.

'Talk to him, I suppose.' Her voice was tired. 'Although I don't know whether it's going to do any good. It's been hard to get any communication out of him at all lately.'

'Has he been – you know – acting strange?'

'Not that I've noticed. Damn it, I hardly see him, Tom. He's always in the city, hanging around at that bloody magazine. Straight after school every day. That's where he'll be now.' She looked at the tablet on the table. 'It's probably where he got this.'

The magazine. Paul had told Gallagher all about it one evening. It was a flimsy publication being run on a shoestring from a tiny office in downtown Dublin. Devoted almost entirely to the city's club scene, it had been given the title *Dave*, which was an amalgam of *dance* and *rave*.

'Preferable to the alternative,' Gallagher had suggested to him, 'which would have been *Rance*.'

Dave was gaining in popularity and starting to make money. The office was above a designer clothes shop owned by the wife of one of the city's most successful DJs and it was he who was funding the enterprise. Someone called Max, positively ancient at twenty-four, was the editor, depending largely on the help of contributors and avid volunteers like Paul who were not sure whether they were in show business or journalism but they were enjoying it, whatever it was.

Paul's particular talent was computers.

'I wish my mother didn't object so much,' he had

confided to Gallagher. 'It's a great place. There's a buzz about it. I feel like I'm right at the heart of something. And now they've asked me to set up a website for them. Fantastic.'

Gallagher had glanced through the magazine and had not understood a word of it. He felt very old when it came to stuff like this. To him, dance music was orchestras with music stands and lacquered couples in sequins and evening dress doing the foxtrot.

Techno, that was another matter altogether. And now there was something called drum and bass. How the hell did they follow it all, knowing where one trend ended and another began?

'Look,' he told Kate, 'don't get upset. It may not be too serious. Kids experiment sometimes, you know.'

'What – are you saying this is all right?' she asked sharply.

'No, no. Nothing like that. I meant – he seems much too sensible and too involved in other things, like this whole computer business, to get himself hooked into some sort of idiot drugs scene. Maybe this is the first. Maybe—' he thought for a second or two '—look, Kate, Paul's not stupid. If he was really into this stuff he wouldn't leave it in his jeans for the Wednesday wash where he'd know you were bound to find it. Maybe— maybe he's kind of deliberately forgotten about it. Is it possible he's seeking a bit of attention? Maybe he wants you to notice him.'

Kate looked at him with both indignation and alarm.

'Are you saying I neglect him?'

'Of course not. But I know how difficult it is for you,

running a business and being a single parent. And now I've come into the picture, occupying your time, too. Maybe he feels left out.'

Kate put her head in her hands.

'It's been so hard. Everything I've done – it's all been for him.'

'And he knows that. You've done a fine job of bringing him up. He's well-adjusted, clever, mature for his years, independent – or so we all think. What if he feels that we take him for granted?'

They sat thoughtfully and he squeezed her hand to comfort her.

'Look, do you want me to talk to him?'

She shook her head. 'No, I don't think so. I've got to do this on my own. It wouldn't – you know – feel right, you doing it. Almost as if I was putting you in a position—'

He knew what she meant. The ground rules and the boundaries of their relationship were less than clear.

'No, sure. You're right. You've got to do it. I understand that. I just thought, well—' He shrugged.

'Thanks for the help. What you said – you may be right. I should talk to him, get it all out in the open.' She smiled. 'Anyway, old FBI habits probably die hard. You'd only end up giving him the third degree.'

The kitchen door startled them as it opened.

Paul Forrest was seventeen but could have passed for twenty. Gallagher did not see much of Kate in him and he figured that every time she looked at the boy she saw the shadow of her late husband.

He was tall and bony with a strong nose and blue eyes. His blond hair was not cropped short in the style favoured by the majority of kids his age – they were like rookie GIs, Gallagher thought – but was longer and fell softly over his ears. He wore jeans and a sweatshirt and he carried a Puma sportsbag which would contain the school uniform, crammed in and crumpled among the textbooks.

Standing in the doorway, the boy got the picture at once: the expression on the faces, the tiny object on the table.

Gallagher stood up, feeling suddenly awkward and intrusive.

'Hi, Paul.'

'Hi,' the boy muttered in return, then turned away from them and went to the fridge. He lifted an opened bottle of milk and took a long swig from it.

Gallagher looked at Kate.

'You want me to stick around?' he said quietly.

'No, it's fine,' she said. 'You go on. It'll be all right.'

'Call me?'

She nodded.

He walked to the kitchen door, opened it, then turned.

'See you guys later,' he said in a cheery tone that was as thin as a bubble.

As he drove away relief settled over him and he admitted that he was glad Kate had turned down his offer. Christ, what would he have done if she had accepted? Delivered another lecture?

Half a mile down the road he thumped the steering wheel and cursed his cowardice.

He was a man who in a long career had got the truth out of crooked congressmen and kidnappers, had turned espionage suspects and mob guys into informers, yet he had flown out of the door of that house to avoid having to confront a seventeen-year-old boy about one little tab of E. Jesus, what kind of behaviour was that?

He sat at a temporary traffic light on Sandford Road, waiting for it to turn green. Half of the carriageway was out of action while it was being excavated. More goddamn road works.

Damn it, what did he know about teenage boys and their problems, anyway?

But no matter how he rationalised it, he could not prevent the familiar spectre of guilt coming forward to confront him.

The light changed and he put the car into gear again, joining a queue of traffic that was going nowhere.

He should have insisted on staying. She could have dealt with the problem on her own, if that was what she wanted, but he should have remained in the house while she did, just so that she would have known he was there for support.

Nothing had moved for at least five minutes.

A few hundred yards ahead there was a pub he had been to once before. He would have a drink while waiting for the congestion on the roads and in his head to clear. He took the first available turn on his left and browsed through the streets beyond until he found somewhere to park.

Noise and laughter met him at the door. The place was designed to look like an old stagecoach inn, a watering hole for weary travellers, which was appropriate in a way. There were fake oak beams with horse brasses and wooden panels giving a tariff in gold leaf paint of imaginary coach fares from Dublin to Galway and Cork.

A television set mounted high on a bracket blared from

a corner of the bar and refused to play along with the illusion.

The barman was an efficient big fellow with red hair and no time to talk. Gallagher knew the type. In the past he had interviewed people like him as potential witnesses. They saw everything, yet they saw nothing.

'Yes, my friend, what can I get you?'

'Bottle of Bud.'

When it came, he declined the offer of a glass, handed over a five-pound note and scooped up the wet change that was slapped on the bar in its place.

He moved towards the television. Three men drinking pints stood below it with their heads tilted back, looking up uncomfortably. They were in working clothes of cotton shirts and dusty jeans. The news was on and they were waiting for the sport.

The newsreader was a man in a double-breasted jacket stiff with authority. He read the introduction to a report from the *Dail*, the Dublin Parliament.

'There were angry exchanges across the floor of the House on the subject of crime prevention, in particular how to combat the twin problems of drugs and vice. The row came during questions to Ministers, when the recent incident involving the television journalist Marcus Kelly and the Dublin businessman Sean Donovan was raised again.'

There was video footage of the proceedings. Judging by the empty seats, the members, Deputies as they were known, had not exactly been queueing up to attend.

There was a clip of one of them, Ben Caffrey, the Opposition spokesman on Justice.

'Are the police going to bring any charges as a result of the Kelly incident,' he wondered, 'and does the Government and in particular the Justice Department intend to provide them with any new funding to deal with what is quite clearly the increased menace of drugs and prostitution on our city streets?'

He sat to await a reply. The Minister for Justice was in Strasbourg at an international conference on human rights, the reporter explained, so the response came from his deputy. It seemed as if Caffrey believed that in the top man's absence he would find an easy target. But he had picked one capable of shooting back.

The junior Minister was a striking dark-eyed woman in her very early thirties. With her slim build and carefully tailored silk suit, she would have been the focus of attention in any room but she was a breathtaking attraction in a drab debating chamber where dullness of speech and an absence of style prevailed.

She answered succinctly.

'Criminal investigations are a matter for the *Gardai* and any proceedings which might result are a matter for the Director of Public Prosecutions. As for the second part of the question, the police budget has been established for the year ahead and it is entirely the prerogative of the Commissioner to allocate funds in whatever order of priority he sees fit. However, the Minister for Justice and the Commissioner are in regular contact and they keep matters under review.'

She sat and waited. The first questions were always just an opening burst, a few shots in the air to make sure the weapons were working. The real skirmish came in the follow-up.

Caffrey's name was called by the Speaker and he stood once more. In the previous Government he had been the Justice Minister himself. A new election could not be far off and he had high hopes of returning to the office which he believed was rightfully his. These people were only interlopers, especially this – this woman.

There was disdain in the set of his face. He buttoned his jacket and stared across the floor. 'Might I ask the Minister whether her Government does not feel it is imperative to provide extra funding for a police force which is already beleaguered? Criminals are running rampant on the streets, without any fear of legal restraint, crime is taking place before our very eyes, the public are alarmed. Does this Government not understand the need to do something to provide assurance? And if they do not, surely it is time there was a Government in power who are capable of dealing with this issue?'

He gave it a full dramatic rendering and as he sat down there were cries of 'hear-hear' from the seats behind him.

His opponent took her time, waiting for them to quieten before she got up again. She had a folder in her hand and from papers in it she read out a set of figures. They were statistics of violent crime, robbery, details of arrests and convictions for drugs-related offences. Then she listed another set of figures in which criminal activity clearly appeared to be reduced, whereas the number of arrests and convictions had gone up significantly.

She turned to the Speaker. 'The first set of figures is for the last year in which the members opposite were in Government and when none other than Mr Caffrey himself was in charge of the Justice Department although—'

she turned to her colleagues – 'that is an image which most people will find hard to conjure up.'

The Deputies on her side laughed.

'The second set of figures, which show a substantial improvement, are the figures for the year to date and are, of course, the result of the concerted efforts of the *Gardai* and the Director of Public Prosecutions, encouraged and supported by this Government.'

She put the folder down and spoke with more force. 'There *is* a Government in power dealing with this issue. Not only dealing with it but committed to it in a way which exposes the incompetence and lack of will which characterised the stewardship of Deputy Caffrey and his merry band.'

There was a chorus of approval all around her, as well as a cheer from the three drinkers in front of the television. And when a political correspondent appeared on screen to deliver a summing-up they had no need of him. They had their own expert opinion on offer.

'Great operator, eh?'

'Great lookin' woman, certainly.'

'Do you think she's giving that oul' fella one?'

'Who – your man Caffrey? Would you catch yourself on?'

'I bet they're all pokin' her.'

'Jaysus, wouldn't you?'

'Feckin' sure I would. I'd poke you just to get at her.'

Gallagher felt his face reddening as their laughter crackled round him. He swallowed the remains of his drink and put the bottle down, a little too hard. The barman looked up with a raised eyebrow when he heard the sound.

The three men heard it, too. They swung round and were baffled by the glare Gallagher directed at them. There was a moment when he almost said something but then he turned on his heel and left.

As he unlocked the car he calmed himself. It wasn't their fault; they didn't know about Emma.

It was the only time he got to see his daughter – when she popped up on television.

Chapter Five

A battered Nissan van in steel grey drove along the Ballyfermot Road with Vinnie Dwyer at the wheel.

Its number plates declared that it had been registered in County Cavan four years ago but in reality it was of a slightly more recent vintage. The plates themselves had been on it only since yesterday, shortly after it was stolen from a builder's yard at Blanchardstown, on the northern edge of the city. Several lengths of wood, which Vinnie had not bothered to clear out, still lay in the back.

It was eight o'clock on Sunday morning and most of Ballyfermot was still asleep. But, like a jungle, it was never entirely still. Day and night its worst dwellers prowled it, causing hate and fear and squalor.

Not that any of this worried Vinnie, whistling softly between his teeth along with the radio as he eased his way round the half-ramps set into the road to prevent excess speed. On the contrary, he thrived on it, especially the fear part.

He was a son of Ballyfermot, born there thirty years ago. Although he lived a few miles away now he was still one of its most savage predators and perhaps the most unsettling thing about him was the fact that he did not look it.

There was no ear-ring, no stubble, no tattoos, no narrowing of the eyes and puffing-out of the chest to signify that he was a hard lad. Instead, Vinnie was brown-eyed and cheerful and handsome when he smiled, although it made him look a bit chubby in the cheeks.

In contrast to this appearance, he could, when the occasion demanded, perform acts of outrageous brutality and he would maim or kill without pause, scruple or any perceptible change in his outward demeanour.

He had served time in the past for robbery but not for crimes of violence which was why there had been no cause for the State to subject him to any kind of an examination of his mental condition. There was no doubt that had there been such scrutiny, it would have established that Vinnie was a psychopath.

He drove past pubs and bookmakers' shops and kebab joints and games arcades, all covered with shutters and metal grilles. A couple of gaunt youths with the shivers were hanging around outside a corner shop which was open for business but most of the people on the road this early were of a type for which Ballyfermot was not notorious. They were middle-aged or they were elderly and they were making their dutiful way to Mass where they would pray to God for deliverance from the madness they so often saw around them.

If you turned off either side of the road, you entered the real Ballyfermot, row after row of two-storey dwellings built on vast tracts of land and housing tens of thousands of people: huge families, dysfunctional families, single-parent families, no-parent families and, in some cases, perfectly normal families trying to get on with their lives.

Off to the right of Ballyfermot, there was the Naas dual-carriageway which would eventually take you to Limerick and Galway and other points west. Away on the far side of that road was the edge of the Phoenix Park, more than seventeen hundred acres of it, the biggest city park in Europe. This morning, its landscaped gardens, its woods and its meadows were vibrant with spring. Deer grazed on the dew-moistened pastures and the joggers had been out since dawn. In a couple of hours the zoo would be opening. And somewhere amid the park's green splendour, the Irish President would be having breakfast in the elegant residence which the State maintained for him. So, too, would the United States Ambassador, within the secure walls of his own particular eighteenth-century mansion.

But all of that might as well have been in a parallel universe.

Ballyfermot had been constructed in the 1960s to provide new homes for the families living in appalling conditions in Dublin's slum houses and tenement buildings. But once they had been transplanted to this environment many of the Dubliners of the inner-city felt rootless, deprived of their familiar, albeit grim, surroundings and alienated by their new ones.

Thus had begun Ballyfermot's slide. The solution became a problem.

Vinnie made a left turn off the main road, then another, then a right, until he was deep into the most inhospitable territory. His was the only vehicle moving and, for the most part, it was the only one capable of doing so. Strange cars of mixed parentage and no wheels stood on wooden blocks. In a parking bay, there was the rusting carcass of a burnt-out Ford Sierra, long since separated from its rightful owner.

But in this, as in all jungles, it was animal life which dominated. A dispute involving Dublin County Council's sanitation department had been going on for four weeks with the result that there had been no refuse collections in all that time. Soggy debris from overturned bins littered the road and packs of scary mutant dogs scurried from street to street, rummaging for scraps.

Stopping outside a house which appeared derelict, wooden sheeting over broken windows, Vinnie turned the engine off and got out. He was dressed in dark blue overalls and he could have been there to read the electricity meter or fix the gas, except that neither of them was connected in this house, at least not officially.

He walked up the short path through the gap where a garden gate had once hung before being uncoupled years ago during a dispute between two families and flung through somebody's front window. The lock on the front door had been hacked off through repeated forced entry but something was propped behind the door to keep it shut. Vinnie gave a shove and felt resistance so he decided to go round the back and try the kitchen door instead. It was unlocked.

The kitchen floor was covered in a film of grease and it was sticky under foot. There was no table and there was no cooker, just braids of wiring jutting from the wall where one had stood once upon a time. The only domestic appliance was an electric kettle on a work surface at the sink beside a collection of tin foil trays containing the slimy remains of an ancient Chinese take-away.

He stood for a moment with his head cocked as he listened to scuffling noises, sounds of haste, coming from upstairs.

'Dezo,' he called. 'It's me, Vinnie. Are you there?'

He went into the hall and found where the kitchen table had gone. It was what had been blocking the front door.

A young man appeared at the top of the stairs. He wore jeans and was barefoot and he finished pulling a tee-shirt over his head.

Dezo stammered when he was nervous.

'Jay-jay-jaysus, Vinnie, I didn't know who-who it was.'

There was a room to Vinnie's left and he looked into it. The floor was bare and the room was empty apart from a stained grey settee, its undulating shape indicating that the springs had gone. An old copy of the *Star* left open at the racing page lay beside it and there was a milk bottle, almost empty except for a substance at the bottom which looked like cottage cheese. A rucksack lay in a corner.

Vinnie did not wait for Dezo to come down but made his way up the stairs towards him. The wood creaked under his heavy boots.

Dezo was about twenty-two and scrawny with lank, unwashed hair normally tied back into a pony tail. Track marks and sores on his bare arms imprisoned him just as much as if they had been a cell.

'Vi-vinnie, this is—'

'Unexpected surprise, eh?'

Vinnie beamed, still looking round.

There was a noise from a room on his right and he stepped into the doorway.

Beside a rumpled bed stood a girl, not more than sixteen or seventeen, pale and hollow-eyed. She wore a bra and pants which had been white once and she was thin to the point of emaciation, with thighs like wrists. The room was rank with the odour of unwashed bodies.

He smiled again.

'Ah, Aileen, me darlin'. Fresh and well you're looking.'

He seemed to study her for a moment. Then he turned back to Dezo.

'Come on. Get dressed, the pair of you.'

Dezo had come back into the room and was pulling on a pair of sneakers. No socks.

'What's, what's the score, Vinnie?'

'He's got a job for you. Something that might put a bit of money your way.'

'Great,' Dezo said, less nervous now. 'Tell us what it is.'

Vinnie shrugged. 'Can't. Don't know. He wouldn't tell me. He just said to come and get you.'

The youth stared at him. 'What's with the overalls?'

Vinnie looked down at himself and plucked at the rough cotton. 'This? Ah, nothing. A bit of manual labour to do later. No rest for the wicked.'

The girl had got into jeans and a grubby sweatshirt which said Nike on the front but was nothing of the kind.

'And he said to bring both of us?' Dezo asked.

'Yes, why not?'

Dezo looked at her. 'You – you know – okay?'

She nodded.

Vinnie led the way down the stairs, whistling through his teeth once more, but he started to laugh when he saw the table in the hall again.

'Christ, Dezo. That's some barricade you have there, eh. That'll keep people out all right. My arse, it would. I walked in the back door. And what are you worried about anyway? Sure there's fuck all here to steal.'

They pulled the table out of the way and went out of the house, leaving the door ajar.

Dezo looked a little agitated.

'All the same, Vinnie,' he said. 'I don't like the thought of somebody breaking in.'

Vinnie threw his head back and laughed.

'Jesus Christ,' he said. 'What the fuck are you talking about? Sure that's what you did.'

They climbed into the Nissan. There was room for all three in the front. Aileen sat in the middle. Vinnie turned to her and winked as they drove off.

As they passed the entrance to a passageway which led along the backs of some of the houses they did not notice a figure which had ducked in there once it spotted them. When they had rounded the corner and were gone from sight, it re-emerged.

Out of the shadow of the entry, the figure revealed itself to be a young man of about twenty, sturdy and of medium height, dressed in chinos and a denim jacket.

Dermot Davis did not look abused and sickly like his sister, Aileen, or her boyfriend, Dezo, but then he did not see heroin as life's sole purpose. In fact, he had never used it at all and the more he saw of what it did the less likely it became that he ever would.

He was not like Dezo. Dezo was a dealer, dividing and bagging the heroin in a string of different houses, although not this one. He and a team of pushers sold the stuff and gave the proceeds to Vinnie, for which Dezo got a small cut.

But he had also developed what he thought was the bright idea of cutting out some of the gear and selling it for himself while diluting the rest even more than usual to make the amounts look the same.

It was dangerous. What if Dezo got found out? More and more, Dermot wanted to get Aileen out of there, back home to Waterford where she belonged, which was why he had come to Dublin to find her, but he knew he would have to bide his time, work on her gradually, otherwise she would just disappear again. In the meantime he would try to keep her alive.

In his hand he held a flimsy blue carrier bag which contained a fresh pint of milk, a loaf, a small packet of butter and some tea bags. He had gone to get them while Dezo and Aileen slept.

As he had watched the couple over the past few weeks their slumber had often looked more like coma and he worried about them vomiting and choking to death. He had checked them this morning before leaving. Each day they seemed to deteriorate a little more and the shadow of disease loomed larger than ever in the room.

Dermot had never seen Vinnie Dwyer before but he had guessed who he was, even before he heard Dezo using his name while getting into the van.

Aileen had talked about him. He was a spooky kind of guy, she said, laughed a lot, seemed good fun, but everyone knew what he really was, everyone had a story about something he had done, each tale more bloody than the last.

Dermot did not like the look of any of this.

He walked towards the house, glancing back over his shoulder once, just in case. The road was still empty but people were beginning to come to life behind their grimy walls. He could hear a baby howling. A second one joined in. Music began to blast from a house further down the street and then came a woman's voice – '*Turn that fucking thing off!*'

He had warned Dezo of the consequences of being caught and he hoped that that was not the reason for Vinnie Dwyer's unusual early call. In the end, though, Dezo would have to look after himself; what he got up to was his own affair. But Aileen – she should not be involved in any of this. Where was Dwyer taking them?

There were practical matters to be attended to first of all. He would have time to worry later. For the moment he would work on instinct.

He had left the house by the back door, which he had unbolted, but now he just strolled in the front. He walked straight through to the kitchen and stood looking around. On the window ledge he spotted what he wanted. A chisel.

He grabbed it and went into the front room where he shoved the settee to one side. Its castors rattled across the bare floor. Where the settee normally stood, there was a section of floor board which was not nailed firmly in place but had been left to look as if it were. Dermot prised it loose easily then lay with the side of his face on the floor and stretched his arm in as far as it would go, across under the more secure woodwork, until his hand touched something. He grasped it with his fingers and tugged.

He pulled out a Dunnes Stores shopping bag.

As soon as he opened it he could smell the money.

It was in half a dozen bundles of much-fingered notes of mixed denomination, each in a rubber band, and there was a small plastic bag of pound coins as well. He would count it later but he knew from talking to Dezo that there was the best part of five grand there.

He put it all into the rucksack. Someone might come back looking for this but neither he nor the cash would be here when they did.

The van was a few miles along the dual carriageway when Vinnie turned off to the left.

'Whe-where are we going?' Dezo asked.

'You'll see when we get there.'

This road led to an industrial estate which was in the process of being built. The Dublin outskirts had many such business parks, all eating away at the soft fringes of the countryside. On weekdays, the area was alive with the sound of excavating, of drilling and pipe-laying, but on this Sunday morning it was quiet. None of the buildings was yet occupied, most were still shells, if not just bare frames of steel girders, and it would be some months before the first tenants moved in.

Vinnie stopped at a gate which appeared to be tightly secured by a huge lock but was not. He unhooked it and pushed the gate open, then got back into the van and drove in.

A blue Mazda was parked alongside a long low warehouse

which had a gaping hole where the doors would eventually be.

'That his car?' Dezo inquired.

'Yep,' said Vinnie and drove right in.

He turned off the engine and there was a moment of silence.

'Right, everybody out,' he said. He hopped to the floor and went round to the back of the van, opening the rear doors and taking something from inside as his passengers stepped down.

'Where is he?' Dezo asked.

The baseball bat hit him viciously in the back of the knee and he buckled with a gurgling cry that came from deep in his throat.

Aileen screamed, her arms jerking in shock like a string puppet's. Vinnie held the bat in his right hand and swung it forearm, striking her hard on the side of the neck.

She crumpled to the concrete floor as if her whole body had broken apart from within, then lay still and silent with her head at an uncertain angle. Her eyes were open and they had rolled up to expose the whites.

Dezo was groaning in agony but he was trying to crawl towards the open doorway. Vinnie ignored him for the moment and crouched to study the girl.

'Fuck,' he said, disappointed. 'That didn't take long.'

He straightened up.

'Ah, well. Better make sure.'

He held the baseball bat above his head with both hands, then brought it down and smashed Aileen's skull.

Deep red blood flowed across the floor behind him as he walked over towards Dezo.

'And now, my boy,' he said, 'I'll show you why it's not a good idea to rip off Sean Donovan's gear and sell it for yourself.'

He twirled the bat and got a good grip on the handle.

He would start with the other knee.

An hour later, the van stood some miles away at a landfill site, a municipal dumping ground.

Vinnie had brought his own rubbish from Ballyfermot.

Seagulls flapped and squawked along dunes of decaying waste which stood waiting for the bulldozers to come and plough them into the ground. A fire was smouldering somewhere and bits of charred paper blew in the wind.

A fragment fluttered past Vinnie and into the shallow pit towards which he was dragging Dezo's bloody and broken body. He had him by the feet and he hauled him along with his face in the mud.

At the edge, Vinnie stopped and looked down. In a pool of brown water with an oily sheen on its surface lay the gnarled frame of an old pram. He put his foot against Dezo's side and rolled him down to join it, then he went back to the van for Aileen.

When they were both in the pit, he stood for a moment studying them. The girl had fallen right across Dezo so that he was practically submerged in the water. Once they were found, the message would be clear to anyone who might even for one moment think of following in Dezo's footsteps: you're all disposable.

He got into the van and went back to the warehouse, driving right into it again. There was blood all over the floor now and some was spattered up the wall in the corner where he had finished Dezo off.

There were two cans of petrol in the van and he emptied most of the contents over its interior. When he had finished, leaving the van's rear doors wide open, he went out to where the Mazda was parked and took a bag out of the back. In it were clean jeans and shoes. He took his overalls and boots off and threw them and the baseball bat into the van.

Dressed afresh, he got into the Mazda and brought it round to the doorway to leave it with the engine running.

From the floor of the warehouse, he lifted an empty milk bottle. He poured some of the petrol into it then soaked a rag and stuffed it into the neck. He stood near the door and gave a last look round, before he took a lighter from his pocket. He lit the petrol bomb and hurled it into the back of the van.

With a whoosh, great sheets of flame billowed out of the vehicle. Vinnie gunned the Mazda and he had barely reached the gate before the van exploded, taking part of the roof of the warehouse off.

'Woo-hoo!' he shouted with excitement.

Out of the industrial estate, on the main road, he slowed down, slipping easily into the traffic, then headed at an even speed in the direction of Sean Donovan's house at Tallaght.

He realised after a couple of minutes that he would have to make a stop along the way. He had a lighter but he had no cigarettes.

Donovan's home was in a private residential development. There were ten houses in a small cul-de-sac, all of them built of yellow brick, with colourful gardens and neat lawns, although the one at the end, towards which Vinnie now headed, was a little less well-tended than the others.

In fact, it was a mess, with grass which only the wind tamed. Weeds smothered the flowers as they struggled towards the sunlight. Sean Donovan was no gardener.

There was a for sale sign at the house beside it and at the one opposite, too, but the sellers did not have a hope of getting a buyer, not while the neighbour from hell lived there.

Vinnie pulled up into the short driveway and got out with a couple of Sunday newspapers. He did not ring the doorbell but went round to the kitchen and walked in.

Donovan was in a satin dressing gown. A mug of tea in his hand, he leaned against the work surface where a monitor showed what the security cameras were surveying. At the moment the screen gave him a black and white version of the parked Mazda but now it switched to the back doorstep.

'All sorted out?' Donovan asked.

'All sorted out,' Vinnie confirmed. 'Lesson learned, I'd say.'

He threw the papers on the table.

Donovan sniffed.

'You smell of petrol. What's all that about?'

'I know I do. I better wash my hands,' Vinnie said, heading towards the bathroom. 'It's nothing,' he called over his shoulder. 'Just a wee problem with a van.'

There was the sound of running water and soap being lathered.

'What time's your flight? Half one?' Vinnie asked.

'Half two.'

'For God's sake, that's plenty of time. By the way,' he said, coming back into the kitchen, drying his hands on a pink towel. 'They're writing about you again.'

Donovan was sitting at the kitchen table with a newspaper spread in front of him.

'I know,' he said. 'I've just found it.'

Chapter Six

Gallagher had not slept. He was unshaven and his eyes were red-rimmed.

The letters had arrived yesterday, Saturday.

Both on the same day. Wham, bam.

He picked them up from the kitchen table in his apartment although he could recite their contents by now. He had read the letters over and over again, including several times during the night.

It did not make any difference; the words were still the same. His money had gone.

His early retirement package from the FBI had been generous. But he had never been particularly prudent when it came to financial matters; his mental energies had always been devoted to the job. In all his years in the United States he had never owned a house or an apartment, always renting, and so when it came time to move he had nothing to sell, nothing to cash in.

He had put some of his retirement money into the purchase of this little flat along the seafront road at Sandymount and he was paying off the remainder through a mortgage. He had a monthly FBI pension cheque which was proving to be less than adequate on its own but a broker in New York had invested the remainder of his money, about $30,000, in property development.

For a while now he had been thinking that maybe it was time he got out of that deal, took his profit, and invested it all nearer to home. His broker would know best. Gallagher had written to him a few weeks ago to ask how his investment stood.

It was a letter from New York that he had opened first, thinking that perhaps this was the reply. Instead, it was from someone else in the firm.

'*I regret to have to inform you . . .*'

For a second he thought someone had died. By the time he got to the end he figured that that might have been easier news to take.

The broker had disappeared. With him had vanished several million dollars in client funds, including Gallagher's thirty thousand.

There was no investment, no interest. It was all gone.

No one knew the whereabouts of the broker, the police were on the case, as was the Securities and Exchange Commission. The words on the page passed in a blur.

While he was trying to take it all in, he had opened the second letter. It was from his bank manager here in Dublin.

'May I draw your attention to the fact that at the close of business yesterday, your account was in debit to the amount of £3,237.41, which is £737.41 in excess of your permitted overdraft limit. I would ask you to make an immediate lodgement in order to reduce this figure and to make an appointment at your earliest convenience so that we can discuss your financial situation.'

He read it again now and his hand trembled as he put the letters down. The shock had not eased.

He looked at his watch for the date. His pension cheque would be in tomorrow, Monday, thank goodness, but it would not keep the tide back for long. Because it was the weekend, there was nothing he could do. Tomorrow he would contact New York to find out what chance there was to squeeze anything out of the situation. But he did not hold out much hope. He had seen this kind of thing happen to people before.

Damn it, he had been careless.

He had better call the bank, too. Jesus, he knew things were tight but surely not this bad. From a drawer yesterday he had dug out bank statements for the past three months, realising that he had not even bothered to open the last one he had received. There it all was – the steady drip, the build-up of debt through his own neglect.

He felt cornered. He gazed around the room.

What if I have to sell this place?

The idea pulled him up short. Where the hell would he live? He could not impose himself on Kate and moving in with Emma was out of the question.

He went to the window and looked out but it seemed as if the view did not belong to him any more. Away over to his left, pink and white like giant sticks of candy, the thin chimneys of the Coolock power station pierced the sky and exhaled streams of smoke into its soft white clouds. All along the shore in front of him, the tide was out, gone impossibly far towards the horizon, and where the sea had been, patrols of oystercatchers and redshank had taken over, stabbing the wet sand in search of sustenance.

The morning was clear and sunny but he felt the storm clouds gathering in his head.

The phone rang.

'Tom,' said Alan Warnock. 'I really am very, very sorry.'

Gallagher frowned. Alan did not know about any of this. What was he talking about?

'Sorry about what?'

'The paper,' he said. 'You've seen it?'

The paper. He had totally forgotten that his article would be published today.

Emma Gallagher turned when she reached the end of the indoor pool, pressed the soles of her feet firmly on to the smooth tiled wall and propelled herself into her last length.

Head down, her arms cutting through the water, she swam with ease and strength, just as she had when she was the Irish universities' women's freestyle champion a little over ten years ago. She swam with the same determination with which she did everything in life, going straight for her objective, never for a moment pausing in its pursuit.

Those who were on her side called it dedication but those who were not would describe it as ruthlessness. There had always been the two disparate views of her but they were held particularly strongly by people who had known her first of all in her previous role as a lawyer, a member of the State Prosecution team seeking convictions in the criminal courts, and now by those she encountered in the progress of her political career.

The huge windows in the wall of the poolhouse were

shielded by long panelled blinds but shafts of the Sunday morning sunlight streamed through the spaces and across the surface of the water that seethed behind her.

At the side of the pool, there was a table and several lightweight chairs. A man in a white towelling robe sat in one of them watching her, squinting slightly against the sun. A cafetière stood on the table and he sipped from a small china cup. A mobile phone was near his hand. He was never far from it.

He was a healthy-looking man in his early forties with a pink glow to his skin after his own swim and greying hair which had gone into tight curls from being immersed in the water.

Fergal Mulryne was leaving her to it. Useful swimmer though he was, he had no intention of trying to compete. He liked to watch her, anyway; he loved the graceful power she demonstrated.

If Mulryne looked pleased with himself, it was with good reason. After several moderately successful business ventures, he had begun a new one a few years ago, importing ceramic tiles from Italy so that he could supply them throughout Ireland and the UK, and he had followed this by opening a number of shops which specialised in expensive household fittings.

His enterprise had made him a lot of money, with the result that he had an apartment in Milan and he had this house, high in the seclusion of the Wicklow hills. Until recently, it had been the home of an American film director, one of the small colony of movie and show business people scattered in comfortable and expensive houses around the neighbouring countryside. Ardmore studios nearby was the centre of the Irish film industry and Ireland itself had become an increasingly popular location. In addition, the Government offered attractive tax breaks for film-makers and there was the unique appeal of the legislation enacted many years before which allowed artists and writers to live in Ireland without paying any income tax at all.

Not that any of this was of any benefit to Mulryne but there were those who reckoned he contributed as much to the well-being of the country as anyone in the film business. There was his charity work, a portfolio of noble causes ranging from Aids awareness to cerebral palsy, and to all of which he gave a precious portion of his increasingly scarce free time.

How he managed it all was a marvel but his selflessness had not gone unrecognised. Last November he had won one of the People Of the Year awards, presented to him by the Prime Minister at the annual gala dinner in Dublin which was a highlight of the Irish national calendar. And if all that was not enough to make a man happy, there was his relationship with Emma Gallagher, emerging now in front of him with rivulets of water flowing down her flanks.

She wore a tight bathing cap and a gleaming black swimsuit that was like a second skin. She pulled the cap off, tossing her head from side to side to liberate the waves of dark hair.

'Enjoy that?' he asked.

'Perfect,' she said, a little breathily.

She smiled at him and then she lowered the straps of the swimsuit from her shoulders and began to peel it off.

The roseate nipples puckered as they became exposed. Her body was firm and well-maintained and although she kept herself in shape, swimming here regularly, working out a couple of times a week at a fitness club in the centre of Dublin, she did it for pleasure and not out of obsession and so she had not developed an excessive, hard-bodied muscularity.

Naked, she bent over Mulryne and kissed his ear as she reached past for her own robe which lay across a chair behind him. Her body was unperfumed but her skin smelled cleansed and pure.

She wrapped herself up and sat to drink the coffee which he had already poured. She looked at her watch. Eleven. God, that was late.

Last night they had gone out to a restaurant with friends who lived near Bray, as she did, and later they had come back here. When Mulryne was in the country, they ended up either in this house or in her home but she liked the luxury of this place, such a change from her own small cottage, and she adored the pool.

She had woken early to find him lying there looking at her. When he saw her eyes opening he had begun to stroke her softly with his fingertips, the way she liked him to, agonisingly, barely a touch at all, an electric sensation on her skin, and when she could not stand it any more she had rolled over on to him, reaching down to find him hard and eager.

Afterwards, they had both fallen asleep, she deeply and without the intrusion of a dream, and they had woken again not long ago. But damn it, she had things to do, things to prepare for tomorrow.

The phone beside Mulryne rang and he answered it.

'Hello?' he said and then, 'oh, hi, Tony.'

He looked towards Emma as he spoke the caller's name, indicating that this was likely to be for her.

It could be only one person.

Tony Goulding was not just the Minister for Industrial Development and Technology, he was also the Deputy Prime Minister. More than that, he was Emma Gallagher's patron, the man who a few years ago had convinced her to give up her career in the courtroom and take up the other love of her life, politics.

Goulding had led one of the old Irish political parties himself but his had been merged with two other groupings to form Democratic Nation, a party created before the last election and now the party of Government. It was as a Democratic Nation candidate that Emma had stood at a by-election for a safe east-coast seat from which a sitting member was retiring. Now, the blink of an eye later, she was a junior member of the Government.

Apprehension nudged her. She admired Goulding enormously but she had become deeply fond of him, too, seeing in him something of a surrogate father. Nevertheless, he was also one of the few people in life whom she sometimes found intimidating. He had power and an ability to make things happen; there was her own rapid elevation as evidence of that.

He had promised to help her make her mark in Government and in return he expected a loyalty which she was happy to give him. She was a member of *his* team rather than that of the Prime Minister. It was also through Goulding that she had met Fergal. That was another thing she owed him.

'Yes she is,' Mulryne said in answer to the expected question. 'I'll put her on.'

'Morning,' Emma began as she took the receiver, realising that she actually felt guilty that Goulding knew exactly where to find her, a little girl who had been caught doing something naughty. 'I've just had the most lovely swim,' she said, as if that was the only reason she was here. 'You should—'

'Have you seen *Dublin Sunday* this morning?'

'No,' she said, flustered, 'I haven't, not yet. I—'

'Then I suggest you do,' he interrupted, 'after which you will call me back and tell me what the bloody hell is going on.'

There was a click and a dialling tone and she was left holding the receiver and wondering the same thing herself.

He had seen the paper now, all right. After Warnock's call he had gone to the shop to get a copy, opening it on the way home, then standing there in the street, horrified, when he saw what Warnock was apologising for.

He looked to where it lay open on the table at an article he had written.

It set out to be his analysis, as an experienced professional in the world of law enforcement in the United States, of how the Irish authorities were handling their own current law and order problems. It was topical, of course, because of this incident in the street which was causing such outrage, but he had not gone into that a whole lot, only to express his concern about what he felt was the real problem, the apparent willingness of the Government and the police to let the media do their job for them.

It looked, he had written, as if they condoned and approved of the continual harassment of people alleged to be involved in criminal activities. But pursuit by the media was not a substitute for proper, rigorous investigation, nor was it the way to ensure conviction since if anyone was eventually charged they could claim with reasonable justification that prior publicity had ruined their chances of getting a fair trial. He had given a couple of examples of US mob figures who had managed to get off the hook that way.

Gallagher had acknowledged, however, that the Government had made some gestures towards dealing with the problems posed by organised crime although he reckoned they were not enough. The creation some years ago of a Criminal Assets Bureau had been a worthwhile endeavour but the harsh truth was that enterprising criminals would always find loopholes and new ways of secreting their money.

The Government did not seem to recognise this, he said, and no one seemed to care except when there was a major crime of some kind which could not be ignored. Even then, there was no real debate on the issues, just vitriol thrown across the floor of the House.

The article went on in that vein but he could not bring himself to look at any more of it. What pious posturing it was.

He glanced again at the picture which the paper had used to illustrate it. They had picked the most unflattering one they could find. It was of Emma making a speech somewhere, mouth open and arm raised, an expression on her face that was almost wild.

The caption below it read: '*Politicians – concern about crime or just an opportunity to throw vitriol?*'

The political stance of *Dublin Sunday* placed it in alignment with the main party of opposition and not Democratic Nation. There had been government coalitions in the past, sometimes of three or more parties, but they were often uncomfortable relationships marred by acrimonious disputes both in private and in public. The merger which had formed Democratic Nation, a whole new party rather than a loose alliance, had been a way of establishing a group which would be a real power in government but its opponents loved to find cracks in its façade.

Gallagher had been used to provide one.

He and Emma had not spoken for two months but when the telephone rang he knew who it would be.

She did not announce herself or say why she was ringing.

'What the hell are you playing at?' she snapped. 'What are you trying to do to me?'

'I'm so sorry. I didn't know anything like that would happen. If it's any consolation, I feel let down, too.'

'You just made a fool of me. You made a fool of both of us, as a matter of fact. And I've had to answer for it to the Deputy Prime Minister, thank you very much.'

Gallagher frowned. 'But you can't be held responsible for something a newspaper does?'

'Of course not. But that isn't the point. I know we don't talk much or have much contact but surely you might have had the decency to let me know you were planning to attack the Government of which I'm a member? And, damn it, attack me, too. What the hell does that look like?'

He groaned inwardly. 'I wasn't trying to do either of those things. I was simply stating what I believe to be the rights and wrongs of a particular issue and what I felt about how it was being handled. If it was an attack on anything, it was an attack on the whole political system. It wasn't about you, Emma.'

'Well, it is now, isn't it?'

'Please believe me,' he insisted. 'I wouldn't do anything to deliberately embarrass you in any way. I wrote the article before all that business in the House the other day and I – well, it just didn't dawn on me that this would happen. I didn't think they'd use a picture of you. I'm sorry.'

'Not half as sorry as I am,' she said, sounding more hurt than angry now. 'God, you're such a fool.'

The words wounded him.

'Look,' he said, 'Do you want me to get them to fix it next week? An apology or something?'

'No,' she sighed, 'there's nothing to apologise for. It's too clever for that. There's nothing I can do that won't draw attention to the thing all over again. I just – I just wish you'd thought about what you were doing.'

'It won't happen again.'

'But the damage is done, isn't it? I'm the one who's going to have to answer the sarcastic questions from reporters. Any truth in the rumour that your father's putting his name forward as an opposition candidate in the next election – I'm sure even you can imagine the sort of line they'll take.'

A thought struck her. 'Oh and another thing – if anyone rings you, don't even think of giving them a comment.'

She rang off.

He stood at the window with the dead phone in his hand and despair in his heart. His financial problems were insignificant now compared to the pain of his daughter's contempt.

In the distance, a couple of people in anoraks and rubber boots were poking around on the muddy shore. He looked at their faraway shapes and thought that for all of Emma's life that was exactly what he had been: a remote figure, intruding on her every so often before going again.

Now he was back for good and she did not want to know him. And after today a reconciliation was less likely than ever.

But what had he expected?

He unplugged the phone from the wall socket and sat down, staring out to sea. The beachcombers were walking this way. The tide was starting to come in.

When it turned again many hours later, with the afternoon light dimming in the sky, he was still sitting there and Kate Forrest was ringing the bell. As he opened the door to her, he could see in her face that he looked terrible.

'I've been trying to call you all day,' she said. 'Is there something wrong with your phone?'

'I unplugged it,' he told her, walking back into the flat. 'I didn't want to talk to anybody.'

'Alan rang to tell me what happened.'

'Oh, did he indeed?'

'He's very cut up about it. You should know that. He feels he's let you down. I was worried. I thought I'd come and see how you were.'

'Well now you know,' he said. 'I'm absolutely one hundred per cent goddamn marvellous. Tell him he can put that on his fucking front page.'

His anger was like a slap in the face.

'Well fine,' she said. She did not need this. 'In that case, I'll leave you to it.'

He pulled himself together.

'God, Kate, I'm sorry. It's not your fault. It's – Christ, everything's a mess. Emma rang earlier, very angry. I think this is going to drive her even further away from me.'

She looked at the anxiety in his eyes. He put his hand to his mouth and nibbled feverishly at a fingernail. She felt uncomfortable.

'I'll put the kettle on,' she said.

Chapter Seven

At the age of nineteen, he had been reading law at Trinity College in Dublin and on the verge of winning a scholarship to Harvard. He was also going out with an arts student who was tiny and lively with auburn hair in a hippie frizz.

'Emma's mother,' Kate said, bringing two cups of tea in from the kitchen, 'what was her name again?'

In the past few months of their relationship he had not wanted to go into the past, always stopping at the doorway and instead veering off towards the more gratifying area of his daughter's successes. Through Alan she knew something of the missing years but not what Gallagher felt about that long part of his life.

Tonight it seemed as if he was inclined to talk. Yet, as he did, she felt a tension that she tried not to let him see. There was something about his mood. It was brittle, as if he were on the edge of something, and she wondered if that was the way he had been before his breakdown.

'Mary,' he said. 'Mary Norris.'

'That's right,' she said, remembering now. 'Do you ever hear anything of her?'

He shook his head. 'Nothing. When we got divorced a while ago she re-married. She had a long relationship over the years with somebody but they couldn't get married until the divorce laws changed. They're living in South Africa now. Emma hears from her, I'm sure. They were very close. *Are* very close.'

'Do you ever think things might have been different if you'd given it a chance?'

'It never had a chance,' he said, almost in a whisper, but there was bitterness in his tone.

She waited and said nothing. He fell silent and looked past her to the window. The deep pinks were darkening over the horizon as the evening descended.

'Do you remember when I went to Harvard?' he asked abruptly.

'Vaguely. It's a long time ago. I remember Alan saying you were a lucky so-and-so. Mostly I remember my mother saying it was a scandal you were off in America, dumping your wife and daughter at home.'

'What did you think?' His eyes examined her face.

She shrugged awkwardly. 'I don't know. I was fourteen or something. More worried about bad hair days. You were just Tom to me.' She gave a little smile. 'I was sorry you'd got married, though. I'd always kind of hoped—'

She paused when she saw he was not really listening. 'Oh, never mind.'

He was searching the gathering dusk where his memories were.

'It was the day I got the news that I'd won the scholarship. I went round to her house with the letter. Pretty dumb, when I think about it now, but I was so overjoyed.

What do you think? – I asked her. And then she came straight out with it. *I'm pregnant.* Just like that. *I'm pregnant.*'

He sipped his tea and looked into the cup, as if noticing for the first time what he was drinking. 'I could use something a little stronger than this.'

'No, tea'll be fine for you,' she said firmly. 'Drink and anxiety are bad companions.'

'Nevertheless—'

He got up and went to the kitchen and when he came back there was a glass of whiskey in his hand. She smelled the sharp fumes and for the first time in ages she felt as if she wanted a drink herself. It was obvious that her weakness had not occurred to him. She drank some more tea and allowed the moment to pass.

'Harvard,' he said, after the first sip. 'Yes, that was my dream. It was all I could think of. I had tunnel vision. And being so preoccupied myself, I just didn't see how obsessed *she* had become.'

You can still be preoccupied, Kate thought, but she did not say it.

'Even then, when she told me, it didn't dawn on me straight away. It didn't occur to me that she'd got pregnant deliberately, in order to keep me here.'

'And so you got married.'

'Madness. I felt carried along in a tide. The wrath of the parish priest. All the pressure of the two families and Mary, who had got what she wanted. There was such a stigma about unmarried mothers. Sin – a disgrace in the eyes of God – I remember being told stuff like that a lot. The liberal sixties took one look at Ireland and moved on,

I reckon. And abortion – well, you didn't mention the word, although everybody knew about all the girls who slipped quietly off on the boat to England. Not that Mary had the slightest intention of doing anything like that.'

'So, Harvard then. How come—'

'They were very flattering. I told them I had to turn the offer down but they said they'd hold it open for a full year in case I changed my mind. We moved in with Mary's parents and I worked behind a bar for a while to earn a bit of money. And then Emma came along. Mary chose the name. I had no say in it.' He drank some more. 'Just the way I had no say in anything else. Nineteen-year-old law students who've been shotgunned into marriage and feel they're missing the chance of a lifetime in America don't make very good fathers. Mary and I fought all the time. After a while even she admitted that it had all been a big mistake.'

'She'd cheated you – is that what you thought?'

He weighed it up. 'Cheated – but not exactly robbed. Harvard was still open to me; the year's grace hadn't expired. Eventually Mary agreed that it was best to let me go. She'd got a job in her uncle's solicitor's office at that stage, working as a secretary, so that meant a bit of extra cash coming in. I guess she concluded that in the long term her life would be better off without me.'

'What about her parents? Your own parents?'

'They thought I was a disgrace, just like your mother did, but they also thought I was making Mary's life a misery here. So I went. Couldn't wait. Jesus, what a self-centred shit I was.'

'You said that, not me.'

He looked sharply at her. 'Well, Christ, Kate, I was only a kid. A whole life and a career in front of me that I didn't want to lose. I felt as if – as if America had given me my soul back, you know? I didn't want the kind of domestic commitments that had been dumped on me.'

He was veering from self-condemnation to self-defence. It was hard to know how to respond but she decided to stand her ground rather than just humour him.

'Maybe you should have thought of that before – you know.'

He raised his hand. 'Sex education lecture not necessary, okay?'

'If you say so.'

'I wasn't a complete asshole. I didn't forget my responsibilities altogether. I studied damn hard and I put in hours of graft in a whole bunch of part-time jobs – I'm a shit-hot short-order cook – I ever tell you that? At any rate, that helped the bursary I was getting, plus there was a small allowance from my dad, who was about the only friend I had. I don't think he ever told my mother about it, God bless him. Each month I sent money home.'

'But you never had any real intention of coming back, did you? Once there, you were always going to stay if you could.'

He looked at her with a kind of desperation. 'You don't like what I did, do you, Kate? But please don't dislike me for it.'

'Tom, it's not for me to judge—' she started but he had moved on.

'I knew for sure that I wanted to stay when the FBI came into the picture. By then I'd developed a fascination with organised crime. I'd written a thesis on what I'd observed as the limitations of US law enforcement at the time. I got it published in a Washington law periodical but what I didn't know was that the kind of new legislation I was suggesting, involving seizure of assets, targeting the proceeds of crime, was already being developed on the quiet. A few months before my graduation I was called to the office of the Dean of the Faculty and found two guys from the Bureau waiting for me, telling me my thesis had impressed a lot of influential people who'd read it and how would I like to join their legal department.'

The memory of his moment of recognition thrilled him anew. She could see it in his eyes.

'They made it sound very attractive – citizenship, rapid progress in Washington – and there was only one decision I wanted to make. So I came back to Dublin to discuss it with Mary because there was no future in the Bureau for me if my personal affairs weren't in order.'

'And I assume she didn't stand in your way.'

'Not at all. She was terrific about it, better than I deserved. And that's how it began.'

'But all those years – both of you with your lives in some kind of dreadful limbo . . .'

'The job, you see. It was everything to me. There was nothing else.' He paused and shook his head. 'What a fool. I supported Mary and Emma, provided for her education, but she wasn't the first thing in my thoughts each day. Sure, I came home a couple of times a year but the more she grew, the more she seemed to grow away, becoming more of a stranger to me, and her mother would certainly have done nothing to change her attitude. But it was what I deserved. I was no father to her, always so impatient to get back to the States again to my career. My damned career.'

He took a gulp from his glass.

'And now I want to make it up to her and she won't give me a chance. She doesn't need me, Kate. She made that clear. When I told her I was coming home, she said she couldn't stop me but she never had a father before and she didn't need one now. Can you imagine how much that hurt me?'

'You came back, nevertheless. It was still the right thing for you to do. To come home.' She sat forward and put a tentative hand to his cheek. 'Give her time. It's difficult for her. She'll come round in the end. She's punishing you for not being here. It's – it's like Paul. I think he's punishing *me* for the fact that he doesn't have a father.'

He stared at her while the words registered with him.

She saw his expression. 'Oh yes. Apparently it's all my fault.'

'God, Kate, I'm so sorry. And so goddamn selfish. I didn't mean to dump everything on you. You have worries, too. How could I have forgotten?'

She smiled and stood. 'I'll clear up.'

She lifted the cups and brought them out to the kitchen, leaving him sitting there with an almost empty glass. As she ran water into the sink, she felt a tightness in her chest. It always came with stress and she had no shortage of that. There was the pressure of work, her problems with her son. And now this. Tom's road to recovery was a long one, longer than she had realised. Could she cope with it?

A bottle of Power's whiskey stood on the table where he

had left it. In its amber glint she saw both an invitation and a threat.

In front of it, side by side, were two opened letters.

She knew she shouldn't.

As she read, an image of her dead husband and the financial disaster that had killed him flickered in her consciousness for a moment.

A shiver passed through her.

She gathered herself and went back into the living room. He smiled at her and she returned it, a little weakly, feeling sorry for him and hoping that her face would not reveal what she had done.

Chapter Eight

'When this is over, I want to retire.'

Grant sipped his Perrier. 'That's what you always say.'

'And you never let me do it,' Leslie said.

With the breeze in their faces, they sat on the deck at the back of Grant's weekend house on Long Island, looking down through the trees towards his private jetty and beyond that to the yachts bobbing softly at anchor.

They had just enjoyed a farewell lunch to mark Leslie's imminent departure to Europe. There had been only the two of them, apart from the cook who had served it. Here, away from the others, they could talk freely and intimately.

'When it's done, we'll discuss it,' Grant said.

'No, Michael, I want to talk about it now.'

Grant looked at him and wondered if he had had a little too much wine.

'All right then.'

'Always there is one last payment,' Leslie said.

'I hate to sound like Heywood Corbett,' Grant interrupted, 'but that kind of cuts both ways.'

Leslie acknowledged the point. 'I accept what you say. I

have been handsomely rewarded over the years but still I feel I am in your debt. I think it is time you declared that debt closed.'

The two men looked at each other. There were things that did not need to be spoken, things from the past.

'I am on the verge of putting in place an important new phase of your operation,' Leslie said. 'But more than that – you have afforded me the opportunity to avenge a great wrong that was done. The thing that has haunted me all these years. When I have taken care of everything, I will have drawn a line under that part of my life.'

Grant turned towards the view. 'Perhaps you're right. You've always emphasised the importance of succession planning. Perhaps it's time I thought of who will succeed you.'

'You don't need to do that. *You* have everything it takes, Michael. All I ask is to be allowed to retire. With dignity. And with honour satisfied.'

Grant put a hand on his arm. 'All right,' he said. 'That's how it will be. If all goes well with this venture.' He smiled. The subject was closed. 'So – Europe. It's a long time since you've been back.'

'Forty years,' Leslie said. 'I was barely twenty when I came to this country. Alone. My parents dead and my brother killed in the revolution.'

'How about some more wine?' Grant asked.

'Please. Just a little.'

Grant got up and went into the house to fetch it. Leslie put his head back. He could hear the distant growl of a plane and he watched its jet stream drawing a thin white line across the blue of the sky.

There had been 200,000 of them, refugees like himself, stumbling across frozen fields at night, their pasts and their futures in little satchels and suitcases, making their way towards France, the United Kingdom, the United States – the countries which had failed them by not intervening but which were now havens of safety.

He had made it to Austria and then to Italy where he had got on board a ship heading to New York. A distant cousin had vouched for him and taken him in and for the first few months he had tried not to let the city overwhelm him. He wanted *it* to work for *him*, not the other way round. He had immersed himself in learning about America, how the Government and the Constitution operated, the country's laws, its economy, its tax system. And, of course, its language.

Young Gabor Laszlo, as he still was, had always been good with languages but figures were his real talent. He had the ability to grasp mathematical concepts very quickly and he possessed a gift for being able to work out difficult problems in his head. His brain was like an accountant's ledger or, these days, like a computer spreadsheet, with debits and credits all firmly in place in its memory banks.

The cousin, a man in his fifties, ran a restaurant on the lower east side, more of a sandwich bar for passing workmen and a few elderly people from the old country. It barely held its own. Gabor volunteered to have a look at the financial position and in a very short time he had things on an even keel through accounting methods which were more creative than they were legal but which were discreet and unlikely to start alarm bells ringing with the IRS.

The cousin was overjoyed and during Friday night card sessions with his friends he spread the word that here was a boy who could do wonderful things for you.

Thus it had all started. Forty years ago. Forty years of planning, of politics, of knowing who to work for and who to avoid, who was on the way up, who was on the way out, eventually reaching a position where he could influence such events himself.

Grant came back with a fresh glass.

'Heywood Corbett still doesn't like you very much,' he said.

Leslie sipped the chilled wine and shrugged. 'That doesn't matter to me. *You* are the one who should watch out for him. He is a weak link. A weak link threatens the whole chain, makes it vulnerable to pressure. Perhaps you should think about that.'

He looked at Grant and saw that the thought was already there.

Grant raised his glass. 'Bon voyage.'

As he packed that night, Leslie smiled to himself. It would take a little time but it was inevitable. Heywood Corbett was gone.

The suitcase open on his bed was not large but it was big enough for one, especially a man who liked to travel light. The clothes he was packing into it were light, too: silk and linen shirts with short sleeves, lightweight cotton trousers, canvas deck shoes, a baseball cap, even a couple of pairs of bermudas. In a bulky wash bag, among the soaps and toothpaste and shaving equipment, there was insect repellent and high-protection sun cream.

It was not the suitcase of a man setting off for Zurich, which would be his first stop in Europe. It was more the suitcase of a man planning a trip to Florida, a short spring holiday in the sun.

Or so he intended people to think.

He was aware that although he kept his activities discreet, the agencies of law enforcement took a considerable interest in him. It would be foolish to book a flight to Zurich. As soon as he did, the FBI would find out about it and they would contact Interpol and the Swiss who might well refuse him entry and stick him on the return plane.

No, that was not sensible.

A flight to Florida, on the other hand, was a different matter. He had rented a house overlooking the sea at Palm Beach and that is where he would appear to be staying for the next few weeks.

The journey there might be uneventful but it was just possible that there would be a problem along the way. His suitcase, for instance. It would not be the first time that his baggage had arrived at its destination after he had or that it had somehow got mixed up with the cases from another flight for fifteen minutes or so.

In either circumstance, it allowed the FBI time to go through it, to see what secrets it held. But they had never found any, nor would they now, he told himself as he folded a silk pyjama jacket into a neat square and patted it into the case.

There. Complete. The real clothes he would purchase elsewhere.

He zipped the case shut and lifted a soft leather shoulder bag from a chair. It contained essentials for the flight, including a couple of books, but there was one thing more to go in, something very precious to him and which he would never be without.

He opened his bedside drawer and took out a photograph in an antique frame. He ran his fingers gently over the woven silver surface, looking at the face in the picture, then closed his eyes for a moment.

The photograph always brought the agony back. Always.

The face was that of a young man in his twenties with hair of deepest black, short and neat and brushed hard back from his face. The lighting in the picture cast a subtle shadow over his sallow skin tones. He was smiling but the smile had not parted his full lips. And the eyes. The eyes, under heavy brows, carried the message that there were secrets within.

Alex. My son. How much I miss you.

Alex Leslie had been dead for nearly four years. Since then, his father had kept the photograph in the drawer, concealing it there because he could not bear the thought of seeing it suddenly on a mantelpiece or a shelf or a cabinet, the memory stabbing at him when he was unprepared. But it would go with him now because he could not stand to be apart from it.

He eased himself slowly into a chair and continued to caress the frame. There was not an indentation in it that he did not know and it was as if the gentle movement of his hands was summoning the past.

Chapter Nine

On this occasion Tony Goulding was in his role as Minister for Industrial Development and Technology but the fact that he was also the *Tanaiste*, the Deputy Prime Minister, provided additional prestige.

He stood with a handful of lesser dignitaries, like the Lord Mayor, on a dais at the front of the huge exhibition hall at the Royal Dublin Society grounds at Ballsbridge. Before him were row upon row of trade stands and hundreds of people waiting to hear what he had to say.

It was not a particularly high podium and so most of the people, especially those at the back, were unable to see him in the flesh. But it did not matter. Thanks to monitors on each stand and several video walls mounted around the hall, they could see his face wherever they were. It was an impressive display of televisual communication but it was out of the age of steam compared to some of the concepts which would be revealed in the coming weeks.

Goulding was about to open the third WONTEC, the annual world information technology convention. Before its launch two years ago, some of the organisers had come up with the working title of WINTEC but others felt this sounded too much like just another Microsoft innovation. Bill Gates might have conquered the world but not all of his opponents had come out of the bushes to surrender.

So a slightly more neutral acronym had emerged and although it had once been remarked that the alternative sounded like a stir-fry, it had stayed as WONTEC. Gates himself was due in Dublin in two days' time to give a lecture at University College, and other gurus of IT would be appearing at seminars and debates in various centres throughout the city.

Goulding's face with its shining, beefy features beamed from the video screens. He was a man who might have been described as verging on elderly although he preferred to think of himself as being in late middle age. He had wary eyes and carefully tended silver wings of hair and WONTEC's presence on these shores was an enormous coup for him.

The first convention had been in California, the second in Japan and now here it was in Ireland. There had been puzzlement and a slight snootiness in some quarters when the venue had been announced but to the more informed observers it was no surprise at all.

For years Ireland had been welcoming computer firms and gaining a reputation as a kind of silicon island. It was a country with an enterprise culture and one that provided attractive arrangements, like low corporate tax, for industries thinking of putting down roots, particularly those industries looking to the future of new technology, of which Ireland aimed to be a world patron.

Industrial development and the jobs which went with it had been the key to Democratic Nation's electoral success.

It was why, when the Cabinet was being formed and Goulding and the Prime Minister were discussing which post he should have, he had been firm about creating this one for himself.

In his chosen area of responsibility, Goulding had come to be seen as something of a magician and even though he had the strategies and successes of previous Governments to build on he always managed to make it look as if the credit was his and his alone. Securing this convention in the face of vigorous international competition was most definitely a personal triumph and in the speech which he was about to make, he would add to the achievement with the announcement that another American software company was going to set up shop, this time in County Mayo.

Not all of the delegates to WONTEC would hear the speech although, of course, it would be available on-line if they wished to pick up on it later. Some of the delegates had not even arrived yet while others had already sought out the charms of Dublin's pubs and hotel bars where they were downloading pints of Guinness and glasses of Bushmills whiskey.

It was unlikely that many of them would bother to pick up a local paper, except perhaps to look at the entertainment listings, although since they no longer considered newspapers to be a primary source of information it was more probable that they would get what they wanted from the website created especially for the convention or from other pages on the net.

If they had looked through the papers, however, they could not have avoided seeing one story which had gripped the local media and which might conceivably have given them a different take on Dublin life from the one they were experiencing in its hostelries.

Even in a place used to occasional instances of violent crime, this one had a particular shock value. Two battered corpses had been found in a rubbish tip on the outskirts of the city. The bodies were that of a girl and a young man. The girl's skull had been smashed and it seemed as if the man had been systematically beaten before his skull was crushed, too.

The police were appealing for information but there were no leads as yet, although the identities of the couple had been established. The girl was from Waterford and had left home months before to live in Dublin, exactly where, her mother did not know, but she knew her whereabouts now, that was for sure, having just had the appalling task of identifying the remains.

Some weeks ago, the girl's brother had also left home, according to reports, with the intention of coming to Dublin to try to find her but there was no sign of him now either and the police had issued a description. There was no photograph to go with it because his mother had only a couple of childhood snaps. He resembled thousands of young men in this city and the *Gardai* did not hold out much hope of finding him if he did not wish them to.

Nor were they at all convinced that he was still alive.

The dead man had been known to the police. He came from north Dublin and he had spent too much of his short life in and out of young offenders' centres and prison for a succession of offences involving robbery and possession of drugs. Both the victims had been users and it was generally assumed that in some way their habit had precipitated their deaths.

One crime correspondent had been talking to 'sources' and had reported that the police believed they knew who might be responsible but they had no evidence to link this person with the crime. The murders were also believed to be connected to the discovery of the burnt-out remains of a stolen van in the shell of a warehouse on an industrial estate. On the floor of the building the police had found extensive patches of dried blood.

In addition, they had found the house in Ballyfermot where the couple had been squatting and they had tried to talk to the neighbours. But that was a complete waste of time as usual. Ballyfermot was a place where people told the police nothing, no matter what, and so if there was anyone who had seen or knew anything they were certainly not going to reveal it.

Unless the brother turned up, alive, the prospects for solving this one did not look good.

But none of this was occupying the attention of the WONTEC fraternity who were still streaming into Dublin airport from major cities throughout the world.

Among them were five men whose ages ranged from twenty-five to forty. They were ordinary-looking men, indistinguishable from all the other delegates, and their arrival would arouse no particular interest. In the unlikely event that it did, they each had ID from a minor subsidiary of Hurll Inc, the American computer giant.

They had not travelled together. Three of them had American passports and had flown from New York, Boston and Los Angeles. The other two had come from

London and Paris and carried European Union passports which allowed them to walk straight out of the airport without being stopped by Customs and Immigration.

They had been chosen as much for the anonymity of their appearance as the technical expertise which they possessed. They needed to blend with their surroundings and for that reason they were all caucasian. There were no blacks or Asians among them or men of Latin origin. Dublin, although proudly cosmopolitan, was in essence a white city.

The group had a leader, a man who wore glasses.

It was not Parrish's first visit. He and two of his companions had been here before.

Their destinations were several of the city's hotels, the bigger and more crowded the better, and so only major hotels had been selected. It had not been easy finding the right accommodation. Many of the hotels had been fully booked for some time but in the end appropriate arrangements had been made. None of the men would stay in one hotel for more than two days before moving on to another one.

Transport was not a concern. Two cars had been left at the airport for them and hidden in secure compartments under the back seats was all the equipment they would need for their stay.

In the days following their arrival, they would do their homework, get to know the geography and wait for their moment to come.

Gallagher sampled the cool tartness of his Guinness, then licked the froth from his top lip. In a painting above his head, the thin face of James Joyce observed the ritual from behind his glasses.

Gallagher's companion had a pint of Guinness, too, and he was using it to help swallow a large portion of humble pie.

Although he was the same age, Alan Warnock had not worn as well. He was a small man, bald and over-weight, but he had his sister's mellow brown eyes.

They were just off Grafton Street in Davy Byrne's, one of Dublin's most famous pubs, the noisy watering-hole for literati past and present, where wide-eyed tourists wandered in looking for an atmosphere which the regulars all took for granted. Gallagher and Warnock were perched on stools at a marble shelf along a wall decorated with brass light fittings in the shape of daffodils. It was as if spring had come into the pub with them but it had not done much to lighten their mood.

'Listen,' Warnock said when they had both taken the edge off their thirst, 'thanks for coming. I, eh – I didn't want us to fall out about this, you know? I was just as shocked as you were about what happened.'

Gallagher gave a surly shrug. He did not want to go over his problems with Emma again.

'Well, for what it's worth,' Warnock continued, 'it's made things kind of difficult for me, too.'

Gallagher gave him a sceptical look and waited.

'It was a bloody sub-editor trying to be clever. I gave her your piece and then came the row in the *Dail* and I suppose she went – *aha, time for a bit of fun here*. The paper hates Democratic Nation, you know.'

'I had noticed.'

'If I'd known what she'd done, I'd have killed the picture but I wasn't there when the page was being put together. I nearly died when I saw it.'

'So,' Gallagher said, 'how's this a problem for you? I'd have thought the editor would have given you a raise.' He sipped his drink slowly.

A choking cough from a nearby table distracted them. A man with a plate of oysters had gone red in the face and his companion was hammering him on the back.

'Too much Tabasco,' Warnock diagnosed before going on. 'The editor heard I'd torn a strip off her. So he called me in and told me she'd done a brilliant job. Very enterprising, very imaginative, he said, just the sort of person who knew what the paper was all about and I was to tell her that and if I didn't watch myself I might find she'd been given my job.'

'So what did you do?'

'What do you think I did? I told her the editor thought she'd done well but it didn't mean that I thought the same and then I went out and got stinking drunk. I'm not getting any younger and I've got the mortgage to pay, you know. I can't afford to make principled stands. You go from being *enfant terrible* to old fart overnight in this business and no one wants you. Anyway, I wanted you to know. I apologise. And now I owe you one. I mean that.'

Gallagher was finding it hard to remain indignant with his old friend, as he knew he would. As well as that, there was a cheque from *Dublin Sunday* on the way and he needed the money. His appointment with his bank manager was looming.

'Okay, then,' he said, 'lend me twenty grand.'

'Yeah, right,' Warnock said with a laugh. 'Nice one. What would you like – pounds or dollars? Maybe you could think of something a bit more realistic, like – why don't I buy the next round.'

Gallagher downed his pint with determination.

'All right. Why don't you buy the next round?'

Chapter Ten

Days later, a clutch of taxi-drivers stood gossiping beside their vehicles outside Dublin Airport's arrivals hall. It was early evening on a March day that had been sharply sunny and there was still a lot of warmth and light in the sky.

The doors parted and a slightly-built man with dark glasses and grey hair emerged, pushing a single suitcase on a trolley. The first driver was leaning back against his car, arms folded over a stomach straining against a cotton shirt that had once been the right size. He levered himself upright.

'Yes sir,' he said. 'A taxi, is it?'

The man looked at the row of vehicles and saw that this one, a white Toyota, was as good as any.

'Yes,' he said. The driver was already reaching for the suitcase. 'Can you take me to the Shelbourne Hotel?'

'The Shelbourne,' the driver confirmed, opening the boot and putting the case inside. 'No problem at all.'

He opened the back door and Gilbert Leslie eased himself in.

The driver hummed cheerily as they negotiated the road

system through the airport complex and then made their way out onto the dual carriageway taking them to the city. He glanced in his rear-view mirror at his passenger but the dark glasses meant that he could not see the man's eyes and could not tell where he was looking.

He had noticed the accent.

'You're American, then?' he asked. He was one of the breed of Dublin taxi-men who did not consider that their job was just to drive. The driving was secondary; the conversation came first.

'Canada.'

The driver nodded his acceptance of the correction. 'Business trip, is it, or pleasure?'

'Perhaps a bit of both.'

'Aye, well, sure you might as well enjoy yourself while you can.'

'That's right,' Leslie said with finality. The discussion was going no further. He turned his head to gaze out of the window.

They reached the Dublin outskirts in a silence broken only by the dispatcher's voice issuing instructions on the radio and by the driver muttering under his breath at some of the idiosyncrasies of his fellow motorists. They drove on towards the heart of the city and down to O'Connell Street, an impressive boulevard with trees lined all along the centre and statues to people Leslie did not recognise.

But what made him sit up was the sight of the flags.

On each side of the street strings of triangular green pennants laced the buildings from top to bottom, like ships dressed overall in ceremonial display.

He leaned forward. 'What are the flags for?'

From the mirror, the driver's eyes looked at him to see if this was a joke.

'Never hear of St Patrick's Day?' he said. 'Not long to go now.'

Of course. For some crazy reason, Leslie always associated St Patrick's Day with New York, the parade along Fifth Avenue, the green beer and all the drunken jollification. But Dublin – this was the authentic celebration. What had he been thinking of?

'Stupid me,' he said. 'It must be the jet lag.'

They crossed O'Connell Bridge, drove on round the perimeter of Trinity College, up Kildare Street towards St Stephen's Green and then they came to a halt in front of the hotel.

'There we are, sir,' the driver said. 'The Shelbourne.'

Leslie got out and looked up at the handsome building. It had stood there since 1824 and had been built so that there would be somewhere for the Anglo-Irish landed gentry of the time to wine and dine and eventually lay their heads when they came into the city from their vast country estates. Many of them would have had their own town houses but not every owner of such a mansion could afford to maintain it all the year round. The Shelbourne had been a godsend to them as well as a stroke of entrepreneurial genius on the part of the man who had built it.

It had been named in memory of an eighteenth-century British Prime Minister, Lord Shelbourne, whose family had previously owned that portion of the Green on which it was sited. But time and history had moved on, perhaps most noticeably in the irony that it was in one of the hotel's big first floor rooms in 1922 that the Constitution of the Irish Free State was drafted, a project supervised by the legendary Michael Collins.

The driver took the case from the boot and handed it into the custody of a red-faced porter wilting in the heat of his uniform of thorny grey tweed jacket and waistcoat. Leslie paid the driver and tipped him.

'Thank you very much, sir,' the man said with genuine gratitude. 'I hope you enjoy your stay in Dublin.'

'Oh, I'm certain I will,' Leslie assured him.

At the reception desk, he announced himself as Mr Gerd Schenk from Toronto and filled in his Canadian passport details on the registration card. He could see that the hotel was busy. On the way he had noticed posters proclaiming the international technology convention, which was now in full swing.

It was a long time since he had left the house at Westchester.

The journey had been complex. First there had been the decoy trip to Palm Beach from which he had then departed in a somewhat undignified manner in the back of a laundry van. After that, using the Schenk passport, he had flown to Toronto where he had picked up a new suitcase and clothes of Canadian purchase.

From there he had flown to Zurich to visit a banker and deliver instructions. Then he had gone to Amsterdam to meet certain key businessmen and tell them what was expected of them.

In both cities he had been greeted almost with awe. It was as if the power of what he represented radiated from him. It was a feeling he liked.

Once he had registered, the porter took his case and led him to a tiny lift of ancient wood and gleaming brass. They went up to the third floor, along a corridor with creaking boards under soft carpet, and Leslie was shown into a small suite.

Once again he found himself at a hotel window overlooking a park. St Stephen's Green was a small island of tranquillity in the midst of the bustling city traffic and the entrance to it was guarded by the tall statue of a man of imposing form and a style of dress that seemed to be early nineteenth century.

Leslie turned back to the room. The sitting-room portion was quite tiny, really just an extension to the bedroom, but it was comfortable. The bathroom, when he inspected it, was fresh and clean. He wondered how much time he would spend in these rooms and he thought of everything that he would sanction and organise and initiate from this quiet sanctuary with the muffled sounds of Dublin outside.

Tomorrow it would all begin. The removal of the first pawn from the chessboard. Then all the others. Until the final sacrifice.

The one he had come for.

He lifted his case on to the bed and unpacked it.

All in good time.

He would sleep long and late in order to shed the debilitating effects of the journey but first he felt like taking a short walk. The park was invitingly near and he was intrigued by the statue. When he got to it, he found that it was to a man called Wolfe Tone, one of the first martyrs to Irish freedom, who had led a poorly organised rebellion against the English in 1798 and subsequently died in prison.

Leslie did not believe in foolish, heroic gestures guided only by raw emotion and not by sense or strategy. That was what had doomed both Tone's rebellion and the uprising in his own country in 1956.

Ireland's eventual independence had been gained by stealth and cunning minds as well as bloodshed. And look at the transformation which time and persistence had brought about in Hungary. In his thoughts he glimpsed Budapest, the river and the bridges across it. Zurich was the nearest he had been for forty years. He wondered if he would ever go back.

Just inside the entrance to the Green there were two more statues: ragged, brittle-looking human shapes, one holding a cup from which real water flowed down to where the other might drink it. It was a reminder to all who passed by of that great Irish tragedy, the Famine. Here, too, was a country which had come a long way.

He let the pathways lead him where they wished. It was light enough for there to be birdsong in the trees still. Two stout magpies strutted on the grass, examining it carefully as if looking for a comfortable place to sit.

All of a sudden, he was out of the Green again, this time on the opposite side of the square to the Shelbourne, and he found himself looking across the street at a row of imposing buildings. He waited for the traffic lights to change and then walked over to see what they were.

There were name plates outside each and he saw from this identification that they were all Government departments. There was no obvious security presence, the area was not cordoned off, and he was amazed at how they were just here, in the middle of the city, with such casual confidence.

There was the Department of Foreign Affairs, a proud edifice with pillars at its front door. Just along from it, No 72 St Stephen's Green, was an unattractive modern construction, six floors of dull concrete and glass. A sign on the front door told motorcyclists to remove their helmets before entering.

Leslie looked up at the words etched above the entrance. Department of Justice.

He gave a little smile. I could almost see you from my room, he thought. Such a compact city. Everything so near, so near.

He felt as if he had just walked across a stage in the final moments before the curtain went up.

Chapter Eleven

As the theme music faded, Marcus Kelly waited for the floor manager to announce that the show was a wrap and then he turned to each of his two guests to thank them.

Neither the Deputy Lord Mayor of Dublin nor the city's Assistant Police Commissioner felt much like shaking his outstretched hand, not after what he had concocted on this programme, so instead they walked straight off the set to where the make-up would be wiped from their flushed faces, telling each other that it would not be the last Mr Kelly would hear of this.

Kelly watched them go, feeling triumphant and totally unconcerned.

Fuck them anyway.

Tomorrow was St Patrick's Day and he would go down to his local where he would get drunk like everyone else and the people there would all tell him what a great fellow he was and he would glory in their admiration. And he had been particularly good tonight – that was the important thing.

Tonight's *The Kelly Inquiry* had dealt with joy-riding, a

major problem in Dublin, with hundreds of cars being stolen each year, many of them taken into the big housing estates where they were raced around the streets before being wrecked, burnt-out or stripped of everything that could be removed and re-sold. He reckoned he had exposed official policy on the subject, as personified by his two guests, as worse than useless.

But the Assistant Commissioner had become incensed by the surprise package which Kelly had produced for them.

There was no point in doing a programme about joy-riding unless you saw people actually engaged in it, so Kelly and his cameraman had been on board a stolen car when its fourteen-year-old driver had whirled it hazardously around the roads. It had been gripping stuff, no doubt about that, and they had interviewed the kids about why they did what they did and what sort of kicks they got out of it.

When they got to the studio discussion, the Assistant Commissioner, who had not known what the film contained, had accused him of encouraging young people to break the law.

'You have actually assisted in the commission of a crime yourself,' he said, gesticulating angrily, 'and I will personally make sure that the police pursue this matter.'

It had got hot and heavy after that but Kelly had come out on top in the end because he was infinitely more at home in a television studio than they were. And no matter whose side the viewers were on, they were certain to tune in again next week. That was what mattered and that was what had made him Ireland's number one television journalist.

He disentangled his earpiece and thanked the crew, then left the studio himself, wondering whether to get his own make-up off now or wait until he got home. Whoever did it would have to be careful with his nose. After Sean Donovan's infamous headbutt it was knitting all right and the swelling had gone down but it was still tender.

He would have a drink first. There was no one in the hospitality room when he got there so he poured himself a glass of soave. It was a bit warm but it would do. He had just put it to his lips when the door flew open.

Dan Corrigan, RTE's Controller of Programmes, was freckle-faced and had hair like rusty wire. Dressed in jeans and a sweater, he had just driven in from home and he was standing on the ledge of his self-control.

There was a low tremble in his voice. 'What the fuck are you playing at?'

Kelly feigned innocence. 'What are you talking about?'

'You know perfectly bloody well what I'm talking about. What attempts were made to clear all that joy-riding stuff with the editorial management?'

Kelly shrugged. 'There wasn't time.' He took a drink.

'Wasn't time, my arse. You deliberately didn't let us in on the detail of this programme. Oh yes, you told the Head of Department about the subject matter and the running order, who the contributors were, that sort of thing, but you didn't tell him about the film. And do you know why you didn't? Because you knew that if we'd heard what you were up to we would have said no.'

He walked forward and stood head to head with Kelly. 'And do you know why we'd have said no? Because we're funded in part by public money, we have responsibilities to our viewers and to our governing body, the RTE Authority, we have obligations to—'

'Ah, for Christ sake, don't give me all that crap,' Kelly broke in. 'Don't talk to me like I'm some sort of a fucking public meeting. The truth is – you hide behind all these fucking obligations because it saves you having to do anything. The biggest decision you ever take in your life is – is deciding whether you're going to wear black shoes or brown ones.'

In spite of himself, Corrigan looked down at his feet. He was wearing an old pair of trainers. They were grey.

'You wouldn't know a good programme if you saw one,' Kelly said. 'And that was a fucking good programme tonight.'

He stabbed a forefinger in Corrigan's direction and some of the wine splashed from his glass on to the floor. 'Just check the calls from the viewers. Check the overnight figures tomorrow morning. Check what it says in the papers.'

He put his glass down. 'And then maybe it'll sink in that it's my programme which is keeping the likes of you in a fucking job.'

He walked past him and across the room to the door.

Corrigan turned, enraged. 'Now, listen here, Kelly. Don't you ever talk to me—'

'Ah, fuck off,' Kelly said over his shoulder and slammed the door behind him.

The sound echoed in his head as he walked down the empty corridor and out through the reception area to the car park. It was well after 11pm and the rows of vehicles in

119

it had thinned out long ago. His white Audi stood out like a beacon. He pressed the fob on his key-ring and the doors unlocked with a squeak and a blink of tail-light.

His blood was racing. He had no time for these people. They knew nothing about good television and they were paying him and his production company fucking buttons to make a series that was raking in the viewers.

Money. He was not getting enough of what was due to him. But that was another story, something he would have to deal with at another time.

He drove out of the car park, heading left towards the road that would take him home, then realised he had forgotten about his make-up. He was sweating slightly as a result of the excitement and it would ruin his shirt. He yanked his tie off and opened his top button, feeling a welcome freedom from constriction.

It was about five miles from RTE to Kelly's apartment at Killiney along the seafront. His was one of three sumptuous flats in a converted Victorian residence on a hillside with trees clustered behind and the sea spread out in front. On a good day, it reminded him of the Italian coast and on a bad day it was still bloody good.

He punched his home number into the car phone and heard his own voice answering. His wife was either out or she had gone to bed and put the machine on. He stuck Celine Dion into the CD player.

It always infuriated him how many junctions and traffic lights there were on this road. It was a cause for celebration if you got beyond third gear. He sat at a red light, waiting for it to change, tapping the steering wheel in time to the music and feeling himself cooling down at last.

On his right, there were the houses of Frascati Park and the big shopping complex which had been built to serve them. Frascati Park. A memory of some builder's Italian holiday. What would be next? Cabernet Sauvignon Avenue? He thought of the wine he had abandoned back at the studio. Soave Street, perhaps?

The light went green and he put his foot down on the accelerator, turning left into a more residential road. He shot along it faster than the speed restrictions allowed, not noticing that a car which had been a few vehicles behind him at the lights had also turned in this direction.

He slowed down when he was nearer home. The house sat off a winding hillside road so narrow that it was virtually impossible for two cars to pass. Further up the hill, someone appeared to have a visitor. In the shadows he could see that a dark car was parked, tucked up onto the pavement.

He swung in through the open gateway and his wheels crunched over the deep gravel which covered the turning area in front of the building. There were three double garages off to one side and he went slowly towards his, at the same time lifting the remote control box from the dashboard and clicking it to open the door.

Nothing. Bloody nuisance but it had happened before. An erratic signal or something but it always worked in the end.

The security lights round the house had not come on either. Maybe there was a power failure.

He tried again. Still nothing.

Once more.

Bollocks.

He would have to get out and open the bloody thing with a key. So much for the wonders of modern science.

He opened the car door and it pinged softly to tell him he had left his lights on but he knew that anyway because how else was he going to see the lock in this darkness? He left the door open and walked forward, fumbling through his key-ring for the right one.

As he did so, two figures eased gently out of the shadows behind him.

Although they trod as softly as they could, the gravel made silence impossible and Kelly heard them. He wheeled round, dazzling himself with the glare of his own headlights, and raised his right hand instinctively to protect his eyes.

The shotgun blast shattered the silence of the night with a roar like a cannon.

It blew Kelly's chest apart and propelled him backwards into the garage door. He hit it with a metallic crash and fell in a limp bundle.

One of the figures crouched quickly in front of him with a pistol in his hand and shot him twice in the head, just behind the ear. Then they both scurried back to the road.

The parked car in the shadows had been joined by the one which had followed Kelly home and they waited with their engines running. When the men were on board, the vehicles sped off in separate directions.

Lights were coming on in windows, voices were wondering what on earth was going on and the soft but insistent sound from the white Audi continued to remind its driver about the headlights.

Chapter Twelve

At six thirty the following morning Peter O'Neill, the Prime Minister, *Taoiseach* in the Gaelic, was behind his desk.

It was St Patrick's Day and he had not expected to be here at all, never mind at such an early hour.

His itinerary for the day was, first, a reception at Dublin Castle for a group of American Congressmen paying an emotional visit to the land of their ancestry, then he would take up a conspicuous position in front of the GPO in O'Connell Street so that he could wave at the parade and be filmed doing so. After that it was off to his constituency north of the city where he was due to hand out the prizes at a junior Irish dancing festival.

But murder did not take St Patrick's Day into account. Especially this one.

In the normal run of things, crime, even a killing, would not have necessitated his personal attention but the death of Marcus Kelly was different. The newspapers spread out across the big desk and the three men sitting on the other side of it attested to that.

Conor Hogan was the *Garda* Commissioner. He was a

man with an unusually broad nose, the legacy of member-ship of the police boxing team many years ago, and it contrasted with the tiny mouth which nature had given him as if to discourage him from saying too much. It had not been effective; Hogan liked to hear himself talk.

Eamon Savage, the Minister for Justice, was a tall, heavily built man in his sixties with a frequent look of disdain, usually from over the top of his half-moon glasses. He bore such an expression this morning, largely because of the presence of the third man, Tony Goulding, an individual for whom he had no time. What they were discussing was none of Goulding's business and he resented the fact that the *Taoiseach* had invited him to sit in although he would wait for a more appropriate moment before saying so.

O'Neill himself, sitting across from these three robust figures, was a considerable physical contrast. He was much younger for a start, in his early forties, and he was a lot smaller. He had fine features and a soft, clear complexion but fatigue had taken up residence in the skin below his eyes.

He picked up a tabloid from the pile of newspapers and then dropped it again as if it had bitten him.

'Christ, look at this.'

ST PATRICK'S DAY MASSACRE – it read.

'Technically, it wasn't St Patrick's Day at all,' Goulding said, 'never mind that it wasn't exactly a massacre, either.'

'But since when did the facts ever get in the way of a good story?' the Commissioner wondered.

Savage brought them all up sharply.

'This is going to be very difficult for us,' he said.

'*Taoiseach*, I think the Commissioner should tell us what is known so far and where that might take us.'

O'Neill nodded. 'Of course. By all means.'

It did not take the Commissioner long to do so.

Marcus Kelly had departed from RTE shortly after 11pm and judging from the time the shots were heard he had driven straight home.

He gave a slight smile. 'We've established who he talked to at RTE before he left there. It seems he had quite a row with the Controller of Programmes and before that he'd had a confrontation with the Deputy Lord Mayor and one of my Assistant Commissioners. The whole country witnessed most of that particular little fracas live on air but we're not suggesting that any of these three gentlemen, much as they may have disliked Mr Kelly, would have gone as far as this.'

O'Neill took a short cut. 'Sean Donovan?'

The Commissioner nodded. 'Obviously a suspect, yes, but he's out of the country at the moment. In Amsterdam, we understand.'

'Handy, that,' Goulding said. 'The perfect alibi. It probably makes him more of a likely candidate, wouldn't you think?'

'But it doesn't help the police much,' Savage pointed out. 'This was a professional job. There seem to have been two cars involved or, at least, two cars were heard driving away from the scene, and the shooting itself was rather skilfully done. If Donovan hired a team to do it, it's going to be very hard to prove.'

'And it's going to be very hard to find them, too,' the Commissioner said.

'Does he have—' O'Neill pondered on the words – 'associates? Cronies, accomplices – whatever you like to call them?'

'There are a lot of people who are connected with him on and off. Drug pushers, prostitutes, pimps, that sort of thing. He doesn't keep a staff as such, apart from a girl who answers the phone at his official place of business, his so-called property company, a scruffy wee office down near the quays. But he has a sort of bodyguard who drives him about and does all the rough stuff for him, we suspect. A fellow called Vinnie Dwyer. We spoke to Mr Dwyer earlier this morning, got him out of bed. But he's got a solid enough alibi and we've placed him in a pub in Tallaght at the time of the shooting.'

O'Neill chewed the inside of his bottom lip as his eyes drifted across the sea of newsprint.

'Wait until the editorials start,' he muttered. 'And the guest columnists.'

'Like Mr Gallagher perhaps, my junior Minister's father,' Savage said. He turned towards Goulding. 'I don't know why you took it upon yourself to handle that particular matter. I would have thought that was my department – quite literally.'

'Perhaps,' Goulding said. 'But let's not forget that I'm the Deputy Prime Minister, the *Tanaiste*, and since I was the one who encouraged us all to take Emma Gallagher on board the team, I thought I was the best person to sort the matter out.'

'That may well be so,' Savage replied, 'but don't you think—'

'Look, let's leave this for now,' O'Neill said. 'We've got

more pressing matters to attend to.' He turned to the Commissioner. 'Where do we go from here, Conor?'

Hogan did not allow his satisfaction at the friendly familiarity to show. It was as if the Prime Minister were rewarding him for being well behaved while the two naughty boys sat there squabbling over a toy.

'It will be quite a storm for us to ride out, *Taoiseach*,' he said. 'We *have* been making progress on Donovan, in spite of what some people might think. A substantial case is being built against him – not in relation to this murder, of course. The Criminal Assets Bureau is almost ready, as I understand it, to go to court with an application to freeze certain of his assets, houses and other property, which they believe are the proceeds of illegal activity. It will then be up to Donovan to prove that they're not.'

'Good,' said O'Neill. 'At least that will be something. How quickly can they go ahead? Tomorrow?'

Savage joined the conversation hastily. 'If I may point out, *Taoiseach*, it's really not that simple. As you know, the CAB isn't just a police operation. It involves the Customs and Excise and the Inland Revenue, for example, as well. It's crucial that they are fully prepared before they go into court. It would be a dreadful mistake to come up with a rushed and incomplete application which would be thrown out by a judge. It's happened before and I think we'd all prefer that it didn't happen this time.'

O'Neill looked at him. Savage was a bit dull and pompous but he was a unique kind of politician, in O'Neill's increasingly jaded view, one who was less interested in expediency and hanging on to his job than he was in doing it properly. For a while O'Neill had fooled himself that he was of the same breed but the power and the things he had to do to retain it had claimed him eventually.

But he *was* different, he insisted to himself now, and he had become Prime Minister in order that he could *make* a difference.

He was not part of the tribal structure left over from the Civil War; the party he led had been created so that the country could break away from that. His own roots were not in the Republic of Ireland at all but in the North, although he had been living here since his late teens, when his parents moved the family away from the Troubles.

He had been hailed as the leader of a New Party for a New Age, which was the slogan they had used during the last election campaign. That is what people had voted for, particularly the young who saw in him a fresh hope. So why was it that he did not feel hopeful any more?

The fact was that the power had become the objective, not the myth of doing things for the good of the country and the people. And in order to stay in power, he needed the old blood, not the new.

He looked at Tony Goulding. In particular, he needed him.

Goulding was a man who could quell a backbench revolt or muster one just as quickly, always the king-maker, never the king, and maybe he was right. You lasted longer that way.

And then there was the small matter of the General Election. The decision on when to call it was looming ever nearer and some of his Government's commitments were still unfulfilled, particularly the final round of privatisation of State and semi-State industries.

But now there was this damned murder. It would take up too much of his time and if it were not handled properly it might mean the difference between staying in office and being dumped.

He looked at the Justice Minister again. He was right about not rushing the Criminal Assets Bureau but time was running out.

'I hear what you're saying but let's see if they can get a move on, shall we?'

The Commissioner had something to say. '*Taoiseach*, if I may—?'

O'Neill gestured to him to proceed.

'Like all of us, I'm concerned with how this will play in the media but let me point out that I'm a policeman and not a politician.'

'Which means?' O'Neill wondered.

'Which means that if there are questions about the performance of my force I will feel obliged to put things into some sort of context.'

'Go on.'

'It's a matter of record that I've expressed concern in the past about how we are funded—'

'Oh, not this again,' Savage said.

'—And I may feel I have to do so once more if the issue comes up. We are simply not adequately financed for everything that is required of us. It's easy to point to a growth in convictions and say that everything in the garden's rosy but the morale of the force is steadily being ground down by the pressure and the extent of the work they have to do – and I'm not even including the anti-terrorist activity that goes on along the border counties.'

'You operate on an agreed budget,' Savage said.

'An imposed budget,' Hogan corrected. 'A budget agreed by you and inflicted on me. Savings targets that grow all the time. How can we be expected to cope with that?'

He leaned forward towards the Prime Minister as if to distance himself from the other man. 'There are two things for which we desperately need more money and I've made a strong case for both of them before. One is technology. Our IT system is creaking at the seams. There are plans to upgrade it but that's not happening as quickly as necessary. The second is transport. We need more vehicles on the road, a more convincing presence that will reassure the public and which will deter casual crime.'

He sat back and turned to address the Justice Minister. 'I'm not talking about running costs to help us more or less stay where we are. I'm talking about solid development money that will stand us in good stead for the future. And when are you going to wake up to the fact that – well, let's be honest – your welfare's as much at stake here as the rest of the country's.'

'Now, hold on a minute—' Savage began.

'Can we look at budgets?' O'Neill inquired quietly.

The Minister was pained. 'But we've gone through all this. We can't just keep dishing out—'

'Let's look at budgets,' O'Neill said, his tone more decisive. 'I'm happy to revisit this at Cabinet.'

'I don't think the rest of our Ministerial colleagues will be too happy about that,' Savage pointed out in a final rearguard action. 'It will mean other areas being trimmed.'

'Well, let's see how it goes.'

O'Neill looked at the Commissioner and raised his eyebrows in a question.

'I'd be most interested in the outcome, *Taoiseach*, yes. That sounds very encouraging,' Hogan said.

'Good.'

So the Commissioner would not be a problem and would not feel the compulsion to engage in unhelpful public controversy. But O'Neill did not like being black-mailed, nor did he like having to humiliate Savage like this. If they had the good fortune to win the election, Mr Hogan would find himself enjoying a rather unexpected early retirement.

'Okay, then,' he added, 'let's get on with the day. I'd better have a word with my Press people. Do you think I should say anything more about this?' A statement of condemnation had already been issued in his name in the early hours.

Goulding shook his head. 'No, I think you should let the Commissioner and his team handle it.'

O'Neill broke the meeting up but Goulding stayed behind after the other two had left.

'That Hogan's a smart bastard,' he said. '*I'm not a politician*, indeed. He could teach a few of them a thing or two.'

'We'll see,' O'Neill said, tidying up the newspapers.

'Look, Peter, do you think Savage is up to this because, frankly, I have my doubts. He wasn't exactly sure-footed just now, was he? Christ, he should have had Hogan on board long ago, one way or another.'

O'Neill gave him a look. The animosity towards Savage was obvious and Goulding never missed an opportunity to get the knife in.

'I'm not dumping him, if that's what you're suggesting,' he said firmly.

'He might be a liability if things get rough. You might want to think about someone who could handle this sort of thing better.'

It infuriated O'Neill that Goulding never treated him with proper deference, never seemed to be aware of exactly who it was he was talking to. This time he was not going to let him get away with it.

'I said I'm not dumping him. I've just been forced to cause him intense embarrassment in order to buy the Commissioner off and I'm not very happy about that, not happy at all. He'll get an apology and an explanation from me in private. He's a good man, an honourable man, and don't bother trying to enlist me into your own little hate campaign.'

Goulding stood up and shrugged.

'Suit yourself,' he said with apparent unconcern and walked to the door.

He reached it as it opened inward. Eamon Savage stood there.

'There's some more news,' he said. 'Sean Donovan's son has been shot.'

Chapter Thirteen

Donovan sat cramped between two sleeping business-men in row ten of the flight from Zurich to Dublin. He was still finding it hard to believe.

It was as if with the snap of someone's fingers he had woken up to find that everything that had happened in the past couple of years had been a dream.

Even Amsterdam, which he had visited many times before, had been alien territory to him. He had checked into the Scandic Crown hotel as arranged and waited for his mobile to ring. All evening he had sat there with a steak from room service and a bottle of Scotch, staring at the phone, checking every now and then to make sure it was switched on.

The people he was due to meet did not use land lines or conventional offices for their business. They met in hotel rooms like this one, in bars around the Leidseplein or in some of the more exotic establishments off War-moestraat. On one occasion he and other entrepreneurs, from London, Berlin and Paris, had been taken to a fine house with a view over the IJsselmeer where they found quantities of cocaine and heroin available for inspection

133

and there they had put in their orders for several months ahead.

He was in Amsterdam now because demand on the streets of Dublin was increasing and because it was time to talk about new routes, to arrange new drop points and ensure a steady means of supply.

He liked the place anyway; he liked the way they entertained you, providing women who would do things you only dreamed of.

The morning after his arrival, he had tried a couple of numbers, both of them for mobiles, but they seemed to be unobtainable. At least, that is what he presumed the Dutch voice was telling him. He tried calling Dublin to make sure he had the arrangements right but, oddly, Vinnie's mobile was switched off.

That night he had gone on a tour of the bars and the clubs that were familiar to him, searching among the crowds for faces he might know.

Nothing. Until one am.

It was a place of dim discretion. It had bamboo curtains and there were crude paintings of Chinese dragons on the walls. He had been entertained there before when business had been dealt with satisfactorily. Now he sat at the back, away from the glimmer of red light from the lamps on the tables, peering around the room to see who was there.

No one was looking in his direction. There were no more than ten customers, all of them watching the two Eurasian women on the tiny stage, transfixed by their sinewy bodies and by the things they were doing to each other.

It was then that he had heard a laugh. There was a woman, dark-skinned, Cuban. She was in a thin dress that concealed nothing and she was draped over a heavy-set man who was slumped in his seat in drink.

He knew her.

He remembered the red slash of her mouth as it had enveloped him, remembered the sheen of her body on satin sheets.

He remembered the smile of the man who had opened his arms and said: 'Take her, Sean. She's yours.'

That was one of the men he wanted to see. Right now.

As he stood up, the woman spotted the movement from across the floor of the club and even in that paltry light she knew him, saw him begin to move towards her, and knew why she had to get away.

The emergency exit. She made a run for it but her heels were ridiculous and Donovan was quicker. He caught her and hauled her back, his hands biting into her bare arms as he forced her down the metal staircase that led to the lavatory.

Donovan's strength belied his stature. Now it was reinforced by rage.

He slammed her face several times into the rough stone wall above the urinal and then let her fall to the wet floor.

'You'll be dead in ten minutes if you don't tell me what's going on,' he said.

The door bounced open. The man she had been sitting with stood there, dishevelled and unsteady.

'Get the fuck out of here!' Donovan shouted and the newcomer backed away as hurriedly as his condition allowed.

On the floor, the woman groaned. Donovan crouched over her. Blood covered her face from a smashed nose and torn lips.

'So what's your choice?'

'I – I don't know anything,' she gasped. Donovan straightened up and kicked her in the ribs.

She whimpered like an animal.

He waited for a moment, then bent towards her. 'Well?'

'You're – being – closed down,' the woman said. 'Don't hurt me again.' Her English was adequate but her voice was barely audible.

Donovan grasped her hair and lifted her head. He stared into her ravaged face. 'What's that?'

'Closed down. Finished. That's the – word.'

'What are you talking about – closed down?'

She shook her head. She did not know much more. 'They talk about someone from New York. Someone has come here. No more deals with you – all finished. That's the order.'

'Someone from New York?' Donovan echoed. 'Who?'

The woman shook her head wearily. She was barely conscious. 'All I know. Somebody big. Word is you're marked.'

She looked up at Donovan. One of her eyes was closing and the flesh around it was becoming discoloured.

'Nowhere to hide. You a dead man.'

He stared at her for a moment, startled, then he let her go and she slumped back to the floor. As he came out of the lavatory and walked up the stairs, he saw two Indonesians with grim faces hurrying in his direction. He pushed open the emergency door, ran down an alleyway and turned into the street, keeping close to the shadows until he was well away.

He stopped after a while and took a few deep breaths. There was blood on his hands and they were trembling. Violence always excited him but now he felt fear adding another dimension. He headed back to the hotel, haunted by what the woman had said, the feeling that some unknown presence was watching him.

In his room, the red light on his telephone was flickering to tell him he had a message. It was from Matt Clancy, his solicitor in Dublin. He called the lawyer at home and woke him up.

'Jesus, I can't talk to you here,' Clancy said. 'Give me a couple of minutes. I'll go downstairs and get my mobile and I'll call you back on yours.'

Donovan was in the bathroom, scrubbing his hands in agitation, when the phone rang.

'Right,' Clancy said. 'Some bad news. I've got word that the CAB are about to move on you.'

'What does that mean?'

'It means they'll go to court to get an order to freeze your assets. Your bank accounts here, all your property.'

They would not get everything. There would still be money in camouflaged accounts that they knew nothing about.

'When's that going to happen?'

'A day or so. You'll get official notification. But if you're not here, then it'll be hard for me to fight the application when it comes to court. It'll look like you've skipped the country.'

'I don't know that I want to come back,' Donovan said.

'I've got a feeling it isn't very fucking safe.'

'Listen, there's more,' the solicitor said. 'Two people have turned up dead in a rubbish dump. Their heads were smashed like tomatoes. One of them's a young lad involved in a bit of dealing. The other one's a girl. The word on the street is that it's down to you.'

Donovan tensed. 'What's the guy's name?'

'Harkin, I think. He had a nickname—'

'Dezo?'

'Yes, that's it.'

'Jesus,' Donovan said. 'That bastard Vinnie. Where the fuck is he?'

'He's nothing to do with me,' Clancy told him. 'You're my client – he's not. I don't want to have anything to do with that character. What I want to know is – when are you coming back?'

'I don't know,' Donovan said. His eyes flicked nervously round the room. The walls seemed to be closing in on him. 'I'll call you tomorrow. And find Dwyer, whether you want to or not.'

He tried Vinnie's phone again himself. Still no luck.

You have nowhere to hide. You're a dead man.

Get out of here.

He had packed up immediately and moved on, finding a small room at the Ibis, the big hotel at Schipol airport. Instinct told him that if the net was tightening at home he had to get the rest of his money. And so the following morning he had flown to Zurich.

He checked into the Marriott and took a taxi to the bank. It was off the bustling Bahnhofstrasse, below which were deep vaults holding immeasurable quantities of gold and silver. Somewhere down there, too, was stored six million US dollars that belonged to him.

The bank was an office with soft carpet and panelled walls and the dignified quiet of an undertaker's showroom. Its public face, once you had rung the doorbell and been allowed access, was a receptionist smiling politely from behind her desk.

He gave her the account number and produced the letter of authorisation he had received when opening the account a year ago.

'I need to speak to this man,' he said, pointing to the signature on the letter.

'Please excuse me for a moment,' the woman had said, leaving the room and taking the letter with her.

Two minutes. Three minutes. Five. He paced the room in impatience, scowling occasionally at the security camera that watched down on him from a corner.

And then she had returned, accompanied by a little man who had his letter in one hand and his glasses in the other and who was most definitely not the person who had welcomed Donovan's business with a handshake when he had first crossed the threshold.

The manager, if that was who this was, put his glasses on and peered at Donovan with curiosity.

'I'm not sure I understand,' he said. 'You say you have an account here?'

'Of course I've got an account here,' Donovan repeated, raising his voice to a level which was not customary in this cocoon of a room. 'Why are you asking me this? I opened an account a year ago. I've been here several times since, depositing cash. There's six million dollars of my money in here. What's your problem?'

The manager gave a little shrug. His expression was dismissive.

'The problem is that this letter appears to be a forgery. It would seem to be the notepaper of this bank, that is true, but it has not been signed by any employee of ours, never mind by me as manager. And apart from that, the account number is meaningless.'

He gave a wintry smile. 'Let's just say that you appear to have made some mistake.'

'There's no fucking mistake.' Donovan stiffened and clenched his fists.

'Oh, I think there is. Fraud is viewed very seriously here in Zurich and unless you would like me to ask the police to have a look at this, I think perhaps you should leave.'

Donovan took a step forward. 'Listen here, you little—'

The manager stood back and a door in the panelling opened. Two armed security guards entered. They had shoulders like oak beams and they seemed to fill the room with their bulk.

'I don't think we have anything further to discuss,' the banker said. He looked at the guards. 'Perhaps you would ensure that this gentleman leaves the premises as quickly as possible.'

As they marched him towards the door, Donovan did not resist. They could have broken his arm with a flick of the wrist.

Outside he had stood looking at the heavy wooden doors now shut forever to him, realising that he had been robbed.

You're being closed down.

But who was behind it? Who had the power to involve the bank itself, because that was certainly what had happened here? The letter was no fake, of course not, and if the banker had really thought that it was, then he would have had the police there in a flash.

Who was there who knew so much about him? In his mind he skimmed through a gallery of faces.

Vinnie? No, not Vinnie, for Christ sake. Ridiculous. His sudden disappearance was suspicious, certainly, but he did not have the brains or the clout for anything like this.

But could he be involved in some other way?

Whatever this was, he thought as he hailed a cab back to the hotel, it was way beyond the reach and the influence of just about everybody he knew. You needed status, a lot of it, to pull off something like this.

Someone from New York.

But he had never had any dealings with anyone in New York.

In the hotel room, he poured a Scotch from the mini-bar and called Clancy. The office was closed and the answering machine was on. He was puzzled at first and then he remembered it was St Patrick's Day.

He called Clancy at home, gave him the number of the hotel and waited.

'Jesus, Sean,' the solicitor said when he rang back, 'you must come home.'

'What is it now?'

'Marcus Kelly's been murdered.'

'What?'

'Somebody blew him away with a shotgun outside his

141

apartment building last night.'

'Jesus Christ. Who—'

'I don't know. But I'll give you one guess who everyone thinks it is.'

Donovan tried to take it in but Clancy had not finished. His voice softened. 'Listen Sean. There's something else I've got to tell you. Now – they think he's going to be okay but – well – somebody's shot your son.'

Donovan could not speak.

'They found him in an alleyway in the early hours,' Clancy said. 'He'd been given a bit of a going over and there was a bullet in his thigh. By the time the police and the ambulance got to him he'd lost a lot of blood and he was on the critical list for a while but it looks like he's going to pull through.' There was silence. 'Sean, are you there?'

Fintan was thirteen. Donovan found himself praying.

It was the one thing guaranteed to bring him back to Ireland.

He watched a stewardess striding down the aisle of the plane and when she reached him he asked her for a brandy.

He was heading into something. What, he did not know but he could no longer stay away. Somebody wanted him to be in Dublin, not roaming around the continent.

God, if he ever got his hands on whoever did it.

But whoever had harmed the boy had done so in order to reach the father.

They were sending him an invitation. And it was the thought of Fintan lying in intensive care, Fintan, the only human being on this earth whom he could genuinely say he loved, that gave him no option but to accept.

The plane touched down with a gentle bump.

As it began to taxi towards the terminal, Donovan finished his drink and tucked the empty glass into the magazine flap in the back of the seat in front of him. He looked out of the window. Out there was his city, his hunting ground. The difference now was that he felt like the prey.

But he needed to see that boy.

When the cabin door swung open, he was one of the first off. With his overnight bag in his hand, he strode along the corridors of the terminal, following the route for Irish nationals, his open coat billowing like a cape.

He breezed through the green Customs channel for those with nothing to declare and made for the open doors that led to the arrivals concourse where Clancy had agreed to meet him in the absence of Vinnie, who had disappeared off the face of the earth. As always, people were waiting, watching for relatives or business colleagues in the trickle of passengers coming through. They stood in groups behind sash barriers that prevented them blocking the doorway.

There were a lot more than usual, Donovan thought, and he saw now that there were television cameras and stills photographers among them. Probably waiting for a movie star or a rock singer coming off a flight from New York or somewhere.

He spotted Clancy at last, a lean man with an expensive overcoat and a dark moustache. At the same moment the solicitor began to hurry towards him.

A voice shouted, 'There he is.'

The pack surged forward and to his horror Donovan realised who they were after.

Clancy grabbed him by the arm and started to propel him through them. 'Don't say anything,' he grunted. 'Let me do the talking.'

They were almost crouching as they ran the gauntlet. Cameras were flashing and microphones were jabbed at them. Questions were being hurled like missiles.

'Have you any comment to make about the murder of Marcus Kelly?'

'Have you any idea who shot your son?'

'Is it true that you're worth twenty million?'

That last one was just the stupidest thing Donovan had ever heard. He felt like stopping and hitting somebody but Clancy had his arm in a firm grip and so he said nothing and kept going.

Outside the airport building, the lawyer had a driver waiting in a car with tinted windows. He helped Donovan into the back and then turned to face the mob with both arms raised to stop their head-long rush.

'Let me just make a couple of things clear,' he said. 'If you're not already aware, I'm Mr Donovan's solicitor. Mr Donovan has come back early from a business trip abroad because of what has happened to his son and like any concerned father he's now rather anxious to get to the hospital to see him. So I'm sure you'll respect his privacy there.'

Some chance, Donovan thought. The photographers were still trying to take pictures but all they were getting were reflections off the windows.

Clancy scanned the faces in front of him. 'The second thing is that both Mr Donovan and I will be watching what you put on television and what goes into the papers. Let me remind you that Mr Donovan has not been charged with anything, he is not wanted for any crime. If we find anything defamatory in anything published by any of you we will not hesitate to issue writs for libel and, believe me, the results could be very costly.'

He turned to get into the car, then added a parting word of advice: 'Perhaps you'd better apprise your editors of that fact.'

He opened the door and squeezed in beside Donovan. The car drove off.

'The CAB application is tomorrow,' Clancy said. 'I just heard this afternoon.'

Donovan's mind was elsewhere. 'How the hell did they know I'd be on that flight?'

'Who can tell? A tip-off from somewhere.'

'Apart from you and me, who knew?'

'Well, let's assume you didn't tip them off yourself and let's assume—' he put his hand on his heart – 'that you take my word for it that I didn't. So, let's see.' On his fingers he began to tick off the possibilities. 'I spoke to your ex-wife, so she knew. I informed the CAB that you'd be in court in the morning, that you were coming back tonight. I didn't say where you were coming from exactly but it wouldn't be hard for them to find out. That's about it, I guess. Oh and, distasteful though it was to do it, I managed to make contact with your friend Vinnie who appears to be answering his phone at last.'

He turned to Donovan. 'So pick any one.'

Donovan said nothing but looked straight ahead with a cold, malevolent stare.

Chapter Fourteen

The river Liffey divided Dublin north and south. The quays ran along each shore but where once there had been warehouses and ship-chandlers, the support structure of the seafaring trade, new blocks of apartments were rising expensively with terraces and picture windows that looked across the river and the city.

Just behind the north quays, there remained a maze of ramshackle streets and run-down properties which housed timber stores, car-repair shops and an array of little offices from which businesses of often obscure purposes operated. One of them had a painted wooden nameplate, beginning to fade, which announced that it was the premises of Donovan Properties, at least those properties in which the owner did not conceal his involvement.

It was two in the morning and St Patrick's Day was over. There was just the hangover to come. The area was quiet. The sounds of timber being cut or metal being hammered would not begin again for another six hours but in the darkness, when the shutters were fastened and the locks clasped, it was common for the sounds of other business to take their place.

146

It was here, in these streets and alleyways, that junkies sometimes came to score and hookers lifted their skirts in the shadows for their furtive clients.

But not tonight.

Two unmarked police cars and a van pulled up at the front of Donovan Properties. A third car blocked the alley at the rear. Like shadows, the night people slipped away. But they need not have worried. The police were not interested in them.

The officers emerged from their vehicles almost before they had stopped, men and women, some in uniform, some in plainclothes, several of them armed. From the back of the van came an officer with a black labrador that pulled eagerly against a strong chain.

The front door did not provide much resistance to the sledgehammer which hit the lock and then they were in and up the dusty wooden stairs to Donovan's office. A swift kick and they were inside. They switched on the lights and began to search.

At a glance, they could see that it would not take long. There was a desk with three drawers on each side, a filing cabinet and an ancient armchair. The dog went straight to the desk, sniffing frantically at one set of drawers and then at the back of the desk. The animal began to whine excitedly.

'Good girl,' said one of the detectives, a young man in jeans and a bomber jacket.

The drawers were locked but he jammed a screwdriver in and the lock gave with a crack. There were papers, letters, rent books, but he did not even glance at them. Instead, while a colleague restrained the dog as it tried to bury its nose into the desk, he pulled out all the drawers and set them on the floor.

At the back, in the open space that was left, he found what they had come for.

They got lots of anonymous tip-offs. Often they were just grudge calls or hoaxes, someone trying to make trouble for whatever reason, but sometimes they were worth pursuing. The fact that Donovan's name had been attached to this one had made it irresistible and it had not been hard to persuade a judge to sign a search warrant.

Well worth the effort. Taped to the floor of the drawer space were a dozen small plastic bags, about the size of sachets of sugar, and containing a white powder.

'Too much to be for personal use,' the detective said with a smile as he took a radio handset from his jacket pocket.

Several miles away, in the southern suburbs of Tallaght, his message was received in the three unmarked cars that were parked at the entrance to a cul-de-sac. As in the city-centre operation, another car was parked at the rear, in a narrow road which ran along the hedge at the bottom of Sean Donovan's wilderness of a back garden.

The Superintendent in charge of the raid lifted a handset from his lap.

'Right,' he said. 'Let's go.'

His car led the way, bounding over the ramp with a second car behind it while the third moved up to block the gap. At the house, they drew guns and covered both front and rear doors.

The Superintendent rang the bell. There was silence as they listened and then he spoke into the handset again.

'Okay.'

Sledgehammers hit front and back doors almost simultaneously and the raiding party swarmed into the house.

Upstairs, a figure appeared at a bedroom doorway.

'Freeze!' the Superintendent shouted. Torches and guns all pointed in the one direction.

Someone thought it was a good idea to switch on the light.

Donovan stood motionless, blinking from sleep and the sudden brightness. He wore a vest and underpants and he had a gun in his hand, although he held it carefully away from his body, dangling it from his thumb and forefinger as if it were tainted.

'Drop it,' the Superintendent advised and he did so. It hit the carpet with a soft thud. Two men hurried forward and cuffed his hands behind his back as the Superintendent announced to him that he was being arrested on suspicion of being in possession or control of a quantity of dangerous drugs.

'What is this? What are you talking about?' Donovan asked, looking pained, then listened as brief details of what had been discovered in his office were explained to him.

He gave a guffaw. 'Do me a fucking favour. Do you think I'd be so fucking stupid as to leave gear lying around like that? Who put it there? Did you do it yourselves?'

One of the younger officers began a menacing move towards him.

'Leave it.' The voice was firm and low, like a dog-handler, and the officer stepped back. The Superintendent pointed at the gun on the floor. 'Have you got a licence for that thing?'

Donovan cocked his head. 'Well, now, what do you think? Who's likely to give me one of those, eh? No, as a matter of fact, I found it lying in the back garden tonight. Someone must have thrown it there. I was going to hand it in tomorrow but you beat me to it.'

'That's another charge, then,' the Superintendent said, smiling at him. 'Not your night, Sean, is it?'

It was not his morning either.

There was not much chance of getting bail but Clancy tried it anyway.

At ten am he stood with his client in front of a District Justice to hear him charged with being in control of dangerous drugs, namely a quantity of heroin, and with having an illegal firearm.

Donovan looked rough. There was dark stubble on his chin, his hair was unkempt and he wore the trousers and open-necked shirt which the police had allowed him to put on before taking him from his home. Overnight, he had been stuck in a cell at Tallaght police station but he had not slept, not while his imagination was racing.

Even if he had wanted to sleep, it would have been difficult because of the constant parade of young *Garda* officers peering in at him as if he were some rare species of animal which had just been captured. What did they think this was – fucking Jurassic Park? On one occasion he had leaped from his bunk with a roar when he saw a face at the slat in the door and it had closed again bloody quickly, that was for sure.

But the truth was – it was exactly how he felt. Hunted and now caged. And what else was in store for him?

The courtroom was packed with reporters and many more waited outside.

For Dick Mitchell, the young lawyer pleading the police case, it was an unexpected venture into the limelight. After being called at home early this morning to be briefed, he had finished his tea and toast in a hurry, then he had showered and washed his hair before putting on the smart dark suit his wife liked and the Missoni tie he had bought a few days ago in FX Kelly's in Grafton Street.

There was just a chance that a camera lens might stray his way as he walked into court. So far, no such luck. But perhaps someone would notice him on the way out.

He stood to apply for a remand in custody.

'If I could explain to the court,' he said, 'further investigations are required in this case. Certain matters, namely the discovery of heroin in premises owned and under the control of the defendant, came to light only in the early hours of this morning, as a result of which the defendant was arrested at his home where he was found to be in possession of an illegal firearm. We will be seeking a remand in custody while those investigations proceed.'

It was Clancy's turn. The magistrate turned towards him and raised his eyebrows.

'We are requesting that bail be granted in this instance,' Clancy said. 'If the court pleases, the evidence against my client is purely circumstantial. There is no proof that he had anything whatsoever to do with the substances found on his premises, nor was he there at the time they were discovered, and we will be strenuously denying the charges.'

He looked at something in his notes before continuing.

When he spoke again his voice had softened.

'In addition, may I submit that it would be unnecessarily punitive to keep my client in custody at this time. The court may be aware that Mr Donovan's son is in hospital as a result of an appalling shooting incident. Fortunately the child is improving but I'm sure this court would not wish to deprive Mr Donovan of the opportunity of visiting as often as possible, indeed remaining at the bedside.'

'What about the weapon, Mr Clancy?' the District Justice wondered with what sounded for all the world like idle interest.

Clancy shuffled his papers. 'The – eh – weapon came into my client's possession, as he has already indicated to the police, by accident. He found it in the garden at the rear of his home where it was most likely dumped by someone seeking to get rid of it. Mr Donovan had every intention of handing it in but when he heard his house being broken into early this morning he reached for the nearest form of protection, which happened to be this weapon.'

He sat down to sniggers from the press bench. The District Justice silenced them with an acid glance.

Mitchell was on his feet again. 'We would vigorously oppose bail. These are most serious charges and not the only matter before the courts in relation to this man. He spends a lot of his time travelling between Ireland and various parts of the continent in pursuit of rather dubious activities, to say the least, and if he were granted bail the State would be concerned about the very strong likelihood that he would fail to turn up.'

He turned towards Clancy with a condescending smile.

'However, we have no wish to prevent Mr Donovan from visiting his son in hospital and we would be happy to facilitate such visits, under police and prison officer supervision, of course.'

The District Justice nodded. He had heard everything he needed to.

'I will remand him in custody for seven days.'

Before he had finished speaking, Clancy got up. 'In that case, we would ask to be given leave to appeal.'

'As you wish, Mr Clancy.'

The reporters scrambled out of the courtroom, switching on mobile phones and hitting the pre-programmed numbers for their newsrooms. The story would make the next radio bulletins and the early edition of Dublin's sole evening paper. Two television reporters scribbled sentences which would form the basis of their pieces to camera and photographers hurried to the side of the court building where there was a yard from which it was most likely that the prison van, with Donovan on board, would emerge.

As a consequence, when Dick Mitchell came out at the front a short time later with hair brushed and his tie straightened, there was no one there to see him and no one to care.

In a cell below the courtroom, Donovan paced the floor while Clancy sat and watched him. He had asked for five minutes with his client and so the prison officers waited outside the door.

'The Criminal Assets thing has gone away for the time being,' Clancy said. 'I got a message just before we went into court. They're not going to proceed today. Obviously, they're going to save that one for a few weeks, try to get a better case. And guess what – the police have nabbed Vinnie Dwyer. They're questioning him, too.'

'There's a few questions I'd like to ask that bastard myself.'

'Well, I'm afraid you'll have to wait your turn.'

'What about the bail?'

Clancy shrugged. 'I'll try and get a hearing at the High Court this afternoon or maybe tomorrow. But it's not going to be easy, not after you pulled that damned gun.'

'Yeah, well, it could have been anybody, couldn't it. How was I to know it was the bloody cops?'

He walked to the brick wall and kicked it sharply in his frustration. The violent thud of contact made Clancy wince.

'It's closing in on me, all this,' Donovan muttered. 'Closing in on me.'

Abruptly he turned. There was a hungry look in his eye.

'But I had an idea in the night. There's someone I could talk to.'

Chapter Fifteen

At eight o'clock that night, with the evening sun warm on his shoulders, a grey-haired man wearing a battered panama hat rose stiffly from a kneeling position beside a rosebed at the back of his handsome house in County Kildare.

He had left the doors onto the terrace open and he could hear the telephone ringing. He turned and looked down the long garden to where his wife was almost hidden among the hydrangea, well out of range. He would have to answer it himself.

Lionel Purcell, or to give him his full title, Mr Justice Purcell, stepped up onto the terrace. The phone was still ringing. Whoever was calling was not taking no for an answer.

He kicked off his muddy brogues and walked into the morning room. The phone was on a table beside a picture of his daughter and two of his grandchildren. It had been taken last summer in the garden he had just left so reluctantly.

He lifted the receiver. 'Purcell,' he announced.

He did not recognise the voice that addressed him. Later

he would tell the police that it sounded like someone trying to speak with a Dublin accent but not quite succeeding.

'If Sean Donovan doesn't get bail, one of you judges will be a dead man. He'll not be convicted of anything either, do you understand?'

Purcell did not.

'I beg your pardon?'

'Let me put it another way,' the voice said.

There was a moment of silence and then Purcell heard four sharp bangs in quick succession. The caller rang off, leaving him standing immobile, holding the phone to his ear.

It took him a second or two to realise that he had been listening to gunshots. When he did, he went straight to the drinks cabinet and poured himself a large brandy. Then he rang the police.

He was not the only judge to receive a surprise call that evening, complete with similar threatening sound effects. There were half a dozen more, all of them to numbers which were supposed to be ex-directory, an alarming fact in itself since it signified a lapse of security somewhere, and all of them delivering variations of an ultimatum that Sean Donovan should not only get bail but that he should eventually walk free.

By midnight, Commissioner Conor Hogan had informed the Justice Minister, Eamon Savage, and for once they were of the same mind: a bit of extra vigilance around the judges, more police patrols past their homes, that sort of thing, but nothing too conspicuous and certainly no mention of any of this in the media, otherwise it would be exaggerated into panic in the streets. It would also tell

Donovan that his crude intimidation worked and it would alarm the judges even more.

But in spite of this instruction, someone somewhere slipped the news to Ben Caffrey, the Opposition's Justice spokesman, who was only too willing to pass it on to the morning papers and make himself available for television interviews.

'A ring of steel,' he would demand on the early news bulletins. 'Nothing else will do if we are going to protect these honourable members of our judiciary from such appalling threats.'

By agreement with the Prime Minister, roused from sleep to be given the bad news, including the fact that Caffrey knew what had happened, Savage did not offer his presence to the media, reasoning that any agreement to appear might run the risk of substantiating his opponent's anxieties. Instead, he left it to the police to confirm in a brief statement from *Garda* headquarters that there had been some anonymous telephone calls which they were investigating. Nothing more than that.

'Are you sure you've got this one covered, Eamon?' the *Taoiseach* asked him before he drifted back to sleep.

'Absolutely,' Savage said.

Hours before that conversation, at ten o'clock, Vinnie Dwyer collected his mobile phone from the officer who had been holding on to it and stepped out of the Bridewell *Garda* station in Dublin city centre. He stood at the door for a second or two, then looked at his watch and smiled. The pubs were still open and he could do with a pint.

It was the third time in a week that the police had hauled

157

him in and the third time they had been forced to let him go, as he knew they would.

The first had been after he had killed Dezo and the girl but they had nothing on him – no witnesses, no forensic evidence they could use against him, no precise time of death – and he was not the sort to crack under their intimidation tactics.

On the night of the Marcus Kelly murder, they had got him out of his bed to bring him here again but he had a real solid alibi that time, in the shape of about half the clientele of the New Western Inn at Tallaght, and they could not link him with that particular matter in any way. Now they had arrested Sean Donovan and so they had decided to bring him in once more, this time to see if he could shed any light on Donovan's activities.

He could have complained. He could even have refused to accompany them to the station and challenged them to arrest him. But instead he had gone along with them, confident that nothing would come of it.

He had not even bothered to ask for a solicitor. He had just sat there whistling and drumming his fingers on the table every time they asked him a question. Some of the top boys came to talk to him, too, a couple of superintendents among them, but in the end they knew he was not going to help and so they had let him stew for a while before sending him on his way.

He walked to a taxi rank and told the driver to take him to Tallaght. Less than half an hour later the cab dropped him outside the New Western.

It was done up like a barn and built on the site of what had once been a farm, in the distant days when Dublin was a much smaller place. Huge cartwheels were set into the exterior walls. The car park had a white picket fence around its edges and a fake well in the centre. The whole building was floodlit in orange by lamps cemented into the ground and the sound of mid-tempo country music reverberated in the air.

Vinnie pushed open the doors and went in. There were two hundred punters in the place, easily. Spread out in the big room were thirty tables, all occupied, and a huge bar ran along one side like in a saloon. An army of waiters fanned out from it, delivering trays which were impossibly loaded. Many of the customers were in the same condition.

On a small stage, a woman with a hard yodel in her voice sang an old Patsy Cline number. She had once been a star of sorts and she could still pull a crowd. Accompanying her was a hairy guitar band who looked as if they would be more at home with something heavier.

At the bar, a group of young men with shaved heads and tattoos on their necks looked alien in this environment. They sat on stools in a semi-circle and ignored the music loudly.

When they saw Vinnie, they began to cheer.

'Here he comes. Beaten the fuckers again.'

'Jaysus, Vinnie, you're great. A pint, is it?'

They slapped him on the back and sat him down.

Customers flowed past them in steady streams and so Vinnie and his cronies did not notice the young man who came into the bar a minute or so later. He was dressed in motorcycle leathers and he placed his helmet and gloves on the floor beside his feet while he ordered a bottle of Miller and gazed around him.

He seemed to give Vinnie barely a glance but nevertheless that was where his attention was focused. Vinnie was rarely out of his sight and never out of his thoughts.

Not since he had killed his sister.

There was no evidence, of course; no one had actually witnessed the murders of Aileen and her boyfriend, but Dermot Davis knew, just as sure as he was standing here now, just as sure as he had known in his bones that something bad was going to happen that Sunday morning when he saw them driving off.

It had surprised and shocked him that he had not cried when the bodies were discovered. Instead, he had found himself gripped with a cold rage. It was still there, like ice in his blood, keeping him calm and clear-headed while he planned what he had to do.

He had not wanted to be found. He had moved around the cheap hotels and hostels near Connolly railway station in the city, thinking it through. He had not gone to the funeral, either. That would have meant police and endless questions that he did not want to answer and he did not have time for that or for anything that would divert him from his task.

The grieving would have to wait. There would be moments for that later, when this was done.

With a portion of the £5,000 from under the floorboards at Ballyfermot he had bought the motorcycle that now stood outside the pub, nothing flashy and conspicuous, a small second-hand Suzuki. Then he had set about finding Vinnie.

It had not been difficult. On the occasions when Dezo and Aileen had talked about him, they had mentioned some of the places he frequented: pubs, a couple of snooker clubs, and in particular this monstrous bar. He had been able to follow Vinnie to where he lived, a flat above a video shop in Tallaght, and he had been in a café across the road from it when the police came this morning to pick him up.

He had tailed them to the Bridewell and then he had simply waited, wondering how long they would hold him, hoping Vinnie would not be charged with anything, because that would mean he was out of reach. He had been about to pack it in for the night, get his bike and go back to his seedy hotel when Vinnie walked out, free as a bird.

Dermot ordered another beer. He was tired and this would be his limit. It was an hour now since Vinnie had come into the pub and he and his companions were downing drinks at a hell of a rate, shouting drunken conversation at each other over the sound of the band.

The expression on Vinnie's face changed.

'Hold on a minute,' he said, 'there's my phone.'

He took the mobile from his pocket and as he answered it he got off the stool and stood stiffly with his hand cupped over one ear.

'Right,' he said. 'Okay. As soon as I can.'

He rang off. 'Lads, I've got to go. Wee bit of business.' He looked across the counter to the barman. 'Paddy, can you get me a taxi?'

Dermot thought Vinnie looked sober all of a sudden.

He left his drink and went out into the car park. It was getting cold but it was a relief to get into the air, away from the smoke and noise. He put his gloves and helmet on, straddled the bike and waited, wondering who or what could have summoned Vinnie away with such urgency.

The taxi took only a couple of minutes. At this time of night, there was a regular procession of them to and from the pub and as it drove off, Dermot followed at a discreet distance. He recognised the route they were taking and it was no surprise when the cab pulled up outside the video shop.

He cut his lights and engine and from a vantage point beside a newsagent's on the opposite side of the street, he waited and watched.

Something a bit strange. When the taxi drove off, Vinnie made no attempt to take out his key. Instead, he stood where he was, shuffling on the spot in the increasing chill.

Now there was a car.

It drove past Vinnie on the opposite side, then swung round in a U-turn and pulled up beside him. It was a black Peugeot saloon, driven with speed and skill. A rear door opened and Vinnie got in.

The car zipped away from the kerb and its tail-lights were already fading in the darkness before Dermot managed to kick his motorcycle into life.

Chapter Sixteen

Tom Gallagher sat across the desk from his bank manager and wondered which of them was more embarrassed.

'What about re-mortgaging, something like that?' Gallagher suggested wildly.

He had put on a tie and a suit and sitting in this tiny office crammed with filing cabinets he felt like an overgrown schoolboy being carpeted by the headmaster.

Noel Meehan shook his head. He was in his early thirties, a chunky scrum half who played rugby at the weekends, and he had just taken over at this small branch.

'Not a good idea,' he said. 'You don't want to lumber yourself with heavier financial commitments for a short-term gain. Look, Mr Gallagher, the bank's concern is that you don't slip further into trouble. That's why I wrote to you. Overdraft facilities on a current account are granted on the basis that there's a regular flow of funds into it and that you're in the black for most of the time. In your case, you've been in debit for the past three months.'

He looked down at the figures in front of him. He hated this sort of thing. He had hoped that the man would have made things easier than this, that he would have come in with a solution to the problem, but instead he had arrived with a horror story about someone embezzling his investments and he had more or less thrown himself on the mercy of the court.

It would not be sorted out today.

'I'll tell you what,' he said. 'We both need to think about this. The bank will stick with you for the moment. Your cheques won't bounce or anything but—' he looked sternly at Gallagher '—that doesn't mean you dash out to buy a new car or something like that. In the meantime, I'll try to put together a few options for you and you'll have to give it serious consideration yourself. You need to look at your lifestyle, what you're spending and ponder how you might increase your income.'

'Get a job, you mean?'

'That's one way,' Meehan said. 'Although I accept that that might not be easy at your age.'

Gallagher was stunned. Meehan fidgeted nervously. 'I'm sorry,' he said, 'I didn't mean that to sound quite the way it did.'

Gallagher felt written off. As he left the bank, he imagined that the eyes of each teller and customer were on him. He had been humiliated, not only by what Meehan had said but by his own inadequacies. He had no idea what he was going to do.

He drove to Sandymount, parked and walked back towards the flat along the shore path. He gave a sudden shiver and pulled his collar up. The sunlight was bright but there was a cutting breeze from the sea, a brusque reminder that winter's departure was relatively recent. He watched a man and a woman try to summon their dog out of the water. A black labrador, young and skittish, it scampered up the muddy sand to them, then stood and shook itself. The couple laughed and leaped back from the torrent of spray.

He was taking his coat off and hanging it in the hall when the phone began to ring.

'Is that Mr Tom Gallagher?'

An unfamiliar voice.

'Yes?'

'Good morning, You don't know me. I'm Matt Clancy.'

True, the name did not mean anything.

Clancy explained. 'I'm a solicitor here in Dublin. I represent a Mr Sean Donovan.'

There was a pause. Gallagher frowned. 'Sean Donovan. *The* Sean Donovan?'

'You could put it like that, yes.'

He had seen on the news this morning that Donovan had been arrested on drugs charges and there had also been a report about anonymous threats to judges. The wording had been careful but listeners would have been left in no doubt that the threats were somehow linked to Donovan's current difficulties.

But why on earth—?

'Sure you've got the right person?'

'Oh yes indeed. I should explain. Mr Donovan was very impressed with an article you wrote a little while ago in *Dublin Sunday* about how he was being hounded by the media. You remember the one?'

How could he forget? 'Yes, I know what you're talking about,' he said.

'Well, Mr Donovan is very keen to meet with you. He thinks you're one of the few people in this country who have been fair to him of late and he's asked me to fix up a visit.'

'A visit?'

'Yes,' Clancy said. 'Unfortunately, he's being held on remand in Mountjoy prison until his appeal for bail is heard so you would have to see him there. I can arrange that. You can come in with me.'

'Look,' Gallagher said, a bit thrown by all of this, 'I can't imagine for one minute why Sean Donovan would want to see me and, frankly, I can't imagine there's anything I'd want to say to him. So – thanks but no thanks.'

'Come on,' Clancy urged. 'This is kind of important to him and it could be important to you, too.'

'In what way?'

'Well, I'd have to let Mr Donovan explain that himself.'

'Sorry,' Gallagher said. 'I really don't want to have anything to do with him. And look – maybe you'd better pass on the message that I wasn't exactly rooting for him in that piece I wrote. I don't have any time for guys like him. I was just trying to give the authorities something to think about.'

'I see. Well, I'll come back to you on that.'

'No,' Gallagher said quickly, 'don't bother. Just forget it.'

He did not take his own advice. The call stayed in his mind all morning. He checked the telephone book for a Matt Clancy, solicitor, and found one. He wrote the number down, not that he was going to do anything with it, but – damn it, it was all very strange.

Emma. That had to be the connection, that Donovan knew exactly who he was and was somehow trying to gain ground for himself through what he thought were Gallagher's close ties to the Justice Department. But if that was his game, then it was a pretty pointless one.

It was early afternoon and he was standing at the window with a cup of coffee when Clancy rang again.

'Look,' he said, 'I know you told me not to bother you with this but I've been to see Mr Donovan again and he insists that I give you another call. I find this a bit embarrassing.'

'Have you ever heard of harassment?' Gallagher asked.

Clancy did not react. 'I've been asked to ring you again to tell you that Mr Donovan has some information which you might find interesting.'

'Information? What about?'

'I don't know. He hasn't confided in me. He says he'll only talk to you. All he'll say is that it's big stuff. Those were his very words. Big stuff.'

Gallagher scratched the beginnings of stubble on his chin. His curiosity was like an itch and there was only one remedy. Donovan would have figured that, too.

'Okay,' he said, finally. 'What way do—?'

'I'll come for you at six thirty,' Clancy said. 'Give me your address.'

Just after seven, Clancy parked his Lexus in a street off the North Circular and they crossed the road towards Mountjoy.

An avenue led up to a door which was the entrance to a brooding fortress of dark Victorian brick. On either side of the avenue, parallel to it, there was a row of houses which had once been warders' homes but were now empty and decaying, their roofs stripped of slates and lead and their rotting wooden beams open to the elements.

Yet in the avenue itself, spring was vivid. Two rows of sturdy cherry trees bloomed gloriously and as Gallagher and Clancy passed by they walked over pink blossom scattered in their path by the evening breeze.

Once through the door, Gallagher found himself in a darker world.

It was a very long time since he had been in a place like this but his senses filled with recognition.

There was a smell of cleaning fluids and age and an oppression hung heavy in the air, like impending thunder. It was in the sound of doors slamming and of distant footfalls on stone floors. They were all incarcerated here, jailers and jailed alike, and there was a feeling of insecure control, a fragile balance of power that could shift at any time.

Donovan and his solicitor were allowed to meet for a consultation in an ante-room and not in the main visiting area where prisoners and their relatives sat face to face, watched by warders with searching eyes. In this room, a prison officer sat against a wall and smoked while Gallagher and Clancy took seats at a thin table and waited.

A door opened and someone was ushered in, a small man in shirt and trousers. It was Gallagher's first sight of Sean Donovan in the flesh and he was not impressed.

Even in the old days, his encounters with some of the legendary Dons had been disappointing. He had found them almost uniformly seedy, fat old men with oyster eyes and mealy skin. They dressed in shiny suits cut from expensive silk in the wrong colours or else they wore stained trousers and rough cotton work shirts, looking as if they did not have a dime in their pockets.

Below them, the standard of wear and wearer fell further, from the *capos* right down to the button men, those little Mussolinis who ran small bits of the operation under orders from on high and took care of the dirty work, the shootings and the beatings.

Donovan would have been one of those. He was a low-life, Gallagher reckoned, and most certainly not the genius of organised crime as portrayed by the media and as he probably believed himself to be. Undoubtedly he would have some criminal cunning but it was not hard to make money in the short term out of drugs and prostitution if you were prepared to take the risks and if you had a brutal nature to enforce your will.

Donovan sat at the table in front of them and stared at Gallagher, apparently getting the measure of him. Some would have found this intimidating. Gallagher did not. He thought he looked like an untidy little man out of his depth.

Donovan's eyes flicked towards his solicitor for a moment.

'What have you told him?'

'Only what you said. That you have some information.'

'Yeah, that's right.' He turned to Gallagher. 'I have some information and I need your help. But I don't expect you to supply it for nothing. There's a hundred grand in this for you.'

'And you can shove it,' Gallagher said. He stood and

pushed his chair back vehemently. He glowered at Clancy. 'Thanks a lot. I'll make my own way back, if you don't mind.' He nodded towards the warder, indicating that he wanted to leave.

Donovan stood abruptly. He grabbed Gallagher's wrist tightly and there was an unexpected strength in the grip.

'Hey, none of that,' the warder said.

Donovan let go. 'Look, I'm sorry,' he said. 'That was a mistake. It was just a business proposition, that's all.' He shrugged. 'It's the way I do things – it's what I'm used to.'

'Is that a fact?' Gallagher turned on Clancy. 'What bullshit. Information I might find useful. You suckered me here so that this little prick could try to buy my help. And let me guess – my daughter being in the Justice Department might have come into it somewhere? Jesus – did you really think I'd go along with this?'

He looked at Donovan. 'You must be desperate.'

'I am.'

The sadness and resignation in the voice stilled Gallagher for a moment.

'Please,' Donovan said. 'Hear me out – five minutes. Then you can go.'

Gallagher stared at him. Up close, Donovan smelled stale and his eyes were bloodshot.

He thought for a few seconds, then gave a curt nod of assent and sat down. 'Five minutes.'

'There are things happening that nobody knows about,' Donovan said quietly, settling into his chair and leaning forward, 'and you're the man who can help me, a man who will understand.'

'Why don't you just talk to the police?'

He shook his head. 'They won't listen. Not to me. I need someone who'll talk to them for me, a go-between, who'll be a—' He beckoned to Clancy to supply him with the word.

'An honest broker?' the lawyer ventured.

Who are in short supply, Gallagher thought.

A hundred thousand pounds was a lot of money.

'That's it. That's what I want, why I thought of you with your – you know – connections. The FBI and everything.'

'What about your lawyer here?'

'That would be just the same as me talking. You'd be more respectable. They'd listen.'

'So then, what sort of message would I have been taking?'

'You know about the international syndicates, how they operate. I think there's something big going on here.'

The warder shifted position and his chair scraped the floor sharply. Donovan looked round, startled by the sound, and Gallagher could see fear flicker in his eyes like a candle in a draught.

'There's no one I can trust. Even that bastard Vinnie has deserted me.'

Gallagher frowned fleetingly at the unfamiliar name but he let it pass.

'Two years ago I was nothing,' Donovan said, 'just another guy pulling strokes wherever I could, turning over warehouses, selling the stuff off. Then a couple of guys from Holland come to see me, tell me I'm just the person they're looking for, someone who knows how to run a successful operation and keep out of trouble.

'They tell me the drugs scene here is all over the place.

Too many people with a little piece of it, too many shipments getting lifted, either by the police and the Customs or knocked off by other gangs. They need somebody here who can streamline the operation, run it with a bit of efficiency and a bit of muscle and that's me – I'm the guy. Naturally, I jumped at it.'

He threw his arms wide as if flinging a window open. 'And suddenly I'm made. Money to burn and no shortage of advice from my Dutch friends and others, all telling me how to launder it and stash it away in a bank account in Zurich. And for a long time no attention from the cops either. Fucking brilliant.'

His face darkened. 'And then this guy Marcus Kelly comes on the scene and it seems I'm the only fucking thing on his mind. He knows everything about me, what I have for fucking breakfast, how many times I shit every day. How in Christ does he know all this stuff? Who told him?'

He looked at Gallagher as if he might have the answer.

'So where's this taking us?' Gallagher asked.

'Everybody thinks I had Kelly killed. Balls! I had nothing to do with it. Oh, I'd love to have killed him all right. I'd have done it myself, no problem, but I didn't. Jesus, why would I do a thing like that, attract all that heat? Do you think I'm fucking mad? I'm telling you – somebody killed Kelly just so people would think it was me.'

He looked into Gallagher's eyes for a reaction but he did not find one.

'But the thing is,' he went on, 'what made him want to go after me? Where did he get his information? And now all this.' He brushed his hand across the table as if he were sweeping something on to the floor. 'The gear they found in my office. I didn't leave it there – somebody else must have done that so the Guards would find it. And this business about threatening judges. I've got fuck all to do with that. That's crazy stuff, that is.'

'Five minutes,' Gallagher reminded him, to hurry him along.

'Okay. I'm telling you there's somebody big behind this, somebody who wants me closed down. Everything that's happened has been part of a plan to set me up for a fall. They're trying to paint a big fucking picture with me right in the middle of it but I don't know who's doing it or why. When I went to Amsterdam—'

Clancy interrupted. 'Hold on a minute. I think I'd better advise you not to say anything here that you might regret. You've already said a whole lot.'

Donovan waved a dismissive hand.

'In that case,' Clancy said, turning to Gallagher, 'let me just say for future reference that I personally have no involvement in this aspect of my client's affairs. Have you got that?'

'Yeah, yeah,' Donovan answered on Gallagher's behalf. 'He believes you. Who wouldn't.'

He continued with his story, telling of the disappearing business contacts, the vanishing cash and the rumour of someone from New York being responsible.

He omitted to mention the battered hooker in Amsterdam.

'I wasn't going to come back,' he said, 'but then they shot my wee boy so that they could get at me. I couldn't leave him lying in hospital on his own, maybe dying. I had to see him. Thank God he's out of danger now.' He sniffed. 'Not like me.'

Gallagher wondered for a moment if Donovan was actually going to cry. They were always great contradictions, these people, family men who loved their children yet brought them up to be brutes like themselves.

But what the hell was all this about? Gallagher had dealt with enough conspiracies in his time to know that anything was possible but he wondered how much truth there was in all of this or whether it was just the desperate imaginings of a swaggering wiseguy trying to save his own skin. What there was, without any doubt, was a real fear.

But why should he care?

'I'm going,' he said and stood up.

'Just you think about what I've said,' Donovan urged. 'Who are they? Why do they want rid of me?'

Gallagher walked to the door and the warder opened it.

'Find out who benefits if I'm out of the picture,' Donovan shouted after him. 'That's what I can't figure. Who stands to gain?'

Gallagher turned. Donovan was standing at the table, wild-eyed, and Clancy was trying to get him to sit down again.

'You've got to get me off this hook,' Donovan said. 'Wait!'

His eyes searched the bare walls. He held his hands in front of him, clenching and unclenching his fingers, trying to grasp something in the air.

'Tell them I'll give them who killed Dezo and the girl. Tell them that.'

'Now, hold on a minute,' Clancy said. 'Be careful what you say here.'

'And the offer – the hundred K – that still stands. No, I'll make it a hundred and fifty.'

The door closed and Gallagher was gone.

Chapter Seventeen

Gilbert Leslie needed to get out of the hotel.

Dressed in one of the Shelbourne's fluffy towelling robes, he gazed from his window down on to the entrance to St Stephen's Green where morning sunlight dappled the leaves. He had got used to gauging the mood of the city from this viewpoint. Today, as the temperature climbed, he assessed it as relaxed and rejuvenated.

There were men in shirt-sleeves, briefcase in one hand and jacket crooked over the shoulder, laughing as they strolled by. Time was being shunned. Two women in dark glasses waited for a break in the traffic before crossing the road. Skirts seemed to be shorter today, the colours more zestful.

Leslie felt restless. Comfortable though his accommodation was, he had been virtually cooped up in it since he had arrived, dealing with business matters on a mobile phone which had been supplied to him for the purpose and only emerging in the evenings to go for dinner, which he ate alone and rather early, or to meet in secret with some of the other key figures in the enterprise which had brought him here.

One of these individuals he had found to be particularly distasteful. Yet to date the man had been effective and eager to impress. Recent events and others still to take place would ensure his continued loyalty for as long as it was needed.

And then—

And then Parrish and his people would take over and do what they had to.

He had gone to meet Parrish one evening in a pub off Grafton Street. He had found it amiable and pleasantly decorative and they had not felt at all foreign or conspicuous amid the clamour of a bar full of good-natured visitors with clip-on badges announcing that they were delegates to WONTEC.

They had sat at a table under wall lights shaped like daffodils.

'One down,' Parrish had said.

'And the next?'

'In a day or so. As soon as we know who it is to be.'

Leslie reflected. 'The last part of the operation—' he glanced at Parrish '—do you have feelings about what you are being requested to do?'

Parrish gave him a look of curiosity. 'I've never been asked a question like that before.'

Leslie offered a shy smile. 'There are those who think I am an animal for having proposed such a – a—'

'A hit?' Parrish suggested.

Leslie said nothing.

'I am the hammer,' Parrish told him. 'It's not my job to question. You're either in this line of work or you're not. You do it quickly and decisively – whatever it is. Second thoughts, doubts – can be fatal.'

Leslie nodded his agreement and approval. Parrish knew his job. 'Who will you use with you?'

'The best of them. A man called Humble.'

'And is he?'

'What?'

'Is he humble?'

Parrish frowned. He was uneasy with this musing. He liked solid fact. Yes/no answers.

'He will do what has to be done.'

Leslie saw the awkwardness. He smiled and put a hand on Parrish's arm. 'My sense of humour. It is not always appropriate.' He turned to something else. 'We've not yet discussed what happens when all this is over. My – personal – business.'

'Don't worry. It's in hand.' Parrish was more comfortable with this. 'There's been some preliminary reconnaissance already. It's just a question of the timing.'

'And the method.'

'And the method,' Parrish concurred.

Be patient, Leslie told himself now as he came away from the window of his room and began to dress.

He put on a light grey suit, white shirt and a ruby-coloured silk tie. His cheeks gleamed from a careful shave and the judicious application of an expensive cologne.

He went down in the lift, through the bustle of the lobby, where he acknowledged the greeting of the porter, and out into the street. The sharpness of the sunlight made him blink and he put on dark glasses. Then he walked down the steps and turned right towards Grafton Street, feeling his heart lighten.

Spring had always been his favourite, a time of revival, and next to it he cherished the fall with the mood of mellow introspection it induced. His own reflections, whatever the season, had not been joyous over the past few years but this morning he felt uplifted. Things were going according to plan and he could relax for a moment and enjoy his surroundings.

It was mid-morning and Grafton Street, curving downhill, was thronged. It was in relatively recent times that it had been paved over into a pedestrian area and it was hard to imagine how vehicles had ever managed to pass along it.

There were sober-suited businessmen engaged in weighty matters as they walked, glancing approvingly at elegant women emerging from Brown Thomas department store. An elderly busker with sad eyes and an accordion stood outside the shop doorway playing *When I Grow Too Old To Dream*.

Which does not apply to me, Leslie thought to himself.

Further on down the street, another busker was drawing much more interest from the passers-by. He sat on an upturned wooden box and with dexterity he tapped out the blues on a guitar which had a key pad attached to the strings.

Tourists drifted from window to window, many of them dressed in variations of the vacation uniform: lightweight waterproof jackets in bright colours, cotton trousers and deck shoes. Leslie could hear snatches of French and Italian in the air. Spanish, too.

He had the distinct feeling all of a sudden of being in a European capital. That was what it was, it came to him now, why he felt so much at ease. It was all so very different from New York. Here were all these people and yet none of them seemed to be in a hurry. They had time to stop and talk, to laugh and enjoy life.

He spotted an *Irish Independent* billboard outside a newsagent's window.

Threats to judges – latest.

He went inside and bought a copy.

'Isn't that the most wonderful day, sir?' The girl behind the counter gave him his change and presented him with a smile that cost nothing.

He smiled back at her. 'Yes, it most certainly is,' he said. 'Long may it last.'

It was a simple exchange between two people who would never see each other again but as he left the shop he felt his spirits buoyed further by the effortless pleasantry. On a corner, a flower-seller's stall was a rainbow display and on impulse he bought a deep pink carnation and put it in his buttonhole. He would find somewhere to sit and read the paper and find out what the 'latest' was.

When alone, he had not strayed beyond Grafton Street but this morning he decided to wander a little further afield. Signposts pointed him in the direction of Temple Bar which the tourist leaflets in his hotel room had told him was Dublin's bohemian quarter and an interesting place to explore.

He crossed Dame Street when the lights stopped the rush of heavy traffic momentarily and in a few minutes he found himself wandering down cobbled lanes, looking into the windows of eccentrically colourful shops which sold arts and crafts, third-world clothing, ethnic foods. It reminded him of Greenwich Village a little or SoHo but it was much more agreeable. Everyone was so – *so white*. How reassuring that was.

The passers-by were younger, students and back-packers for the most part, yet no one seemed to question his presence and he did not feel like an elderly oddity who had wandered into alien territory. There were galleries and music shops, some playing wistful Celtic sounds, others assaulting the street with a rhythmic barrage of technology. And there were restaurants and coffee shops. That was what he wanted.

He found a bistro with a corner view and went in. There was a small table by the window. He opened the paper. There was nothing new on the judges at all, just a re-hash of what had gone before with one or two additional strident comments from public representatives. 'Latest', he should have realised, was a word newspapers used when they had nothing fresh but wanted to keep the story going.

He put the paper down and lifted the menu from between the salt and pepper. A double espresso sounded good. So did the cakes But he would resist.

Damn it, no he wouldn't. Just for once he would indulge himself.

'Going to a wedding?'

Leslie looked up. A waitress was smiling at him. She was not much more than twenty, not tall either, about his own height, with a torrent of dark curls. She was dressed in a loose white cotton shirt that was a landscape of hills and valleys and he wondered suddenly what its folds concealed.

He realised that he was gawping stupidly at her and had not answered.

'I'm sorry. What did you say?'

'I wondered if you were going to a wedding.'

He looked puzzled for a second and then he remembered the buttonhole. 'Oh,' he said, 'the carnation.' He gave a chuckle. 'No, nothing like that. It was such a nice day that I thought I would brighten myself up.'

'Quite right,' she said. 'Men should wear buttonholes more often. But they're probably afraid that people might think they're gay.'

'Did you?'

'What?'

'Think I was – gay?'

'No – as a matter of fact. Not that it would make any difference to me.'

'But why were you certain I was not?'

'Oh, I don't know.' She shrugged. 'Woman's intuition, I guess. Now, can I get you something?'

'Oh, I'm terribly sorry,' Leslie said. 'Please forgive me.'

What the hell was he doing, flirting with the girl like that? *You old fool.*

'Don't apologise,' she laughed. 'I started it.'

She took his order and told him he would just love the cake he had chosen and as she went off to get it his eyes followed her, watching the slim hips in the tight black skirt, seeing almost the movement of a dancer in the way she walked.

When the order came, he ate the cake and drank the coffee and pretended to read the paper but all the time, as she moved around the bistro, his eyes sought her out, admiring her gracefulness and her confident, easy way with people.

This was the sort of girl his son should have had, not the

bimbos he had surrounded himself with. The *whores*. A girl like this might have made all the difference.

She bent over a table to wipe it, one foot stretched off the ground behind her, and he could not help staring. She turned and saw him before he could look away and then she walked towards him with a grin.

'What did you think of that?' She paused as if to underline the innuendo. 'The cake.'

'It was delicious,' he said, enjoying the possibility that she was teasing him. 'You were right.' He patted his stomach, holding it in at the same time. 'But I don't think it's the sort of thing I should be eating.'

'Oh, I don't know. You seem to be in good shape to me. Would you like some more?'

He waved an admonishing finger at her. 'Flatterer. But I'm not having another piece.'

'How about more coffee then?'

'Yes, thank you. That would be nice.'

She came back and put a fresh cup in front of him. 'I hope you don't mind me asking, but your accent – where are you from? It's a bit unusual.'

'Italy,' he said, 'although I lived in America for a few years.'

'You on holiday?'

'No, business, but I have a little time to myself today. I also have some family connections here.'

'Family connections. Italy. Sounds like the Mafia.'

'Of course,' he laughed. 'I'm the Godfather. Didn't you know that?'

'Sinead,' someone called from behind the counter.

'Sorry,' she said. 'I have to go.'

Sinead. That was her name.

He wanted to know more about her but it was perhaps fortunate that the bistro had become busy. He had already displayed far too much interest so he decided to leave quickly. He finished his coffee and looked at the bill she had left, then he counted out some money, including in it a generous tip.

When he was outside in the street, he regretted doing so. The tip was much too large and it meant that she was bound to remember him.

But then, he thought as he walked away, is that not exactly what you want?

Chapter Eighteen

Gallagher could not wipe his meeting with Sean Donovan from his mind.

Nor could he forget the hundred thousand. Or was it a hundred and fifty?

It had been in his thoughts when he went to sleep last night and he had even dreamed that he had gone to see his bank manager again only this time it was Donovan, with a rancid smile, sitting there in that broom cupboard of an office.

All he had to do was hold out his hand and the money was his but it was an offer he was going to have to refuse. Yet perhaps for the first time in his life he understood the desperation that drove some people. Addicts needing their next fix, stealing, even murdering, to get the money they needed.

The despair that had driven Kate's husband to kill himself.

The thought of drug-dealing focused his mind on Donovan once more. He regretted ever having clapped eyes on the guy and he did not intend to encounter him again.

There was no doubt that Donovan was trying to use him because of his family connection but it was too easy to write him off because of that. Gallagher had seen enough people in Donovan's position in his time, men in fear of the retribution of the Mob or of an unforgiving foreign government, to know when they were telling the truth.

Whatever the reality might be, Donovan sincerely believed that someone was out to get him.

Paranoia? Sure, it might just be that. But sometimes people were paranoid for a good reason.

Part of his own unease was the concern that Emma might somehow find out about his visit to Mountjoy. A report from the prison governor perhaps, filtering up through the system and into the Justice Department – then *kaboom*.

Worse – what if it got leaked to the Press?

A phantom headline appeared in his mind.

MINISTER'S FATHER IN SECRET JAIL VISIT.

It would do nothing at all for their relationship, coming hard on the heels of the *Dublin Sunday* row. If Donovan had told him something earth-shattering, then the visit would have been entirely justified. Instead there were just fragments, eerie suspicions in the mind of a troubled and unreliable man.

Exactly what information was there?

Dezo and the girl. There was that, for a start; Donovan's parting shot. It had clicked with Gallagher when he was in a taxi on the way home – those murders, the bodies of the young couple on the rubbish dump. They had caused shock waves for a short time until the killing of Marcus Kelly had come along to take their place. The public memory was short.

But what of the rest of what Donovan had had to say? He had been amazingly frank about his drugs business, about his dealings abroad and his Swiss bank account, much to his lawyer's consternation. What if there really was a new element now, some kind of power play among criminal organisations?

Gallagher was a little out of touch with who was running what. The Irish drugs scene was developing, there was no doubt about that, but although the major syndicates, the Colombian cartels and others, would be the source of supply, staying far at the back of it all and working through their European associates, they would not dirty their hands with someone like Sean Donovan. He was a bug which could be squashed at any time.

So, supposing for one moment that what Donovan had said was true, that there *was* someone from New York involved here, that he *was* in the middle of some complex conspiracy designed to finish him off, then what had he got himself involved in? One thing was certain – Donovan himself sure as hell did not know.

He would have to call Emma. She would be furious that he had allowed himself to be dragged into this. He felt like a difficult child having to own up to some act of mischief.

He dialled the number of the Justice Department and asked for her office. He had never called her there before. It felt strange.

He was put through to a female voice.

'Secretariat?' she said.

'I'm trying to make contact with Miss Gallagher,' he said. 'My name is Tom Gallagher. I'm her father.'

'Her father – I see,' the voice said, a little sceptically.

'Well now, I'm sure the Minister has your number already, Mr Gallagher, but perhaps I could just take it anyway.'

Gallagher gave it to her. They would check it out to see if he was the real thing.

'I'm afraid Miss Gallagher is actually out of the country at the moment,' the woman said. 'You're – eh – obviously not aware of that.' Her tone suggested that if he was really who he said he was then he would have known. 'It was on the news this morning. She's representing the Government at a conference in Strasbourg for the next couple of days. But I'll certainly give her the message that you rang. She'll get back to you as soon as possible, I'm sure.'

Gallagher thanked her and hung up. He sighed deeply. He really needed to see Emma with this, talk to her face to face, however painful the outcome, but that was not possible.

He wanted to get shot of all this stuff, one way or another. Get it out of his hair.

He had an idea. He looked up the number of the *Garda* headquarters at Phoenix Park.

Like Alan Warnock, Jim Foy was another old boyhood friend with whom he had made contact again when he returned to Ireland, discovering in the process that Foy was now a Chief Superintendent working in the office of the Deputy Commissioner for Operations.

'Tom,' Foy said when Gallagher got through. 'A surprise. What can I do for you?'

'The Marcus Kelly murder, this whole Sean Donovan business and so on. I need to try to talk to someone. Who would all of that come under?'

'What's this?' Foy asked with a laugh. 'Writing some

more scurrilous stuff about us?'

'Christ, Jim – not you, too. It would take too long to explain but no – I'm not.'

'Fair enough. Well now, let's see. You're talking about different people there. It's all the Dublin Metropolitan Area, of course, but a lot of folk would be involved, the Criminal Assets Bureau as well. Let me think – if you want to have a chat with someone who might have the whole picture, your best bet would be the National Bureau of Criminal Investigation. I'd say Chief Superintendent Barrett Greeley would be your man.'

'Where would I find him?'

'He has an office in Harcourt Square. In the city.'

'Great. I'll give him a call. You're terrific.'

He found the number and asked for Chief Superintendent Greeley's office.

'Chief's phone.' It was a woman who took no nonsense.

'I'd like to speak to Chief Superintendent Greeley, please,' he said.

'Can I ask who's calling?' Suspicion now because his voice was not familiar to her.

'My name's Tom Gallagher,' he said.

'The Chief's not here just at the moment,' she told him. 'Can I ask what it's about?'

Gallagher hated that: first being asked who was calling, so that you thought you were going to be put through, then being told the person was not around. He was there all right; just not taking this call. He would fix that.

'Yes. You can tell him I'd like to have a word with him about a man called Sean Donovan. Tell him I've been talking to Donovan and I've got something to pass on.'

'Rrright.' There was uncertainty, then – 'Would you mind holding on for just a moment?'

In a couple of seconds a man's voice came on.

'Mr Gallagher?'

'Yes?'

'Barrett Greeley.'

'Oh, right. I was told you weren't in.'

'I was in another office.' The tone challenged him to prove otherwise.

'Of course. Look,' Gallagher began, 'I should explain who I am first of all. I used to work with the FBI and now—'

'Yes, I think I know who you are,' Greeley interrupted. 'What's all this about Sean Donovan?'

'I've been to see him in Mountjoy and I'd like to talk to you about it.'

'You've been to see him? How come?'

'He sent a message through his solicitor that he'd like to talk to me.'

'And you went?' Greeley sounded incredulous.

'Yes.' Gallagher said, discomfort growing. Greeley was making him feel foolish. 'He told me a few things I thought you should know.'

'Well, then – I'm always interested in anything Mr Donovan has to say. You'd better come in and tell me, hadn't you?'

Harcourt Square was a slightly shabby area just beyond St Stephen's Green. The police building, which housed several specialist units, stood back behind high fencing but when Gallagher presented himself to a young *Garda* officer in a hut at the open gate he found security a bit more relaxed than he might have expected.

The policeman had the sports pages open and a music station on the radio. A pile of boxes stood waiting to be collected by the Stolen Vehicles Unit. In the States, a building like this, the officer would not have been guarding the place on his own; he would have been armed to the teeth and there would have been a gauntlet of electronic screening to pass through.

Gallagher told him who he had come to see.

'Mr Greeley, is it?' the young man said, running his finger down a clipboard. 'The Chief Super?'

'That's him,' Gallagher said.

A car with three plainclothes men drove in and tapped its horn gently. The Guard gave a desultory wave as it went by.

He found Gallagher's name. 'Here we are. I'll just ring up,' he said and picked up the phone. 'Hello, Moya? I've got a Mr Gallagher down at the gate to see the Chief.' He listened. 'Right you are then.' He hung up. 'Somebody'll come down for you.' He stepped out of the hut and pointed to the main door. 'If you just wander on in there, they'll meet you.'

Gallagher did as he was told and strolled inside. Photofit pictures of wanted criminals scowled from a noticeboard beside details of a police golf tournament.

Heels clacked on the floor behind him.

'Mr Gallagher?' He turned to see a small red-haired woman in a belted dress. Her eyes did not welcome him. 'If you'll come with me, I'll take you to see Chief Superintendent Greeley.'

He followed her down a corridor where the doors had

tiny name-plates, some stating the identity of the occupants, others acronyms to denote functions. There was a door right at the end of the corridor, facing them as they approached, and as he drew closer he could see Greeley's name staring from it.

The woman rapped sharply.

'Come in.'

It was a smoker's office, airless and polluted, with windows that were rarely open. But as he looked at the man sitting behind the desk, he saw that that was the least of his problems.

The cropped hair had grown a little but there was still the same suspicion in the eyes which had stared at him from the front row of the lecture room at Templemore.

Greeley saw the recognition and the shock of it. He gestured to a chair on the other side of the desk. He did not offer his hand.

'Yes, we've met before,' he confirmed.

Gallagher sat. An ashtray full of acrid cigarette butts was under his nose.

'This – this is a surprise. I felt bad about not having had a chance to speak to you after our – eh – conversation at Templemore,' he said. 'You weren't at the lunch, I noticed.'

'No, I had things to do,' Greeley said, tidying some papers into a pile. 'I couldn't stay.' There was ash on the desk. He tried to sweep it away but rubbed it into the surface. He dusted his hands. 'Anyway, I didn't have a lot of interest in seeing those young recruits drooling over you.'

'Is that how you saw it?'

Greeley shrugged. 'That's how you played it.' He lit a

cigarette from an open packet on the desk and threw the match into the ashtray.

'So let's hear about Mr Donovan.' The words came out with the exhaled smoke.

There was a notepad and a pen in front of him but as Gallagher told him of his encounter the day before he did not bother to jot any of it down. Instead, he turned sideways in his chair, leaned back and fixed his attention on a Bank of Ireland calendar on the wall. March was the cliffs of Moher in Connemara. Waves lashed the rocks with white foam and gulls drifted in the air currents above, silent for once.

When Gallagher had finished, Greeley turned to him again. 'Well, that's fine, Mr Gallagher.'

'Tom.'

Greeley did not take him up on it. 'I'll get Moya to show you down,' he said instead.

'Hold on a minute. You mean you're not going to give me a response to any of this?'

Greeley considered the question. 'Okay,' he said, 'I'll give you a response. I think you were an *eejit*, not to put too fine a point on it, to go anywhere near Sean Donovan. Now, quite frankly, I don't give a toss what sort of shit you get yourself into but it so happens that I think your daughter's doing quite a good job at the Justice Department. She prosecuted a few cases for me once and she was bloody brilliant. It's none of my business but if she were my daughter I don't think I'd want to do anything that would damage her. Does she know about any of this?'

'No.'

'I didn't think so somehow. That little bastard Donovan has been trying to use you. Look at it: he gets you involved, the father of the Junior Minister, and it all gets out some way or other. So there's embarrassment all round, a real mess, and he claims there's been dirty work at the crossroads, somebody planting drugs, maybe the police even, and then it comes to trial, if it ever goes that far, and he gets off. And don't forget—' he pointed a finger – 'you're the one who gave him the idea in that article you wrote, saying that publicity would endanger a fair hearing. Remember?'

Gallagher did not even try to answer. Greeley was echoing some of his own thoughts.

'For somebody with your background, big shot in the FBI and all, you blunder about through the undergrowth a bit, don't you?' Greeley said. 'At least you didn't take the money he offered you.'

Don't allow yourself to get angry.

He knew Greeley was taunting him, enjoying being able to deliver this rebuke. There was retribution in it for the skirmish at Templemore.

'So you're just going to dismiss everything he said?' Gallagher asked eventually.

'No, I'm not going to dismiss it. It's just that he hasn't told us anything we don't already know.'

'What about the murder of that young couple?'

'Oh, for Christ sake,' Greeley said, stubbing his cigarette out irritably. 'He did that himself. Not personally, maybe, but he had his friend Vinnie Dwyer or somebody do it for him. Dwyer was questioned about it but we had to let him go. No evidence.'

Gallagher picked up the name. It was the one Donovan had mentioned.

'Dezo, the fellow who was murdered – he was one of Donovan's pushers. He was probably found with his hand in the till, maybe taking some of the gear for himself, I don't know. The girl might have been at it with him. Or maybe she was just in the way.'

'But if he was aware that you knew all that, then why would he volunteer—'

'God knows who he might try to finger. The Pope, the *Taoiseach*. Anybody to save his own hide. As for the rest of it – we're certain he was behind the Marcus Kelly shooting although we'll never prove it unless we find the trigger men. And they wouldn't have hung around. I presume you know a professional hit when you see one.'

He had not extinguished the cigarette completely. Smoke from the smouldering filter tip was bitter in Gallagher's nostrils, like the sarcasm.

'So what about Amsterdam, Zurich, this notion of someone from New York?' Gallagher tried.

Greeley lit up again before he answered. 'It may surprise you to learn that we are not exactly unaware of Mr Donovan's connections in the drugs trade and that we have a relationship with police forces in other countries. Maybe you've heard of such a thing. And what if he knew that the idea of someone from New York would appeal to you, you with your big-time criminal organisation obsessions, and so he made up a story about someone being out to get him?'

'So who shot his son then?'

'A lot of people in this city don't like drugs. They think

195

we don't do enough to stop it, so they take matters into their own hands, especially the people in the inner-city areas. As we understand it, Donovan's boy's a chip off the old block, in spite of his age. There have been stories about him pushing drugs to his classmates at school. The police involved in the case think he may have been shot by a few people trying to discourage this sort of practice. Now I don't condone it but if it works—'

He let the thought hang in the air. 'There is one thing,' he said with a hint of a smile. 'I'm delighted to hear that our friend Mr Clancy was involved in this little discussion. We might have a wee word with him. You never know what he might give us if he thought we had something hard on him. It wouldn't do any harm to open up a second front on Mr Donovan.'

Gallagher frowned. Greeley's scepticism was having an odd effect, recharging his suspicions rather than dispelling them.

'The man was afraid of something,' he said. 'I understand your instinct to be cautious, but the man was afraid.'

'And he's got a lot to be afraid of. For once we've got him where we want him and he knows we're damned well not going to let him go.'

'And the tip-off about the drugs?'

'Who knows? Someone with a grudge, maybe. One thing's certain – we're not going to be examining that particular gift horse too closely, not if it gets Donovan off the streets.'

There was a knock and the red-haired woman came in with a folded piece of paper. Greeley opened it and smiled.

'Surprise, surprise. The High Court has just refused to

give Sean Donovan bail. Good. Now, Mr Gallagher, I think that concludes our business. And I do recommend that you have a word with your daughter about what you've been up to. I'm sure you'd rather she didn't hear it from anyone else.'

Outside the building, Gallagher took several deep breaths of fresh air.

His face felt flushed with anger and embarrassment. As he walked past the Guard at the gate and into the street he did not notice the friendly goodbye.

Chapter Nineteen

It was after eleven when Lionel Purcell finally rose from the table, a trifle unsteadily, announced to his dinner companions that he was going and wondered if he was getting too old for this sort of thing.

There were five of them in all. They sampled the fare of Dublin's finest restaurants once a month, awarding their own imaginary stars, sometimes taking them away if there was any perceived imperfection, and with a level of humour redolent of junior school they called themselves the Egon Toast Club.

The restaurants indulged their spoofery and their ebullient behaviour because they were men who were all at a professional pinnacle and they were big spenders. There was Purcell, who was a High Court judge, there was an eminent consultant surgeon, an investment banker, the millionaire owner of a supermarket chain and a best-selling English novelist living in leafy, tax-free Wexford.

Tonight they had descended on La Stampa in Dawson Street, wolfing their way through five courses with a new wine for each, and now they were into the brandy and Montecristos, entertaining each other with social gossip which was as usual of a most defamatory nature and all the more enjoyable for it.

But Purcell was tired and he was going home. They each took it in turn to pay for these jolly outings and it was not his turn tonight. He stood for a moment, his cigar wedged in his hand, then raised his arm and bade them adieu.

He made his way through the restaurant, being careful not to lurch into someone's table or collide with a waiter. The walls were lined with Knuttel paintings which he hated. The rat-faced people in them eyed him with menace.

Someone got him his coat and he dropped cigar ash down it as he put it on. Outside the restaurant, the night air was cool and it made him a little giddy. Across the street, the lights of the Mansion House, the Lord Mayor's residence, glittered like jewellery. Purcell blinked several times and tried to sharpen his focus. To his blurred vision, the place seemed to be on fire.

Still, never mind; someone would look after it.

A dark Mercedes was parked directly outside and the driver, a plainclothes man from the protection squad, got out and opened the rear door for him.

'We're going to good old Herbert Park tonight, Jackie,' Purcell said as he slid inside, 'not to Kildare.'

'Right you are, sir,' the driver replied, although he was aware of that already.

Purcell kept a small one-bedroom flat in a mews in the south of the city. He stayed alone there when business in the courts kept him late, when he wanted a bit of privacy to write a judgement or when he was on his monthly night out with the boys.

If he was going to keep up his membership of their little

club, then he would have to try to arrange that their evenings did not fall on busy court days. This had been a long one and he was far too weary.

Among other things, he had had to listen to an appeal for bail by lawyers acting for that man Donovan. All that bloody nonsense with the phone calls. It had made no difference to his decision; not the slightest. There was no question of granting bail, even if he had set it at what, ten, twenty, thirty million? The charges were much too serious for that.

Threatening the police with a gun. Silly little man. He would be locked up and never heard of again.

They were at Herbert Park within minutes. He let himself into the flat after stabbing the door with the key for a second or two. Jackie came in with him to check that there were no unwanted guests, then called the local *Garda* station to inform them that the judge was home. They would run a patrol round here every half hour or so.

'Very good of you, Jackie,' Purcell said. 'Marvellous driving as always.'

The policeman made sure the burglar alarm was set properly. Under a table in the hall there was also a panic button which would bring the police running if it was pressed. He touched his fingertips to his forehead in a salute and then left.

He held his right hand in front of him and stared at it. Where was the cigar? It seemed to have disappeared somewhere along the way. He spread his fingers and looked at the back of his hand, then the palm, trying to work out how this conjuring trick had been accomplished.

The intercom buzzed.

It might be Jackie. Perhaps he had found the cigar in the back of the car and brought it back. Excellent. He had barely smoked any of it and it was rather a good one, much too fine to waste.

He pressed the button. 'Yes?'

'It's me, sir.' Jackie's voice. He put an eye to the security peep-hole in the door and saw his driver's distorted features.

First class job. Damn cigar might have set fire to the bloody car into the bargain.

He opened the door to the sound of a loud electronic whooping, deafening in the confined space. He had forgotten about the burglar alarm.

Suddenly there were three sharp bangs, then Jackie stumbled past him and fell face forward on to the floor.

That was when he saw the other two men, dark figures whom he did not recognise. One of them had something in his hand and he appeared to be pointing it at him.

'Look here, what's—'

The shotgun roared but he heard little of it in the moment he died. Blood deluged the walls as his chest erupted and he was hurled backwards on top of the body of the dead driver. The shock waves were still eddying when the second man stepped in, stood astride him and aimed a handgun at his head.

It was five am when the Government jet touched down at Baldonnel military airfield on the outskirts of Dublin. Emma's body needed sleep but her mind would not let her have any.

The call to the hotel had come a few hours ago, the

Prime Minister himself waking her from the depths of slumber to tell her that the judge who had refused to grant bail to Sean Donovan earlier that day had been murdered, along with his protection officer.

'I need you back here now,' he told her.

She had sat up with a start as a dream ebbed away. She had begun to mumble something in dozy confusion. 'But the conference. What about—'

'Now!' O'Neill had repeated with force. 'The Government jet is on its way to pick you up. I'll see you in my office the moment you return.'

It was dizzying. On the journey, her mind carried her along like a white water ride with the implications of what had happened and how it might affect her but she forced herself to stay calm.

Let's just wait and see.

She unfastened her seatbelt, lifted her handbag and went into the tiny washroom. In the baleful light, she leaned forward and stared closely into the mirror. There was not much she could do about the red eyes or the bags under them but she could do something with the rest.

She brushed her hair and fixed her lipstick, then dabbed a little perfume on her neck. The ritual, as much as the effect, made her feel a lot fresher. She was wearing a white silk blouse and she fastened the two buttons which she had opened earlier because the plane was hot. She straightened her skirt, brushing her hands down the creases that had formed in it, then went back and slipped into the jacket she had left folded carefully on the seat beside her.

When she emerged from the aircraft, she found two officers from the protection unit waiting beside a black

Mercedes and her case already in the boot. Their faces were grim. They had just lost a colleague and the man he had been looking after and they would be feeling a mixture of emotions at this time. Anger, mostly.

'I'm very sorry to hear what happened,' she said.

'Thank you, Minister,' one of them acknowledged as he held the door open for her.

They drove like the wind and at that hour on a Saturday morning there was nothing to delay them. The gold streaks of dawn were turning to blue, promising a fine day, but she knew this would be her only chance to appreciate it.

The driver radioed ahead to confirm that the pick-up had been as planned and to give their estimated time of arrival. They were in the heart of the city soon, weaving through streets which were almost deserted, but Upper Merrion Street, where Government Buildings was located, was an exception.

There were police on the pavement beside cars which looked important. A clutch of reporters and cameramen stood on a corner, kicking the kerb and drinking coffee from styrofoam cups. They gathered themselves hastily when they saw the Mercedes, swinging cameras onto their shoulders, but she was too quick for them to get much and she was out of the vehicle and into the building in a flash.

Just inside the door, two of the *Taoiseach*'s aides hovered.

'He's waiting for you, Minister,' one said, a little breathlessly, as they walked on either side of her down the corridor. 'Mr Goulding is with him too.'

'You made very good time, Minister,' said the other.

She glanced at them as she walked. There was an added

layer of deference here that she had not experienced before. She had seen it in the demeanour of the protection men, too, and it excited her. The world had turned and she was not the person she had been just a few hours ago.

The door of the Prime Minister's office opened. She did not enter cautiously, slipping round the door as some of the more simpering civil servants did, but swiftly and with the confidence she knew he wanted to see.

O'Neill and Tony Goulding were in shirtsleeves and they looked grey and exhausted. Compared to them she was composed and immaculate and she could see a welcome recognition of that fact lighten the strain on their faces.

'I'm glad you're here.' The *Taoiseach* smiled. He stepped forward, taking her right hand in both of his. She did not feel at all comfortable with such a condescending gesture but she allowed it for a second before taking her hand away.

O'Neill looked at her and in her eyes he saw his mistake. He waved to an armchair beside the marble fireplace and she sat down.

'Now,' he said, levering himself on to the edge of his desk where he sat with one leg crooked over the corner, a pose he favoured when he was trying to appear relaxed but still in charge. He was under the impression, too, that it made him seem a little taller.

Emma looked at his feet. She had noticed before that he always wore good shoes. These were black loafers. There was a buckle on the side which gave them a slightly raffish touch and she wondered if they were his own choice or whether they had been approved by Mrs O'Neill.

'I'll get straight to the point,' he said. 'A little over an hour ago, Eamon Savage came here and I reluctantly asked for his resignation. And, I must say, to his credit—' he turned and looked at Goulding as if to make a point '—he did not hesitate to comply.'

Emma's eyes went to each of the men in turn, trying to surmise what had gone on between them before she arrived.

O'Neill continued. 'Let me say that it gave me no pleasure to have to ask for it. Eamon Savage is an honourable man but in the circumstances there was no alternative.' He gestured in the general direction of the window. 'After last night's murders, they would have been baying for blood out there and I'm afraid there are serious issues to be addressed about his handling of the security arrangements surrounding members of the judiciary.'

'What about the Commissioner?' Emma asked.

It was a good question, O'Neill knew, and in posing it straight away like that she was answering many of his own queries about her.

She was direct and to the point, no expressions of regret and sadness about her boss, the departing Minister. Life goes on. He looked at her as he considered whether to take her into his confidence. He decided he would.

'Eventually,' he said, 'but not yet. Not a good moment for a new hand on the tiller, even if we had strong views on who that new hand should be, which we don't. The Deputy Commissioner has been in the job for only a matter of months and it would be rather a case of catapulting him into a position for which he is not fully equipped. In any case, the Commissioner will only say that he acted as instructed. And with a policeman being killed, too, it might be an unpopular move. No, it had to be Savage alone, I'm afraid. He seriously under-reacted to the threat.'

He stood up. 'And now the next step.'

He moved from the desk to where she sat.

'You'll have guessed, of course. It's very simple but it's also very important. I want you to take over as Minister for Justice. Will you accept?'

Even though it was what she had been expecting, it still surprised her when he said it. She stood, remembering as she did that she was taller than he was. She leaned her hip slightly to one side to make it less obvious.

'I – well – yes, *Taoiseach*. I will. Thank you. I assume this is for an interim period?'

'Absolutely not. I have no doubt in my mind that you would have attained this position in time but last night's events have rather thrust greatness on you a little sooner. I intend that your appointment should be ratified by the President on Monday.'

'Then – I'm – I'm very grateful indeed. I'm honoured and extremely flattered that you've shown such confidence in me.'

'You may not have a lot to thank me for,' O'Neill said. 'It's going to be a rough ride, Emma, but I – we—' he turned to Goulding briefly '—are sure you can handle it.'

'Congratulations,' Goulding said, beaming.

Emma looked at him. Savage had gone and Goulding would have been happy to help dispose of him. He put his arm round her shoulder and squeezed. It was the sort of fatherly gesture she was used to receiving from him, usually in private, a sign of support and affection, but at this moment it felt like a manifestation of ownership.

He had encouraged her to go into politics and she had been delighted and flattered by his patronage because she knew that with him on her side no door would remain closed to her. He had promised her that she would get this far one day, perhaps go even further, and she had told him how much she wanted that and how indebted she would be if it happened.

Sometimes, when they talked alone, she had felt able to confide in him about her empty childhood and she had felt herself turning to him to fill the gap left by her absent father.

Until Tom Gallagher had returned. To confound her emotions and her ordered life.

Her ties to Tony Goulding could not have been any more binding had they been sealed in blood.

And now there *was* blood and the spilling of it had brought her to one of the highest offices in the land.

'Bravo,' Goulding said.

It struck Emma that the acclamation was as much for himself as for her and she wondered what the price would be for this achievement.

Chapter Twenty

Vinnie Dwyer was going to meet somebody. As he made his way through the O'Connell Street crowds in the mid-morning sunshine, he carried a flimsy shopping bag containing a loaf of bread, a bag of apples, a box of cereal and, at the bottom, a couple of items for which there was no known bar code.

He eyed the newspaper billboards casually but did not stare at them. They had got the heavy type out for this one. JUDGE AND DRIVER SHOT DEAD.

Some people were stopping to buy a paper but Vinnie did not. This whole business gave him a strange feeling, anxiety and excitement all rolled into one.

The stakes had got very high and the game was not over yet. Not by a long chalk.

For him it had begun one night a year ago.

He had been asleep in the flat after a couple of games of snooker and a lot of drink. He had been buried under the blankets, still in his socks and underpants, but in spite of the deadening effect of the alcohol something had disturbed him, a wrong sound registering in his head, and he had emerged into half-consciousness to see shadows and shapes moving about in the room.

He had lurched from the bed, propelled by instinct more than intent, but his feet had caught in the heavy blankets and he had fallen to the floor.

He remembered hands on him, pulling at his clothes, lifting him, fists hitting him as he struggled, and then a blanket being put over his head. When it was taken away again he found himself blinking into the light, lying naked on the bed with his hands tied behind him.

Two men, one wearing glasses, stood looking at him. He raised his head a fraction and glanced down furtively towards his dick, as if to reassure himself that it was still there. It lolled on his thigh, a shrivelled thing, and he wanted desperately to put his hands over it in a gesture of protection which for no logical reason at all would have made him feel more secure.

He had never felt so much at someone's mercy in his entire life.

His gun. He thought of that next. It was in a biscuit tin in the kitchen, under a layer of Mars bars that he kept to satisfy his sweet tooth, but they had found it. There it was, an old nine millimetre Browning, in the hands of the man with the glasses who examined it with an amused curiosity, turning it round and round as if it were some sort of museum artefact.

There were three of them and he had never seen any of them before. Two stood beside the bed and watched him silently. They were well-dressed, in suits and ties, but there was muscle beneath. One, whose name was Humble, although Vinnie did not know that, was eating a Mars bar.

He wondered what they saw when they looked at him

but he could not read their eyes. He felt overweight and under-endowed and, frightened though he was, he also felt anger pushing its way to the front of his emotions. He wanted to make these bastards pay for the humiliation they were causing him.

And then, at last, with sinking stomach, he began to wonder why they had trussed him up like this.

If they had come here to kill him they would have done so already. Unless there was something they wanted to know. The thought struck him with sudden alarm.

The third man, the one fondling the gun, started to speak. He sat in a chair drawn up to the bed. He wore an open black raincoat which he kept pulling up to cover his knees. The room was chilly; Vinnie was acutely aware of that. He willed himself not to shiver.

The man's accent was American which for some reason made Vinnie feel more fearful. Flat on his back, he looked at the other two men. Maybe they were all American. But formal introductions or an explanation of any kind were not on the agenda.

'Vinnie,' the man said, as if he were welcoming him. 'At last.'

'Who the fuck are you?'

The man smiled. He knew, as Vinnie himself had the moment he had spoken, that it was impossible, not to say ridiculous, to sound tough and menacing when you were tied up naked with somebody pointing your own gun at your prick.

'I'm sorry we've had to tie you up,' he said, 'but you have quite a reputation for being physical so we've had to do things this way in order that we can have a talk without you, shall we say, disrupting the proceedings. Now – I have a proposition for you but first let me tell you a few things about yourself.'

To Vinnie's surprise, he did. He had an impressive knowledge of his past, however he had gleaned it.

'We know all about you and your friend Sean Donovan,' the man said. 'We've been observing. We see the way he uses you, gets you to do all his dirty work for him, take all the risks. And for what?'

He turned to survey the tiny room, the fading yellow roses in the cheap wallpaper, the chipped chest of drawers with its sticky surface. He sniffed the air as if noticing the fetid odour for the first time.

'This is hardly the Waldorf, is it?'

His companions began to laugh but he silenced them with an abrupt motion of his hand.

'Untie him and let him up,' he said. 'Let him get dressed. No more indignity for Vinnie.'

As he pulled his clothes on with some haste in case they changed their mind, Vinnie listened carefully to what his visitor had to tell him. He heard sympathy and truth in what the man was saying and for once he had the feeling that here was somebody who understood him.

When he had finished dressing, he sat down on the bed again. The man put his hand into his coat pocket and threw him a bulging brown envelope.

'Open it,' he said.

It was full of money. Ten thousand pounds, to be exact, he was informed, and it was just a beginning – 'although don't go throwing it around in case people like Donovan and the cops start to wonder where you got it from.'

All Vinnie had to do to earn it was to make a phone call regularly to someone and supply bits and pieces of information about Donovan. It would all take a little while to develop but in the end, Donovan would be out of the way and Vinnie would be set up with his own operation. And when that happened, the ten grand would be small change. That was a promise.

Vinnie had a feeling that when these people made a promise, of whatever kind, they kept it.

'So, Vinnie. What do you say?'

'What – why me?' he asked. 'Who are you people? What's your game?'

The man laughed. 'It's not really why you. It's why Sean Donovan. But we'll let that pass for the moment. Never mind who we are for now. There'll be plenty of opportunity for explanation as time goes on. You – you're in the right place at the right time and you're the right man. Simple as that. You get things done and you can do what you're told. Don't knock it. So what do you say?'

And of course Vinnie had said yes.

Wise decision, he told himself now as he walked past Clery's department store. There were summer clothes in the window, co-ordinating combinations of shorts and tee-shirts for all the family, arranged in a display involving a deck chair, a beach ball, a plastic crab and a floor coated lightly with sand.

He knew that they would have killed him there and then if he had said no.

So he had stashed the money and he had done what they had asked, making a few phone calls to a guy called Marcus Kelly. It was all a mystery until, when Kelly's television reports hit the air, he had begun to understand what they were doing. Donovan's profile increased so that he became a monster in the eyes of the public.

Soon Vinnie met other people who were involved and bit by bit he got drawn into the scheme.

And then things really started to happen.

Jesus Christ, these people could do whatever they wanted. First, they had blown Kelly away. Used him and then wasted him.

Bang. Just like that.

And last night. Murdering a fucking judge and his protection officer? Unbelievable.

But although these were certainly scary guys, it was the man they had taken him to meet the night he had got out of the Bridewell who had really put the fear of God in him.

They knew he spent a lot of time at the New Western Inn at Tallaght. He had a vested interest in the place. When the bar was being built, he and some of his friends had gone to see the owner, at another pub he ran, and told him that if he wanted the job to be finished on time then it might be as well if Vinnie kept an eye on things for him.

'Just to make sure that none of the workmen gets frightened off for whatever reason. You know what I mean?'

The owner did. He had looked with disgust and a sense of inevitability at Vinnie and his grinning companions, with their shaven heads and tattoos, crowding his attic office. Then he had gone to the safe.

And so it was that the pub had risen without any trouble

and it had opened on the day it was supposed to. In order to ensure that it was a continued success, without any interference from armed robbers, for example, or trouble-makers of any kind, Vinnie and his acolytes retained their role as security consultants.

But the man he had been taken to see did not like it.

Their meetings had taken place in a car out at Black-rock. The man had been waiting there, just him in the back and a driver in the front. It had been hard to see properly but even in the dark Vinnie could sense that this person was not like anybody he had ever met.

Getting into the car, he had felt a nervous prickle on his skin. It was something to do with the clean, almost anti-septic, fragrance that came from the stranger and the way he sat there, upright in the seat, hardly moving, scarcely bothering to look Vinnie's way. At that moment Vinnie had become conscious of the smell of drink on his own breath, the cigarette smoke wreathing his clothes, and he had felt sordid and unclean in his presence.

'Vinnie,' the man had said. 'I felt it was important that we meet. There is much to be done and you – you are a vital part of all of it.'

Vinnie had found courage from somewhere.

'Who are you?' he asked. He had detected traces of something foreign in an accent that was otherwise that of an American.

The man smiled. 'My name is Schenk. That is all you need to know about me. Now, Vinnie, this business with the bar that you are – protecting. It is time it ended, I think. It is petty extortion, much too likely to attract unwelcome attention and, anyway, soon you will have no need of such trivial activities. You must give it up. What do you say?'

And once again, of course, he had said yes.

Schenk delivered the rest of his instructions, from which there could be no deviation. Vinnie was to keep a low profile, stay at home, away from most of his usual haunts, after this whole distasteful business at the New Western had been abandoned. There was to be no getting drunk, with the attendant risk that he might say too much, too unwisely.

'That would be a foolish mistake,' Schenk said. He turned briefly and for a second Vinnie saw the message in his eyes. 'Foolish and final.'

Then he smiled and began to outline how things would work in the future: Vinnie's new and vital role as a distributor, how they would set up mechanisms, retail outlets where a lot of cash changed hands, to help him cleanse the money so that he would not have the police and the Criminal Assets Bureau breathing down his neck.

'You will just have to be patient a little longer and then the whole of this operation will be yours.'

Vinnie had always wondered what Donovan had done wrong and he wanted to ask. He was certain there were things that he was not being told, a much bigger picture of which this was only a small corner, but for the moment he would sit and admire it. Like the man had said – don't knock it.

For the past year he had been doing everything they wanted, supplying all the information they needed to bring Donovan down. Killing Dezo and the girl had been his own idea, to show them that he was a hard man who did not shirk from the really rough work, but he had been admonished for that.

'We don't need demonstrations,' the man he now knew as Parrish had said at a meeting shortly after Donovan had gone to Amsterdam. 'No unnecessary killing. Only when business calls for it.'

Well, it had called for it now all right.

Schenk himself had given Vinnie one more task, one more person to deliver. He felt his heart beating hard at the thought of it.

There was a gap in the traffic and he nipped across the road to the central reservation which divided O'Connell Street down the middle. He stood beside a giant concrete bowl filled with red and yellow tulips and waited for a break in the stream of cars on the other carriageway. Once he reached the far side of the street, he walked a few steps to a big McDonald's. It was packed and noisy and the moist smell of hot food made him hungry. He joined the smallest-looking queue.

'Take your order here?' A girl called her mantra to him.

He asked for a Big Mac, regular fries and a Coke and then carried it to a spare seat over by the wall beside where a man sat on a stool, reading the *Mirror*. A tray of food debris was shoved to one side. The man was about thirty-five, dressed in a jacket and open-neck shirt. On his feet he wore black boots, workman-like and well-maintained.

'Anyone sitting here?' Vinnie asked.

'Help yourself.'

Vinnie put the carrier bag down on the floor between the two stools and opened his Big Mac carton but the fries tempted him first and he began to eat clusters of them.

'It's all there,' he said eventually, looking at the wall.

'The money too?'

'In there.'

The man folded his paper and put it into the carrier bag. As he got off the stool he gave a nervous glance round the restaurant. Vinnie wanted to kick him because the look would have given them away if anyone had been watching. But he was certain no one was.

The man lifted the bag and made his way into the street. Vinnie took a bite out of his burger and looked at his watch. The fucker would have to hurry. He was on duty in an hour and he still had to go home and change into his prison officer's uniform.

There was a lot of money in that bag, not to mention the other stuff. He had better not leave it on the fucking bus.

He took a sip from his Coke and through the big window he watched the other's progress as he dashed across the road. At the central reservation, the fool almost tripped over a motorcycle messenger who was bending over the rear of his bike, fixing something.

Gallagher's Saturdays were getting to be full of surprises.

He shared the shock of this one with everyone else in the country but he felt something else as well: an undeniable sense of pride.

His daughter was now the Minister for Justice. At the age of thirty-three. No, damn it, she was still only thirty-two.

But what a way to get there. He kept the television on all morning. RTE had put together special news bulletins to report on the murder of Mr Justice Purcell and his driver and the resignation of Eamon Savage. There was a profile of Emma in which his own background got a mention in passing. There was footage of her by-election win and a reference to her close friendship with the businessman and philanthropist Fergal Mulryne. And there was a brief shot of her passing through the doors of Government buildings very early this morning.

He wondered how she would handle all of this, whether she was ready for it. He wanted to tell her how pleased he was for her but somehow he did not feel entitled to pick up the phone and call her.

Donovan's name was all over the air waves and the morning papers, with reporters scarcely bothering to conceal their belief that he was behind the murders.

By rights Gallagher should have felt anger at how Donovan had sought to manipulate him but he did not. Instead he saw Donovan's haunted face in the prison interview room. He was finding it hard to accept that the man he had met there had then planned and ordered these audacious killings.

Kate rang, which pleased him.

They had seen each other a few times since the Sunday she had called but he had a feeling that they were drifting, that their natural intimacy was slipping away. They had even made love once, here in his bed, but she had been compliant rather than encouraging and he had felt awkward and clumsy.

Afterwards he had wanted to ask her what was wrong but he had decided not to. He was afraid she might tell him.

'How do you feel?' she asked him now.

'Confused. Overwhelmed. It's great for Emma – a fantastic achievement – but what happened to that judge and the cop was appalling.'

'Have you spoken to her?'

'Spoken to her? Of course not. I'm the last person she'd want to hear from.'

'I wouldn't be so sure. Her own feelings are probably the same as yours. She's human, you know, vulnerable like the rest of us. Why don't you call her?'

'I'd never reach her.'

'Well, try, Tom. Call her at home. Leave a message on her machine.'

He did. He also called the Justice Department where one of the staff, who found themselves at their desks rather unexpectedly on a Saturday morning, told him she would inform the Minister that he had called.

'I can't guarantee that you'll hear from her,' she said. 'I'm sure you understand how it is.'

He understood very well. The task facing his daughter was enormous. Her promotion could be a poisoned chalice. She had a huge flood of public anxiety to stem and she did not have much time to do it.

He sat around all day nursing a dwindling hope that she might call.

She rang at six.

'Hello.' She sounded weary.

'Hell, is it?'

'You've no idea,' she said.

'I appreciate your calling. I didn't expect you to. But I couldn't let the day go by without – well – telling you I was thinking of you.'

'That's nice,' she said.

Kate had been right. He did not hear the usual resentment in her voice. But maybe she was too tired to hate him.

'I got a message that you called before. What was—'

'Oh, it was nothing,' he said. 'I just wanted to talk to you, was all.'

This was not the time to tell her about Donovan. But when – when would he do so?

'Where are you?' he wanted to know. 'Still at the office?'

'I'm afraid so. Another meeting at seven, would you believe.' She paused. 'Listen, em – look, I was thinking.' She seemed to be making her mind up about something. 'Have you plans for this evening?'

'No, nothing.'

'Then, well, maybe – maybe we could have a drink or something. A bit later.'

His heart was beating harder. 'I'd like that. I'd like that very much,' he said.

'You've never been to my house.' She said it as an observation, as if she had just realised.

'No, I haven't.'

'Well, maybe you'd like to go out there and wait for me. I don't know how late I'm going to be but if you didn't mind hanging around, I could send a car for you and it could take you home again.'

'That would be fine – if you're sure.'

'There'll be someone there to let you in. You'll be expected. And you'll see the booze. In front of your nose. So start without me if you feel like it.'

The car and driver were at his door at seven thirty to take him south towards the outskirts of Bray. Emma's tiny house was white-washed and ancient and it sat in quiet privacy beneath a community of chestnut trees. It had once been the gate lodge to an Anglo-Irish mansion which was now an expensive sanitorium where the rich and famous came to dry out.

An anonymous dark van was parked outside when they arrived and a couple of police technicians with overalls and tool boxes and coils of wiring wandered in and out.

'You'll be Mr Gallagher,' one of them said. 'We got a message from the Minister's office.'

'Yes,' Gallagher said. He looked at what they were doing. 'New security?'

'That's right.'

'I guess it comes with the badge.'

'Something like that. We're putting in extra cameras. The burglar alarm's already linked to the local *Garda* station and we're giving her a panic button. Although it didn't do the poor old judge much good, did it?'

It dawned on him what he had said. 'Christ, I'm sorry. I didn't mean—'

'Don't worry about it,' Gallagher said. He wondered how long Emma could remain here in this house. Its remoteness and seclusion would be a continued security problem.

When the men had gone, his driver, too, he listened to the silence descend. In the shelter of the trees, the house was quite dark so he put a couple of table lamps on to light the room. There would have been two rooms once but someone, Emma perhaps, had converted the space into one single open area, the whole width of the house, that served as dining-room and sitting-room combined. It was all there as soon as you opened the front door.

The furniture was a mixture of traditional styles and he wondered if Emma's mother had donated some of it to her before she went off to South Africa. High-backed chairs sat round a dining-table that took eight and a pair of deeply inviting settees sat on either side of the fireplace. A couple of newspapers had been discarded on the floor.

He looked around. She had some nice things. There were paintings, a few interesting pottery pieces, and at one end of the room a tall cabinet full of hand-blown glass in rich colours.

There were photographs, too. Emma in school uniform. Emma and her mother at her graduation. Emma and her mother dining somewhere, toasting each other by candlelight. Emma and Fergal Mulryne in sweaters, strolling on a west of Ireland beach.

There were no pictures of him. It was as if he did not exist. It made him feel like an intruder, creeping about in her private world. But then – she had invited him here. Maybe there was a chance that things could change.

He found the drink arranged on a trolley under a painting of a Venetian canal and when he had helped himself to a decent Scotch he sat down on a settee. It was a comfortable home, he thought, pleasantly cluttered, not untidy, but it gave the impression that the person who lived here did not spend much time in it. It told him nothing about Emma at all; there was nothing that he could take away and add to his own sketchy picture of her.

He picked the *Irish Times* up off the floor and was amazed to find no mention of the Purcell murders on the front page. Instead, the main story concerned the impending decision on the privatisation of the airports, currently run by the semi-State agency Aer Rianta whose management team had put together one of two competing bids.

Gallagher frowned, then looked at the date. It was a week old. A lot had happened since then. He set his glass down and turned the television on.

He awoke, shivering, to find that the late football was on and Emma was standing looking at him with her hands on her hips.

He sat upright.

'I must have dropped off.'

'Hours ago, by the look of you.'

He stood up. She was tall; she got that from him but she had her mother's looks. It was in her eyes and the softness of her skin. They stared at each other, neither of them knowing quite what to do. He wanted to embrace her, convey some sort of affection, but there was a barrier between them.

'How's your glass?' she asked.

'Fine.'

She went to the drinks trolley and poured a Scotch for herself.

He surveyed the room once more, for her benefit. 'This is very nice,' he said.

'Thanks. I don't get to see a whole lot of it. Even less in the future, probably.'

'Well, I feel very – privileged – that you asked me to come here.'

He looked towards one of the pictures of Emma and her mother. She saw where his glance was directed and waited.

'Do you hear much from your mother?' he asked her.

'She rang this morning, as a matter of fact. The story was on CNN, apparently.'

'Any developments?' he asked. 'As you see, I kind of missed the evening news.'

'Well, no one else got killed today so I suppose that's always something.'

'This is a very tough job for you. What are you going to do?'

'Well, I might get someone to take a wander into Mountjoy and dispose of Sean Donovan. That would ease the problem for a start.'

Donovan. He just could not tell her. No way. He gulped the remains of his drink.

She took his glass from him and misread the look on his face.

'Oh, for goodness sake,' she said. 'I'm only joking. Don't panic.'

She gave him a fresh drink and they sat, on opposite settees. 'But, all kidding aside, I'm going to have to do something to fend off the calls for God-knows-what – tanks on the streets, maybe. That's what they'll be at in the *Dail* next week, not to mention the papers tomorrow.'

She froze with her glass to her lips and looked at him over the rim. 'You're not writing anything by any chance, are you?'

'No – not at all.'

'Glad to hear it.'

'When did you learn what had happened?'

She told him about the *Taoiseach*'s call to Strasbourg, the flight back, the dawn meeting and the whirlwind which had swept her along all day. She told him she had had a lengthy meeting with the *Garda* Commissioner and his most senior operational officers.

Gallagher wondered anxiously if Barrett Greeley had been among them.

'And then, in the midst of all this, I had to have a session with Tony Goulding about other Government matters which I'll now be involved with.'

Her eyes clouded over. 'The reality is we'll never get these people, not unless they're planning to hit someone else and we get wind of it. The Guards have no idea – oh, we all know it's Donovan all right – but they've no idea who this team is. They're good – quick and efficient. They hit the judge and his man the same way they hit Kelly. The guns have no history and there's zilch coming from the streets. Zee-roh. No one's ever seen anything like it.'

'What about the Minister – I mean, your predecessor – Savage? Have you spoken with him? There's a lot he's going to have to live with.'

She shook her head. 'He called it wrong. It's that simple.'

'My problem is – I see everybody's point of view these days. I understand how tough it can be.'

'Well, I'm afraid I can't afford that luxury.'

They wrapped themselves in an awkward silence for a moment.

He sat forward. 'Emma, there's so much I want to say to you. You have a lot of anguish, a lot of bitterness—'

She stiffened slightly. 'Look – do you think we really want to open this up now?'

'Perhaps not, but it's just that since I've been back I

haven't had the chance to talk properly to you. I just want you to know how much I regret not being a proper father to you. If I could re-write history, I would. If I—'

'Would you? Would you really?' She looked at him in doubt. 'If you had the chance again, would you really stay here in Dublin with my mother and me instead of going to Harvard?'

He shifted uncomfortably. 'It's not that simple. It's a question—'

'It seems simple enough to me.'

'Emma, your mother and me – it would never have worked. Surely she must have told you that over the years?'

'She had a lot of things to do over the years. A lot of responsibilities. Making excuses for your absence wasn't one of them.' She sighed then sat back into the softness of the settee. 'I'm too tired for this.'

'You're right. Maybe not the time or the place. I should go.'

She did not argue with him.

She had kept her car and a driver waiting outside to take him home when he was ready. An unmarked police car was also parked where its occupants could observe the house. Security was tighter now.

She opened the door and as she did he leaned over and kissed her quickly on the cheek. She looked startled but she said nothing.

'Look after yourself,' he said.

It was after midnight by the time he got home and when he let himself into the apartment he could see the red light on his answering machine blinking in the dark. He rewound the tape, took his jacket off and threw it on a chair.

When he heard the voice, he swung round and stared at the thing as if it were alive.

It was Donovan.

He could not make out everything the man was saying. He must have been using a mobile phone because it kept cutting out in mid-sentence but there was enough for Gallagher to hear the sounds of deep distress.

'You've got to help me,' Donovan said.

Was he crying? Drunk?

'This isn't me,' the voice on the tape said, confusing Gallagher for a moment. 'None of this is me. But I know what they're doing.'

It broke up again and Gallagher strained to hear.

'. . . Wasn't . . . judge . . .'

The voice came back more clearly. 'First you create the problem – then you solve it. Or you make it look that way. That's what I think this is.'

Donovan laughed, a disjointed, unsettling cackle. There were some more words but Gallagher could not make them out and finally there was nothing.

He played the tape again, then once more and this time he wrote Donovan's words on his notepad, finding a clean sheet and tearing off the page where he had jotted Matt Clancy's number down.

First you create the problem – then you solve it.

Chapter Twenty-One

He woke at eight thirty with the phone ringing and a head muggy with sleep.

He had lain awake until after five, due to a combination of his usual insomnia and his thoughts about Donovan's bizarre message.

He picked up the phone.

'Why didn't you tell me?' Emma said quietly.

He swung himself out from under the quilt and sat on the edge of the bed.

'Tell you what?'

'That you went to Mountjoy to visit Sean Donovan.'

He looked at his bare feet on the carpet and felt the blood draining down towards them.

No avoiding it now – when it was too late.

'I planned to. But I couldn't, not last night.' He lifted his head abruptly. 'Wait – how did you know?'

She was silent briefly. 'You haven't heard?'

'Heard what? I was fast asleep until the phone rang.'

'Donovan's dead.'

Shock tingled on his skin.

'Dead? How do you mean – he's dead? He rang me last night.'

'He did what?'

'He rang me. There was a message on my answering machine when I got back.'

'Jesus Christ!'

'So how—'

'He was found dead in his cell at six o'clock this morning. Overdose of heroin, by the look of things. The syringe was beside him. The police and the prison authorities want to know how he might have got it so they've been checking his list of recent visitors. Not many – just the two. You and Clancy, his solicitor. The Commissioner thought I should know.'

'Emma, I—'

'So,' she persisted, her voice steely calm and all the more unnerving, 'someone will want to talk to you about it. They'll want to talk about this call of Donovan's now, too. What did he want?'

'Just rubbish. I couldn't make a lot of it out. He was using a mobile and it kept breaking up.'

'Do you have the tape?'

'Yes.'

'Then I suggest you let the police have it. Let them decide whether it's rubbish or not. Don't you think?'

'Yes, you're right. Of course.'

'I'd like you to get into your car and take the tape and yourself down to Harcourt Square. Think you could do that? I understand you already know where it is.'

Acrobats in the pit of his stomach. 'Greeley?' he asked.

'Greeley,' she confirmed. 'I gather you've met him already.'

'Yes.'

'So the police knew you'd been to see Donovan but I didn't?'

'When you were in Strasbourg, I tried to call—'

'I asked you about that. You told me it was nothing.'

'It was just – the circumstances of last night. Being in your home. I couldn't. Emma, I'm so—'

'No!' She stopped him. 'Don't tell me you're sorry. I don't want to know that you're sorry. Just – just do what you're told and get down to Harcourt Square.'

'Okay.' He felt about six years old.

'Christ, look at the time. I've got a meeting with the *Taoiseach*. Won't that be nice for me?'

She rang off.

He sat with his head in his hands and misery creeping towards him from every corner.

Greeley treated him like a criminal, performing in front of two of his subordinates who stood to one side and watched with fascination, spectators at a blood sport.

'When you visited Donovan,' he asked, 'did you bring anything in with you? A briefcase, anything like that?'

'What are you suggesting?'

'Just answer the question, if you wouldn't mind.'

'No. Nothing.' He felt a nervous itch below his collar.

'And what about Clancy?'

'He had a briefcase but he didn't open it. At least I don't recall that he did.'

'Now think about that. You're sure? He didn't pass anything to Donovan?'

'No. A warder was watching, too. It wouldn't have been possible.'

Greeley lit a cigarette and inhaled sharply. It took an eternity for the smoke to re-emerge. His eyes studied Gallagher almost lasciviously, savouring his embarrassment and discomfort.

'So let's hear this tape then,' he said at last.

Gallagher had brought his answering machine with him. It was compact and not difficult to transport. One of the officers turned it on and they listened.

'Well, what do you think?' Greeley asked his men when it had finished.

'Hard to say, sir,' one ventured. 'He sounds a bit wired.'

'Wired. Yes, that's a good word,' Greeley said. 'What time was the call made?' he asked Gallagher.

'The machine clocked it at eleven ten. What time does the medical examiner reckon Donovan died?'

Greeley's laugh was scornful. 'Oh, well, I think that kind of information is a matter for us. Don't you think so, lads?'

The detectives smiled uncomfortably and shuffled their feet.

Gallagher had another question. 'Was Donovan a user?'

Greeley laughed again, this time at the persistence.

'Jesus, you haven't got the hang of this exactly, have you, Mr Gallagher? You see, the idea is that I ask you the questions, not the other way round. I'm sure even the FBI do it like that. But maybe you've forgotten.'

He drew on his cigarette and relented for a second. 'What the hell – I suppose there's no harm in telling you this much. The bastard's dead anyway. Yes, he did a lot of heroin once upon a time.'

'Any recent evidence of use?'

'Ah now, I think you've asked enough. We don't want you trying to take over our investigation. Giving you a taste of the old days, is it, all this? Remembering what it was like to be in the big time, eh?'

Gallagher reddened. Thus far but no further.

'Look, Chief Superintendent, do you have a problem here? Why don't you clear your throat and spit it out? Okay, so I went to see this guy in prison. Not a crime. Unwise, maybe, but I was curious about why he wanted to meet me, as you might have been yourself. Anyway, as you'll recall, we've discussed this already, right? Then last night I get home and there's a message on my answering machine. So here I am again, with the tape, trying to be of help.'

His unexpected forcefulness silenced them.

He opened his arms in an accommodating gesture. 'What I'm trying to do is have a conversation here – one professional to another – and you can let me in on this if you want. If you don't, fine, that's okay, too. But I don't have to sit here and take a lot of sarcastic crap from you just because you've got a hair up your ass for some reason.'

He stood and looked towards Greeley's men. It was a safe bet they had never heard anyone speak to their boss like that before. He saw it on their faces.

'Now, if there's nothing else, I'll be on my way.' He walked to the door.

'Just one more thing,' Greeley said as he opened it. 'If

you're planning to leave Dublin in the next day or so, perhaps you'd let us know before you do. I'm sure we'll want to talk to you again. It's always such a pleasure.'

You asshole, Gallagher thought. He turned to say something then changed his mind.

Chapter Twenty-Two

L ong before two thirty on Monday afternoon, the
visitors' gallery overlooking the Dublin Parliament
chamber was packed.

Gallagher was lucky to get a seat. There were only one
or two left, over in a corner, which was not the best of
positions, and he could just about see the front benches
where Emma would stand to make a statement. He did not
mind being in the midst of a crowd of other onlookers; it
meant that if she were to glance up in his direction, then
she might not notice him.

He had never been inside the *Dail* before and it
reminded him oddly of a Baptist tabernacle he had once
visited out in the mid-west, a case involving the kidnapping
of the Pastor's daughter. They found eventually that the
Pastor had done it himself, faked an abduction. He had
raped and strangled the girl and buried her body in the
basement of the church.

Nice man, Gallagher thought wryly. No longer with us.

The chamber was carpeted in a deep blue with rows of
brown leather seats curving in a horseshoe and tiered
sharply. Only a few of them were still vacant, apart from

234

the Government front bench which would not be occupied until the last moment when the *Taoiseach* and his team entered. He could not see the Opposition, who sat right underneath his vantage point, but he could hear the rumble of voices as they prepared for battle.

At the head of the chamber was a tall desk like a pulpit where the Speaker of the assembly, the *Ceann Comhairle*, sat to preside, the green, white and gold flag of Ireland hanging limply on a pole to his left. High behind him was the Press bench with reporters arranged in a long line like judges in an Italian court. There were nods and winks to cronies below.

Gallagher could feel the sense of expectation in the air. In spite of what had happened between him and Emma, he had not been able to keep away. He could not bear being absent on such an important day in her life. He had missed too many of them in the past.

The gruff voices in the chamber below him grew noisier and he saw that the Prime Minister and his front bench were slipping into their seats. Emma was to O'Neill's left and a man he recognised as Tony Goulding, the Deputy Prime Minister, was on his right.

His daughter wore a blue suit which matched her surroundings and in her lapel she had a large silver brooch with a Celtic design. Her face looked pale and determined. She placed three buff-coloured files at her left hand and she checked that their contents were in order.

A lot had happened to her today already, Gallagher knew; he had been following every news bulletin. The House had met briefly this morning to ratify her appointment and then, with motorcycle out-riders leading the way, she had been swept out to the Phoenix Park, to the residence of the President, where she was presented with the seal of office.

Now here she was, about to speak in public for the first time about the events which had led to her elevation.

'Do you mind if I squeeze in beside you?'

Gallagher looked up to see a man smiling at him. He had dark curly hair going grey and skin that was lightly tanned. His face looked familiar. Gallagher moved out into the aisle to let him in and got the connection as soon as he sat down again.

'You're Fergal Mulryne, aren't you?' he said.

'Yes, that's right,' the man acknowledged.

Gallagher held out his hand to him. 'We've never met. The name's Tom Gallagher. I'm Emma's father.'

Mulryne eyes widened. 'Really? Oh, my goodness.' He shook the hand. 'I'm delighted to meet you.'

Mulryne was dressed in a quietly impressive green-grey suit of a delicate weave. Next to him, Gallagher felt scruffy in a beige linen jacket that was just a little too rumpled. They talked for a bit while there was some preliminary business on the floor and then they heard the voice of the Speaker.

'The Minister for Justice,' he called, then sniffed and blew his nose.

Emma rose slowly, her head up, scanning the benches opposite so that they could see her composure and her confidence. Only then did she begin to speak.

First she went through the events of Friday night and what was known about the murders. She offered her condolences to the Purcell family and to the family of the protection officer. She made no attempt to minimise the situation, but spoke of it as an extremely grave matter.

'It is an insult to the entire country,' she said, 'a blow against democracy and against freedom itself.'

There were hear-hears from her own benches but silence from the opposite side of the chamber. She had chosen words with which no one would disagree. She linked the Judge's murder, as the Press had done, to the killing of the television journalist, Marcus Kelly. The method of assassination had been exactly the same.

'I can assure this House that the *Gardai* are exploring every possible avenue and using every possible resource in the pursuit of the persons responsible. However, it is only fair to point out to the House what an enormous task this is. These were professional killings which we believe may have been carried out by persons from outside the State, hired and brought here for this specific purpose, and the assassins may already have left the country. In that event, it will be extremely difficult for the police to establish their identity and to bring them to justice.'

'So you're giving up before you start?' a voice cried from the Opposition side.

'Order!' the Speaker insisted.

'It would be wrong of me to mislead this House,' Emma went on, 'or to raise false hopes that arrests might be imminent in this case. But I have every faith in the skill and professionalism of the *Gardai* and I can assure them of the full support of my department as they go about their investigation.'

She opened one of the files and slipped a sheet from it. 'I would like now to turn to the issue of the man Sean

Donovan who was found dead in Mountjoy prison early yesterday morning. Mr Donovan, who was on remand on charges of possessing drugs and a firearm, died from an overdose of an unusually high grade of heroin which would have been instantly fatal once injected.

'The police are investigating this incident in an attempt to determine the nature of Mr Donovan's death but today I am also announcing an inquiry which will be carried out by a team from my department and from the office of the *Garda* Commissioner and which will bring recommendations to me with a view to introducing new measures to eliminate the availability of illicit drugs in prisons. I am convinced that whatever the circumstances of this case, it is vital that we put measures in place which will have more than a short-term effect.'

She gave a long look around the chamber. 'I am sure the House is well aware of the extensive speculation in the Press linking the late Sean Donovan with these murders. Let me state to the House that there is no hard evidence to provide such a connection and with Mr Donovan dead it will be extremely difficult to establish one unless the actual killers are found. But let me also say that in the light of his death, the police do not anticipate any further occurrences such as the appalling acts of murder we have seen.'

She shut the file, a symbolic gesture indicating that if the case was not exactly closed officially, it was, in effect. She picked up another folder and addressed herself to the Speaker, as was the custom of the House. The Prime Minister listened with his arms folded, staring at his knees, but Goulding had turned his head and was watching her performance with approval.

'*Ceann Comhairle*, I have spoken here before with some pride about this Government's achievements and its record on crime.'

There were disgruntled noises from across the way.

'I would like to say to this House today that, while much has been accomplished, there is much more that needs to be done. In particular, in the short time available to me I have identified the clear need for a radical review of development funding for the *Garda Siochana*. To that end, I have this morning made recommendations to the *Taoiseach* and the Cabinet and I am pleased to say that they have been approved. I have established a number of priorities, measures which will have lasting benefit and are not a panic attack brought on by the awful matters which I have raised this afternoon.'

She lifted a sheet from the new file. 'The first step is to review training and recruitment into the police force to ensure that we get only the best and the brightest and that they receive the most up-to-date training in order to cope with modern-day crime. The second is to speed up existing plans to replace the current, rather antiquated, *Garda* computer system and replace it with a new, state-of-the-art communications network where vital information will be readily and instantly accessible throughout the country. The first stage of this will be on line before the end of the year. The third is the gradual improvement of the quality and type of vehicles which are currently used by the police force.'

She looked up. 'And finally, I have agreed with the Commissioner that there should be additional manpower in those areas of police operations where it is most needed, in particular Serious Crimes and Drugs.'

She turned to the Speaker again. '*Ceann Comhairle*, over the next few months, the Commissioner has agreed to conduct a review of the entire policing strategy in urban areas. Although the record on detection and conviction is good, there is simply too much crime, a lot of it petty crime, and we must find ways of preventing its spread.'

She put the folder down and stood with her hands by her sides. 'On a personal note, if I might add, I find myself appointed to one of the most crucial offices in Government in the most extraordinary and most dreadful circumstances. I intend to carry out the functions of this office with vigilance and vigour and both those elements are present in the measures which I have outlined today.'

She looked round at the benches behind her and then allowed her gaze to sweep over the entire chamber. 'The people of this country need to feel that law and order, their security, is in safe hands, that it is a number one priority for their Government. Let me assure the country today that that is very firmly the case.'

She sat to the sound of praise from her own side. O'Neill leaned sideways and muttered his congratulations. Someone in the bench behind bent forward and patted her on the shoulder. Emma shuffled her folders into a neat pile and waited.

Gallagher realised he had been practically holding his breath throughout. He exhaled with relief.

Mulryne looked at him and raised his eyebrows. 'Well, what about that, eh?'

'Indeed,' Gallagher said. Emma had been busy. She had put together an extensive package and he wondered how the Government was going to pay for it. Other departments would be losing something along the way, that was for sure, but nobody had asked that yet.

This had been a speech that was as much about Emma as about anything she planned to do. There had been no mention at all of Eamon Savage, no tribute to the work that had gone before. *Le roi est mort.* She had told the country that she was here now and that she planned to stay.

'Deputy Caffrey,' the Speaker intoned. There was a tickle in his throat and he took a sip of water from a glass in front of him.

The Opposition spokesman rose to take his turn and launched into a spirited attack on the Government, the Justice Department and the police for failing to take adequate measures to prevent the murder of Mr Justice Purcell, in spite of the warnings which he, personally, had given that more needed to be done.

'The truth is,' he said, 'that we are all at the mercy of criminals and their gangs now and there is nothing that the police can do about it. Even protection officers are being killed. The Minister has confessed her impotence to this House but she has tried to obscure the fact with a shopping list cobbled together in haste as if she were trying to get to the supermarket before it closed.'

There were 'tut-tuts' and mutterings of 'shame' from the Government side. Emma gave a little smile; his sexist, patronising attitude would not endear him to anyone.

Caffrey gestured to the House with an open palm. 'Naturally, I welcome measures which will improve the quality of our police service. But we have not heard today exactly where the money is coming from. No doubt that will be revealed when we hear where the cuts have been made in other departments.'

He narrowed his eyes and stared across the chamber. 'I see the Minister for Education looking a bit glum. What has he lost, I wonder?'

There were subdued chuckles behind him.

'But there is a question which I would like to put to the Minister for Justice, something which has been brought to my attention and which requires an answer.'

He paused to let the tension build. 'Is it true that the Minister's father visited Sean Donovan in Mountjoy prison last week and could she explain to the House what the purpose of his visit was? What exactly was the relationship between Donovan and Mr Gallagher?'

There were gasps. Reporters looked at each other, baffled. On the Government back benches, members were shifting uncomfortably. Gallagher wanted to disappear. Out of the corner of his eye, he could sense Fergal Mulryne looking at him.

Caffrey sat down and the Speaker turned towards Emma. 'Minister, do you wish to respond?'

'Thank you, yes.' She stood and Gallagher saw that in her hand she had the third of her folders. 'It is true that my father visited Sean Donovan at Mountjoy last week. The meeting came about as a result of contacts with Mr Donovan's solicitor and as I understand it my father saw him because there might have been some journalistic benefit. As it turned out, that wasn't the case and the visit was a very short one.'

Caffrey sprang to his feet. 'Is it true that the Minister's

father has been interviewed by the police in connection with their investigation into how Mr Donovan may have had access to drugs?'

All around, voices were getting louder.

'Order!' the Speaker called. The tickle in his throat turned to a cough.

'My father informed the police of his visit as soon as it had taken place – that was before Mr Donovan's death. And, yes, he has spoken to them again since then.'

'And is it also true that Donovan actually telephoned the Minister's father at his home just hours before he died?'

Caffrey's voice was rising but Emma's remained steady. Someone had been talking out of school, Gallagher thought, and he wondered if Chief Superintendent Greeley was the big fan of Emma Gallagher that he had made himself out to be.

'Yes,' Emma said, 'that is true. My father received a message on his answering machine late on Saturday night. He has also informed the police of that fact and passed the tape of the call to them.'

She sat down. Caffrey spread his arms to the House. 'Here we have a serious matter, a very serious matter indeed. How are the people of this island expected to place their faith in a Minister whose own father has obscure and dubious connections with one of the most vicious criminals this country has ever seen?'

He pointed his finger angrily across the room at the Prime Minister whose head was bowed as if in prayer. 'If she has any sense of decency at all, the Minister should resign immediately and the *Taoiseach* should go to the President and ask for a dissolution of Parliament so that there can be a General Election in which the people can express their feelings about the mess these people have got us into.'

He sat to cheers and the stamping of feet.

The Speaker called for order, his face getting redder. He picked up the hand bell which sat in front of him on the desk and rang it with force. Emma caught his eye; there was something else she wanted to say.

'The Minister for Justice,' he announced.

There were jeers and whistles from across the room as she got up once more. She raised her voice.

'I think the country can see very clearly from this performance what the real tendencies of the members opposite are but let me add to their knowledge.'

She opened the third file just enough so that those with a sight of it could glimpse what was inside. There were photographs, maybe three or four, yet it was impossible to make out any detail in them.

'As I'm sure everyone is aware, the late Marcus Kelly had devoted a lot of time to investigating the affairs of Sean Donovan. What his investigations revealed was shown on prime-time television. I think it will interest members of this House to know that at the time of his death, Mr Kelly was researching another programme about Mr Donovan, focusing on prominent figures who were clients of some of Mr Donovan's more upmarket call girls.'

The voices around the room grew louder and more excited and the Speaker swung his bell angrily.

'Or-der!' His voice cracked on the word.

Tantalisingly, Emma eased the photographs out of the folder a little more. Some of the reporters were leaning dangerously over the edge of their dais, straining for a better look. Behind Emma, heads were bobbing and weaving as Deputies tried to do the same but on the Opposition side, they could merely sit and wait out the discomfort.

Emma continued, the whole debating chamber hanging on her every word. 'I have learned that as part of his research, Mr Kelly observed certain people leaving a house near Leeson Street.'

The Speaker did not like this and thought he should stop it.

'I must insist that the Minister confine herself—' He coughed violently.

Emma needed to be quick. 'And on three separate occasions he observed a prominent member of the Opposition front bench. I make no further comment other than to suggest that if anything's a connection with Sean Donovan, then that is. Perhaps the Opposition should put its own house in order before having the gall to level half-baked accusations and innuendo in this direction.'

She sat down amid pandemonium, slid the photographs back into the file quickly and put it with the others. Members were on their feet, shouting and waving hysterically across the floor. Some of the reporters dashed to the phones; others could not decide whether to follow them or not, afraid that they would miss something if they did.

The Speaker rang his bell. His voice had gone. He pointed angrily at Emma for having carried on when he had ordered her to stop. O'Neill and Goulding did not speak to her but their smiles said it all.

Not actually naming anyone had been a clever move, Gallagher thought. It meant that the newspapers would speculate wildly, while getting themselves in knots trying not to libel anyone in the process. And then they would follow the Opposition's big names around, waiting for them to stray off the beaten track.

One thing was certain: there would be a lot of detours. No one who might remotely fit the bill would want to be seen within miles of Leeson Street.

It also meant that his own misdemeanour, if that was what it was, would be overshadowed completely. He looked towards Emma. She knew how to play dirty and he wondered how she had managed to get her hands on this information.

Then again – maybe there was no information at all. What if it was just a smokescreen designed to cause panic? When he thought about it, she had not actually mentioned photographs, had she? Everyone would assume that was what she meant because she had photographs in the file in her hand.

He watched her sitting there calmly, a stillness in the eye of the storm, and he wondered if she was not clever but cunning.

'Well,' Mulryne said, 'what did you think of that?'

'I don't know,' he answered. In Mulryne's voice there was a note of pride and triumph and he found that he was not able to share it.

Chapter Twenty-Three

D ublin Airport was used to invasions. St Patrick's Day, rugby matches, Eurovision Song Contests, it really made no difference. The hordes streamed in from across the globe and then on to their various destinations. It was when they were leaving again, all at the same time, often in the midst of a peak period for Irish holiday travellers, that things got difficult. Conga lines of bodies and baggage weaved through the departures concourse, tempers and patience running on empty. And when flights were delayed, it did not bear thinking about.

The WONTEC convention was over and the airport had already had a couple of overloaded days but one or two visitors had been wise enough to leave it until the initial rush had cleared.

Among these stragglers were three men. They arrived at the airport individually for flights which were separated by several hours. Like everyone else who had been to WON-TEC, they were laden with souvenirs. For most of those who had taken part, these would be fond memories for a time before being stuck in a box as recollection faded and put in the attic to gather dust. But the mementoes which these men carried would go into the nearest trash can once their bearers reached the end of their journey.

Their tickets indicated that they were returning from whence they came. One was going to Paris, one to London and one to Boston but there would be onward destinations after that and new identities to take them there.

They were leaving two of their number behind, the men named Parrish and Humble. The final phase of the operation, the one which had so outraged Heywood Corbett in New York two years ago, would be handled by them.

And then they had a job to do for Gilbert Leslie.

The morning after the *Dail* sensation, which was what the papers were calling it, Gallagher rang Alan Warnock at his office.

'Remember you said you owed me a favour?'

'Yes?' Warnock conceded, a little hesitantly.

'Well, here's your chance. And don't panic – it won't land you in any trouble. And it won't cost you any money, either.'

'In that case, fire away.'

'I'm interested in finding out a bit more about Marcus Kelly.'

'Oh, really?' Warnock's attention was aroused. 'Now, why would that be?'

'Oh, just something that's been at the back of my mind. I'd like to know how he operated, what his background was. Think you could manage that?'

'Just something that's at the back of your mind, eh? Nothing to do with your conversation with Mr Donovan, I suppose?'

'No,' Gallagher said casually. 'Curiosity, that's all.'

'Of course,' Warnock said, not believing him for a second. 'Well now, I could probably give you most of it off the top of my head because everybody ran profiles of him when he got killed. But yeah, I could get you that.'

He lowered his voice until he was almost whispering. 'Come on, Tom, what's all this about? Anything to do with yesterday – the pictures? Who's in them? Everybody wants to know.'

'Look, that's nothing to do with me. Why don't we talk about this later? Can we meet this afternoon?'

They arranged to see each other at five in Mulligan's, the big rough-and-ready pub that was a favourite haunt for newspaper people. Gallagher got there first and sat at a table, sipping a cool pint and thinking about Sean Donovan.

He would take some convincing that the man's death had been self-administered.

Whether external forces were responsible or simply other prisoners with some kind of a grudge was another matter. If he had killed himself, then what was the likely scenario: that he was a rampant psychopath who had ordered the murder of Marcus Kelly and a judge before finally cracking up completely and committing suicide? Possible – but not probable.

And then there was the easiest explanation of all – that Donovan had simply overdosed on his own stuff and that his death was an accident. It was a common enough occurrence among drug-users but to Gallagher it felt wrong.

Whatever the cause and whatever conclusion the police

finally came to, there were going to be no tears for Donovan. It was good riddance and no would care how it had come about. The country's number one bad guy was dead and people could breathe more easily. That was the signal Emma had given: the case was closed and there was no further reason for alarm.

But Donovan's strange references continued to echo in Gallagher's head and now there was something else, put there by Emma herself when she spoke in the *Dail*.

Marcus Kelly.

Find out who's to gain, Donovan had said.

What was all that about?

First you create the problem and then you solve it.

Was it not Marcus Kelly who had created the problem, or at least had first drawn attention to it? Donovan had wondered about Kelly, hadn't he, where he got his information, how he came to embark on this crusade?

He put the brakes on his train of thought. What was he doing? Accepting everything that Donovan had told him?

Warnock breezed in and greeted several people on the way to Gallagher's table where a pint sat waiting for him. He took a long pull on it before he spoke.

'So, come on, then. Out with it. Who's in these pictures?'

'I'm the last person you should ask.'

Warnock saw the rueful look. 'Don't tell me, let me guess. Your visit to Mr Donovan didn't go down too well?'

Gallagher shook his head.

'Aha,' Warnock said. 'At least you can't blame me for that one.'

He pulled a spiral-bound reporter's notebook from his

jacket pocket. 'So tell me why you want all this stuff on Kelly?'

'To be honest, Alan, I don't really know.'

Warnock studied him and decided he was being truthful. 'Fair enough. But if it leads to anything I might be interested in, maybe you'll tell me.'

He opened the notebook. 'Right now.' He took another slow draught from his pint. 'Lovely. Marcus Kelly, then. Like I said to you on the phone, a lot of it's been written about already but the interesting thing is that when you start to talk to people – casually, you know – you begin to get a slightly different picture.'

He laughed. 'I remember once, a paper I worked on before this, out in the Midlands, the farming editor died. He was a sort of a legend in local journalism and the editor asked me to get tributes to him. You know – humorous anecdotes from members of staff, people in the community, because he was such a *much-loved personality* – in quotes.

'Jesus, it was a nightmare. Everybody I asked had a tale of horror about how mean he was. He went out somewhere with a photographer once, some story or other. He took the photographer in his car and then charged him for the petrol he'd used. Incredible. I had to make half of it up in the end although the truth about the stingy old bastard would have been much more interesting.'

'And what's the truth about Kelly?'

'The thing about Kelly is that no one ever seemed to like him – not that that's necessarily unique in this business, but people do seem to have found him to be a rather creepy individual.'

He looked at his notes. 'Let's see – he had this production company, still on the go, presumably, called Marcuscreen. You'll find it in the companies registry office. Nothing strange about it. I looked it up for you to save time.'

'I'm obliged, Alan. Looks like you've gone to a bit of trouble.'

'Oh, think of this as an investment. Anyhow, Marcuscreen has just three directors. There's Kelly himself, his wife, Frances, and someone by the name of George Levy. Mean anything to you?'

Gallagher shook his head.

'Me neither. They've been doing a profitable line in corporate video and so on, some one-off independent documentary programmes here and for the BBC up in the north, but the big showpiece, of course, has been Kelly's own series for RTE, the *Kelly Report*.'

'*Inquiry*,' Gallagher said. 'I think it's called *The Kelly Inquiry*.'

'Whatever. Who's doing this, you or me?'

'Sorry. Go on.'

'Some time ago, the Government put a big squeeze on RTE, saying they should increase the quota of programmes by independent producers – you know, not their own staff people – all part of a drive to widen the base of the television industry. The finger was being pointed at factual programmes and news and current affairs so RTE invited offers.

'That was when Kelly came along with the idea for his – *Inquiry*.' He elongated the word and gave Gallagher a look. 'And it would seem that one of the reasons RTE signed him up was because what he was offering was remarkably cheap, much more economical than anything anyone else was suggesting, and apart from that, editorially, it was the kind of thing they wanted.'

He sipped his drink. 'Now, from everything I've heard, Kelly was known to be extremely fond of money so it seems a bit strange to learn that he was doing a series for peanuts. Maybe he had plans to up the ante – I don't know. A bit late now. At any rate, the series started off cheap and cheerful – or maybe not so cheerful, come to think of it – discussion programmes about abortion, alcoholism, all the usual worthy, boring stuff, but then he gets his teeth into Donovan, up jump the ratings and away we go. Best thing on television in this country. No doubt about it.'

'What about this fondness for money?'

'Indeed. I'll come to that. Kelly came from Carlow originally, went to UCD, worked in print journalism here for a while, then worked for RTE as a staff reporter oh—' he waved vaguely in the air '—years ago, don't know when exactly, but nobody liked him then. He knew how to rub people up the wrong way and people felt there was something, you know, *flaky* about him – I suppose you could say.

'Then he got a job with some obscure satellite channel on the continent, working a news beat on the financial markets, moving between Italy and Switzerland, and rumour has it that he had some funny friends over there.'

'What sort of funny friends?'

Warnock looked at him as if it was unnecessary to explain, especially to him.

'You know – *funny*. The sort of people you used to come

across all the time. There are rumours that he might have done a few people a few favours, running little errands, carrying little packages across various borders under the convenient cover of his television work.'

'What are you saying – drugs?'

'Drugs, maybe. Not buckets of snow anyhow.'

'Well, well,' Gallagher said with a smile.

'I know,' Warnock agreed, sitting back in his seat with the same thought. 'Hypocrisy's a wonderful thing.'

He returned to his notes. 'But then so are rumours, wouldn't you say, and that's what most of this is, don't forget. Anyway, that was our friend Kelly until a couple of years ago when he came back and started Marcuscreen. And here he is, home to Dublin, in all the right restaurants, flash car, nice clothes, great apartment. Money from somewhere. So maybe the corporate video business pays a lot better than I thought it did. Are you having anything?'

They had finished their drinks.

'Why not.'

'Two pints, when you get a minute,' Warnock called to the barman. When he turned and spoke to Gallagher again he had developed a stage English accent.

'I have of course, my dear Watson, been detecting the unmistakable odour of sour grapes emanating strongly from some of the people I've been talking to, you understand.' His voice returned to normal. 'People in this business get very jealous of colleagues who do well. They like to think ill of them, spread stories. It makes them feel better about their own lack of achievement.'

The drinks appeared on the bar and he went to get them.

'There's no doubt about it,' he said when he came back, 'if you were to go outside there into the street and ask anybody to name the first journalist who came into their head, they'd probably come up with Marcus Kelly. Alan Warnock's name would be pretty far down the list, anyway, that's for sure. I doubt if my own mother would even think of it.'

'Oh, I don't know,' Gallagher said. 'She might – eventually.'

Warnock ignored him. 'But Kelly did a hell of a number on Sean Donovan. Everybody agrees that his ability to uncover what seemed to be cast-iron information was absolutely remarkable. Other reporters covering the crime scene had nothing like it – which is leading them to wonder, of course, especially now that he's dead, just how he came by it. Was somebody using him to do their dirty work for them?'

He hunched his shoulders and went into a bad Boris Karloff. 'Rival master criminals from the sinister depths of the underworld, perhaps? Heh, heh.'

Gallagher looked pained. Warnock straightened up again. 'Frankly, I wouldn't put it past the cops myself. Stranger things have happened. So there you go. What do you think? Interesting, isn't it?'

'Like you say, there could be a lot of sour grapes in there. Good old-fashioned jealousy.'

'Oh sure, but then again—' he sipped his drink '—maybe there isn't.'

Chapter Twenty-Four

G ilbert Leslie admonished himself.
 You are weak.

He had been to the little Temple Bar bistro twice since his first visit. Tonight would be his fourth. And his last. There could be no more of this nonsense.

But he liked to see her face, that was all, and what harm was there in that.

Vialli. That was the name he had invented for himself.

'I don't know your name,' she had said one evening as she took his order. 'I like to know what to call my regulars.'

'Guillermo Vialli,' he had told her.

She had repeated it, savouring its syllables, the soft cadence. 'I love Italian names.'

They had talked in snatches after that and he had learned that she was not a waitress by choice but had been a student before dropping out of university because she wanted to be an actress. She was working in the bistro, long hours, so that she could accumulate the money she needed for drama lessons.

He smoothed his hair and dabbed fresh cologne on his

cheeks and set off from the Shelbourne at a brisk pace. He did not know if she would be there but he knew he would be deeply disappointed if she were not. That had happened already, a couple of nights ago. He had forced himself to eat a morose salad and had not lingered.

But tonight? He opened the door and stepped in.

There she was.

The little table where he had first sat was free and she was serving a couple at the one next to it. She had her back to him and she did not see him enter or notice him approach.

'Good evening, Sinead,' he said softly as he eased his way past her.

She turned with two main courses in her hand and smiled.

'Mr Vialli,' she said with some pleasure. 'Back again?'

'Can't keep away,' he joked, except that it was true.

'I'll be with you in a moment,' she said and returned to her customers.

'Don't worry. There's no rush.'

The bistro was normally quiet in the early evening, a lull between the bustle of the day and the clamour of late supper, but it seemed particularly so tonight, he was glad to see. Perhaps they would have the chance to talk some more.

Candles flickered on empty tables. She served him a chicken and pasta dish and he drank a small bottle of San Pellegrino with it.

From the other side of the serving hatch she watched him.

It was not the food or the ambience that brought him

here: he came to see her. She had seen how he responded to her, how his face could reflect her smile.

She made a decision.

'So how was your day?' she asked when he had finished and she was taking his plate away. 'Would you like to see the sweet menu? Coffee?'

'Oh, busy – you know. No sweet, thanks. A double espresso. How was yours?'

'Just finishing, thank God. You'll be my last customer tonight with any luck.' Her eyes widened and she put her hand to her mouth. 'Oh, I'm sorry. I didn't mean—'

He laughed. 'Don't worry about it.'

She brought him his coffee and paused by the table.

'Look, I don't want you to take this the wrong way, but I was thinking of going for a drink when I've finished here and I wondered, if you're doing nothing yourself – well . . . would you like to join me?'

He studied her. Her head was slightly to one side and the question was still in her eyes. What had prompted it? Did she feel sorry for him? Did she think he was a lonely old man, dining alone?

Or was it possible . . .?

No, that was an idle hope.

'That's kind,' he said, 'but I'm sure you're meeting someone. Friends, perhaps. I can't imagine you're going off somewhere all on your own.'

'I am tonight. I just want to go and unwind for half an hour. But look – if you'd rather not—'

'No – I'd love to,' he said, *too quickly*. 'I'm really not at all familiar with Dublin pubs. Perhaps I need a good guide.'

He paid his bill and she suggested that he wait for her outside for a moment rather than in the bistro itself, just in case the other girls – well, he knew how it was.

'I understand perfectly,' he said, although as he waited and saw people pass by with a glance at him, a man hanging around on a street corner, he began to feel uncomfortable and conspicuous.

But it was just a drink; that was all.

The door of the bistro opened. 'At last,' she said. She was still wearing the uniform of white shirt and tight skirt but she had put on short black boots with heels that made her taller and she had her hands buried in the pockets of a leather blouson.

He was not sure whether he liked the outfit. For a second he thought she looked tartish and he had not expected that at all but then she smiled and he was reassured.

'Ready?' she asked.

She did not explain where they were going but he soon found that it was not far. They walked round a corner and down another, narrower, street and then she was pushing open the door of a pub.

'Here we are,' she said.

It was dimly lit and full of young people who were, at the very most, a third of his age. They clutched beer bottles and tried to hear each other over the sound of electronic music pounding at a frenzied pace. A couple of people nodded to Sinead and looked at Leslie as if he had strayed in from another galaxy.

This was not the place for him to be.

She leaned towards him. 'What do you want to drink?' she shouted.

He shook his head. 'Nothing.' He did not like raising his voice but he had to. He frowned and gestured at his surroundings. 'This . . . how can you unwind here?'

'You don't like it?' She was bobbing up and down to the music.

'It's dreadful.'

She saw his consternation and laughed. 'Okay then. That's all right. We'll go somewhere else.'

Outside in the darkening street he paused to let the hammering in his head stop.

'My God,' he said. 'I cannot believe how loud that was.'

'Somewhere a little more relaxing, perhaps?'

Another corner, another street and now she was at the door of a small hotel. The lobby had a marble floor, palms in big terracotta pots and a porter in a Napoleonic greatcoat.

The bar was to the left, dim as before, but this time there was a warmth from the soft lighting and the music was piano jazz seeping from the speakers. They found a table in the curve of a banquette. A waiter in a waistcoat with a hand-painted design greeted them with half a bow.

'What would you like?' Leslie asked.

'A vodka and tonic. No ice, thanks.' She took her jacket off and put it on the seat beside her.

'A vodka and tonic,' he repeated. 'And bourbon – do you have bourbon?'

The waiter bowed again. 'Bourbon – yes sir.'

'Then I'll have a bourbon and iced water.'

The waiter left and Leslie surveyed the room. At other tables, there were other twosomes, holding hands, speaking softly like lovers.

Like lovers who should not be, he thought at once, wondering if they had noticed him and this girl and what assumptions they had made.

'Bourbon? I thought you'd have – I don't know.' Sinead gave a little frown. 'What do Italians drink?'

'Oh, the same as everybody else. A lot of wine, perhaps, scotch, gin, brandy. I like the occasional bourbon. I suppose it's a hangover from my days in America.'

'How long did you live there?'

He would answer only so much, even though everything he told her would be a lie.

'Eleven years. I worked in the motor industry in Detroit and then I came back home to Milan to do the same thing there.'

The waiter brought the drinks.

Leslie lifted his glass to her. '*Salut*,' he said.

'*Slainte*,' she responded and clinked her own glass against his.

They drank. 'So, tell me,' he said, relaxing into the seat, 'how are the acting plans going?'

She told him about the course she hoped to get into, about auditions for small parts at the Abbey and the Gate, walk-ons, about menial backstage jobs she had once done and how she sometimes woke up in the mornings and wondered if it was all worth it.

He wondered where it was that she woke.

'Of course it will be worth it,' he said. 'If it is what you want and you want it badly enough then you will succeed. But it is good to have thoughts of doubt sometimes, to sit quietly and assess things. If the goal is the right one for you, then you come out of that with new determination and conviction. Is that not so?'

'Yes,' she said. 'I suppose you're right.'

He would ask her.

'This is very pleasant,' he said, sipping his bourbon, 'very pleasant indeed, but I felt a little concerned that I've taken you away from where you really wanted to be. Perhaps there was somebody in that other place – a friend—'

She chuckled gently at the awkward route he was taking.

'Why don't you ask straight out? Do I have a boyfriend – or maybe even a girlfriend?'

He had not thought that she might be homosexual. The notion shocked him and played across his features.

She noticed. 'No – no boyfriend. And I'm not gay. There's an *ex*-boyfriend, though, but he's working in Australia for a year. While he's gone, I'm looking after his flat for him – rent free, which is very nice because it helps with my savings for the drama course.'

'I wasn't prying,' he said. 'At least I didn't mean to.'

She patted his hand. 'You're very nice, Mr Vialli, do you know that? A really nice man. There can't be many left.'

They had another drink and she insisted on paying for it. It was when she began to stifle a yawn that he looked at his watch. They had been there for an hour.

'You're tired,' he said. 'I'm sorry.'

'No, it's fine. The drinks have unwound me – unravelled me, more like.' She stretched her arms above her head with her fingers locked together and the movement pulled her shirt tight over the substantial shape of her breasts.

'But, yes, you're right, I am tired. Time to go home. I'm very much looking forward to being off tomorrow, I can tell you. I'll have a nice long lie-in. Maybe I won't get up at all.'

She lifted her jacket and he helped her into it. They went outside into the night. It was colder now and quite dark. He could hear more of that awful music punching the air from somewhere nearby. Four young men staggered past, singing a football song. One of them dropped an empty beer can on the ground and they began to kick it about, cheering as it clattered and banged across the cobblestones.

'Listen, how would you like to walk me home?' she said. 'It's not very far.'

About ten minutes later, they were outside an old red brick warehouse which had been gutted by a developer and turned into a dozen small apartments. She unlocked the street door and they stepped into the hallway.

At the bottom of the stairs a couple of bicycles were chained to the banisters. There was a snatch of canned laughter from a television somewhere. On the bare stone floor were fliers which had fluttered down from the letter-box. A pizza delivery service, a weekend of folk music, a rally on behalf of political prisoners in Central America all rasped under their feet like a sand dance.

It was warmer in here and Leslie shuddered suddenly with the change in temperature.

'I'm on the next floor up,' Sinead said. 'Will you come in for a moment? Tea or coffee? Or I might be able to find something a little stronger?'

'I shouldn't,' he said. 'I should really—'

'Oh, come on.' *Don't be silly*, her tone said. *Are you afraid of me?*

The apartment looked larger than it was because of the

way the space was used. It was only a bed-sitting room with a tiny bathroom off it and an alcove for a kitchen but it was on a split level with the sleeping part raised slightly from the rest of the room and reached by a couple of steps.

The floor was polished wood under multi-coloured hessian rugs. The walls were new brick instead of old and they had been painted a buttercup yellow. Sinead flicked a switch at the door and a couple of lamps came on, up-lighters that mellowed the shading.

'Have a seat,' she said, indicating a settee. It was covered by a heavy green throw with a beaded fringe. She smiled at him and as she did the lamplight caught something in her dark eyes and Leslie thought for a second that the softness had gone from them.

He sat down and looked around. On the walls were framed posters of theatrical productions.

'This is very agreeable,' he told her.

'Not bad for free,' she said, taking off her jacket and throwing it over a chair. She bent over a low cupboard and when she stood up she was holding a squat bottle of Cointreau and a couple of small glasses.

She displayed them to him. 'Will you?'

'Perhaps just a small one. Thank you.'

She took her boots off. She was not wearing tights, just little socks which she peeled off and tossed on to the floor like woollen snowballs. She settled beside him on the settee with her legs tucked under her.

He drank some of the liqueur and on its warm, slow journey it bathed the edges of his reserve. They talked a little and he felt a curious sense of security, as if she were harbouring him from the world outside.

Afterwards. This sort of moment would be much better when he had accomplished everything that had brought him to Dublin. But that would not be possible.

It was time to leave.

He stood up. 'I must go,' he said.

She stood, too, smaller now in bare feet.

'No,' she said. Her voice had become a hoarse whisper. 'Don't.'

Her eyes fastened on his and she reached towards him. He gave a sudden start as he felt her hand sweep slowly down between his legs. He stirred in her grasp.

She let go and stepped back from him but he could still feel her touch, like an imprint, and he could not speak.

'You don't want to go,' she said. 'Not just yet. Not when there is more.'

Immobile, he stared as she began to undress, unbuttoning the blouse carefully, then opening it wide and easing it off her shoulders. She was sturdy and her breasts were heavy and when she had unfastened her bra and dropped it to the floor, she cupped her hands under them, showing him the nipples, wide and dark.

'This is what you would like, isn't it? I can give you things – up there.' She inclined her head towards the raised level where the bed waited. 'Whatever you want. And afterwards,' she smiled, 'well – you're such a generous man, I know. You just might want to consider how you could help me with my drama lessons.' She inclined her head coyly. 'Don't you think?'

She moved towards him again. 'Come on.'

There was a light somewhere at the back of Leslie's brain, sudden and sharp. He blinked and then found that there was a red frame round everything in his vision and that what was within it was misshapen. Her face had become strangely distorted. The room itself had turned into a tunnel. His heart was pounding and there were sharp needles of heat stabbing at the rim of his cheekbones.

So disappointing. So very disappointing.

Why did it always have to be this way? All of them the same in the end.

The first had been the girl who had betrayed Karel, his brother.

Another night. Another country. Long ago.

Men with weapons breaking in. Soldiers in rough Russian uniform filling the tiny house with their anger as he, Gabor Laszlo, stood alone at the bottom of the stairs and in a state of terror he hoped they would not see.

But it was not him they had come for. It was his older brother whom they sought. And when he told them he did not know where Karel was, they hit him with their rifle butts and clubbed him to the ground, kicking him and cursing at him as he lay there, but still he did not tell them. Even though he knew.

As they had beaten him, he had tasted his own salty blood in his mouth and felt waves of nausea and blackness sweeping over him and then a new voice had cut through the shouting of the others and the beating had stopped.

Through his blurred vision, he had seen someone bending over him and then the voice said something in Russian and suddenly they were gone, out into the blackness, leaving the door hanging off its hinges, and when he felt the cold slithering across the floor and beginning to wrap itself around his battered body, he had struggled painfully to his feet.

He had often wondered why they had not taken him with them, to be dragged into the headquarters of the ARVO, the Hungarian secret police, then beaten and tortured before confessing to crimes of which he had no knowledge before being taken out to a scarred wall in a courtyard and shot.

There was no logic to any of it. No logic dictated why one person should live and another die. It all turned on the moment.

They did not find Karel the night they came to the house in Budapest. They found him two days later when he turned up to meet the girl in the City Park and they were waiting.

He had been foolish. Gabor had told him so, ages before; no woman was worth the risk. But Karel revelled in risk.

Like most of those most closely involved in the fighting, he knew it was over and that they would find him eventually unless he fled. If he did not leave the country, then he would die. But he wanted to see her first, one last time, to try to persuade her to come with him. America, perhaps, France or Italy. So he had sent her a message and she had been sitting on a bench in the park, as he had told her to, and he had pedalled slowly towards her on his bicycle.

And then there were men in trench-coats and soldiers with rifles. They were behind bushes, climbing out of vans, and the girl was standing – standing and backing away from him – and he set off fast across the grass, but there were shots, people screaming, and he fell with three bullets in his back.

He did not die immediately, not until the ARVO had taken him to the secure hospital wing that they used for their own purposes, and there they questioned him and inflicted more agony before the final blackness took him.

Gabor never saw his brother alive again but there were

those who told him what had happened in the park and who knew how it had come about.

And so he had watched the girl, puzzled because he could not understand why she had done what she did.

He had followed her for weeks, waiting for the moment when he could ask her. He discovered her address, one room in a tall building of smutty brick, and he would watch from the shadows of an alleyway across the street. By day he would trail after her, seeing her strolling with soldiers, laughing, her head thrown back and her dark hair tossed in the wind.

Why? That was all he wanted to know.

One night he had stood in the cold of the alleyway with the pain of the frost in his ears and in his fingertips, observing a young Russian officer leave the building in his warm coat and thick gloves and his shiny boots. After a few minutes Gabor had crossed the road, pushed open the unlocked front door and climbed the long flight of stairs towards her room.

It might have been all right if she had not been drunk, if she had not devoured him with her eyes as she leaned on the open door frame in a dressing gown of huge red poppies made out of a thin fabric that he did not know was silk.

She had no idea who he was, seeing only a handsome boy of nineteen with dark hair and bright eyes. In turn he had seen an altogether different woman from the one who had laughed in the street and in his brother's heart. And then she reached out and grasped his arm and pulled him into the room.

There was the smell of heavy perfume and the slightly sour odour of drink.

Sometimes it came to him unexpectedly, as if carried in

the wind, and when it did he would stop and remember.

It was here – now. In a room in Dublin.

At the end, on that night in Budapest, he had been between her legs, emptying himself into her, and as he rose he saw that she was dead across the bed, the marks of his strong hands red and raw on her throat, and he knew that this was what he had come for, not to ask her anything at all.

What he had done that night had been buried and forgotten along with his old life, until another night twenty years ago in a hotel in Miami and another girl. So young and beautiful. The same dark hair and dark eyes.

He knew that she had been paid for, that she had been provided for him, but her affection and easy conversation were a brilliant act and he had gone along with it, allowing himself to be transported into a world that did not exist but which would be real for one night.

But then she had said something or looked at him or touched him – he had no clear recall of what had caused it – perhaps all three – and he had seen the decay beneath the glitter so that he was once again in a bleak and barren room in Budapest and as he straddled her his hands were on her throat and there were sharp, awful choking sounds coming from her.

There was no sexual contact that time, no unseemly mess, just the body. They took it away, the people who had paid for her, and dumped it somewhere. They could do anything they liked. They owned the hotel and they owned the town.

But he would have been seen with her in the hotel restaurant and so they moved him to a different room so that the police would find nothing.

It was months later, when he was back in New York, that

they came to talk to him. By then the girl's body had been found and identified and the police had tried to piece together her movements up until the time she was last seen.

Yes, he confirmed to them, he had been in Miami on the day in question, a business trip because he was a management consultant to some hotel-owners down there. Yes, he had been introduced to a young lady and had had dinner with her. But no, he had not seen her after that.

And when the police inquired further, there were those, a United States Senator among them, who swore that at the approximate time of the girl's death he had been with them and no one else.

He had thought it was over.

He stood back and pulled his trousers up, fastening them with trembling hands which still had the feel of her throat on them. He was breathless through exertion and shock.

She lay across the settee with her legs apart and one foot resting on the floor. Her skirt was rolled up to the waist and the knickers he had torn from her lay beside her head. Her hair was spread out behind her like a fan and her dead eyes stared past him towards the buttercup wall.

In the lifeless face he saw his own destruction.

No one should know he had done this.

Think.

Parrish. The others. They did not know about her or the bistro. He had never mentioned it to any of them and so when her death was discovered they would not associate it with him.

The police. The police would trace her movements. The

staff in the restaurant – perhaps they would remember him but did they know that he and the girl – Sinead – *no, he could not think of her with a name now* – that he and the girl had gone off together? She had tried to keep that from them. Perhaps that was helpful, although he might be remembered as a customer she had talked to earlier in the week.

Fool. Fool.

That first bar. She had been known there. Some of her acquaintances would remember and perhaps try to give a description. What about the hotel? If anyone remembered, would they come forward and risk public revelation about their own furtive assignations?

But the waiter – he might remember. Leslie saw him in his colourful waistcoat, carrying the tray with her vodka and his bourbon.

The bourbon. He would remember the drink and it would trigger a memory of the man who had ordered it and as his heart sank into a pit Leslie knew without a shadow of a doubt that the waiter would be able to give the police a very good description indeed.

Think.

She had offered him sex so she was not expecting to be interrupted. Therefore it was probably true that she lived here alone.

He had time.

His fingerprints were on file somewhere in the FBI's records as a result of investigations long ago. What had he touched? Very little really.

With a cloth from the kitchen, he went over every likely surface but he had only moved from the door to the settee so it was not difficult to cover the possibilities. Using the cloth, he took the bottle of Cointreau and put it back in the cupboard. Then he took the two glasses into the kitchen, washed and dried them carefully and set them in the cupboard, too.

The girl. What would he do with her? He saw something glisten like a snail trail on the inside of her thigh and it disgusted him. There was little he could do about that, nor did he propose to try. His semen would be anonymous, with no previous DNA connection to lead them to him.

But they could get fingerprints from skin now.

He went into the bathroom and came back with a flannel and some soap that smelled of freesia. He bent slowly over her and with a kind of reverence he lifted her head in his hands and tenderly washed her bruised throat at the spot where he had strangled the life out of her.

When he had finished, he left the soap and the cloth back and took some tissues from a box, using them to switch off the light and close the door gently behind him.

There were other arrangements to be made. When he got back to the hotel, he made a call from his mobile. After that, he rang downstairs to reception and told them to make his bill up. He would be checking out in the morning.

Chapter Twenty-Five

On Saturday morning, Gallagher just caught something on the eleven o'clock radio news. It had started by the time he turned it on.

'. . . *Subject of much speculation since the allegations by the new Justice Minister on Monday. This report by our Political Correspondent, Eugene McCann:*

'*Mr Seamus North's decision to resign, not only from his role as the Opposition spokesman on finance but as a member of the* Dail *itself, comes at the end of a week in which there has been widespread speculation about the identity of the prominent politician alluded to by Emma Gallagher. Although his statement says merely that he would like to devote more time to his family and to private interests, it is known that he has had several meetings with the leader of the Opposition in the past few days as a result of specific references to him in certain newspapers . . .*'

With or without photographs, Emma had her victim.

She had started a feeding frenzy and he wondered how she felt about her achievement. Frankly, just at this moment, he did not care to ask. What she had done was unsavoury; it was smear politics and it had upset him to see how readily she had indulged in it.

You weren't here.

She had grown up to be the person she was because of him. It would have been different if he had been dead. She would have coped with that – raged about it, certainly, blamed him for dying – but instead she had had a father whom she had known was alive yet who preferred to be somewhere else, not with her.

What right had he to be displeased with her for turning out the way she had? What right had he to disapprove of her bitterness, her cynicism, the way she reached out and grabbed what she wanted?

Give her time, Kate had said. But time would not alter her personality. That had been moulded over the past thirty-two years.

He dialled Kate's number. She had been in England on business for part of the week and she was due back. Paul was old enough to be left to fend for himself while she was away but Gallagher had called with him anyway one evening and they had gone out to the cinema together.

The boy would turn out all right; he had no doubt about that. They had even got to talk about his father, cautiously at first and then more openly. Gallagher had seen the anger and resentment in him and the grieving he still had to do, in his own good time.

She answered. 'You're back,' he said. 'Good trip?'

'Except that after I came home last night and parked my car, somebody put a brick through the windscreen. A couple of other cars in the street got the same treatment. Drunken hooligans. Apart from that, as Mrs Lincoln might have said, it was fine. Now I've got to meet somebody in the

Shelbourne for coffee and I'm waiting for a bloody taxi that hasn't arrived.'

'Anybody I know?' He hoped it sounded like casual curiosity, not anxious prying.

'The man who runs the company in Paris that I do business with. He's over for the rugby match.'

'Oh right.' Ireland were playing France at Lansdowne Road. 'Hey,' he said, 'I've got to go into town a little later myself. Why don't I meet you at the Shelbourne when you've finished and then maybe we could go for lunch? I could take you home later.'

It was a while since they had talked properly. It was time they did.

She thought. 'Yes, okay. That would be nice.' Something else came to her. 'Oh, and thanks for keeping an eye on Paul when I was away. That was good of you.'

'I wasn't keeping an eye on him – or at least I hope he doesn't think that. I enjoy his company.'

When he got into the city he found that as usual the area around St Stephen's Green was impossible. Not a space. Neon arrows pointed in the direction of the multi-storey car parks where the NO SPACES signs were lit, reminding him of the boards outside American motels.

He drove around the Green a couple of times, getting hot in the car, and then cheered quietly to himself as he saw someone pull out of a gap just opposite the Department of Foreign Affairs. He put money in the meter, threw his jacket into the back seat, then locked the car and turned into the park.

He wore a short-sleeved shirt and as a breeze scampered by it tickled the hairs on his forearms. In the grassy areas between flowerbeds vibrant with colour, people had arranged themselves in the sun. Girls with loose cotton skirts rolled up to their thighs lay flat on their backs, shoes and bags neatly to hand. Eyes shielded by dark glasses, their faces were turned up to the heavens in worship, with expressions that bore a haughty disregard for everything else around them. In a clutch in the centre of the grass four youths sat indian-fashion, stripped to the waist, with redness beginning to glow among the freckles on their backs as they eyed the girls pointlessly then turned in on themselves to mutter and giggle.

He emerged from the Green at the statue of Wolfe Tone. In front of the Shelbourne the incoming and outgoing tides were converging. There was a large touring coach with German numberplates and from the luggage bay underneath it, suitcases were being disgorged into the street. Behind was a dark blue BMW with its boot open. A slim man with thin black hair curling long into a froth at the back of his neck was lifting a soft suitcase into it.

Just in front of Gallagher there was a public telephone point where a woman was having an angry conversation. She hung up with finality and strode off. Gallagher's gaze followed her momentarily.

Beyond her, on the other side of the street, a porter had opened the rear door of the BMW and a man was getting in.

Gallagher saw only the side of his face for just a moment but he saw the shape of the nose, the sleek sheen of the hair, and as the man slid into the seat he thought he got the impression of a slightness of build.

It was enough.

His heart seemed to have climbed high into his chest and it pounded against his breast bone. In the sunshine there was gooseflesh on his skin.

He stood absolutely still in the centre of the pavement and stared at the car. It was a shiny, impenetrable shell, yet he believed that the very look of it told him something.

It was on the move. Right indicator on, out and round the luggage blockage into the traffic. In the one-way system it had two choices: it could go straight on, heading into south Dublin, or it could follow the curve of the park.

Gallagher suddenly felt exposed and highly visible. His only cover was to change direction and walk back the way he had come. As he did, the BMW passed him, moving swiftly, taking the route around the Green. It was only feet from him now but he could not turn and look at it without being noticed. All he could do was glance surreptitiously to the side as it went by but he saw only a distorted reflection, a blur of colour that was his own shape, the trees in the park and the statue of Wolfe Tone.

It had almost disappeared round the corner before he remembered to look at the numberplate.

96 D – he did not get the rest. The car had been registered in Dublin that year; that was all that meant.

The palms of his hands were clammy and he felt his legs losing their strength. He turned back into the welcome refuge of the Green. He needed to find somewhere to sit.

He had glimpsed a face from another lifetime.

The sight of it had been fleeting and fragmentary, impressionistic rather than precise, but it had screeched across the surface of his memory like chalk on a blackboard.

Someone from New York.

There was a bench just inside the entrance. Bird droppings had dried on the slats but he did not notice them.

In his mind's eye, he saw it all, what he always tried to avoid seeing, what came to him in dreams he could do nothing about. But he was awake and it was there now, in the light of day, almost drained of colour, as if he were seeing it through the lens of the surveillance camera they had installed in the downtown hotel room that night.

Gallagher himself had picked the hotel as a venue because he had seen how easily it could be watched, how comfortably every approach, every route away from it could be covered, and because he knew how important tonight was.

It would be the last step in a long-drawn-out and dangerous operation of entrapment.

Gallagher saw the faces of Gaines and Dobchek, two of his best field agents, young and eager, like the faces of the recruits down at Templemore. They had been posing as Irish terrorists trying to buy arms from an American dealer and tonight they would bring him a deposit, $20,000 in a soft leather overnight bag. In turn they had asked him to bring a sample.

But although the sample would have been enough for an arrest, it was not enough for Gallagher. He wanted everything. He wanted to know where the rest of the merchandise was and he wanted Gaines and Dobchek to persuade their man to take them to it.

They would not go alone, of course. Other agents would be listening and watching, thirty of them in all, in cars and vans and in a helicopter. Then there was the SWAT team, poised and ready.

Gallagher was racing, racing. Alone in his office looking out at the glittering Manhattan night the juices were flowing. He was so near to a great prize.

Important though it would be to close down an illegal arms operation, it was not his only goal – not when the dealer's name was Alex Leslie, the only son of Gilbert Leslie, for decades the great strategist who had helped crime become more organised, more international and more impenetrable than ever before.

Leslie himself seemed untouchable. Yet tonight, Gallagher hoped, would finally be their chance.

Alex Leslie ran a haulage business in New Jersey. The company had been set up for him by his father and its legitimate operations were profitable but it was merely a front, however lucrative. Through it, using the network of international contacts Gilbert Leslie had established, Alex had become a successful conduit in the world arms trade.

He could not have done it on his own. He did not have the brains of the father; everyone knew that. Somewhere, deep in the background, Gilbert Leslie was pulling the strings.

But if they caught the puppet – then they might have the puppeteer, too.

Gallagher had fought hard to gain control of this one. There had been a great deal of resistance from those running the counter-terrorism programme but in the end, because of Gilbert Leslie's significance, the Director himself had approved a joint operation with Gallagher at its head.

And as he looked down towards the Manhattan streets Gallagher knew that if this was successful it meant an open door for him to Washington, the real centre of power.

He was impatient to get there.

He had given Gaines and Dobchek their final briefing, just the three of them together, except that as they sat with him they looked at each other nervously and he saw an anxiety that was not normally there.

Their pitch to Leslie, he had suggested, would be that there were people back in Ireland, the people who had sent them, who were concerned with the slow progress of these negotiations. Samples of merchandise would not satisfy them; the agents had been given instructions to ask to see the quantity.

They would appeal to Leslie's understanding: it wasn't they who were insisting, as they were sure he would appreciate, but they were being pressed by their masters at home.

Gaines had frowned and told him they were uncomfortable about pushing Leslie to take them the rest of the way. He was a difficult fish to play and they had taken time and care to get him to this stage. He was also dangerous and volatile.

But Gallagher had insisted. He had waited long enough.

This surveillance operation had been planned in great detail and put in place, he had assured them, with their safety in mind. It would be their finest hour – until the next one, he had joked, putting his arm round them, cajoling and encouraging with his usual mock blarney.

He praised Gaines and Dobchek to the skies. How well they had worked their way into Leslie's confidence. How brilliant their Irish accents were although hadn't they a good tutor. More laughter. But in their faces he had seen their unease. At that moment he should have allowed them to back off, to play it their way, but he did not.

And now Gallagher saw himself in a surveillance van.

It had been raining in Manhattan and although it had

stopped the streets were slick and wet and traffic passed by with a sticky swish.

On the monitors in the van he could see Gaines and Dobchek waiting in the room. Their movements were fidgety, tense. Dobchek turned the TV on, then off again.

Through the microphones hidden in the room, they were able to talk to the van but the van could not talk back. They carried no handsets in case Leslie searched and found them and although the room itself was wired, they were not, since it was always Leslie's practice to frisk them when he arrived.

He was coming.

A car passing by the front of the hotel slowly, then driving on.

And here it was again, back round the block, slowing and then stopping. A man got out and Gallagher would see the dark features of Alex Leslie, the hair like night, an Adidas sports bag that appeared heavy in his hand.

He entered the hotel and when his car drove on, Gallagher issued the order for someone to follow it. Two agents pulled out but as they did, they cut across the path of another car. Both vehicles braked and there was a brief squeak of tyres in the wet.

The eyes of the drivers met in a moment of unmistakable, mutual recognition.

This was no ordinary car, passing by innocently and unaware. It was Alex Leslie's back-up vehicle, checking the surroundings for trouble.

The car sped off and the agents followed. Their radios crackled with information that no one wanted to hear, spreading fear and dread in the airwaves and all around the men in the surveillance van.

But if Leslie's back-up men saw something, what could they do about it? How could they warn him if he was in the hotel on his own? And then the van picked up a radio signal from somewhere. It was a voice – 'Heat. Get out of there.'

Damn it, Leslie had a radio receiver, probably with an ear-piece . . .

Gallagher's mouth went dry.

On the monitor, in the moment before he ordered the SWAT team in, he saw Leslie enter the hotel room.

Agents were flooding into the building, pouring down the stairs from a room on the floor above, but Leslie was calm and unhurried, putting his hand into the Adidas bag which was already open. Gaines and Dobchek stood to greet him and Gallagher could hear their welcoming voices.

Leslie taking something from the bag now.

The squat shape of a Mini-Uzi in his hands.

Leslie shooting. A short burst for each. Two bodies falling backwards, arms outstretched.

And then he saw Leslie grab the case with the money from a table and vanish from his vision and he could not see anything of what happened next, although he could hear a long burst of shooting somewhere, just on the edge of the range of the hidden microphones.

In front of him there was only the stillness of the room, one body on the floor and the other one across a chair, and then he saw other agents coming in, fast at first, then stopping in their tracks when they saw what was there and what he would see himself when he went in.

He would see the killer's body, too, sprawled on a blood-soaked corridor carpet near the back stairs where the pursuing agents had cornered him.

★ ★ ★

On a tree opposite where Gallagher sat, a chaffinch called loudly, trying to attract the attention of anyone who would listen, but he did not hear it.

Instead, he saw himself visiting the homes of two young widows with redness in their eyes and anger in their hearts. And he felt their hatred, saw the depth of it in their faces, because of what he had done to them.

He blamed himself just as much as they did. He felt self-loathing and disgust at how he had disregarded the fears of their husbands.

Their dead husbands.

In the end it had been an accident, a simple slip, which had caused it all, yet it was he who had ordered the car to go in pursuit, he who had masterminded the entire operation. He who shouldered the guilt.

None of it had brought him one single step nearer his quarry. In subsequent examinations of Alex Leslie's papers and business records, nothing was found that might incriminate his father.

Nor did the FBI ever find a single weapon of the batch Gaines and Dobchek had been trying to buy. Only the gun which had been used to kill them.

There had been questions to answer, a painful interview with the Assistant Director in Charge, and there was a report which he had to write in a hurry because in Washington the Director himself wanted to see it.

Then there was the despair of the funerals, tears and rain in a damp cemetery, the cold faces of his colleagues looking at him as if he had ceased to exist.

It was from that day that Gallagher began to crumble, falling away from himself like the sodden pieces of clay that rolled down into the graves of Gaines and Dobchek.

At night, in the darkness, Gallagher began to see Gilbert Leslie's face. But it always vanished when he clawed his hand towards it.

At meetings, his mind would wander. The sight of their bodies, posed strangely in that hotel room, was always there. On a TV set in a bar, when he had had too much to drink, he saw it once, although what everyone else saw was a basket-ball game. No matter who you are, the barman had said as he showed him into the street, you can't come in here and throw bottles at my TV set. Next time it would be the police.

Alone in his office, he shuffled the papers around on his desk each day, alternating one tidy pile with another while the out tray remained empty. Letters and reports were unsigned, decisions not taken.

He could not sleep. The agonies came to him over and over. Once, he had even telephoned Mrs Dobchek to tell her how much he regretted what had happened but she cried hysterically down the phone. It did not occur to him that there was anything odd about making a call like that at three o'clock in the morning. He just wanted to make things better.

Since he could not sleep, there was no point in being in bed so he got into a routine of lying there for a little while before getting up at about two am and dressing, tidying an apart-ment that was never untidy, then getting into his car and driving around the lower reaches of Manhattan, looking at the people still on the streets, wondering who they were, occasionally stopping them to ask and seeing their fear when he sometimes felt the need to produce his gun to reinforce his inquiries.

He would reach the office at about four thirty, startling the night duty men, who felt eventually that they had to put in a report to their administrator about his bizarre hours.

Soon, during the day, routine meetings and operational planning sessions were held without him and he did not even notice. Sometimes people came to find him and discovered him asleep at his desk. After a while they did not bother to seek him out at all.

He was offered leave which he refused to take and then a psychiatrist came to talk to him. Gallagher saw him a couple of times, answered his questions as best he could, but he did not have a lot of time; there were places he had to go and he had left his apartment in a bit of a mess. The whole place needed to be cleaned from top to bottom and when he had that done he would get people in to go over the office. It was filthy.

The psychiatrist sat in his chair, looked around the impeccable, gleaming room and nodded. He understood.

It was depression, brought on by the trauma of great loss. He was incapacitated by grief and guilt and he could not carry on this way. He had to receive proper treatment.

While that was being arranged, something else in Gallagher cracked.

He assigned agents to watch Gilbert Leslie round the clock, follow him wherever he went, and in such a way that Leslie would know what they were doing. But after only two days of this, the order was countermanded by the ADIC and Gallagher was asked to go home and stay there until further notice.

Instead of obeying this instruction, he summoned two puzzled agents and got them to take him up-state to Westchester County. When they arrived, with no explanation from Gallagher of why they had come, they parked outside a pleasant house with black wooden shutters and a well-kept garden.

He told them to wait in the car while he went to the door.

When Gilbert Leslie opened it, Gallagher punched him in the face and knocked him to the floor. He pulled Leslie to his feet and hit him again, this time hard in the pit of the stomach.

He was reaching for his gun when the agents got to him and dragged him away.

Leslie did not sue. He would undoubtedly have won if he had but the FBI would have fought dirty and his normally low profile would have been raised in a way that he and his friends in business would have found undesirable.

For Gallagher, it was over.

One morning, a piece of paper was placed in front of him and he signed it without entirely realising what it was. It was his agreement to take early retirement on medical grounds.

They did not dump him, exactly. There was the pay-off and the pension and they picked up the medical bills for a while, too.

It took him a long time, a lot of care, but gradually he had begun to improve. And then, two years after he left the Bureau, he took the last big step and moved home to Ireland, leaving the cause of his downfall behind him.

Until today.

He shook his head to clear it. Could it really have

been Gilbert Leslie or had he simply made a mistake? Might it have been just a hint of resemblance colliding with what was always hiding round a dark corner in his mind?

He felt calmer now. He held out his hand and looked at it. It was steady. He got up from the bench and began to walk back towards the Shelbourne.

Yet Sean Donovan's words were lodged in his mind, too, immovable, reminding him with the regularity of a time check.

Someone from New York.

He came out of the Green and half expected to see the BMW in front of the hotel again but it was not. He crossed the road and went in.

In the lounge to his right there was chatter and the clink of crockery. Waitresses carried silver trays with delicate smoked salmon sandwiches. On each table there were miniature daffodils in tiny pots. A vast chandelier glistened like frost out of season and caught the light that flashed through the windowpanes from passing cars.

He spotted Kate at a table in a corner by the fireplace with a tall man of forty-something, wearing a blue blazer. She did not notice him at first. She was relaxing in a high-backed armchair, her legs crossed and her hands in a steeple in front of her. The man leaned forward across the table, explaining something with a smile, the gestures of his hands shaping it.

Gallagher was about to raise his arm and signal across the room when she threw her head back and laughed. Then she saw him and waved. The man looked in his direction and raised a slim glass of champagne to his lips. There was a glass of iced water in front of Kate.

As Gallagher walked their way, Kate straightened up in the chair.

'Tom,' she said, 'you're here.' She gestured to her companion. 'Tom, I'd like you to meet Philipe Foucaud, the business associate I told you about.'

Foucaud stood, buttoning his blazer, and gave a little bow before he shook Gallagher's hand. His fair hair was flecked with grey.

'I'm delighted to meet you,' he said. 'May I get you a drink?'

There was an extra seat but Gallagher did not take it. 'Look, I don't want to get in the way,' he said.

'Not at all,' Foucaud assured him.

Gallagher fidgeted. He pointed backwards over his shoulder. 'I'll be back in a moment,' he said. 'There's something I need to attend to first. Please excuse me.'

He went out towards the hall again, a perturbed Kate watching him go.

At the reception desk, a young woman was tapping something into a computer. When the stutter of her printer began, she looked up.

'Can I help you?' The tag on her lapel said her name was Adeline.

'I hope so,' he said. 'I thought I saw someone I knew just a couple of minutes or so ago when I was coming into the hotel. A man, about sixty-ish. He was getting into a blue BMW. Seven series, I think. The man I'm thinking of is called Gilbert Leslie. Have you had anyone of that name staying here?'

She looked at him and then down at her screen and he

heard the keyboard begin to click again as she checked the register.

'No,' she said, studying what appeared, 'no one called Leslie, I'm afraid.'

'Well, then, could you give me the name of the gentleman who just checked out?'

She became less helpful, retreating behind hotel policy. 'I'm sorry, sir. I really can't give out information about our guests. A specific name, yes, perhaps—'

She let it hang and he stared at her for a second, trying to think of some way round this, but he could not. It would be there, right in front of her, but there was no way he could see it. On the other hand, he might simply be wrong; there was always that.

Behind him a couple waited to check in, tubby Americans in golf caps.

'If there's nothing else, sir—'

'No, nothing. Thanks anyway.'

He moved away and went back to the lounge. When he got there, Foucaud had gone.

'Where's your friend?' he asked Kate.

'Gone to meet some of his compatriots in Grafton Street and then head for the match.' She looked at him with concern. 'What's wrong with you? You seem a little edgy.'

'No, it's nothing,' he said. 'I thought I saw someone I used to know, that's all. Now – where will we have lunch?'

Chapter Twenty-Six

On Sundays, the bistro opened between eleven am and nine pm but Damian Fox, the owner and chef, wondered if it was worth it.

Last year, in his first year of operation, he had not opened on Sundays at all but then he had seen that other establishments in Temple Bar did and that there were people around, potential customers, particularly from March onward, so he thought he would give it a go. So far, it had not been what you might call a brilliant success.

It was quiet this morning but it might pick up for lunch. He took a tray of fresh ciabatta out of the oven and breathed in its hot, doughy sweetness.

And where was Sinead?

It was eleven thirty and she should have been here half an hour ago. But then, if she did not turn up he would not have to pay her. He had two waitresses here already, Carmel and Julie. He looked out from the kitchen. Two customers, drinking re-fills of coffee and reading the Sunday papers. A waitress each. What service that was.

Still, it was not like Sinead. She was one of the more reliable girls. He had never known her to just not turn up.

Staff telephone numbers were written on the kitchen wall so he dialled hers. He did not know how long he let it ring but it was enough; you could have run the length of O'Connell Street in that time.

Carmel came into the kitchen. She was a bony girl with hair like ginger fluff and she and Sinead seemed to get on all right.

'You wouldn't know anything about Sinead, would you?' he asked.

'No word from her yet?'

'No. I phoned her a moment ago and got no answer.'

'That's not like her.'

'Just what I was thinking. Listen, since we're not too busy, you wouldn't go round to her place and knock on the door, would you? Maybe she's sick or something.'

'I'll do better than that,' Carmel said. She opened a cupboard door and took a key ring from a nail. There were two keys on it. 'She keeps this here as a spare just in case she ever forgets her own. I'll be able to let myself in if I have to.'

'Okay,' Damian said. 'Don't be long.'

It was not far. Sinead had shown her the flat once. It was lovely, not big, just a nice size for one, and she wished she could have a place like it herself instead of having to share with three other girls she did not particularly like and who kept borrowing her stuff without ever asking for it. That and bringing men back for parties on nights when she had been working late and all she wanted to do was go to bed. On her own – thank you very much.

A thought loomed.

She had wondered about Sinead. There had been a wee

man in the bistro a couple of times, an Italian, Sinead said he was, and she had been fussing over him a bit. She had done that with a couple of men before, always the mature type, and then she would turn up one day in some new outfit or other, like that leather jacket which must have cost a fortune.

Carmel had asked her once.

'How can you afford these things?'

She had smiled and winked. 'Ah now. Some of us have it.'

Carmel wondered about Sinead.

She let herself into the apartment building and walked up the stairs to the first floor, then checked that she had got the right door.

There was a bell. She pressed it and she could hear it ringing just on the other side but when it stopped there was no sound of movement beyond. She tried again, then she rapped on the door a few times.

'Sinead. Sinead, are you in there? It's me, Carmel.'

There was still no response so she opened the door with the key.

She saw the body instantly, right there across the room on the settee, and from the way she was lying and the cold, almost blue colour of her face and the awful empty stare, she knew Sinead was dead.

And then she wondered if there was anybody else in here.

She pulled the door shut with a bang and scrambled back down the stairs and out into the street, running and tripping over the cobbles, back to the bistro where she burst in and blurted it all out to Damian.

He picked up the phone.

★ ★ ★

Only a matter of weeks after being promoted, Inspector Frank Dolan now found himself in charge of a murder case. He had been involved in a couple before, stabbings in the street, that kind of thing, but this was the first time he would be actually running the investigation.

The medical examiner told him that it looked as if the victim had been strangled manually and raped and that she had been dead for at least twenty-four hours. So that gave somebody a head start. Very unpleasant.

There was no evidence of a break-in or anything being disturbed or stolen, which pointed to the likelihood that the killer was someone she knew. They went over the apartment for fingerprints but that did not turn up much although Dolan harboured the hope, very slight, of getting latent prints from the bruised skin on her neck before the body underwent a post-mortem.

The fingerprint people tried but there were no traces at all. If there had been any, then with the normal shrinkage of the skin after death, they had been distorted or had simply disappeared.

The flat belonged to a young man called Kennedy who was working in Australia. A check showed that he had not been back for six months and he confirmed to the police in Adelaide that the girl was living in the apartment and looking after it while he was away.

Dolan spoke to Damian Fox, the owner of the bistro where she worked. He was a slim man in a white tee-shirt. Dolan smelled the aromas in the kitchen and looked at the cakes in the display cases and wondered how Fox managed to stay so thin. Dolan was putting on weight.

'Exercise and worry,' Fox told him. 'Especially the worry. That will curb your appetite every time.'

'So what's worrying you?' Dolan wondered.

'This.' His eyes roamed swiftly over his premises. 'You've no idea how hard it is to keep your head above water. And with this murder – Christ, I don't know what effect it's going to have.'

He told Dolan he had last seen Sinead on Friday evening when she finished her shift. He also gave an account, which his wife and his staff could support, of his own whereabouts from that time. 'Since you're bound to ask,' he said.

The young waitress called Carmel, who had found the body, was in a state of shock, yet there was something about her, Dolan thought, an unwillingness to hold his gaze for long, that he felt he would like to pursue. When she recovered enough for him to do so, she told him about the little Italian man who had been in on a couple of occasions in the past week and then again on Friday night and that he had left at about the same time Sinead did.

Dolan felt sure that that was not all, that there was something more. But it would wait for the moment.

Sinead's parents, Robert and Maura Patterson, came down from Donegal, which was by coincidence Dolan's own home county, and through talking about familiar places and some rather tenuous mutual acquaintances he was able to ease things a little for them, although not much.

Their daughter was dead, for Christ's sake.

Mr Patterson, an accountant from Buncrana, identified the body. Mrs Patterson brought pictures, some of them taken by a local photographer when Sinead was in an amateur drama production in the year she left school. For just a moment, Dolan could see the joy and the hope that had been in her.

The story made the news bulletins on Sunday night and the papers the next morning. They released one of the pictures, one that showed her at her most attractive and vivacious. If someone out there knew something, then the sight of it might encourage them to share the information. The murders of children and pretty girls always tugged the heart strings when there were good photographs.

On Monday morning two young men who knew Sinead came forward to say that they had been in a pub on Friday night when she had come in with an elderly guy, about sixty, maybe. She and the man had left again fairly quickly.

Dolan checked with Carmel and, yes, that sounded like him. But he still felt sure there was something else that she was not saying.

It was not until Tuesday evening that they got the best description of all, from a waiter who worked in a small hotel nearby. He had been in Birmingham since Sunday, visiting his brother, travelling over on the ferry from Dun Laoghaire to Holyhead, and did not see a local paper until he got back.

'It gave me a hell of a shock when I spotted her picture,' he told Dolan.

He had noticed her in the bar before with men who were, well, a bit oldish, really. When he said it, he averted his gaze, just like Carmel had done.

'She's dead,' he told Dolan. 'I don't like to say . . . it's an awful thing . . . but I used to wonder what she was up to. It looked a bit – dodgy, you know?'

Dolan went to see Carmel at the bistro before it closed. When she was certain no one else could hear, she told him of her suspicions about the men Sinead seemed to like to cultivate.

Great, Dolan thought. How the hell do we trace this lot?

But they had Friday's man to find first, which would be hard enough. A growing number of people from various European nations were living and working in Ireland now, French, Italian, German, Dutch, Spanish, not to mention the steady tide of tourists drifting in and out, and the place had been full of French people at the weekend, all in town for the rugby match and all safely back home by now, no doubt.

The waiter was able to give them good descriptive detail. It had not been anyone he had seen her with before and it was the drink that he remembered first. Bourbon and iced water. It helped him give a picture of the person who had ordered it.

As they compiled a computer image of a man, about sixty, sleek, well-kept hair, eyes of a light colour – grey, blue, the waiter was not sure – Dolan tried to convince himself that they were starting to get somewhere.

They distributed the picture to Dublin police stations and the media that night.

Disaster struck the next morning.

One of the papers had sent a reporter to talk to the traders and residents of Temple Bar to get their reaction to the murder. After all, this had been a girl who both worked and lived there, like a growing number of people did. The place had become a community of its own.

One person, anonymous of course, told the paper of their fears that there might be a sex maniac on the loose and that a lot of the young women were in fear of their lives. Whether anyone actually said any such thing or whether the reporter made it up was a bit academic in the end.

On Wednesday morning, there it was:

SEX KILLER MAY STRIKE AGAIN – FEAR.

Out at the *Garda* headquarters in the Phoenix Park, Commissioner Conor Hogan flung open the door of the office of the Deputy Commissioner Operations and stuck the paper on the desk in front of him.

'We had better get a result here,' he said. 'Pronto. The new Minister's been on the phone already to inquire whether she should be worried about any of this.'

'Christ, that's a bit *hands on*, you might say.'

Hogan snatched the paper back and scanned it again. 'I have told her – no, it's just a lot of media hype and we're on top of it. She's going to London for the regular meeting on terrorism with the British Home Secretary and I've said I'm certain we'll have made some progress by the time she comes back. Right?'

'I'll make sure of it, Commissioner.'

'And I want this damn *sex killer fear* nonsense stopped.'

When the door had closed, the Deputy Commissioner Operations picked up the phone and roasted the Assistant Commissioner in charge of the Dublin Metropolitan Area for not keeping him in the picture.

And following that short and one-sided conversation, the Assistant Commissioner called Chief Superintendent Barrett Greeley.

'Yes, I know, I know,' he said in response to Greeley's anguished wail. 'I know you've got the fucking judge's murder and the Donovan case and every other fucking thing but the Commissioner wants this one sorted out and I want you to make sure it happens. Who's looking after this case?'

Greeley checked the computer and groaned when he saw. A first-timer.

'I guess I am now,' he said.

Chapter Twenty-Seven

The damage to her car had put Kate Forrest in the mood for replacing the thing altogether. She had got the windscreen fixed quickly but she was still finding minute pieces of glass wedged into the folds of the upholstery and under the floor carpet and just being in the vehicle made her feel tense and uncomfortable.

So on Wednesday, her usual day off, she embarked on a tour of the showrooms of various south Dublin car dealers, seeing what they had to offer. Gallagher volunteered to do the driving and they went in his untidy little Renault. She would not be getting one of those but then she should not blame the car for the way it was being driven.

A couple of times she had to point out that the lights were against them and on one occasion he almost clobbered a cyclist by driving too close.

'Are you okay?' she asked him. 'You seem a bit preoccupied. Do you want me to drive?'

'No,' he said sharply. 'I'm fine.'

He was not fine; she was not blind. His mind was somewhere else, not with her. It did nothing to assuage her growing worries about his health. His problems with

299

Emma and his financial difficulties would not be helping him, either. Maybe they should discuss it. But she did not know how he would respond. She found herself less at ease in his company than before.

He had been extremely odd when he had seen her in the Shelbourne with Philipe. Was his mood today anything to do with that?

The encounter had given her a lot to think about because it was at that moment that she recognised how much she was being drawn to Philipe. This was more than just a business relationship; there was something stronger between them that neither had yet admitted to. But she recognised, too, that part of the attraction was the stability she saw in Philipe and that she did not see in Tom Gallagher.

That did not stop her feeling deeply for Tom and worrying.

Their lunch on Saturday had been an uncomfortable event, with her trying to make conversation and him going off somewhere inside his head. When he had taken her home in the afternoon he had not stayed long. She had telephoned him on Monday night, just to say hello and because she was feeling guilty about her feelings for another man. She had found him short on communication but he had offered to be her driver today and she had accepted, in part to see how he was.

Not good. There was an invisible wall around him and she wished she knew what lay beyond.

From behind it, Gallagher searched for a face and a blue BMW. But since Saturday the only place he had seen Gilbert Leslie had been in his dreams, during those brief periods when he had actually managed to get some sleep.

He wondered if he should tell Kate what was on his mind. Could he do so without opening up everything that had happened in the past? Or was it time he did that at last?

He hesitated.

At about five thirty they ended the search, she for a new car and he for a fantasy, and they went back to the house at Ranelagh, burdened with brochures and indecision.

Paul was there with school books spread out in front of him on the kitchen table. He put a full stop at the end of a sentence and looked up. He had not realised Gallagher was there.

'Oh, hi. Bloody revision,' he explained. 'The exams start tomorrow.'

'Hi,' Gallagher said quietly and wandered off in the direction of the living-room.

Kate and Paul looked at each other and she gave a shrug that said *don't ask*.

'Right, who's for a cup of tea?' she inquired.

She brought a mug to Gallagher and found him on the settee in front of the television. The news had started.

She could not let this go on. 'Look, Tom,' she said, 'I think it's time we—'

'Wait – shut up a minute!'

He stood up abruptly, staring intently at the screen, and raised his hand to stop her speaking. Startled, she put the mug down and followed his gaze. Paul came into the room to see what was going on.

It was another report about the murder of a girl in Temple Bar at the weekend. They were showing a computer impression of a man the girl had been seen with on the evening she died. The face looked cultivated and almost serene, Kate thought, not like a murderer at all.

'It is believed the man is foreign, possibly Italian,' the reporter said, 'and the police are anxious to interview him in order to eliminate him from their inquiries.'

And now here was the reporter with the evening sun on him, live from a little square in Temple Bar, talking to Chief Superintendent Barrett Greeley who had something to say about the way the case was being reported.

'While everyone's appalled by the murder of Sinead Patterson,' he said, 'I think we have to get things into perspective and that's why I've been horrified by some of the reports I've read in the Press, these suggestions that there's a sex killer on the loose who may strike again. This is utterly insensitive and irresponsible journalism which has no basis in fact whatsoever.'

'So you're saying the man's unlikely to strike again?' the reporter asked.

'Well, we don't even know that it *is* a man.'

'You're looking for a man, aren't you?'

'That's a normal part of the investigation. We're not saying he's the killer. Look, it would be totally wrong for me to speculate. We have the appalling murder of a young woman to solve and we intend to do so quickly. This has been a single incident, horrifying though it was. I want to reassure people here in Temple Bar and throughout the Dublin area that these scares are unfounded.'

He had finished. The reporter had not.

'But you can't say for certain that the murderer won't strike again?'

'I – eh – I can't say that, no. But I think it would be foolish to—'

'I'm afraid we'll have to leave it there, Chief Superintendent,' the reporter said, turning to the camera with a complacent smile. 'And now back to the studio.'

The next item was about farm workers in the west of Ireland seeking a pay rise.

Gallagher looked at Kate and Paul. They were staring at him uneasily, without any understanding of what was going on, and he realised that he was smiling stupidly.

The shadow of self-doubt had been blown away. The computer impression had done that. Although it was not exact – the hair was not quite right and nothing could ever properly convey the effect of the grey eyes – it was enough to confirm the identity of the man he had seen.

Someone from New York.

Gilbert Leslie. That's who it was. He was sure of it. What was he doing here? What connected him to Sean Donovan?

'I'm sorry,' he said to Kate. The moment had arrived and he could avoid it no longer. 'I didn't mean to shout at you. Look, you'd both better sit down. There are things I should explain.'

He stood quietly for a moment, ordering his thoughts. They sat expectantly, as if waiting for a performance to begin.

When it did, it was a revelation.

First he told them about Leslie, who he was and what he was, and in the telling he felt a release, as if a poison was draining away from him. Then he told them about Leslie's son, the incident in which he had died, and his own subsequent mental collapse.

That was harder, as he knew it would be.

All he had ever told Kate was that he had retired from the FBI due to ill-health. He had admitted having a breakdown which had led to severe depression but he had never been specific about the cause. Since he had come home to Ireland, he had not spoken to anyone of those black events. He looked at Kate to see how she was responding but found it hard to interpret what was in her gaze.

When he told them of the deaths of Gaines and Dobchek he felt the shame again, the guilt, but as he spoke he knew that this was better for him than what he had been doing before, trying to hide it all away.

He recounted to them what Donovan had told him, his insistence that someone from New York had been sent to shut him down. Now there was Donovan's own strange death itself, as well as the murders of Marcus Kelly and Mr Justice Purcell.

Finally he came to the man he had glimpsed outside the hotel last Saturday, how the face he had seen had disturbed and haunted him until he had seen the picture on the news bulletin just now.

'It's not just the resemblance in the computer impression; it's the circumstances. A girl strangled.'

He remembered things. Incidents, crimes, dates, he could turn them up like a card sharp dealing aces.

'There was something in Miami years ago, the murder of a hooker. The FBI became involved on the fringes because an organised crime figure was a possible suspect. Gilbert Leslie again. He had been with the girl for a time the night she disappeared but he had an alibi that was fireproof. The case was never solved and no one was ever charged. I wonder if the file is still open? I suppose it was a long time ago.'

Paul was excited. 'Tom, this is fantastic. It's – it's like some movie.'

Kate did not share his elation.

She felt shock at first, then irritation and now she felt a little sad. She looked at Gallagher and thought that she did not know him at all. She had had no idea of the secrets he harboured. She had spent the last few days feeling bad about what might be between her and Philipe Foucaud but it would scarcely have troubled him, had he known. What was eating at him was this man, Leslie, or whatever his name was, the obsession of the past.

'That time, when I met you in the Shelbourne,' Gallagher said, 'I checked with reception but there was no one by the name of Leslie and they wouldn't let me know the name of the man who'd just left.'

'Then if they had no one called Leslie, maybe it wasn't him,' Kate said.

'But, Mum, he wouldn't have been using his own name, would he?' Paul turned to Gallagher. 'What are you going to do?'

'I really should tell Emma about this. Unfortunately that might not be easy since she's in England. It was on the news before you came in. She's at a meeting with the British Home Secretary and she's taking part in some debate or other at Cambridge after that.'

'So then—'

'So then that leaves bloody Barrett Greeley,' he said. 'Again.'

'Wait a minute,' Kate said. 'Isn't it possible you might have made a mistake?'

'Of course it's possible. Do you think I haven't agonised over that for the past few days, wondered if I was cracking up again? That's what you're thinking now, probably.'

He looked at her and she blushed.

'No,' he said, 'Gilbert Leslie's real, flesh and blood. He's here. I know it.'

Kate sighed. 'I just thought – if you're wrong and you go to the police – it might be embarrassing.'

'Mum, I think Tom knows what he's talking about.'

She turned to look at her son. There was a challenge in his face. He was lining up against her. Getting at her again.

'Is there any way I can help?' he asked Gallagher.

'You're not getting mixed up in this,' she said. 'You don't understand.'

'What don't I understand?'

How could she explain something that he seemed to be choosing to ignore – the obsession that drove people, the demons Tom had spoken about? Yet as she looked at Gallagher, she saw that the gloom had left him and that there was a brightness in his eyes. It would be hard for Paul to accept that there could be anything – *wrong* – with this man.

'This isn't some make-believe adventure story, Paul,' she said.

Gallagher walked forward and took her shoulders in his hands.

'That's right, Kate. It's not make-believe. It's reality.'

He smiled at her. His eyes urged her to believe him but he could see that she did not.

She eased herself out of his grasp and he realised to his dismay that there was something more in the simple movement. She was backing away from him to somewhere beyond his reach.

'Okay, Tom,' she said softly. 'You know best. You must do what you think is right.'

Chapter Twenty-Eight

He watched the late news in his own place and video-taped it and was no less convinced about the computer picture when he saw it the second time. And the third and the fourth.

A third and a fourth whiskey, too.

In fact, the picture seemed to take on even more of Gilbert Leslie's physical characteristics every time. That was his imagination, he realised. Because he knew the man, he saw more than was there. Particularly in the eyes. Those grey eyes, bled of colour and feeling.

The Chief Superintendent's contribution to the bulletin was now just a short sound bite; the questioning had not been retained. Even Gallagher, who was no fan of Greeley's, thought that what the reporter had done earlier was unfair and irresponsible.

He rode an emotional wave and fought to stay afloat.

Kate and he were going no further.

He should have talked to her a long time before today.

That face was on the screen again. 'You,' he said out loud. 'You're to blame for this.'

Gilbert fucking Leslie was at the root of all his problems.

And now he was here in Dublin. And for what? Hardly a vacation, that was for sure.

Fuck him. Fuck Barrett Greeley, too.

He poured himself another drink and then he fumbled through the telephone book to find the number of the Bureau of Criminal Investigation at Harcourt Square.

'I am about to hand you the greatest criminal in the history of the universe and you had better damn well be grateful for it,' he said, then dialled.

It was just after ten when he got there. Greeley was still in his office. He rarely left much before eleven these nights. There were no acolytes this time; just Greeley and the cigarette fog. Gallagher blinked as it stung his eyes.

The Chief Superintendent looked at him with suspicion and sniffed.

'Did you drive here, Mr Gallagher?' he asked.

I'm drunk.

'Perfectly,' Gallagher said.

'I would doubt that,' Greeley ventured, lighting another cigarette, but he did not pursue the matter. 'So then – this is getting to be quite a regular thing, isn't it? First Sean Donovan, now this murder in Temple Bar. You've got information about *that* now, you tell me. What – did the late Sinead Patterson leave a message on your answering machine, too?'

Gallagher gritted his teeth and leaned across Greeley's desk. 'Listen, you asshole, it's taken a lot for me to come here.'

'The best part of a bottle of whiskey, I'd say.'

'Look, don't fuck with me.' Gallagher put his elbow on the table and pointed his forefinger at him. 'This is important. And when it's over you're going to be Mister Fucking Supercop, believe me.'

'I can't wait,' Greeley said. He was tiring of this. 'Okay, let's hear it. I'd like to get home before tomorrow.'

Gallagher laughed. 'You won't want to go home at all, not when I tell you about the man you're looking for. His name—' he paused '—is Gilbert Leslie. Now, it might not be a name that will mean anything to you so I'll explain.'

Greeley exhaled a lungful of Marlboro and looked at him. 'No need. Gilbert Leslie, real name Gabor Laszlo, originally Hungarian, came to the United States in the Fifties, believed to be a consultant to the leaders of organised crime, never been convicted, semi-retired. How's that?'

Gallagher sat back. 'Very good,' he conceded. 'I'm impressed.'

'So why would it be him?'

'The computer picture. Look at a photograph of Leslie, get the FBI in New York to send you one. It's him. You'll see. Ask them about a case in Miami, oh – about ten years ago. Leslie was questioned about the murder of a girl, a hooker. See if there's any resemblance with this case. I don't know if the file's still active or not. However, that's not all.'

He looked at Greeley. The policeman's stare was blank behind the smoke curling from the cigarette in his fingers.

'Remember Donovan – what he said about someone from New York closing him down? I know it's Leslie he was talking about.' He slapped Greeley's desk sharply with the tips of his fingers. 'I know it's Leslie and you know why? Because I saw him.'

'You saw him?' Greeley's eyes widened.

'Saturday morning. Outside the Shelbourne. He was getting into a blue seven series BMW. I only got the year on the registration – 96-D. I thought – you know – I wasn't sure. It was just a glimpse. I asked at the hotel if they had a Mr Leslie there but they said they hadn't. He'll be using another name, of course. Then I saw the photofit and, well—'

He sat back with the palms of his hands outstretched, as if he were handing it all over.

Greeley had stubbed his cigarette out and was scribbling notes.

At last he was taking an interest.

Gallagher relaxed but his mouth felt dry. 'You think I could have a glass of water?'

'Sure.' Greeley stood and went to the door. 'How about a cup of coffee maybe?'

'No, water'll be fine.'

The Chief Superintendent left for a second and came back with a paper cup from a cooler. Gallagher sipped it and then remembered.

'So, how come you know so much about Leslie?'

'We keep in touch with things,' Greeley said, folding his arms and leaning on the desk. 'We're not the rednecks you think we are.'

'I never—'

Greeley waved his protest away. 'Let's just forget it.'

'You'll check all this, then. Find out about Leslie?'

'Of course.'

'Because if he's here,' he said, 'there's something very big going on. This man is major league. So what's he doing in

Dublin?' He sipped some more water. 'The girl – he's made a mistake there which will let you get to him. But Donovan – he was only a worm, for Christ sake. There has to be something else, something, I don't know—' he searched the yellowed ceiling for clues – 'something on an enormous scale if it has brought him here in person. It's got to—'

Jesus.

He had not considered the most obvious thing.

The realisation crawled over his skin.

He reached for the paper cup with a tremor in his hand. Greeley saw it.

There was a knock at the door and two uniformed officers came in.

'Ah, thanks, lads,' Greeley said and stood. 'These two gentlemen are going to take you home. One will drive you in your own car. I really don't think you should be driving it yourself, do you?'

Gallagher had become very quiet.

'Are you all right?'

Gallagher sipped the water and nodded but he could not speak because he was consumed with the thought that Gilbert Leslie had come to Dublin because of him.

Chapter Twenty-Nine

They buried Sinead Patterson in a tiny graveyard on the Inishowen peninsula. It was an afternoon full of birdsong; a day for living, not dying, Inspector Dolan thought.

He had come in part out of sympathy because he had felt her parents' grief like a wound, in part out of professional need so that he could cast an eye over the mourners and in part simply because it was Donegal.

Sinead had two sisters. They were younger, girls drained of tears, clutching their mother in mutual succour.

Damian Fox was there, thin in a black suit that billowed in the hillside breeze. Dolan saw Carmel the waitress holding a hat by the brim. They looked discomforted by the occasion and the unfamiliar environment, city folk uprooted temporarily.

Afterwards people told the Patterson family how sorry they were and then trickled away down the winding graveyard paths, leaving them with their depleted souls.

Those were the images which Dolan brought back with him to Dublin eventually, along with a reaffirmation of his love for the rough-hewn passionate beauty of the county in

313

which he had been born. He brought nothing at all which would help in solving Sinead Patterson's murder, other than the certainty that when they caught the man they were looking for and learned what happened that night it would cause those who loved her to grieve afresh.

When Gallagher's phone rang on Friday morning, it startled him.

It was almost as if its very tone had become more shrill, jangling nerves which were already on edge.

He was convinced that Gilbert Leslie's presence in Dublin had something to do with the fact that he was here, too. The paths of their past were so entwined, so much was left unfinished between them, that there had to be a connection.

But exactly how he fitted into Leslie's plans, whatever they were, and how it all linked to Sean Donovan and everything else that had happened he had no idea. Did Leslie want him dead? If so, then presumably there had been ample opportunity already – or was he waiting for some other moment?

There was one plus point: Leslie would not be aware that Gallagher had seen him.

Every time he left the apartment, he tried to find out if he was being followed, using techniques learned many years ago which would expose a watcher without revealing the discovery. But there was no one tailing him, nor was there anything strange about the cars parked in the vicinity of the apartment. He noted their numbers and movements as best he could.

On the table in his living-room were scattered half a

dozen pages of notes. On one sheet he had written the names of Marcus Kelly, Sean Donovan, Mr Justice Purcell, Gilbert Leslie, Sinead Patterson. Lines in thick marker linked them in different permutations like some molecular structure.

There were question marks, heavily underlined, but there were no answers.

He wondered how Greeley was progressing. Maybe this was him on the phone now.

'Hello?'

It was Emma.

'You're there,' she said. 'Make sure you're still there in twenty minutes. I'm coming to see you.'

Her voice was clipped, terse, and he wondered what was going on.

Then it came to him. Suddenly Barrett Greeley's face loomed in his thoughts and he understood why he had heard nothing.

She was as good as her word.

Twenty minutes later, a black Mercedes pulled up at the kerb and the Minister for Justice got out and strode up to his front door. He heard the bell and looked down from his window to see her standing there frowning into the wind gusting off the sea.

When she stepped into the apartment she stood for a second looking round. She had never been there before. A big bookcase and hard brown furniture. Words and wood. An old rug covering the floor.

She saw the notes strewn across the table, picked them up then let them fall again.

'Let me assume the reason for this visit,' he said. 'You

heard I've been to see Greeley again.'

She swung round to face him. 'This business with you and this man Gilbert Leslie. The Commissioner's been to see me. He told me that you went to visit Chief Superintendent Greeley at Harcourt Square the other night, that you were drunk and that you came out with some cock and bull story that it was Gilbert Leslie who killed the girl at Temple Bar and that you'd actually seen him coming out of the Shelbourne.'

Her expression was incredulous.

'It's not a cock and bull story at all,' he protested. 'It's true. Greeley was very interested in what I had to tell him. He knew a lot about Leslie, too, which I have to say surprised me.'

He felt angry and confused.

'He knew about Leslie,' Emma explained with slow sarcasm, 'because after your last encounter with him he did some digging of his own into your background. As a result he was able to find out the reason for your leaving the FBI, your mental breakdown, and the whole history of your – *interest* – in Mr Leslie.'

By *interest* she really meant *obsession*. That was clear.

'That prick.'

She laughed. 'Call him whatever you like, he's only doing his job. In all fairness to him he did actually check everything you told him, including the murder of that girl in Miami, although he's still waiting to hear more from the police there.'

She stood right in front of him and looked hard into his eyes. 'But you didn't see Gilbert Leslie. You just didn't. You hear me? A guy like Leslie – you know he's the sort of person your people would keep an eye on. That's why I can tell you, totally reliably, that Gilbert Leslie is on holiday at Palm Beach in Florida and has been for a couple of weeks.'

She paused and watched her information sink in.

'Now will you get off this thing,' she said.

'It can't be true.'

'But it is. It is true, god damn it. Several police forces and the FBI have confirmed it. What more do you need?'

He got up and walked towards the window, as though moving away from her would change everything.

'You've got to think about what you're doing,' she said. 'This thing with Sean Donovan – it hasn't been good for you.'

He glared. 'What – you think I'm nuts? Imagining things?'

First Kate, now Emma.

'No, I think you made a mistake. You saw someone who reminded you of Gilbert Leslie and your imagination went into overdrive. I suppose that's understandable, considering everything that happened in the past, but you've got to try to take a hold of yourself.'

She paused.

'Let me put it another way.' She put her hand on her chest. 'It's all a bit embarrassing. The Commissioner, Chief Superintendent Greeley – these are busy people with a lot of responsibilities. So am I. When my father starts getting drunk and getting in the way, it creates big difficulties for me.'

'Drunk and getting in the way?' It stung him. He turned to the window again. 'I know what I saw,' he said.

His defiance detonated a small charge in her.

'Okay, I've done my best now but I'm telling you. Keep out of it.'

He swung round. 'He's here. Believe me.'

'Don't you listen? No, of course you don't, what am I talking about. It won't matter what I say. You've done nothing but screw things up for me – the – the article in the paper, then the whole bloody stupidity of visiting Sean Donovan and now this. That's a hell of a list of accidents, you know. You couldn't do better if you tried.'

The emotion welled in her. The first tears were waiting to spring free but she was damned if she was going to let them. The words would be enough and they were tumbling downhill in an avalanche.

'What's your plan – because I won't let you into my life you've decided to ruin it for me? Are you jealous, by any chance? That I'm making something of myself without your assistance? Mr fucking big shot FBI-man who wrecked his own life with his damned obsessions and his uncontrollable ego?'

It had been waiting a long time but it was out now.

'No more chances,' she said, pointing an angry finger. 'Any more of this stuff and I'll make sure they do you for wasting police time.'

She stormed out of the apartment and slammed the door. Just outside, she took a tissue from her pocket and dried her eyes. She stood in the downstairs hall for a full minute. By the time she got out to the car she had recovered herself.

Chapter Thirty

Dermot Davis found it hard to believe how easy it was. He thought he had set himself an impossible task, following Vinnie Dwyer's movements night and day, but it had not been difficult at all and since the time the big car had collected Dwyer in the street and whisked him away somewhere it had been even more of a piece of cake.

The fact was – Vinnie hardly went anywhere now. He had made a trip into the city centre to meet someone in a McDonald's that Saturday morning but apart from that he had not strayed beyond a half-mile radius of his flat.

Dermot could have sat an exam on the subject of Vinnie Dwyer's day.

Vinnie came out of the front door of the flat at about one and went into the video shop to return last night's viewing. Then he turned left, down the street to the corner shop, and came back with a bag of groceries and a racing paper.

He stayed at home for about an hour before emerging again. This time he turned right, to the bookmaker's. The rest of the afternoon he spent alternating between the

319

bookie's and the pub next door to it. At about six, sometimes with winnings in his pocket, sometimes not, he would return to the video shop to make his evening selection before wandering into a Chinese takeaway and coming out with a carrier bag containing his supper.

Once, Dermot had drifted into the bookmaker's himself and placed a bet, seeing Vinnie studying the racing pages and the TV screen and being greeted like a local hero by most of the people who passed his way.

Dermot's horse lost. Not a day for an outsider.

On another occasion, he had almost gone to pieces when Vinnie himself had come into the greasy spoon from where Dermot carried out his surveillance. He had sworn the game was up, that Vinnie knew everything and had come for him. But all the man wanted was chips and a hamburger which he ate at a table behind where Dermot sat and imagined he could feel Vinnie's eyes boring into his back.

At night, Vinnie stayed home, alone mostly, but sometimes people came to call. Some of his cronies from the New Western Inn stopped by with packs of beer and one night two young women came in a taxi.

It had got to the stage where Dermot felt he did not have to watch the flat all the time and that he could predict where Vinnie would be at a given moment. Yet he felt certain, too, that his quarry's dismally boring routine would not last forever. Sooner, rather than later, it would change.

He would have to act before then.

There was also the question of how much longer he could use the café as a vantage point. No one bothered about a motorcycle courier dropping in from time to time but they noticed if he sat there for hours. So Dermot was forced to spend a lot of time on the move.

That had additional advantages. It had allowed him to develop a series of circuits of the surrounding area which took him past Vinnie's front door every twenty minutes and gave him a range of alternative routes from which he could choose when the day came.

And it would be day, he had decided. He would not do it at night.

He restricted his visits to the café to a cup of tea in the morning and the afternoon and sausage and chips at lunchtime, although that still gave him a problem. A couple of real motorcycle messengers were using the place, nodding to him when they came in, and he had noticed them talking about him to the staff. The couriers all knew each other but they had not recognised this member of the species, in spite of his familiar plumage. They had radio receivers, too, squawking intermittently as they ate, and Dermot felt conspicuous in his own uninterrupted silence.

It was time he made his move.

He was meeting a man tonight, in a pub near his dingy hotel. He had found out from the old soak who ran the place which bar was most likely to be used by the criminal fraternity, although in this area he could just as easily have gone out into the street and thrown a stone at random. It would almost certainly have hit somebody who had done time for something.

He had been to the recommended pub a couple of times, cultivating one of the barmen to whom he had given £50 by way of a calling card and a request to pass the word that there was something he was looking for.

As a result, two nights ago, he had met someone. A getting-to-know-you session to make sure that neither was a cop.

Dermot told him what he needed, that it had to be the right size because of where it had to fit, but he did not say why he wanted it, nor was the question asked.

He knew that he had been followed back to his hotel afterwards but they would not have been able to tail him when he went out again in the morning because he took a route which would have shaken anyone off.

When he returned in the evening he discovered that someone had been through his room.

'Did you see your friends?' his drunken landlord asked him. 'They came knocking your door this morning.'

There had not been much in the room for them to search and they would not have found the money; it was in a luggage locker at the central bus station.

He would need some of it tonight so that he could make his final purchase.

He hoped he had passed the test.

Gallagher was running out of friends and places to turn.

Kate, Emma, Greeley.

Greeley? He had never been a friend; what was he talking about. But for one gloriously hopeful moment Gallagher had believed he was an ally, ready to fight his battles with him.

He felt alone and adrift yet still stubbornly certain that he was right.

You could also be cracking up, like everyone thinks you are.

True – but he gave himself some reassurance with the notion that if that thought had occurred to him, then there was probably nothing to worry about.

That made him smile.

Nothing to worry about.

The things Emma had said.

She had wounded him deeply. He could not even turn to Kate for solace now.

Instead, he concentrated his thoughts on Gilbert Leslie. He had done things alone and against the odds before and here he was doing it again.

The first thing was to shove out of his mind all this stuff Emma had told him about Leslie being at Palm Beach. That had to be a mistake and somehow he would prove it, although if the police were not going to look for Leslie, then he certainly did not have the resources to do so himself.

What he could do was try to work out what Leslie was up to.

To that end, he could pace around the apartment talking to himself and writing things on pieces of paper, an exercise which he reckoned had gone about as far as it could, or he could try and talk to someone else.

The person he had in mind was a bit of a forlorn hope but that was the only kind of hope he had left.

Chapter Thirty-One

Just after noon on Sunday, Gallagher waited in the lobby of the big golf hotel at Portmarnock, north of Dublin along the curve of the coast.

He sat with a small pot of coffee at a table by a window, looking over the folds of the links at the little knots of golfers dotted far away in blobs of colour. To the south, shimmering slightly in the heat haze that rose from the course, were the twin chimneys of the power station which he was used to seeing much closer at hand from the windows of his apartment.

He drank his coffee and waited.

It said something for Eamon Savage that he had agreed to meet him at all. The name Gallagher would not be one to bring him joy unconfined whenever he heard it.

Savage lived at Malahide, not far from Portmarnock, and through Alan Warnock Gallagher had obtained his ex-directory phone number.

Warnock had been beside himself with curiosity.

'Eamon Savage? You want Eamon Savage's number? First you ask me about Kelly and now you want to talk to Eamon Savage? Jesus, Tom, what's going on?'

324

'Alan, honestly, I can't tell you. I just need to talk to him about something. Please bear with me. I promise I'll fill you in on it when I can. Give me a day or two.'

He had left a message on Savage's answering machine on Friday evening and had given up all hope of hearing from him when to his surprise Savage had called last night, wondering a little brusquely what Gallagher wanted. Gallagher had been enigmatic and reluctant to talk on an open phone line but had used words like *important* and *urgent* and he had a slightly embarrassing feeling that he might even have referred to *a matter of life and death* at one point.

However he had achieved it, he had managed to entice this appointment out of him. He looked round the lobby. He was its sole occupant, apart from a couple of young women behind the reception desk. It was spacious, with comfortable settees in soft tartan fabrics. Bright sunlight beamed down from a glass ceiling onto a marble floor.

Yet it was still the lobby. Elsewhere in the hotel, there were other places, bars and lounges perhaps more private, but Gallagher had a feeling that in choosing to meet here, Savage was keeping him at arm's length.

A man in a pink jumper was teeing off. A rather poor drive, Gallagher thought, although he was no expert himself. He had tried golf once, many years ago, but because he was not instantly and instinctively good at it, he had abandoned it as a waste of time. In his life he had never had room for half-hearted pursuits.

Doubt clenched itself like a fist in his stomach.

On the way in the car, he had rehearsed what he was going to say but as he had outlined it in his head it had seemed less and less convincing, even to him. What was it going to sound like to anyone else – the ramblings of a fruitcake, which is what other people considered he was, his daughter included? Kate, too, probably.

However, he was certain Savage would at least listen since some of the events he wanted to talk about had been instrumental in ending his Ministerial career. How he might respond was another matter.

'You must be Mr Gallagher.'

He had been so wrapped up in his thoughts that he had not noticed Savage approach. He looked up to see a large bulky man in a yellow Pringle sweater assessing him cautiously. There was a young woman with him.

Gallagher stood.

'Yes – sorry – I was miles away.'

The woman was heavy-set. She wore glasses and her father's gaze. Savage did not attempt to introduce her.

'I'll give you ten minutes,' he said. 'My daughter and I have to be somewhere at one o'clock.'

'I'll bring the car round and wait for you,' she said and strode away without any acknowledgement of Gallagher's presence. He was in enemy territory.

Savage sat.

'Can I get you anything? Coffee or a drink?' Gallagher asked him.

'No, nothing. Let's hear what it is you have to tell me.'

'First,' Gallagher said, 'I really appreciate the fact that you've agreed to see me. I thought—'

Savage interrupted him with a gesture of his hand. 'I agreed to see you out of curiosity as much as anything else. Your call to me was, to say the least, unexpected and the conversation last night was bizarre.'

'Let me try to explain a little about myself first,' Gallagher said.

'Don't bother. I'm well aware of your background. It came up when your daughter's name was being put forward as my junior Minister.'

Gallagher looked at him and wondered how much he knew, whether that meant all of it, but Savage's face gave no indication.

'What you could explain,' Savage said, 'is why you've come to *me*. I'd have thought you'd have been more likely to speak to your daughter or the police about *matters of life and death*, as you put it so melodramatically last night.'

'I did – without a great deal of success. The police think I'm bananas and my daughter thinks I'm a menace.'

Savage raised his eyebrows, surprised and a little amused by Gallagher's candour.

'Well, then, we'd better see which of those I opt for, hadn't we?'

'Okay,' Gallagher said and began. He told Savage first of all about Gilbert Leslie, a few sentences that encapsulated a lifetime of crime but could not do justice to Leslie's eminence in that world. Then he outlined his belief that Leslie was the man responsible for the Temple Bar murder.

He told him about Sean Donovan and Donovan's story that someone from New York was involved in a conspiracy to finish him off. He told him about going to Barrett Greeley and about his disagreement with Emma.

He hesitated momentarily. 'I should also tell you,' he said, 'that when Greeley's people checked on Leslie's current whereabouts they were informed that he was still in the United States. On vacation in Palm Beach, to be exact.'

'So this could all be bollocks then?' Savage said. 'Just your imagination – and a complete waste of my time?'

Gallagher shook his head. 'It's not. Leslie's here – I know it. No matter what they say.'

Savage opened his arms out in a gesture of submission. 'Well, I don't see how I can help you.'

'I need to find out what has brought him here and where I fit into it. We go back, Mr Leslie and I. I find it hard to believe he could be in Ireland without there being some connection with me. And I need to know what the big game plan is.'

Savage's daughter was walking across the floor of the lobby. She stopped and tapped the face of her watch and he nodded.

'Just another couple of minutes. I won't be long.'

When she had gone, Gallagher continued, talking quickly. 'Leslie's not here because of some pissy little local Dublin drugs war. This is a guy who plays a bigger game. He's like a – a chief adviser to the President of IBM or somebody. Everything that's happened – all the murders – Marcus Kelly, the judge – they're all linked to him in some way and I've got to find out how. I thought that from your perspective in the Justice Department, having your finger on the pulse of this place, you might be able to give me some idea of what a criminal like him might want here.'

Savage examined him from under his brows. 'Not to mention the fact that I'm also one of the few people you can approach without running the risk of it all getting back to your daughter, I suppose. Am I right?'

Gallagher gave a reluctant nod.

'You've never been able to shake this man, have you?' Savage said.

'I don't understand what—'

'I said I knew about your background. I do – all of it. When your daughter was being appointed I had some of my people make inquiries. I know about your breakdown and the cause of it.' He levelled his gaze. 'Your former colleagues in the FBI were very helpful. They left nothing out.'

'I see,' Gallagher said. He felt as if he had been frisked and something incriminating had been found on him.

A waiter came to the table and put down a saucer containing the bill.

'I really don't think I can be of much assistance to you, Mr Gallagher,' Savage said. 'Let's look at what you've told me. For once, though it pains me to say it, I agree with your daughter. You've got nothing to go on but the mutterings of a vicious criminal, now deceased, and a glimpse of a man who looked for a moment like this Gilbert Leslie – the same Gilbert Leslie who is reliably reported to be still in the United States.'

He gave Gallagher a look that was an appeal to his good sense.

'I think you should leave all this to the police,' he said. 'Go home. Take things easy.'

Gallagher threw some coins into the saucer. 'Don't patronise me,' he muttered.

'Okay, then, I won't.' Savage leaned back in his seat. 'So let me tell you something. If I thought for a moment that there was anything more substantial in this, not just a whole load of supposition and your own – shall we say – *preoccupation* – then I would be very interested indeed. And I would be interested for one simple reason – namely the possibility that there might be an opportunity in this to discredit your daughter.'

Gallagher bristled with resentment. She was still his daughter. But he said nothing.

'For a politician,' Savage went on, 'I've always been rather bad at the actual politics. I got involved because of a genuine belief in doing things for the good of the country.'

'Very noble of you.'

Savage side-stepped the sarcasm. 'Naïve, maybe, but there you are. I believe in appointing people on merit, because they have ability, not because they're sycophants or because they toe the party line. I chose your daughter as a junior Minister because she was the right person for the job. If I'd followed my own personal prejudices – been a little less *noble* – she'd still be on the back benches. For a start, I don't particularly like her and secondly I chose her in spite of the fact that she was being pushed in my direction by that bastard Tony Goulding.'

From the microphone behind the desk, one of the receptionists paged someone. Her voice sprang from a speaker on the wall above their table and Savage waited until she had finished.

'From the day and hour she was appointed, she made no secret of the fact that she wanted my job. Damn it, at meetings in my office I could practically see her looking round the room and working out how she was going to decorate it when the time came. Well, she can do what she likes with it now – I've got a feeling she won't be there very long.'

'What makes you say that?'

'Our party's not going to win the next election – no way. All that stuff she's been doing to throw dirt at the Opposition – it won't work in the long run. People will want a change. Apart from that, now that she's got the job, she'll realise more than ever that she's only there to do Goulding's bidding.'

Gallagher frowned.

'It was Goulding who persuaded your daughter to get into politics,' Savage explained.

'I knew that – yes.'

'But he doesn't do things out of any sense of philanthropic duty, let me assure you. He buys people, he owns them, and sooner or later he calls in the favour. And if the debt isn't paid in full, then—'

He made a slicing motion across his throat.

'The streets are littered with former Ministers and others who fell foul of him. Most of the current Cabinet are his poodles, one way or another. I was never one of those but your daughter will make up for that. Let's see how she does.'

He slapped his thighs, then stood up to go. A smile flickered.

'You know, Mr Gallagher, if I was as immersed in conspiracy theories as you appear to be—'

He paused for a moment and then shook his head to dispel whatever notion had just crept into it.

'Good day to you,' he said, then turned and walked away.

When he had gone, Gallagher had the curious sensation that they had scratched the surface of something important. But he had no idea what it was. The feeling stayed with him until his phone rang later that afternoon. It was Fergal Mulryne, with something else for him to think about.

Chapter Thirty-Two

W ithout knowing it, his mother had given him the
idea.

He changed out of his school uniform first and then
started to look through the papers on the desk in her study.
She would not get home for hours and by the time she did
he hoped to be in the city.

If he found what he was searching for.

Over tea last night she had mentioned it, thinking he
would be interested because it involved computers. It was
in some paperwork which she had brought home: a letter
about a snap survey being carried out on behalf of *Bord
Failte*, the Irish tourist board.

'They do these all the time,' she said. 'Pay a fortune to
consultants to carry out research for them. You should
maybe think of something like that after university, joining
one of the big firms. The money would be good and you
would enjoy it.'

She had shown him the letter. *Bord Failte* had sent it to all
Dublin travel agencies as a matter of information. Hotels in
the city were participating in what was known as a survey of
travellers, logging details of people staying with them in a

two-week period that included St Patrick's Day. The information would include nationality, length of stay, onward
destination, if known. The data would be collated by a
consultancy firm who would try to assess what it told them
about Dublin as a popular St Patrick's holiday venue.

She might have brought the letter to work with her this
morning.

No, there it was.

He photocopied it on the fax machine, then shoved the
copy in his pocket and ran out of the house towards the
bus stop.

He was certain Tom was on to something. Perhaps all
the more so because his mother was so sceptical. Okay, so
he had been ill once, a long time ago, but there was no way
he would start simply imagining things, conjuring visions
out of thin air.

The office where the magazine *Dave* was produced was
on the second floor of a thin three-storey Georgian building in South William Street, the heart of Dublin's garment
district. At street level, up a short set of worn granite steps,
there was a shop run by the wife of the DJ who owned the
magazine and it specialised in women's fashion that was
avant-garde and not for the faint-hearted. On the top floor,
behind a frosted glass door, an ancient bespoke tailor
carried out their alterations as he had done for previous
tenants through fifty years of *haute couture* trends that had
been and gone and come back again.

Paul opened the office door. Urgent electronic music
hammered the air but he paid no heed to it. As always, the
place was an untidy shambles where people came to hang
out, which was how he had first become involved himself.

No one seemed to mind them coming in to drink the coffee, use the phone or listen to new CDs.

He said hello to a couple of people and stood around, watching for a computer terminal to become free. He could have used the one at home, of course, but somehow he felt this would be safer.

He sat down in front of the screen.

He did not waste time trying to get into the Shelbourne. It had an e-mail address but he knew its system would be largely an internal one, perhaps linked to the hotel's parent company, the Meridien group, although with little room for access.

The consultancy firm was the way to do it. Cracking its computer security would be relatively simple for someone with his skills and ingenuity. He set up a couple of hops to cover his tracks and soon he was in.

At first he was dismayed to find that most of the hotels had provided their returns by group but then he saw that certain significant Dublin establishments had a section of their own. The Shelbourne was among them.

The sighting of Leslie had been on a Saturday. Paul had the correct date. He also estimated that Gallagher would have been there somewhere around twelve noon.

He scrolled at speed through the lists in front of him. He wanted to do this quickly in case somebody came along and asked him what he was doing.

There it was. The Shelbourne's file.

Once inside he proceeded more slowly. There was a whole lot of stuff in which he had no interest. It was names he was looking for.

There were three Saturday departures between 11 and

12. Two of them were women, French. The third was a man called Schenk with an address in Toronto.

There was no one by the name of Leslie. The receptionist had been telling the truth.

He clicked on the upward arrow and went back.

Mr G. Schenk. Could this be him?

Sifting through the rest of the data, he found that this Mr Schenk had registered just before St Patrick's Day, ten days or so previously. A long stay.

Detail. His fingers clicked on the keyboard and the mouse. He needed more information.

Here we go.

The booking had been made by telephone and a Visa card bearing the name Gerd Schenk had been used. The call had been from a number in the United States, not Canada, as he might have expected. There was an area code, a number and a telephone extension – 2740.

He could feel a pulse beating in his temple. He turned to the throbbing room that he had managed to ignore until now.

'Phone book. Where's the phone book?'

He spoke to no one in particular and no one answered him amid the noise. He got up from his seat and shuffled through a pile of discarded newspapers and magazines until he found it.

'Hey, are you going to surf that bloody net all day?' someone asked. 'Other people might want to use the thing, you know.'

'Hold on,' Paul said, 'nearly finished.' He downloaded the information and then closed down.

There was a room off this one where it was quieter. It

was normally used by Max but he was not in today. It was no tidier but there was a phone and he shut the door to keep the noise low.

From the directory he discovered that the area code, 804, was for Virginia. He checked his watch. Five pm in Dublin. That would make it noon over there.

He thought. First he programmed the *withhold* facility so that no one could detect his number and ring back. Then he dialled.

It rang four times, long American warbling rings that seemed to add to his excitement, and then a woman's recorded voice said: 'This is the Foundation Bank of Richmond. If you are calling from a touch-tone phone you may enter the extension you require at any time.'

Foundation Bank – what was that? He hesitated for a second and then he pressed the numbers. 2 – 7 – 4 – 0.

He waited. The extension rang. Once. Twice.

'Yes?'

It was a male voice, unwelcoming.

Paul said nothing. He stood there in silence, trying not to let his breathing be heard by a man on the other side of the Atlantic.

'Hello. Is someone there?' the voice said.

Would he hear from the sound of the line that this was long distance? Paul rang off hastily and stood beside the phone with his beating heart.

What the hell was he playing at? Jesus, what on earth would he have said to that man, some guy in a bank somewhere in America?

What was the Foundation Bank of Richmond? He had never heard of it although he was well aware that the

United States was littered with obscure little banks of one kind or another. Did Schenk work there?

It would be a hard nut to crack; bank security always was. It was possible that he was capable himself but he was sensible enough to recognise that there were hackers out there who were much more proficient and better equipped than he was.

There was one in particular who might help.

He went back out to the main office and waited impatiently for a computer to become available. Larry was using the one he had been on before. He was a part-timer like Paul and he looked after what they laughingly described as filing.

'Larry, I really need that thing,' he said.

'Keep your hair on. Christ, this Manchester United web page is fucking brilliant. Have you seen it?'

'Larry, there's something I've got to do for Max.'

'Sure he's not here.'

'Larry – please.'

He got up. 'What's so bloody important anyway?' he grumbled.

Paul sat down. The net would have the answer, as it always did. He chose a search facility and went to the menu of chat rooms.

It was there that galaxies of specialised interests, many of them weird and not so wonderful, met to exchange information on the subject of their choice or just while away the hours talking nonsense. You could not take part without registering and providing a brief profile of yourself although it was a useless exercise since no one ever revealed their real name and hardly anyone ever told the truth. A quick analysis would have revealed a proliferation of seventeen-year-old blondes from California. In reality, they were most likely to be post-adolescent male loners of uncertain sexual enthusiasms.

Dave was the name Paul had picked for himself some time ago. It was a comparatively ordinary pseudonym. The person he was looking for was called *Gigolo*, a man, he supposed, although that was certainly not guaranteed.

He scrolled down the list of the thousand or so users. Some of them did not have a recognisable pseudonym at all. They were people from a world where letters and numbers were interchanged. They had adopted aliases which were unfathomable and often unpronounceable and in which the letter X was positioned regularly like a road block.

With such a cast of characters, it was not surprising that what they had to say often contained little clarity either. Their conversations seemed to be without context, swirling aimlessly in an invisible pool where normal thought progression had no place and where a mutant sub-language had evolved.

Paul found Gigolo's name quickly but there was nothing against it to indicate which room he was using. It meant he had not logged on.

Not surprisingly, there were several rooms for computer buffs. Paul found the most likely one, where he and Gigolo had conversed before, and went in. Down the right-hand side of his screen he could see the names of ten users who were already there. A heated conversation was under way with capital letters being used as artillery fire and punctuation marks flying around like shrapnel.

He was reluctant to get involved but he needed to leave a message in the hope that someone would pass it on if Gigolo made an appearance during the night – or was it day in his part of the hemisphere?

He had no other way of making contact. It was a strange quirk that in an age of greater world communication than ever before, with access to all sorts of information available in an instant, many of those most skilled in the technology were people who were obsessive about privacy and anonymity.

He began to type.

I need to talk to Gigolo.

Has he been heard from today?

Someone called Baltha4U replied.

HELLO, DAVE. NO GIGOLO. ANYTHING YOU WANT TO TALK ABOUT TO ANYONE ELSE? HOT CROSS IS HERE. VIPER, TOO. AND ME.

They were all nutters, Paul reckoned.

Don't think so. Spread the word.

Dave wants to talk to Gigolo. Same time tomorrow.

He left the room and logged off. The screens that the others saw, wherever they were in the world, would show that he had done so.

He had chatted to Gigolo many times before. He did not know his real identity, just that he lived in New York City, the only personal snippet Gigolo had ever revealed. Of course, even that might not be true.

Gigolo was one of an elite band of *supernerds* who specialised in hacking into apparently impregnable computer systems. They had no desire to obtain the secrets within: just the need to prove that no doors were barred to them.

Very few were. Gigolo might like a new challenge.

The following afternoon, when Paul told him about his interest in the Foundation Bank of Richmond, he accepted it.

Chapter Thirty-Three

Fergal Mulryne had taken on the role of peacemaker.

'Can I come and see you?' he had asked when he phoned Gallagher. 'I think it's important that we talk.'

He had arrived later in the afternoon, a maroon Daimler pulling up soundlessly outside the apartment building. He had stood in Gallagher's living room in an exquisite pure wool jumper and dark slacks. 'Very cosy,' he said, looking around. 'Very compact.' He walked to the window. 'And what a wonderful view.'

Gallagher had poured wine for them both and waited.

'I'm worried about Emma,' Mulryne had said. 'This row that the two of you have had—'

Gallagher raised an eyebrow.

Mulryne lifted a hand in reassurance. 'Now I've no idea what it was about – she didn't go into that – but I know that she's been deeply upset by it. Tell me it's none of my business if you want but here goes – I think it's awful the way the two of you seem to be pulling each other apart and I just can't stand by and watch it happen. I want to do something to stop it.'

Gallagher saw concern and determination in his eyes

so he decided to level with him.

'I've tried to get closer to her,' he confessed. 'It just doesn't work. Circumstances – things have happened – that have made matters worse.'

'Look, I know she feels bitter about a lot of things but, frankly, life's too short. Now there's something coming up. I've decided to have a drinks party this week, very small and very discreet, to mark Emma's appointment. I don't want to make it a big celebration. Because of the way it's all come about, I don't think anything conspicuous and ostentatious would be a good idea. So I'm having a small get-together, just a few friends, at my house. And you'd be doing *me* a big favour if you'd come along.'

'Does Emma know you're inviting me?'

'Not yet.'

'She won't want me there.'

'Let me handle that. I guarantee you'll be made welcome. What do you say?'

'I'll think about it. Can I let you know?'

Mulryne had given him his private number. And after he had gone, Gallagher, with no one else to turn to, had called Kate.

She listened patiently.

'Well, that's progress,' she said. 'Mulryne would seem to have his heart in the right place.'

'I don't know that I can go. Do you think I should?'

'Of course. You must do everything you can to make things up between you and your daughter – no matter what she's said to you.'

'But what if there's some sort of a scene when I get there?'

'Don't be ridiculous. There won't be any scene. Tom, she's your only daughter, for heaven's sake. You should give it every chance. And what will it look like if you don't go? What if the papers get hold of it somehow and write that you snubbed her?'

He was not convinced. 'I'm not sure.'

She paused and made up her mind. 'Listen, will you go if I come with you?'

He parked outside her house in Ranelagh, admitting to himself that maybe the real reason he had said he might not go was so that she would volunteer to accompany him.

She opened the door, elegant in a silk suit and pearl choker, and he saw in her cool gaze that she had been thinking the same thing.

'I'll just get my bag,' she said as he stepped into the hall. On a table there was a huge vase of spring flowers, filling the space with fragrance and colour. She lifted a card sitting beside it and popped it into her bag.

'They're beautiful,' he said. 'A secret admirer?'

'No,' she told him, snapping the bag shut, 'I just thought I'd brighten the place up. Now – shall we go?'

The spring evening sunlight was warm and confident, turning the wooded hillsides a vibrant green, but in spite of this the drive to Wicklow was tense, their conversation minimal. Kate became a little tetchy when Gallagher took a few wrong turnings before finding the correct one.

Mulryne's house could not be seen from the road. You turned first through the electrically operated gates, which lay open and welcoming on this occasion, and then made your way along a tree-lined avenue. As he drove, Gallagher thought he glimpsed deer in the woodland to his right. Soon the trees were replaced by sweeping lawns, beyond which the house stood, a haughty piece of colonialism, white and pillared.

They were not the first people to arrive. Other cars were already parked to the side, none of them as modest as Gallagher's diminutive Renault.

There were two attendants. He gave his keys to one of them and then he and Kate walked up the steps to the front door. He noticed that there were security cameras in key positions.

At the top, he paused and turned to look at the view. Another car was coming up the drive.

It was a deep blue seven series BMW.

'Tom! Great to see you. And this must be Kate.'

Gallagher had to turn towards his host. Mulryne was in a light linen suit. He shook his hand and found himself being led into the house without having a chance to look back again.

That car?

Emma stood waiting in the big open hall, a glass nestling in her grasp and an uncertainty in her eyes that matched his own. Gallagher could see that Mulryne would have had to use all his powers of persuasion. She nodded to him, then switched her attention to Kate.

Behind him, he could hear Mulryne greeting the driver of the BMW.

'George! Good man. Glad you could make it.'

Gallagher turned. Before him he saw a slim man with thin black hair curling long into a froth at the back of his neck.

For a second he thought he was actually going to lose his balance.

With a slightly quizzical nod, the newcomer acknowledged his obvious interest and then walked on into the house. Gallagher struggled with his composure. He felt his mouth dry, his hands moist. Emma had taken Kate off and was introducing her to someone. He was alone.

Mulryne appeared at his elbow. 'God, Tom, no one's looking after you,' he said with urgent concern. 'Let's get you a drink.'

He put his arm round Gallagher's shoulders and led him through the hall and into an enormous drawing room where people were standing in little clutches. High in a corner he saw a flashing red sensor and the tiny lens of another security camera. The furniture in the room was exquisite, even to his untutored eye, and on the walls there was a fine array of Irish landscapes.

Mulryne waved and a waiter came forward.

'What will it be?'

'Whiskey.'

'We've got Scotch, Irish, single malt—' the waiter began.

'Anything.'

'So glad you came,' Mulryne whispered eagerly to him. 'You were right. She was difficult to convince. But you're here now and that's a start. And your friend, Kate. Lovely woman.'

Gallagher's whiskey arrived and as he drank he looked around the room.

Somewhere in this house was the man who had driven Gilbert Leslie from the Shelbourne? Why was he here? Who was he?

There was a familiar face in conversation in a group

round the fireplace. Mulryne saw him looking.

'Tony Goulding, the deputy Prime Minister,' he said. 'I'll introduce you.'

Goulding levered himself away from the mantelpiece and shook Gallagher's hand with enthusiasm.

'So you're the man we have to thank.'

'I'm sorry?'

'For producing such a wonderful daughter.'

'Oh, I see.'

'She's quite brilliant. I'm sure you must be very proud.'

'Of course,' he said. 'I hope that she—'

His attention was suddenly elsewhere. The BMW driver had come into view again, standing in the doorway with a glass of wine.

Gallagher realised that he had not finished what he was saying and that Goulding and the others were staring at him.

'I'm sorry,' he said. 'You'll excuse me for a moment. You've reminded me that there's something I forget to tell her.'

He moved off and the men resumed their conversation. Gallagher found Mulryne.

'Fergal,' he said, as casually as he could. 'That man over there at the door. For some reason his face is familiar to me but I'm not sure why.'

Mulryne looked.

'Where? Oh, George? That's George Levy,' he said. 'He's an accountant. As a matter of fact, he's your daughter's accountant. Maybe that's how you know him.'

George Levy. Why did the name ring a bell?

And then he remembered.

Mulryne was still talking but there was a roaring in Gallagher's ears which practically blocked out any other sound.

George Levy. The third director of Marcuscreen, Marcus Kelly's company.

As he began to absorb the implications, he felt as if the room were spinning away from him. This man was linked to Kelly and he was linked to Leslie. And now? Now there was a connection with Emma, too. He saw at once where she must have got the information about Kelly's investigations with which she had so shocked the *Dail*.

Once more he could hear Sean Donovan's words echoing in his head.

First you create the problem and then you solve it.

Find out who benefits, who's to gain.

He felt ill. Mulryne had gone into circulation again and he was by himself. Somehow, a little unsteadily, he made his way through the open downstairs rooms and out to a terrace at the back. A couple stood talking and hardly noticed him. They had rested their glasses on a wrought-iron table and the sun had turned the wine in them to liquid gold.

Gallagher rounded a corner of the house, away from their view, and vomited into a bed of roses. When he had wiped his eyes and blown his nose, he made his way gingerly to a garden seat a few yards away and slumped down on it, trying to get a grip on what it all meant.

A new picture, bleak and distressing, spread itself before him on the gently cascading lawns. He thought of the murders which had taken place. Kelly, Donovan, the judge – and a policeman who had got in the way – all of them part of a plan concocted by Gilbert Leslie.

And sipping from this poisonous brew was his own daughter? Could that possibly be true?

First create the problem. It was Donovan who had been created as the problem, sponsored and encouraged by figures from abroad, acting, Gallagher had no doubt, on Leslie's instructions. Kelly had been given the task of turning Donovan into a monstrous criminal creature. The murder of Kelly himself and then of the judge had secured Donovan in that role.

Once created, the problem had then been solved by Donovan's death, which Emma had been swift to suggest would mark the end of the crisis and herald her own arrival on the scene to set the world to rights.

He felt a sudden chill.

Who's to gain? Who had gained more from what had happened than she had, rising meteorically to one of the most important offices in the land?

But ultimately it was Gilbert Leslie who would benefit; that was certain. How he would do so, what complex and lucrative scheme was at the root of all this, was another question.

He looked at his watch. He had been out here for twenty minutes and they would be wondering where he was. He felt like walking off towards the trees, getting as far away as possible from everyone and everything. Instead, with legs that felt leaden, he walked back towards the house.

In the drawing-room, Goulding was still engrossed over by the mantelpiece and, seeing him, the meeting with Eamon Savage came into Gallagher's mind. Goulding had been Emma's most ardent supporter. Was he involved in this, too? Savage had been certain that Goulding had secured Emma's appointment for a purpose. So what was it that she could deliver?

Kate and Emma were walking across the room to him.

'There you are,' Kate said. 'We didn't know where you'd disappeared to.'

'Sorry. I was feeling a bit under the weather so I went outside for some air.'

'You look a bit pale,' Emma said.

'I could be better,' he said, avoiding her eyes. He turned to Kate. 'I think maybe I should go home, if you don't mind.'

'Whatever you think. Will you be all right?'

'Just a bit of a bug, that's all. It'll pass.'

Emma went to find Mulryne.

'Hope you'll be all right, Tom,' he said with an anxious look. 'Is there anything I can get you?'

'No, I'll go home and go to bed. Shake this thing off. It's been working on me for a couple of days, whatever it is.'

Their car was brought round to the front door and they said their goodbyes.

'There's one thing,' Gallagher said, turning to Emma, 'something I almost forgot to ask you. That day in the *Dail* – the photographs in your folder – they weren't anything to do with what Kelly was digging into at all, were they? It was a bluff, wasn't it?'

She gave a coy smile.

'I just happened to have a couple of glossies of office interiors I thought I might be interested in. It's amazing the conclusion some people will jump to, don't you think?'

The sunlight was mellowing as they drove home. In his

mind, clouds were gathering. Along the way, Kate offered to drive but he said no.

When they got to Ranelagh, he stopped and sat staring straight ahead. There was a deadness in his eyes that disturbed her.

'Tom,' she said. 'Have you thought of seeing a doctor again?'

She waited but he said nothing.

She got out of the car and when the door closed he drove off without another word.

Chapter Thirty-Four

The sound of the door buzzer woke Gigolo. He sat up and snatched his watch from the table beside the bed and saw that he had slept in.

'Shit,' he said. His mouth was sticky with slumber. He ran his hands through his confusion of black hair and then scratched the stubble on his chin. He had arranged to meet a couple of guys down at a cyber café in the Village this morning and now he was late.

The buzzer rang again.

'Yeah, yeah,' he murmured. The girl beside him made sleepy sounds but did not wake.

He had slept deeply but he still felt weary. He had spent most of yesterday trying to crack this Foundation Bank place, without a great deal of success, and then, close to midnight, the girl had arrived and he had gone what you might call 'on line' with her instead.

He turned to look at her. She lay on her cheek. Errant strands of her long hair were damp in her mouth and he drew them away gently. He got out of bed and slipped into a cotton robe that was hanging behind the bedroom door.

Everyone called him Gigolo, which was the name he had

chosen for himself because it seemed to signify a happy mixture of his affinity with computers and his prowess with women. His real name was Anton Meyer but his acquaintances on the Net did not know that, nor did they know that his late father was an investment banker who had left him a substantial amount of money.

The inheritance allowed him to maintain a decent but small apartment on East 76th Street in Manhattan, between Third Avenue and Lexington, without having to do anything as boring as go out looking for a job, and it had provided him with the funds to buy the technology that filled the apartment's main room.

The blinds were closed and it was dark, lit only by the spectral light from half a dozen monitors, each with its own screen saver pattern. Gigolo had designed them all, creating them as fish of different species. As he walked through the room it was like being in an aquarium.

In spite of all this kit at his disposal, he had not been able to breach the defences at the Foundation Bank and it irritated him. He had had about as much effect as if he had been hammering a pencil on a steel door.

He had probably stopped at a good time, thanks to the girl. He was aware that even though he had been careful, hopping across half the country, there was a risk of leaving a trail. The bank might have a security system with the capability of tracing unwanted visitors. He would try a different route when he started today.

He opened the blinds, screwing his eyes against the light, as the buzzer went again.

'Okay,' he called out. 'Keep your shirt on.'

He looked through the peephole and saw a mailman

standing outside, with a cap and a satchel. Gigolo undid
the locks and opened the door a fraction but he kept it on
the chain.

'Yeah?'

'Package for you. You gotta sign for it.'

Gigolo could see the parcel in his hand. The mailman
slipped a receipt pad and a pen through the gap at the
door. The spot was marked with an asterisk and Gigolo
signed, reluctantly using his real name. Sometimes it was
unavoidable.

He handed everything back. 'Thanks,' he said. 'Pass it
in.'

The mailman tried to squeeze the package through the
space but no matter which way he turned it it would not
fit.

'Wait,' Gigolo said. 'I'll open this thing.'

He released the chain.

The door was shoved violently against him, knocking
him off balance and back into the apartment.

As he fell to the floor he saw that there were two of
them.

The mailman had dropped his satchel and had taken a
pistol with a silencer from it. The second man was dressed
in overalls and looked like a building superintendent. He
closed the door quickly and when he turned Gigolo saw
that he carried an identical weapon.

He tried to scramble to his feet but the mailman
slammed him hard on the side of the head with the butt of
his gun.

'Hey,' the other man said, taking in his surroundings,
'look at all this shit.'

Gigolo groaned on the floor. There was a mist in front of his eyes and he felt as if there were knives sticking into his brain.

The mailman kept his weapon pointed at him while the second gunman explored the apartment. It did not take long.

'One bedroom,' he said. 'There's a girl in it. Asleep.'

'Bring him in there,' the mailman said.

They dragged Gigolo along the floor, then they heaved him on to the bed.

The girl sat up, dazed and confused, then caught her breath in horror.

Before she could scream, the mailman stepped back, raised his gun and shot her twice in the chest. Blood spattered the bed. Sounds began to rise in Gigolo's throat but stopped abruptly as the second man hit him hard in the mouth.

The girl was dead, slumped back on the reddening sheets, but the mailman came forward and shot her through the left eye to make sure.

Gigolo stared in silent terror, his face covered in her blood and his own. Beneath him, the bed was wet where he had urinated.

'Now,' the mailman said, 'there's a couple of things we need to know.'

Chapter Thirty-Five

Gallagher got drunk. He wandered the streets near his apartment, trying pub after pub until it was night and he was standing in his own gloom at the corner of a bar, drinking pints of Guinness with whiskey chasers.

When he ordered yet another round, the barman asked him if he was sure. He blinked and glanced about him and saw that the other customers were wondering who this stranger was, getting tanked up on his own.

He did not like people staring at him.

'What the fuck are you all looking at?' he shouted.

'Right,' said the barman, 'that's enough.'

He found himself out on the street. Time to go home, if he could find the way. He had booze there anyhow.

He tried to hail a taxi a couple of times but the drivers could spot a troublesome drunk a mile off so they ignored him. But he made it to the seafront road eventually and staggered along it towards his apartment, stumbling into the gutter once or twice.

If they came for him at this moment he would not care. They could do what they liked. He was worthless,

356

he had left a stain on everything he had touched and he had failed everyone. Mostly he had failed his daughter, a woman he did not appear to know at all. Not only was she someone alien to him, she turned out to be a willing accomplice in Gilbert Leslie's conspiracy, whatever the hell that was.

Letters lay unopened inside his door. He had ignored them when he went out this morning and he ignored them now. One of the envelopes had his bank's logo on it. It would be the manager, writing about his little financial problem again. What did it matter.

He found the whiskey bottle and a glass and slumped down in a chair in front of the window. He left the lights off and stared out into a starlit sky while he drank.

The phone rang a couple of times but he just let it. He had already unplugged the answering machine and he sat there listening to the insistent ringing and the silence that came once the caller gave up.

Then he poured himself another drink.

School had got in the way. The last of the exams.

Paul had not been to the *Dave* office for a few days and had no idea how Gigolo was getting on. He was forced to use the computer at home in order to find out.

The search engine came up on screen. All he could do was enter and wait.

The list of users sped past.

Gigolo was in there, in one of the computer chat rooms.

As Paul entered he could see that Gigolo had been watching a conversation but not taking part. Now Gigolo would be able to see that *Dave* had arrived.

HELLO, DAVE. NICE 2CU AGAIN.
WONDERED WHERE YOU'D GOT TO.

Paul typed a return message.

Sorry. Been a bit busy. How's NYC?

COOL.

A quiet talk?

It was a request that they go into a private room, a facility which was a clever creation in the software, where they could converse without other eyes seeing what they had to say. Once they were inside, Paul typed again.

Have you managed to make any progress?

SOME. TAKE IT EASY FOR A MOMENT. WHAT'S THE BIG RUSH? YOU'RE THE ONE WHO HASN'T BEEN AROUND, REMEMBER. I HAVE THINGS TO ASK. I'M CURIOUS FOR A START, YOU HAVEN'T TOLD ME WHY ALL THE INTEREST IN THE BANK.

Paul frowned. Damn. Gigolo had not been at all inquisitive when he had first broached the subject. There was no way he could tell him.

Sorry. Can't say yet. Need to know how's it going.

TOUGH. THE PLACE IS VERY SECURE. CAN YOU TELL ME ANY MORE ABOUT IT THAT MIGHT HELP ME? WHERE DID YOU COME ACROSS THIS MAN SCHENK?

Too many questions. Gigolo was making him nervous.

Sorry. Can't say, he repeated.

DON'T WORRY ABOUT IT. I FIGURE I MIGHT
HAVE SOME ANSWERS BY TOMORROW ANY-
WAY.
HOW'S THAT?

Paul heard the front door close. His mother was home.
This was a good place to stop.
Got to leave you.
Gigolo was disappointed.

THAT'S A SHAME. CAN'T YOU TALK FOR A
WHILE? A FEW MORE MINUTES, MAYBE?

Afraid not. Let's talk at the same time tomorrow.
Paul logged off but he also saved the conversation and
printed it out so that he could read it later. He was not
exactly sure why, but he wanted to look at it again.

Chapter Thirty-Six

A t the age of thirty-five, Bruce Morrow was the young-
est Chief Executive Dublin Airport had ever had but
he did not consider himself to be its most successful. Not
yet.

That accolade would come within days, he hoped, when
the Government accepted the bid from the in-house consortium he led, making him the first CEO of the new,
privatised airports company.

But his group was not the only contender.

There were two approved bidders. The competition came
from a strong international group that caused him some
concern, a consortium called Dhow, composed of several
major interests involved in the computer industry, in banking and, it pained him to acknowledge, with success in
airport management in Australia and southern Asia.

But Morrow felt certain the decision would go his way.
In the unlikely event that it did not, the matter would not
rest unchallenged. He and his board had agreed that they
would seek a judicial review which, at the very least, would
make things messy for the Government and throw an
unwelcome spotlight on their decision-making processes.

Bruce Morrow was one of those active, enthusiastic people who needed little sleep but in this tense period, waiting for the verdict, he found himself waking even earlier each day. This morning was no exception. Once up and dressed, he padded about in socks so as not to disturb his wife, Nicole, and the twins, Rebecca and Emily. They would be awake soon enough, two four-year-olds filling the house with their exuberance before Nicole took them to playgroup and then made her way into Dublin to Holles Street hospital where she worked as an assistant to one of the administrators.

It was a part-time job, just a couple of days a week, finishing after lunch. Then she drove out to pick the girls up and went home. She did not work because she needed the money, that was for sure. It was a question of independence. Morrow understood that and he never questioned it.

He peeped round the door of the children's room and smiled at the identical blonde curly heads asleep on their soft pillows, the floor strewn with last night's toys, left where they had fallen.

They were spoiled rotten, the pair of them, but he did not care. He knew how tough it had been for Nicole, the trauma of two earlier miscarriages. She had waited a long time for this joy and they were both savouring every moment of it. He stepped over towards the children, then bent down and as gently as he could he kissed them both.

He would die if anything ever happened to them.

Downstairs, he lifted his briefcase from the hall, slipped his shoes on and left the house. His home was an old Georgian rectory far into the Wicklow hills. It was a bit remote, miles from anywhere, but he liked the seclusion, the feeling of escape it gave him. It was about an hour's drive to Dublin but the creation of new by-pass roads meant that he could reach the airport without having to go through the city.

The heavy pink blossoms of an early clematis hung from the walls around the door and sunlight glinted from the bodywork of the Jaguar sports car poised in front of it. He eased himself in behind the wheel and the car glided down the driveway towards the narrow country road.

He looked both ways and saw nothing. Out here, there was no such thing as traffic.

From their vantage point in a hidden laneway, three men in a dark car watched him.

'There he goes,' Humble reported.

'An early bird,' Leslie said, leaning in towards him from the back seat, his cologne strong in Humble's nostrils. 'Very commendable.'

He sat back again, feeling the satisfaction that often came to him when he acknowledged the power he had; to decide the life or death of someone he did not know and to do so calmly and rationally.

Yet it was not always like that, was it, he reminded himself.

He had a fleeting vision of the girl dead on the settee. A bad mistake.

And now someone, God knows who, had got hold of the name Schenk and had tried to get into the bank's computer system. The hacker had been found and dealt with but they had established first that he had been acting for another party. Whoever it was would have to be traced – and quickly.

Parrish and Humble sat quietly and obediently in front of him. They knew what was required and what they would have to do in just a few days' time but Leslie had suggested this morning's mission of observation in order that he could emphasize the importance of their task and the consequences of failure.

That could not be countenanced.

Morrow's car had gone from sight.

'Time for you to show me,' Leslie said.

They took a drive, a meandering ramble that led them along the quiet forest roads where there were awkward corners and nasty drops. Near one difficult bend, they stopped.

'This is where we'll do it,' Parrish said.

Leslie lowered his window and peered out. Bramble thickets and beds of ferns clung to the hillside. Down among the trees there was a soft darkness broken in places by an insistent morning sun. A warm woody smell filled the air.

'Splendid,' he told them and after a few minutes they drove back to their surveillance position.

At eight fifteen, Humble made another announcement.

'Here she comes.'

Leslie saw a black Audi estate with a fair-haired woman at the wheel and two blonde children strapped into booster seats behind her. In silence, they followed her along the wooded roads they had travelled a short time before. They did not stay too close or keep her always in their sight. There was no need because they knew where she was going.

There was hardly any traffic on this road. There would

be none at all on the morning when Parrish and Humble would put the ROAD CLOSED sign behind her and then follow to the one which would force her to stop and try to turn.

After a journey of twenty minutes, Nicole Morrow stopped at a house with open grass all around it and safe stone walls too high for small children to climb. Other cars had parked at its gate and children were kissing their mothers goodbye and skipping up its path. A sign in the garden announced that this was the Little People Play-group.

The three men drove past without slowing but as they did Leslie got a good look at the woman and liked what he saw. They made an attractive sight: the natural beauty of the tall young mother, the twins lively and utterly indistinguishable.

He smiled to himself and thought of Heywood Corbett's outrage when he had first suggested this. Corbett's days were numbered. This business with the bank had to have been caused by carelessness. The leak would have to be sealed and then Corbett would pay for the mistake.

But this – there would be no carelessness here.

It could not be better. It would be a poignant final detail, delivered with perfect timing.

The death of his wife and two children would destroy Bruce Morrow and leave him with no stomach at all for a fight.

Emma Gallagher's driver swept along the south Dublin avenues and pulled up outside the entrance to the Berkeley Court Hotel.

It was seven thirty am. She and members of her departmental team were due in Belfast in the early afternoon for a meeting with British Government officials which would last until midday tomorrow. But there was something she had to attend to first because it would be too late to do so when she came back.

She was not looking forward to this.

It had been after midnight when she had finished going over the documents, reading and re-reading them, all the while feeling the discomfort of the decision she knew she had to take, and it was then, in spite of the lateness of the hour, that she had called Tony Goulding and asked him if they could meet over breakfast.

She strode through the big open lobby, acknowledging nods from one or two by-standers who recognised her. She had spotted Goulding's car and driver outside so she knew he had arrived ahead of her. In the dining-room, the head waiter ushered her to him. There was the smell of toast and bacon as she walked to where he sat at a quiet table in the corner, reading the sports pages of the *Irish Independent*.

'Good old Kilkenny,' he said as he folded the paper. 'I have money on them for the championship.'

In Dublin, it was not an unusual sight to see a couple of Government Ministers having breakfast or lunch together or dining with equally well-known faces from the world of industry or high finance. It did not arouse any interest beyond a first glance but head waiters nevertheless ensured that they were given tables where they would be left alone.

Emma had suggested the Berkeley Court because she had not wanted the discussion to take place in either her office or Goulding's. Oddly, away from the curious eyes and ears of their civil servants, this public encounter could be altogether more private.

'I took the liberty of ordering already,' Goulding said as a waiter pulled Emma's seat out for her and offered her the menu.

She did not look at it. 'Just some toast,' she said, 'and some coffee. Thank you.'

Goulding leaned back in his seat. 'You look tired. Is the job giving you the run-around?'

'No, it's not the job. It's – other things.'

'Something personal?'

'No. Nothing like that.'

If only he knew. It was not just a question of her problems with her father. Now there was something else, something she could not avoid for much longer.

She had spent last night alone but the previous night she had slept with Fergal at his house. They had made love and not for the first time she had simply allowed him to—

To fuck you. Face it – that's what it was.

The sex had been active and energetic enough but there had been nothing in it for her. No thrill, no satisfaction. It was a while since she had experienced either. Only when she took the initiative, feeling a sudden sexual hunger, did it do any good. But on those spontaneous occasions it had nothing to do with poor Fergal. Practically anybody would do.

She did not love him. It was time she faced up to the fact and told him. There could be no future in their relationship and it was not fair to leave him under the impression that there was. There was her position to think about, too.

She did not want gossip in the papers about the rather liberal nature of their arrangements.

God, it would not be easy.

The waiter brought a tray with her toast and coffee as well as a robust helping of bacon, egg, sausage and grilled tomato for Goulding.

'You should eat more,' he said as he compared their plates. 'You shouldn't worry on an empty stomach. You'll get ulcers.'

'Tony,' she began, 'there's something I have to say.'

He munched as he waited.

'Go on.'

'I'm indebted to you for a great deal,' she told him. 'You're a man after my own heart. You believe in pursuing your goals with vigour and determination. You believe there's only one chance in this life so we'd better take it now. And you set great store on loyalty.'

'Sounds about right,' he said. 'There should probably be something in there about getting your retaliation in first but you can let that go.'

'No,' Emma agreed, 'that's an important characteristic, too. You're right. Both of us make bad enemies and I certainly don't ever want to be one of yours.'

Almost imperceptibly, his eyes narrowed.

She went on. 'But if I'm going to fulfil your faith in me, if I'm going to have any standing as a Minister and a member of the Cabinet, then I have to act according to my conscience and the decisions I take have to be mine.'

She paused and sipped from her coffee cup. The toast had gone cold and she had not touched it.

'Go on,' he said again.

'Damn it, this is very difficult.'

'Come on, Emma. Get it out.'

'Aer Rianta.'

'Aer Rianta,' he echoed.

'I can't do what you want.'

Tension settled over the table like a sudden frost. Neither of them spoke.

In approximately forty-eight hours the Prime Minister would convene the Cabinet meeting which would decide which way the privatisation of the airports should go.

The two bids had been summarised by experts from the Department of Finance and Goulding's own department. As the newest member of the Cabinet team, Emma had been the last to familiarise herself with the details. She had finished doing so last night. But before she had begun reading, she had been well aware of which way Goulding wanted her to vote.

Even in the maelstrom of that first weekend after the sacking of Savage, he had still managed to find time to brief her on other business, including the privatisation issue, and to tell her in confidence how vital it was that she voted for the bid by Dhow.

'In the short term it will cause tears,' he had told her, 'but in the long run it will be best for the country. I've had private indications from people who are close to Dhow that the individual corporations behind it would be keen to set up other industrial bases in Ireland if the decision goes their way.'

She had always known that Goulding bent the rules. What he had told her sounded like a bribe but if the country was to benefit, then well and good. She could turn a blind eye like the best of them.

But by midnight last night, she was not so sure that a vote for Dhow was the right course of action. And growing in her mind was the suspicion that if they were to succeed there might be more in it for Tony Goulding than for the nation.

'Believe me,' she told him, 'this has caused me absolute agony. The briefing documents are brilliant. Even a non-economist like me can make sense of them. As far as the numbers are concerned, there's not much in it. The Dhow bid's ahead by a couple of million but of course the decision can't depend on cash alone. The business plans have to be solid as a rock, too, and as far as I can see, neither of them could be found wanting in any detail.'

She drank some more coffee and noticed that Goulding had stopped eating.

'I can see why you're attracted to Dhow,' she went on, 'and I'm sure you'll be able to set out quite an impressive stall when we get to talk about this. There are some big guns involved and plenty of experience in the running of airports. But, Tony, look at the skill and strength in the local consortium. There's an expertise and a confidence there that they've derived from years of successful expansionist management. A decision in their favour would be a huge morale boost for the country, don't you think?'

Goulding did not comment.

'I went back and forth, first one way and then the other,' she said. 'Talk about indecision. But in the end I came down on the side of the home team. There's a lot of justice in it if we make that choice.'

She crossed her hands and pressed them to her chest.

'Call it gut instinct if you like. It just *feels* like the right thing to do.'

'It is not,' Goulding said. His words were clipped. 'You're making a fundamental mistake by letting sentiment enter into this.'

He looked around but they were safe from other ears. 'We have to see the bigger picture here. As far as the actual airports are concerned, there's not a lot in it – you're right – the Government gets its money one way or another. But I'm looking to the future. The people involved in Dhow represent all sorts of other industries, too. What if Hurll were to come here, for instance? One of the most rapidly developing players in the world computer industry. What a boost that would be for the country. Can't you see what the long-term benefits are likely to be?'

'You've got no guarantee that anything like that might happen.'

'Believe me,' he said, 'it will.'

She knew at that instant that he had been bought.

Even though she had suspected something, the realisation hit her like a blow.

But she had not gone along with it. On this occasion, she had not followed him blindly.

'I'm sorry, Tony,' she said. 'I've made my mind up.'

'That's your decision then. You're voting for the local management?'

'Yes. And I think I owe it to the rest of the Cabinet to tell them why I'm doing so.'

For a moment his eyes widened and he looked alarmed. Then he folded his napkin and dumped it on the table beside his abandoned breakfast.

He smiled a thin smile. 'You've been decent enough to inform me, Emma. I appreciate that – but then I would have expected nothing less from you. And of course I admire your principles.'

'It's good of you to say so.'

He reached across the table and touched her hand. His skin felt warm and a little moist and she almost recoiled.

'You must do what you think is right. There's nothing more important than that.' He stood up. 'It will be an interesting vote, anyway.'

'Do you think it will be close?'

'I hope not. It's got to be decisive – whatever way it goes.'

Chapter Thirty-Seven

On account of a little turbulence out in the Gulf of Mexico, it was a bit breezy in Palm Beach as the police car made its way slowly along a private driveway lined with the tall trees which gave the resort its name.

The two uniformed officers watched the palms swaying rhythmically and wondered if the weather forecasters were right when they said that this was a storm which would pass right by.

At the end of the drive there was a complex of Spanish-style bungalows, comfortable holiday homes, each tucked away amid its own gardens. Outside one, the officers got out. After they had rung the bell a couple of times, the door was opened by a man of medium height, in his sixties, with silvery hair.

He looked at them warily. 'Police? What can I do for you two gentlemen?'

One of the officers tipped his cap. 'Sorry to bother you, sir. I don't know if you're aware – but somebody got assaulted near here last night. A – eh – senior gentleman, like yourself. His house was broken into, some stuff taken. At the Stella Maris estate just along the road. You know it?'

'Yes,' the man said. 'I do. That's terrible news. Is he all right?'

'A bit shaken up is all. A few bruises. But it could have been a lot worse.'

His companion spoke. 'We're doing a check of the neighbourhood to see if anyone heard or saw anything suspicious.'

The man thought and then shook his head. 'No, nothing. I can't think of anything at all.'

'You were at home last night?'

'Yep, haven't moved from here for a couple of weeks. Enjoying the weather. Although—' He looked beyond his visitors towards the wind in the trees. 'Right now, I'm not so sure.'

'Well, just be careful,' the first policeman said.

'Oh, we got a good alarm system here.' He smiled. 'All kinds of bells and whistles. I'll make sure it's switched on before I turn in tonight.'

'And if you see anything, you'll let us know?'

'You can count on it. Grateful to you boys for stopping by.'

He stood at the door while they got into their car, then waved as they drove off.

When they were out of his vision, they pulled in again. The officer in the passenger seat reached into the glove compartment and took a photograph from it.

The person in the picture had not posed for the shot and would not have been aware that it was being taken. It was not by any means perfect. It had been taken through a window, with a long lens, but it was the most up-to-date photograph they had and it was good enough.

They looked at it for the few seconds it took them to agree and then the driver put the car into gear.

His partner got on the radio. 'We're on our way back.'

'And?' A squawk at the other end.

'And nothing. It's not him.'

Across the Atlantic, it was the early afternoon and Gallagher was out of booze.

From his window, he saw that the weather had decided to regress and that the tide was on the turn. Along the Sandymount strand, rain whipped by a ruthless wind drummed on the backs of walkers scurrying home with their heads down.

He had been dozing in the chair and he was half-sober again. That would not do.

The off-licence would be open.

He left the apartment and hurried down the stairs, not bothering with a coat or remembering to shut the door behind him.

At the *Dave* office in South William Street, Paul was late trying to make contact with Gigolo. Other things had intervened.

It was getting near the deadline for the magazine's next issue, which meant that Max had gone into a fever of activity while he tried to make up for lost time. He had also given Paul instructions on how he wanted the web page updated and that had to come first.

But he had finished now. Paul looked around. Max was in his office on the phone. He raised the search facility on the screen then went to the chat menu. He had just entered the usual room when he felt a hand on his shoulder.

'Listen, you,' Max said.

Paul stiffened under his grasp.

God, what did he want?

Max took his hand away and moved in front of him. He was a short, burly fellow with yellow hair. With his arms folded, he sat on the edge of the desk, almost obscuring the monitor, and glowered.

Paul felt sure the guilt was written all over his face. He tried to smile. 'Hi, Max,' he said, as chirpily as he could.

Max looked at him and shook his head.

Paul glanced furtively to the screen behind him. He could see the names of everyone currently in the chat room.

Gigolo was there.

He might have been waiting for a while. He would see that Paul had arrived at last. He would wonder why he had not said anything.

'I don't know what you're up to,' Max said. 'I can't figure it out.'

Paul felt weak. He looked up at him. 'I don't – what do you—' he began.

'I mean, you come in here practically every fucking day, working away on that web page, and you don't get a fucking penny for it. What's more, you never even ask.'

'I – well – it's okay – I—'

'It's not okay,' Max said. 'So from now on, I'm kind of putting you on the payroll. It won't be much but it'll be something. It'll mean you're no longer working for nothing. But don't tell the taxman about it.'

He put his hand in his pocket and took out some notes.

Paul felt relief beginning to spread over him.

'Here you go.' He stood up and squeezed Paul's shoulder again. 'Thanks for all your help.'

'Gee, Max, thanks. That's great.'

Max moved away and Paul breathed again. He shoved the money into his pocket without looking at it and began to type.

Hi, Gigolo. Sorry. Had to talk to somebody first. Shall we go private?

Gigolo said nothing. The screen showed that he had departed.

'Gigolo leaves,' it said.

In a moment, when he arrived in the private room, he saw that Gigolo was already there. He typed another message.

That's better. So – any news for me?

He waited but there was no response. He tried again.

Have we a problem? Are you giving me the cold shoulder?

Silence.

What was all this? Of course, it was entirely possible that Gigolo had been distracted, just as he had been. Then at last—

SORRY ABOUT THE INTERRUPTION. HAD TO ANWSER THE DAMN DOOR. THE REST OF THE WORLD INSISTS ON INTRUDING SOMETIMES.

Paul froze. His heart missed a beat.

All of a sudden, he knew what was wrong and what it was that had nagged at the back of his mind about their last conversation.

He stared intently at the screen to make sure he had not made a mistake.

No, there it was.

The word ANSWER, misspelt, was like a warning signal.

He thought for a second. Then he typed.

Mebbe we should just forget about this. Drop whole thing.

Gigolo came back.

NO, I'LL GET THERE OK.

Are you sure?

NO PROBLEM. TOMORROW.

Paul racked his brains quickly.

B sure you cover tracks well. Remember old friend Osiris? Getting caught hacking into government research place in Seattle?

DON'T WORRY. THAT WON'T HAPPEN TO GIGOLO.

There was a hesitation.

SIX PM NEW YORK TIME IS GOOD FOR ME. YOU?

I'll try. Uh-oh. Sorry. Duty calls.

Have to break off.

He left the room and logged out.

He looked at the screen with its undulating saver pattern. Suddenly he felt a lot safer away from that thing.

Something very strange and probably very bad was happening.

Tom. He had to tell him.

He picked up the phone and dialled Gallagher's number but found that it was unobtainable. He tried again. Same thing. Then he tried the operator who told him it sounded as if there was a fault on the line.

Damn.

He walked to the window and saw the rain. The street outside was a mess. Several buildings in it were being renovated and cement mixers and piles of sand blocked the pavement at various intervals. Streams of muddy brown rainwater rushed towards the gutters.

He would have to get to Sandymount, find Tom and talk to him, but it would take him ages by bus. A taxi was the answer but he did not have enough money.

Oh yes, he had.

He dug into his pocket and pulled out the cash Max had given him. He counted it. Twenty-five pounds.

Max was right. It was not much but it was something.

Because the rain had brought a sudden rush of business, the taxi took nearly half an hour to arrive and almost the same length of time again to get to Sandymount.

He paid the driver, ran up the steps to the front door and pressed Gallagher's buzzer. There was no response. He went down the list and selected another button, a flat at the top.

A woman answered. 'Yes? Who is it?'

'Hello,' he said. 'I'm sorry to bother you. I'm a friend of Mr Gallagher in flat two. I'm supposed to meet him here but he's not answering his bell and his phone appears to be out of order. Could you let me in so that I can try his door?'

'Who did you say you were looking for?' the woman asked cautiously.

'Mr Gallagher in flat two.'

'And who are you?'

'My name's Paul Forrest,' he said. The name would mean nothing to her but it would make him less anonymous.

After a pause, the front door clicked open. By the time he got up the stairs to Gallagher's apartment, a grey-haired woman was leaning over the banisters, looking down with a suspicious frown.

He smiled at her reassuringly. 'Thanks,' he said. 'Much appreciated. I'm sorry to have to disturb you like that.'

'I don't really like letting people in like this, you know. You never know what sort of criminals are hanging around. Was that you outside in the taxi just now?'

'Yes, it was,' Paul said.

The fact that he had arrived in a cab seemed to mollify her. Burglars and murderers would not travel around like that, presumably. She retreated back up the stairs.

'As I was saying, it's not a very good idea to open the door to complete strangers.' She was still muttering to herself as she went back into her own flat, closed the door and locked it.

'Thank you,' he called after her, then turned to knock on Gallagher's door.

It was ajar.

He tensed and began to wonder what he would find inside.

He knocked softly as he pushed it right open and went in.

'Tom?' he called into the silence, hearing the nervous quaver in his own voice.

There was no reaction. The flat was empty and stinking of stale drink.

He moved through each room. In the living-room he found the phone and saw that it had been unplugged. There was a pile of notes on the table. He saw Gilbert Leslie's name scribbled on them. The bedroom was a mess, the air heavy. In the kitchen, dishes were unwashed and on the work surface there was an abandoned plate of scrambled egg. He touched it with his finger. Cold.

He went back into the living-room and saw the empty bottles at the chair over by the window.

Where was Tom?

He looked out of the window. The rain had not eased; in fact it seemed to have got worse. It had come down over the sea like a shutter and it pounded the surface of the coast road. Cars sloshed past, their windscreen wipers at full speed, and they doused the pavement with water from deep puddles.

He was about to turn away again when he thought he saw something.

There was a figure further down the road, just at the limit of visibility.

He peered. Oblivious to the downpour, someone was sitting on a wall at the edge of the sea. It looked like a man.

Was it possible?

He hurried out of the flat and down the stairs and at the front door he flicked the snib on the lock so that it would not snap shut behind him. He began to run, his sneakers slapping the wet ground, the rain finding another easy human target.

As he got nearer the figure on the wall he saw that it was a man dressed only in shirt and jeans. He was certain now.

'Tom!' Paul called.

There was no response.

'Tom!' he called again and stopped running.

The figure turned. Gallagher was drenched to the skin. There was a vodka bottle in his hand.

Paul was shocked by his appearance. His hair was plastered tight by the rain and his unshaven face was grey and gaunt. For a few seconds Gallagher looked at Paul as if he were a stranger. Then he turned away again and took a drink.

Paul stood a few feet from him, unsure about going any further or what to do. He was afraid that in this state Gallagher might fall into the sea.

Or was that what was in his mind?

'Tom,' he called once more. 'I need your help.'

There was no answer.

'Tom, please,' he said. 'I think I've found Gilbert Leslie.'

Chapter Thirty-Eight

He handed the vodka bottle over easily enough. Paul dropped it into a rubbish bin as they stumbled in the rain back to the flat.

'Leslie,' Gallagher said. 'What do you mean—'

'I'll explain it all in a minute.'

When they were safely indoors, Paul helped him out of his sodden clothes and steered him in the direction of the shower. Then, while Gallagher groaned under its hot stinging spray, he dried himself off as best he could.

'Christ, Paul, tell me what's going on,' Gallagher croaked.

'I will. Just hold on.' He was desperate to tell him. He wanted to pour it all out but he had to be sure Tom was able to absorb it. He had already absorbed so much else.

As Gallagher dressed in fresh clothes, Paul rummaged in the fridge and found bacon and eggs, then he cleared aside the debris and cooked him a hearty fry-up that might help soak up some of the alcohol. He watched Gallagher wolf it down at the kitchen table and he brewed a big pot of tea from which he took a cup himself.

'How long have you been drinking?'

'I don't remember. Gilbert Leslie. Where is he?'

Paul looked at his watch. It was an hour since he had got here. What Gallagher needed was a good twenty-four hours in bed to sleep it off but they did not have the time. He was wreathed in fumes and he looked terrible, his eyes red and bleary, but this would have to do.

Paul sat down in front of him and in spite of his good intentions it all came out in a rush, a cascade of words. Gallagher heard about somebody called Gigolo, about a bank in Virginia and about something in computer-land known as a chat room.

He shook his head to try to clear it, then reached out and put his hands on Paul's shoulders. 'Wait a minute, wait a minute. I'm not getting any of this. Take it slowly.'

Paul took a deep breath and then gave him the whole story, from the moment he hacked into the Tourist Board consultants' computer right up until this afternoon and his last conversation with Gigolo.

There was a fog in Gallagher's brain but in spite of it he could see that the boy had exposed himself to danger.

Paul took a couple of folded sheets of paper from his back pocket. 'I knew something wasn't quite right but I couldn't put my finger on it. Then today I saw what it was. It isn't Gigolo at the other end.'

'How do you know?'

'I spend a lot of time talking to people on the net. You get to know them, their style, how they string words together. It's like recognising someone's voice. Everyone has verbal mannerisms. People writing in a hurry are no different.'

He unfolded the paper. Gallagher saw snatches of conversation which were arranged like a script, with the name of each speaker coming before what they had to say.

Paul pointed. 'It was when he messed up the word ANSWER that I saw it. I remembered then that one thing that distinguishes Gigolo is that he always gets the word THE wrong. It always comes out as T-E-H. I often thought he did it on purpose so that you would know for sure it was him. But look – this guy doesn't. Not a misspelling until we get to ANSWER.'

Gallagher blinked to keep the words in focus. 'It could just mean that Gigolo has cleaned up his act. It's hardly conclusive.'

'Yet the first time I talked to him, when I told him about the bank, it was the same old Gigolo. The same old T-E-H. I didn't save it but I remember it. Still, you're right. Not conclusive. That's why I gave him a test.'

'A test?'

Paul nodded. 'Look at this bit of conversation.'

Gallagher followed where his finger pointed. It was a warning about not getting caught like someone called . . . what was that – Osiris? . . . who had hacked into a research facility in Seattle.

'There's no one called Osiris, no old friend,' Paul said. 'I made him up. I don't know whether there's a Government place in Seattle either. But see the way Gigolo doesn't question any of it? If it was the real Gigolo, he'd wonder what the hell I was talking about.'

He frowned. 'Right about then I began to feel kind of creepy, as if somebody was watching me. And then it occurred to me that that might be exactly what was going on. Gigolo, or whoever he is, has been pissing me about, stringing me along. What if it was a delaying tactic while someone was trying to put a trace on me? He gave a precise time for the next contact – six pm his time, one o'clock our time tomorrow. I'm sure that's when they're planning to do something. Like grab whoever Gigolo's been talking to. So that's when I came here. And found you.'

Gallagher for a moment lowered his gaze and looked at his hands. There was a graze where he had staggered against a wall last night. He felt ashamed of himself and his drunken self-pity, self-destruction, whatever it was.

'You've been very clever,' he said, looking up at Paul, 'although you took a lot of risks – dangerous for other people, too. What about the guys in the office? Or your mother? Did you use her computer for any of this?'

Paul nodded and glanced away, sheepishly. When he had started this he had not thought of consequences, where it all might lead.

'I did it for you, because I believed you were right,' he said. 'I was convinced you weren't – you know – *sick*. I wanted to show my mother she was wrong.'

Gallagher looked at him. Damn it, what had he led the boy into? But there was no time to agonise about that now.

'Right,' he said. 'We've got to send for the cavalry. This time I hope they're sensible enough to come running.'

He stood up and held on to the back of the chair for a moment because his head was light. When he went to the phone, he found it dead and then remembered that he had unplugged it.

'I'll do that,' Paul said and stuck it back in the socket.

Gallagher dialled. 'Chief Superintendent Greeley's office,' he said.

Someone asked him who was calling. 'Tell him it's Tom

Gallagher,' he said loudly, 'and that I've got some information he'll want to hear.'

Greeley came on almost immediately.

'I've been trying to call you. There was something wrong with the phone.'

'I was kind of incommunicado for a while,' Gallagher said. 'Now, look. Gilbert Leslie. He may have been staying at the Shelbourne on a Canadian passport—'

'—and going by the name of Schenk,' Greeley finished for him. 'Stay where you are. I'll send a car for you.'

Just over half an hour later, they were in Harcourt Square. There were four of them: Gallagher and Paul, Greeley and another detective, a chubby man whom he introduced as Inspector Frank Dolan.

Greeley sniffed the air and looked at Gallagher. 'Jesus, what happened to you? Did you go swimming in a brewery?'

'Something like that.'

'Maybe I'd better not ask.' He looked at Paul. 'And who's this?'

'This is Paul Forrest,' Gallagher explained. 'He's the son of a friend of mine.'

'I don't think he needs to be involved in any of this, do you?'

'I'm afraid he's already involved, Chief Superintendent. He's been, shall we say, kind of busy. He's got a lot to tell you.'

Greeley looked at Paul with curiosity.

'Then perhaps we should hear it.' He turned and opened a window behind him. 'But before we go any further, there's something I've got to say. I'd like to apologise to Mr Gallagher for my behaviour towards him. He was right and

I was wrong. Simple as that. I thought I should say that straight off.'

No one spoke for a few seconds. Rain drummed on a tin roof somewhere. The atmosphere became more bearable as the open window and Greeley's apology cleared it.

'We all make mistakes,' Gallagher said.

Greeley resumed his seat and with it his role.

'Now,' he said, 'let me tell you what's been happening at this end and then you can fill me in on whatever it is you've been up to.'

He looked at Paul. The boy's cheeks reddened under his tough gaze.

'We've been going through the needle-in-a-haystack routine, looking for the man who killed the girl in Temple Bar, checking as best we can on foreign visitors who were known to be around at the time. That has meant a trawl of all the hotels in the Dublin area for a start and at this time of year, as you can imagine, there's no shortage of tourists from abroad. As well as all that, there's the big information technology convention.'

He took a Marlboro from a packet on his desk, looked at it for a second then changed his mind and put it back.

'We struck lucky at the Shelbourne. Someone stayed there calling himself Gerd Schenk, from Toronto. Sixty-something. About the same age as the man in the Temple Bar description. But we got word from the Canadian authorities last night that Mr Schenk died four years ago, even though he seemed to have been staying at the Shelbourne for a couple of weeks.'

He looked at Gallagher. 'So, naturally my thoughts turned to you and the famous Mr Leslie. As you know, the

FBI had already told us that Leslie couldn't possibly be here, that he was in Palm Beach, but I managed to persuade the police there to check again. They did so this morning. They went to the house where Leslie's supposed to be on holiday and they found that whoever the guy is that's staying there it isn't him. It's somebody who looks like him all right, from a distance maybe, but it's not our man.'

'A ringer,' Gallagher said. 'Does he know you've made him?'

'Not as far as we can tell. There was a burglary nearby and the Miami police took advantage of it to visit the house and a few others in the area to warn the residents to be on the look-out for anything suspicious. That's how they managed to get up close. If the guy checks around, he'll find there was a genuine break-in in the vicinity and he won't get alarmed.'

Gallagher nodded in approval.

'We also checked this morning on how this Mr Schenk's hotel booking was made. Apparently it was fixed up by somebody ringing from a bank in the United States.'

'The Foundation Bank of Richmond, Virginia,' Gallagher informed him.

'The very one, yes – how did you know?'

Gallagher gestured to the young man by his side. 'Perhaps this is where Paul should come in.'

For the next ten minutes Paul told them about everything that had happened. At the end, Greeley frowned.

'I could give you a lecture about using computers for improper purposes,' he said, 'but I think this is worse kind of trouble, don't you?'

Paul nodded.

'I decided not to contact anybody about the bank yet,' Greeley said. 'I didn't want to run the risk of spooking Schenk – or, rather, Leslie – but he might well have been spooked already, mightn't he?'

The boy looked uncomfortable.

'So you think this Gigolo isn't who he's supposed to be?' Greeley asked him.

'I'm certain he's not,' Paul insisted. 'Apart from everything else, he's been too inquisitive about me. That's not like the real Gigolo.'

'How do you read it?' Greeley asked Gallagher.

'If Leslie's tied up with this bank, then there has to be something wrong going on in there. I think Paul and his friend Gigolo had stumbled on something.'

'I'm afraid that when Gigolo tried to get into the system he may have left fingerprints,' Paul added. 'Then they traced him somehow and got to him and—'

He stopped. He did not want to pursue this.

'And somebody stepped into his shoes,' Greeley said.

No one spoke for a second or two.

The silence was like an act of remembrance. Each of them had a separate mental image of a man they did not know who had been caught up in something he did not understand and was probably now dead because of it.

Paul put his head in his hands. Gallagher put an arm round his shoulders then spoke to Greeley again.

'The contact time tomorrow is very specific. I think they know *where* Paul is, if not *who* he is, and that's what they want to find out.'

Greeley thought of something. 'The FBI are interested

in the possibility that Leslie's in this country. They may well ask for permission to send someone over here.'

Gallagher sat up. 'How would that work?'

'A formal request to the Commissioner.'

'Would the Justice department have to know about it?'

'Absolutely. Yes. The Minister would have to approve.'

'That can't happen,' Gallagher snapped.

'Well, I can understand that you don't exactly have fond memories of the old firm but—'

'It mustn't happen.'

'Why not?'

'Because—' Gallagher was having difficulty with the words. The implications of what he had to say were enormous.

'Because my daughter may be involved in this somehow.'

They sat in the stillness of shock, staring at him in disbelief.

And then he told them about the party at Fergal Mulryne's house and about discovering the identity of the man he had seen chauffeuring Gilbert Leslie away from the hotel that hot Saturday morning.

'The man's name is George Levy,' he said. 'It turns out that he's also my daughter's accountant. Not only that but he was one of the three directors of Marcus Kelly's television production company. So guess where she must have got her information about what Kelly was investigating.'

He looked hard at Greeley. 'Levy is a link with Kelly, he's a link with Leslie and he's a link with my daughter. In the circumstances, she must not be made aware of any of this.'

'Jesus Christ.,' Greeley said. He looked at each of the others, seeing his own fear mirrored on their faces. He felt suddenly very small and vulnerable.

'What can you do to keep the FBI away?' Gallagher asked.

'I'm not sure. Since I've been talking to a contact there already, I could probably talk to him again, man to man, try to get them to hold back on this for twenty-four hours or so. But that's about all. After that they'll come banging on the door.'

Gallagher stared at the floor and rubbed his chin. The stubble rasped under his fingers. 'It doesn't give much time.' He looked up. 'But to do what? Solve several murders? Catch a killer? Get to the bottom of this Gigolo business? Uncover some kind of conspiracy involving my own daughter?'

'Take your pick,' Greeley said.

Gallagher thumped the desk in exasperation. 'Goddamn it, there's something going on here, something very big.'

'Well, of course there is,' a voice chipped in.

Throughout the conversation, Inspector Frank Dolan had stood over by the door without saying a word. Now the others turned to him in surprise.

'Frank?' Greeley queried.

'Of course there's something big,' he repeated. 'It's the airports, isn't it?'

'The airports?' Gallagher echoed.

'Haven't you been reading your papers?' His look suggested they were all fools. 'The Foundation Bank is part of the consortium trying to take them over.'

Chapter Thirty-Nine

As if there had been some sort of signal, they swung into action like a team who had worked together a hundred times before. In reality, Gallagher thought, they were a strange crew: a broken-down FBI-man, an over-worked Chief Superintendent, an out-of-shape Inspector and a boy who was out of his depth.

They were all of them in something deeper than they could cope with. But they did not stop to think about that.

Dolan gave himself the task of digging out everything he could about the airports privatisation and as they waited for him to return Gallagher and Greeley discussed the next step. Paul observed them quietly, almost from the wings. But to his mind they were avoiding the obvious, the thing that would place him firmly centre stage.

'The first thing,' Gallagher said, 'is to go somewhere where we won't be so noticeable.'

Greeley nodded in agreement. 'You're right. The sight of you hanging around the office would make people curious, start a few questions. Since you're what I might call *civilians*, I'd rather you weren't involved at all but I suppose there's not much I can do about that now. I need people I can trust and we need to keep the circle tight for the moment. So consider yourselves temporary and unofficial recruits to the National Bureau of Criminal Investigation.'

Paul cracked a smile.

'There's also the question of safety,' Gallagher said. 'I kind of feel it would be a good idea if Paul stayed somewhere else tonight, not at his own house.'

'Plus his mother,' Greeley added, 'not to mention yourself as well, the one man who can recognise Gilbert Leslie a mile off. I'll put you all up in my place. No problem.'

Wondering where on earth everyone was going to sleep in a four-bedroom house that already had three teenage boys in it, he went to ring his wife. While he did so, Gallagher used another phone to call Kate's office.

It was five o'clock and she had just left.

'Do you think she'll go straight to the house?' he asked Paul.

'No. She told me she'd be a bit late. Something about having a drink with someone after work.'

Dolan came back into the room with a folder that contained glossy documents and photocopied newspaper cuttings.

'Let's take all this stuff and get out of here,' Gallagher said. 'We'll go and wait for her to come home.'

The rain had turned to a thick greasy drizzle as they drove to Ranelagh in two anonymous police cars, Greeley, Gallagher and Paul in one, Dolan behind them in the other. On the way, Gallagher scanned swiftly through the contents of Greeley's folder and what little there was about the Dhow consortium of which the Foundation Bank was a part.

There was a cross avenue near Kate and Paul's house so they parked the cars there, out of the way, then walked back. Paul opened the front door and they went in. In the hall, the flowers Gallagher had seen on his last visit had been replaced by a new display.

Apart from Gallagher, none of them had eaten for a while. Paul took them into the kitchen where he laid out cold ham and cheese and took some biscuits from a cupboard. Then he made his second big pot of tea of the day. Gallagher gulped a glass of water down. He was dehydrated.

Dolan spread his stuff at the end of the table and Gallagher went straight to a copy of Aer Rianta's annual report. It was an impressive document. As well as Dublin, Cork and Shannon, the agency owned Birmingham airport and a chain of Irish hotels. It had also developed a successful network of duty free shops throughout Europe and in other key parts of the world, in particular, the Middle East, South East Asia and the former Soviet Union.

Viewed purely as a report on a year's business performance, all totally legitimate, it was an attractive account. There was clearly a go-ahead management running the show and the prospects for further development were unlimited. But Gallagher read it with another scenario in mind.

He turned to a chart which showed the global spread of Aer Rianta's activities and some of the cities where it had a foot-hold: Beirut, Bangkok, St Petersburg, Karachi.

'Jesus Christ,' he said. 'This could almost be a display of international drugs routes. It would certainly be easy to make it one.'

At a glance, he saw what had brought Gilbert Leslie to Ireland.

'It's brilliant,' he told the others as they gathered round him. 'Absolutely sensational. Acquisition of the airport company would provide Leslie and his people with a ready-made network for narcotics trafficking and money-laundering. It would be the perfect cover.'

He began to pace up and down the kitchen, thumping his fist into the palm of his hand as he spoke.

'There's a huge cash turnover at airports, all sorts of currency changing hands. If you have your own airport, think how easy it would be to establish laundering points in key places, like duty free shops, for instance, as well as everything else an airport has to offer. With a network like that, millions could be laundered every week. 'Then on top of that, there's the opportunity to bring in huge supplies of drugs, right under the noses of the authorities. Not just in Ireland, either, but anywhere else where the airports are under their control. Just consider – how long do you think it would be before the new Dublin owners made an announcement about a contract with some new air freight carrier or other? An airline actually set up and owned by a front for a drugs cartel?'

'What about airport police checks?' Paul asked. 'Customs? All the security scanning that goes on?'

'Not hard to fix when you own an airport. Or several, for that matter, as this Dhow consortium appears to do already. You put your own people in and you buy off some of the others, people in key places. And, of course, every now and then you let a shipment get caught and people don't realise that dozens more have got through.'

He pulled a chair out from the table and sat down. 'This would help Leslie's people increase their hold on the world's drugs supply, provide a whole new laundering system as well. And all the time, the original business, the one built up by hard work and honest sweat, is progressing in the normal way, taking over new airports, perhaps, and making money for the new shareholders, most of whom would have no idea of what it is that they really have a stake in.'

'Many of them wouldn't care,' Dolan said.

'But I do,' Gallagher informed him. 'By God I do.'

It was the first time he had ever been afforded a glimpse inside one of Gilbert Leslie's masterplans before it was finally in place. It was ambitious and audacious and above all it would make perfect and attractive business sense to the people Leslie advised.

Who knew what other respected and established operations cloaked his dark presence. But Dolan was right. The borders between legitimate and illegitimate profit had been eroded. Money was money; who cared where it came from.

'This thing will cost Leslie's consortium, what, about a hundred million dollars?' Gallagher wondered.

'Something like that, paid over several years,' Greeley said.

'So that money goes into Government coffers and it's somehow used for the benefit of the country as a whole?'

Dolan was reading a cutting and gave them a summary. 'The *Taoiseach* says the funds derived from privatisation will be used specifically for education, health and welfare. New school buildings, AIDS clinics, centres for the homeless, drugs rehabilitation units, that kind of thing.'

Gallagher shook his head as he saw the irony. 'Full circle, for Christ sake. Money from drugs being used to repair the damage they caused in the first place. Jesus, how did these people get this far? What kind of help did they have?'

He thought of Emma and felt cold.

Shuffling hurriedly through the paperwork on the table, he found the breakdown of the consortium. Among its members were companies of impeccable credentials – a famous soft drinks manufacturer, a major oil exploration outfit, a computer conglomerate. He found it hard to believe that they could be involved in something as sinister as this. But then it had been Leslie's strategy all along to become so embedded in legitimate business that criminal sources of income were undetectable.

Computers. He pointed to the page. 'There's how they've been tracing you,' he told Paul. 'Right there. I bet they set up the Foundation Bank's computer security system, too.'

'Hurll?' Paul said in disbelief. 'But that's one of the best.'

'Welcome to the new world of organised crime.'

'Hold on a minute,' Greeley said. He looked edgy. 'In order for them to secure this thing, they've got to make sure the Cabinet vote's going to go their way.'

Gallagher nodded. 'That's correct. So they must own someone on the inside.'

'But who?'

'My bet is Tony Goulding.'

'Oh, my God,' Dolan said.

'Don't sound so surprised,' Gallagher told him. 'Money can buy a lot of things. Especially if there's enough of it. Greed, the hunger for power – that sums up Goulding and my daughter, too, I'm sorry to have to say. Goulding's been behind her from the start – with one objective in mind all along. She would have been the last piece of his jigsaw.'

The others listened intently as he went on. 'So you've Goulding and Emma and whoever else he's got in his pocket. I went to see Eamon Savage. I didn't tell you that. He's got the measure of Goulding and if he's to be believed, most of the rest of the Cabinet are men of straw. They'll go whichever way the wind blows hardest. So will the Prime Minister. Savage was a different story. He would certainly not have done Goulding's bidding. And that meant he had to go – to be replaced by someone who would do what was expected of her.'

He stopped. The truth cut deeply.

'When's the decision being made?' Paul asked.

'There's a special Cabinet meeting at six tomorrow night,' Dolan said. 'The plan is for an announcement the following morning.'

'But what about Aer Rianta?' Greeley asked. 'Surely to God they'll not just roll over and let this happen. They've got this guy Bruce Morrow as a chief executive, a bit of a dynamo. He and his team are bound to launch some form of objection, aren't they?'

'Leslie will have thought of that,' Gallagher assured him. 'Believe me. He will have found some way to neutralise them. He doesn't leave loose ends.'

'Apart from Sinead Patterson at Temple Bar,' Dolan reminded them.

Gallagher smiled in agreement. 'Apart from Sinead Patterson. Listen, let's all sit down for a moment. Review where we are, okay?'

Greeley lit a cigarette. Paul searched for an ashtray. 'Look,' Greeley said, 'I don't mind admitting – I'm finding this hard to take in. The scale of it.'

Gallagher saw his anxiety and knew it was justified.

They had uncovered something that could get them all killed.

It was not just a question of keeping Paul and Kate safe; no one was untouchable, not even Greeley or Dolan. There was too much at stake for Leslie and his people and if they had already murdered a judge and his protection officer, executed them deliberately and strategically, then they would not hesitate to remove another couple of policemen who got in the way.

'If it's any consolation,' Gallagher told him, 'this is probably the biggest thing any of us has ever stumbled into, me included. What we do from here on – well, we've got to think about that. But for the moment, we can reassure ourselves with the knowledge that no one is aware of what we know.'

He leaned in towards them. 'Here's how I see it. God knows how long Gilbert Leslie's been working on this. Years. He'll always look for ways to expand the interests of his masters but he's very patient, always careful to make sure he's got it right.'

'Excuse my ignorance, but who are *they*?' Paul asked.

'Organised crime, the mafia, the mob, the syndicate – it doesn't matter what you call them, nothing quite describes the magnitude of what these people control or the lengths to which they'll go to achieve their goals. It's a kind of alternative business world, an alliance of interests, all of it rooted in criminal activities which net billions of dollars around the world each year and make the men who control this – this *thing* – very rich indeed.'

He put a hand on Paul's shoulder. 'Leslie's a thinker. He'll have seen the great potential there is in Europe with the greater trading freedom that the European Union provides, and then there's eastern Europe, what used to be the Soviet Union, all those new markets. Don't forget he's a European himself, born in Hungary. It would be only natural for him to look this way and he's at a time in his life when he might be inclined to get a bit nostalgic, to think about the things he left behind.'

Greeley snorted. 'You're making him sound almost human.'

'Maybe he read something somewhere. Maybe he read there was a new Government here and that they were going to privatise the airports. It would have been enough to get his brain into gear.'

He thought. 'Goulding would have been the first step. How Leslie got him on board, I don't know, but he would have to be the key to it. Then Goulding would have run into a big problem with Eamon Savage. It's my guess that Savage is a man who would not advocate selling to an outsider. Anyway he'd stand in Goulding's way just for the hell of it. He would also have the clout to cause a troublesome Cabinet split and a long-drawn-out delay.'

'There might even be a new Government by then who would rescind the whole idea,' Greeley said.

'Exactly. If this Government fails to get re-elected, then

the whole plan goes with it. But if the deal gets through before the end of their term, then it won't matter whether they get themselves re-elected or not.'

'*Savage must go,*' Dolan mused, as if quoting a slogan.

'Which would not be easy,' Greeley said. 'First Goulding had to find someone who'd be a good replacement and then launch her successfully on the political stage.'

He looked at Gallagher apologetically.

'Donovan was the next step,' Gallagher went on, 'the creation of a bogeyman, a figure everyone could hate and fear. That was how Marcus Kelly came in, brought back from his wanderings in Europe and established with his own production company so that he could become a hot-shot investigative reporter. RTE found him an irresistible prospect with good stuff to offer at a reasonable price.'

'Why was he killed?' Paul asked.

'In that world everybody's disposable,' Greeley said. 'He was useful to them when he was alive and he'd be equally useful dead. Killing him would further blacken Donovan. Meanwhile, Donovan's somewhere on the continent trying to disappear so they shoot his son in order to lure him back here. And then he's arrested for possession of drugs that somebody planted.'

'Thought you didn't believe any of that stuff,' Gallagher said.

Greeley gave him a sour look. 'Times have changed. Right now I wish I'd believed it earlier.'

Gallagher knew what he meant. Other people might still be alive.

'The Judge,' Gallagher said. 'It was Purcell's hard luck

that he drew the short straw. First there were these threatening phone calls and when the judge who refused to give Donovan bail was actually murdered, then Savage was seen to have under-reacted as Minister for Justice and in comes Emma Gallagher.'

He stood up and stretched his legs. 'And it would all have stayed smoothly on course if I hadn't seen our friend Mr Leslie coming out of the Shelbourne.'

'And if he hadn't killed the girl,' Dolan ventured again.

'Jesus, what the hell do we do now?' Greeley asked no one in particular.

They lapsed into an impotent silence. Then Paul spoke up.

'We have to smoke them out. And you know as well as I do that there's only one way to do it.'

They looked at him, surprised by his firmness and aware that he was right. But what he was thinking was dangerous.

Before any of them could speak, there was the sound of a key turning in the front door. There were voices, amused, chuckling. A man's voice first, then a woman's.

'You might regret suggesting this,' Kate laughed. 'You'll have to take pot luck, I'm afraid. Whatever's in the fridge.'

She paused. 'Someone's smoking in here.'

The kitchen door swung open and she walked in. It took Gallagher a moment to recognise the man with her. Philipe Foucaud was neat and handsome in a double-breasted suit of Prince of Wales check. Gallagher was instantly conscious of his own rough appearance.

Kate looked bewildered.

Tom and Paul. Two complete strangers who looked like

the police. The mess on the table. The fog of cigarette smoke.

Foucaud spoke first. 'Hello again,' he smiled at Gallagher.

The flowers. There had been a card the first time. Kate had hidden it in her bag. Now he understood.

'Hi,' he said. 'Back for a replay?'

Kate glared at him. Embarrassment filled the room.

Gallagher looked at Kate and then at Foucaud. 'I'm sorry. I shouldn't have said that.'

It was a stupid and petulant remark. Yet in that instant, seeing the two of them together, he had realised truly that all was lost and it had ignited a spark of last-gasp jealousy.

Foucaud shrugged.

Kate was angry. 'Look, what the hell's going on here?'

Greeley stepped forward, taking charge with a formal air that helped him cover up his discomfort.

'Mrs Forest,' he said, 'my name is Chief Superintendent Barrett Greeley.'

'You're Greeley?' she said in surprise.

'Yes. This is my colleague, Inspector Dolan.' He looked at Foucaud. 'And this gentleman?'

'Philipe Foucaud,' the Frenchman said. 'I'm a business associate and – a friend – of Mrs Forrest.' He gave Gallagher a glance.

'Foucaud? Do you live here in Dublin?' Greeley asked.

'No, I live in Paris. I'm staying at the Shelbourne. Leaving on an early flight tomorrow morning.'

Greeley nodded. 'I'm sorry for the intrusion,' he said to Kate, 'but I'm afraid it was unavoidable. We had to wait for you. I should tell you that thanks to your son Paul here and to Mr Gallagher we've now got a lead that may help us solve a number of murders and prevent a criminal conspiracy being carried out.'

Kate looked at Gallagher.

'You mean – this Leslie business? That man—'

'Frank,' Greeley asked Dolan, 'why don't you take Mr Foucaud back to his hotel? Just have a look at his ticket while you're at it, check the time. And then, sir, I'd appreciate it if you stayed in your room for the rest of the evening. I'll have a car take you to the airport in the morning.'

'Look, what's all this—' Foucaud began.

'No reflection on you,' Greeley smiled. 'Just a safety precaution.'

'Can we get to the cars this way?' Dolan asked Paul, indicating the kitchen door.

'Yes, there's a gate at the back.'

Kate seemed dazed. Foucaud gave her a wistful look as Dolan ushered him out.

When they had gone, Gallagher spoke. 'Kate, we're going to need Paul's help.'

'What do you mean? What has he to do with all of this?'

'For reasons of security, I think it's better if we discuss this elsewhere,' Greeley told her. 'Paul has managed to uncover certain things. But I'm afraid there's a chance that some people may be looking for him.'

Kate put her hand to her mouth.

'He needs to be where no one will find him,' Greeley said. 'I'll explain it to you as we drive. You might like to gather up a few things first. I'm afraid you won't be back here this evening.'

Kate stepped back. 'I'm not going anywhere. Look – why don't you just get out of my house. Leave us alone.'

'We can't, Kate,' Gallagher said.

'You,' she said, glaring at him, 'you're the cause of all this.'

'Mum, please,' Paul said.

She looked at him. 'What kind of trouble are you in?'

'None at all if this is handled properly,' Greeley answered for him.

'Oh my God,' she gasped. Her body seemed to slump as she stood there.

Paul took her gently by the arm. How vulnerable she seemed suddenly. And how frightened.

For him.

He had caused all this trouble in part through his feelings of resentment about not having a father. He had given her such a hard time. When this was over he would make it up to her.

'Come on, Mum, it'll be all right. Let me help you get your bag.'

They left Kate's new Saab where she had parked it just a couple of doors down and went out to the police car by the back way, as Dolan had done. Gallagher and Paul sat in the rear, with Kate in the front. As Greeley drove, heading for his home at Mount Merrion, he outlined everything that had happened, taking his time and guiding her round every turn in the unfolding story.

Her fear spilled out into anger. She swung round to Gallagher.

'Look what you've done,' she shouted. 'Filled his head full of nonsense about the FBI. And now you could get him killed, never mind the rest of us.' Her eyes were on fire. 'You've done this deliberately, haven't you? What did you think – that if you made yourself out to be the big hero with my son, it would get you closer to me?'

'It wasn't that, Kate. I never dreamed that Paul would go off and do something like this. But what's happened has happened. There's no going back now.'

Greeley's house was in a new development made of pink brick that was streaked and sooty from the rain. He pulled into the driveway and turned the engine off. Kate got out and leaned against the car. She began to sob.

Gallagher tried to put his arm around her shoulder but she shrugged it off fiercely.

'Get away from me,' she said through the tears.

There was no one home but there was a note on the kitchen table. Greeley smiled as he read it, then he led them into the more comfortable surroundings of the living-room.

'The wife's gone to visit her sister in Drumcondra and she's arranged sleep-overs for the boys with some of their friends. So we're on our own.'

They stood there, the four of them, looking warily at each other.

Then Paul took over and in a calm and measured way he told his mother what had to be done.

Chapter Forty

Vinnie Dwyer was itchy with impatience. When was it
all going to happen – this wonderful new life of
prosperity that they had promised him? It was driving him
mad, hanging around like this.

This afternoon his frustration had taken him to the pub
down the road for a few pints but when he came back to
the flat he found them waiting for him. The two Americans
with the hard stare. How the hell did they get in? Jesus,
they weren't human.

'Mr Schenk wants you to do something,' Parrish said.
'It's important. Where have you been?'

They would be able to smell the alcohol. 'Went for a
drink, that's all,' he said.

Parrish's eyes showed disapproval.

'There's a woman,' he said, 'name of Kate Forrest. She
owns a travel agency, lives with her son in Ranelagh.'

He mispronounced it *Ran-ee-lagh*. Vinnie corrected him.
Parrish did not indicate that he had heard. He handed
Vinnie a slip of paper with the address of the agency and
Kate's home address.

'Think you could find these places?'

Vinnie looked at the paper. 'Sure. I know where they are.'

'Okay,' Parrish said. 'You're to follow this woman when she leaves work. Stick with her until further notice. If she moves, we want to know about it. We have to know where she is at all times. You got that?'

Vinnie nodded. He was getting irritated with these bastards.

One of these days . . .

'How do I know what she looks like?'

Parrish gave him a description. He also gave him a telephone number to ring once he thought the woman was home for the night.

'Then maybe we'll let you go home, too.'

Humble checked his watch. 'It's time you got moving.'

Vinnie was emboldened by the drink. 'Why me? Why can't you do this? I thought this kind of thing was your territory?'

Parrish's expression was blank. 'We have other arrangements to make. Mr Schenk wants you to do it.' He smiled. 'You're the coming man, Vinnie, so maybe you'd better get on with it.'

He reached the woman's office at a few minutes before five, just in time to see her leave and get into a smart green Saab that he reckoned was brand new. She drove to a snooty-looking lounge bar where he thought he might be a bit out of place in his jeans and bomber jacket so he waited with a pint in a pub across the road and watched from there.

He lingered with the last drops in the glass until it was unbearable. Then he ordered another.

A few minutes later she came out and he saw that she was now with a man in a check suit. The guy had his arm around her waist. When they drove off in the Saab, Vinnie followed, belching from the effects of the beer he had downed in haste rather than leaving it unfinished.

At Ranelagh, she parked outside a house and they went in. Vinnie circled the block and then came back. Fuck it, anyway. These people were not going anywhere tonight by the looks of them. They were probably in there shagging each other senseless already.

He took his mobile from his pocket and dialled the number he had been given. It took a while for someone to answer. It was a man's voice, one he did not know.

'Yeah, this is Vinnie. Who's this?'

'Just give your message,' the voice said.

'Yeah, well, right – she's at home. Brought a man with her. Big fellow with fairish hair. What do you want me to do?'

'Just stay there.' The man hung up.

Fuck this.

He was bursting for a leak. He would find a lavatory in the nearest pub. Have another drink, too. Why not?

Two more pints later, he was back. The Saab was still there.

He found an inconspicuous parking space and settled down to wait, wondering what in the name of fuck all this was about. He resented being kept in the dark.

After a time he began to feel a bit drowsy. He flicked the wipers on to clear the windscreen. The street was quiet. There was just a motorcycle messenger riding slowly past, looking for a number.

★ ★ ★

From the back of her departmental car, Emma stared out at the rain. It had been much more agreeable in Belfast, cooler than recent days but still sunny, and she had been surprised at the miserable wetness that greeted her when she had flown back to Dublin.

A frown flickered on her brow.

She had lunched at Stormont Castle on the outskirts of the city with the Northern Ireland Secretary and some of his senior officials. The castle was the centre of Northern Ireland administration and an office in it had been given over to her and her staff for their temporary use. When she got back there after lunch to prepare for her final meeting, she found a request to ring Tony Goulding.

She got through on his private line straight away.

'Tony, what's up?'

'Ah, great,' he said when he recognised her voice. 'Something important that I can't discuss over the phone. When will you be back?'

She looked at her watch. 'Around seven, I suppose.'

'We need to meet,' Goulding said. 'Somewhere private.' He gave her an address that she recognised.

It was now seven thirty and she was on her way there, wondering what this was about.

The car was climbing the hill of Howth, at the north end of Dublin Bay, creeping round narrow roads overlooked by proud residences which old money had built. On a clear day, which this was not, the view was spectacular, taking in all of Dublin, the coast to Dun Laoghaire and beyond, with the Sugarloaf mountain and the soft peaks of Wicklow in the background. But this evening the drizzle was like a screen.

Ted, her driver, changed down another gear. The hill was getting wilder, gardens gradually giving way to unkempt fields, and it was harder to climb. Near the peak, the houses were fewer. There were dry stone walls and a thick covering of heather that was beginning to turn purple, the faintness of the colour making it almost an illusion.

They turned into a driveway that seemed impossibly steep and narrow but at the top it opened out into a tarmac plateau in front of a large house. Several other cars were already parked there, Goulding's among them, and she could see his driver wiping condensation from the inside of his window. Ted mistook the gesture for a greeting and waved back.

He opened her door for her and she got out, feeling the sudden force of the wind on the exposed headland. She looked up at the house. It was built of sandstone and it had a terracotta-coloured roof. Each room had huge windows so that the entire front of the house had access to the view.

There was someone at an upper window. For a second she glimpsed a man. Someone with grey hair. He pulled back when he saw her looking.

The front door opened and George Levy stood there. Even though this was his house, she was surprised to see him.

'Hello, George,' she said. 'I didn't actually expect that you'd be here.'

His smile was anaemic. 'He's waiting for you,' he said and stood back. When she was in the hall, he closed the door behind her.

'This way.'

There was something strange here.

'What is all this, George?'

He did not answer but instead led her up the stairs where he opened the door to a first floor drawing room.

Goulding was sitting in an armchair turned towards the door. A second man stood at the window. He had his back to her and had resumed his study of what was available of the view. Levy took up a position by the door.

Goulding stood. 'Emma, you're here. I'd like you to meet someone.'

The man turned from the window. At the sight of him her heart began to pound.

She took in the steel grey hair, the pale, soul-less eyes.

But some intuition told her that she should not let her recognition show. She felt as if her legs were turning to liquid and she willed them to retain their strength.

'May I introduce Mr Gilbert Leslie,' Goulding said.

With those words, it was as if some mythical creature had been made flesh, created in this room as a handsome man with fading looks but with an aura of power and menace that nothing could weaken.

In her state of shock she found herself letting him shake her hand. He had short fingers and his grip was dry and firm.

She thought of him grasping the throat of the girl in Temple Bar and she took her hand away again quickly.

Her mind went into playback. Everything her father had said, everything that had happened, all of it seemed to be flashing by, headlong. She looked at Tony Goulding and saw only the slick features, the greasy smile, not the warm paternal figure he once had been.

Her life was ruined. And as she looked at Gilbert Leslie, she knew why he had come.

'As a matter of fact, I used to know your father quite well,' Leslie said, gesturing towards an armchair for her and taking a seat himself.

'Really?' Emma said as she sat. Her legs would not have held her up for much longer.

Leslie's eyes locked on to hers. Was it possible she did not know anything about him? Or was this a feigned ignorance? And, if so, what else might it conceal?

He felt suddenly wary.

Emma saw the look and knew she had made a mistake. She could not pretend she had never heard of Leslie or the part he had played in her father's life; that would be foolish. Yet she knew instinctively that if she were to reveal that her father knew Leslie was here, it would almost certainly mean his death.

She looked at Goulding. He did not know about any of her father's theories. Out of feelings of embarrassment and self-preservation, she had avoided telling any of the people who were closest to her about the things she had believed were only in Tom Gallagher's tortured mind.

She had been ashamed of him. She had scorned him.

You empty-headed fool.

There was lost ground to recover.

She looked at Leslie with a smile, then allowed it to vanish quickly. 'I'm not stupid,' she said. 'I know who you are. And don't patronise me.'

Leslie sat back in his armchair. 'Well, at least that saves a long introduction.'

413

'What I'd like to know,' she continued, 'is what the hell a criminal like you is doing here in this country and what your association is with a Government Minister?'

She knew her indignation would sound hollow. Outside in the rain there were armed police drivers from the special protection unit, yet there was no way she could bring them to her aid. She looked at Levy waiting by the door and she felt like a prisoner. But then her gaze fell again on Goulding, her patron and mentor, and she conceded that her captivity had begun a long time ago.

'Two Government Ministers, as a matter of fact,' Leslie corrected. 'But let me get to the point and not waste any more time. Mr Goulding tells me you intend to vote for the management buy-out. That's rather disappointing. I'm afraid we can't allow such a thing to happen.'

She stared at him. 'You're the Dhow Consortium.'

He nodded. 'In a way. We've spent a great deal of time and effort to ensure that the Dhow bid will have a fair wind. You, Miss Gallagher, have been placed in position for a purpose. Mr Goulding assured us that you would follow his wishes so it would be rather unfortunate if you, of all people, were the one to knock the matter off course.'

Everything that had happened had been designed to secure the take-over. My God, there must have been years of preparation. First her own grooming by Goulding, then the emergence of Sean Donovan and the murderous events that had followed, all choreographed in order to engineer the sacking of the one remaining Cabinet Minister who would have resisted Goulding and who might have encouraged others to rally to his standard.

She felt an inner rage, in part because of these men and

what they had set out to do, but mostly it was directed at herself. Blind to everything except the power that she craved, she had gone along with Goulding, trampling others underfoot to get what she wanted and all the while making Gilbert Leslie's goal the more attainable.

She had not believed her father and his warnings. She had dismissed him like an old fool. But it was she who was the idiot.

It was an extraordinary scheme, outrageous. But it had not succeeded yet. Instead of being an advantage to them, she had become a stumbling block.

What was their plan now? To kill her? No, it would not be that. Too crude. It would cause too much disorder and put the privatisation vote back still further, perhaps forever, if there was a General Election in the interim.

She looked at Goulding and saw that beneath the veneer he was uneasy. Her discussion over breakfast yesterday had forced him to tip his hand and bring Leslie out into the open. That would not have been part of the strategy.

'Well, the matter is very definitely off course now,' she said. 'There'll be no vote at all. Not after I've seen the Prime Minister and the *Garda* Commissioner, which I intend to do as soon as I leave here.'

Leslie laughed. Light, almost a chuckle.

'Don't be silly,' he said. 'You know we can't allow you to do that.'

'How are you going to stop me? By force?'

'No, of course not. What do you think we are? When we've concluded our discussion, you will leave here freely. But let me point something out to you. As you can imagine, we've gone to some lengths to make sure we've got – how shall I put it – all our bases covered. Taps on your phones, that kind of thing. Your father's phone, too. So if there's any attempt to contact the *Taoiseach* or the Commissioner, or anyone else, for that matter, like your father, for instance, then we'll know about it. Such foolishness on your part would have serious consequences, I'm afraid, particularly for him.'

She could not keep the fear out of her eyes.

'Oh, we're not going to kill him,' Leslie said. He paused, keeping her guessing. 'We'll kill his friend Mrs Forrest instead.'

A phone rang somewhere and Levy left the room to answer it. She used those few moments to try to recover herself.

'So you see,' Leslie said, 'the Cabinet meeting will go ahead as planned and, of course, if there's any silliness during it, then, naturally, the same situation will apply.'

In her mind, Emma searched frantically for some hope but she could find none.

'We have Mrs Forrest under surveillance,' Leslie said. 'That telephone call will have confirmed it. So don't think about trying to contact her, either.'

Levy came back into the room and whispered something to Leslie.

'Good,' Leslie grinned. 'And your father would appear to be with her. Both of them where we can keep an eye on them.'

'This is lunacy,' Emma said.

'On the contrary, it is business.'

'But Aer Rianta. Bruce Morrow and the management team won't give up. They'll go for a judicial review of the decision if it goes against them. They'll try to get the whole thing opened up again. You'll never win.'

In Leslie's smile she saw with sinking heart that he would have thought of all that.

'You leave Mr Morrow to me,' he said. 'I think that in a couple of days he'll be rather too preoccupied. A family bereavement, you understand.'

My God. What was he going to do?

She turned to Goulding. 'And you – you have gone along with all of this? Without a qualm? All this murder?'

Goulding shrugged and did not answer but his face had become grey.

Leslie laughed again. 'He's a little reticent, poor man.' He gestured towards Levy. 'George here has been an associate of ours for quite a while. I'm afraid he gave Mr Goulding rather bad financial advice some time ago which might have destroyed him if we hadn't come to his rescue. As a result, he's been rather grateful to us and tremendously helpful. Until now.'

No one missed the menace in the words.

Emma thought suddenly of Levy's connection with Marcuscreen. 'It was you who killed Marcus Kelly,' she said, 'not Sean Donovan.'

'Of course. We made a martyr out of him. That was always the plan, apart from which he had become rather greedy into the bargain. It was a suitable move all round.'

'And me – was it because of who my father is that I was *selected*?'

She made the word sound as if it were part of some hideous experiment.

'Interestingly, no,' Leslie said. 'I discovered exactly who

417

you were only recently when you were drawn to my attention. It was then I decided to come to Dublin and handle things myself.'

Emma felt the anger boiling in her.

'You didn't handle things in Temple Bar very well, did you?'

Something flashed in Leslie's eyes, a hint of alarm. Goulding looked a bit confused. Levy frowned.

'What are you talking about?' Goulding said.

'Ask *him*,' Emma said, taunting. She would have to conceal the real source of her information, that her father had recognised him, but it might cause them some anxiety and cast doubt in Leslie's direction. There was nothing to lose.

'Ask him about the waitress he murdered in Temple Bar,' she said. 'Raped her and strangled her. I knew when I came in here that I'd seen his face somewhere before. It's a match for the computer picture of the man the police are looking for. The foreign gentleman they're so anxious to talk to. They're searching everywhere.'

'Gilbert?' Levy asked.

Leslie threw his hands wide. 'Pay no attention. She's trying to unsettle you. I have no idea what she's talking about.'

He looked at Emma. His stare was so intense that his eyes seemed to be dead, fixed like the eyes of a doll.

At that moment, she saw in his face what would happen when all this was over, the fatal consequences of the fact that he had had to show himself.

But then it was also likely that he had made his decision about that a long time ago.

Both she and Goulding knew far too much to be allowed to live.

A period of time would be allowed to elapse but in the end they would both be disposed of in some way.

Her father, too. For old time's sake.

As she was driven away a short time later, Leslie watched from the window. He had been impressed by her. She had a defiant spirit, anger that was like a flame, but soon it would have to be extinguished.

There were loose ends, still. He did not like that. Goulding had not delivered her, like he said he would, but in order to save the life of the woman Forrest she would do what she was told.

The bank, that computer business. That still had to be cleaned up. Time was running out.

Calm yourself. Everything will be fine. And then . . .

His little leather bag lay on a chair. He reached in and took a set of photographs from it.

It was a long time since he had seen Tom Gallagher and he would never see him in the flesh ever again. That was why he had asked for these pictures.

They were of poor quality because they were frames taken from a video camera, yet he could recognise Gallagher clearly enough. As he stared, he focused his hate on the face in them.

You are the man who killed my son. At last I will have my vengeance.

He turned to the window. It would be a greater retribution than he had ever dreamed of. The father and the daughter.

He looked at the pictures again. Goulding was in them, too, standing at a fireplace with Gallagher and others, a drink in his hand.

Emma sat alone with a whiskey. She had changed into a shirt and jeans because she somehow felt tarnished in her business suit. Outside the latticed windows of her little house, wind rustled the trees and the rain dripped from broad drooping leaves.

They had to be stopped.

She did not care what happened to herself, she was beyond redemption now, but she could not let this thing go on. Yet any attempt to stop it could mean death for Kate, even her father, and with its success there would be more killing. Leslie's ominous reference to Bruce Morrow echoed in her thoughts.

Of course, he could be bluffing; she knew that. But it was unlikely. She thought of the murders he had already sanctioned, each one a specific step in a corporate business plan. And there was the girl he had killed through what could only have been his own animal lust.

She sipped her drink and looked across the room at the telephone she could not use.

At that moment it rang and made her jump.

Some of the whiskey slopped from her glass on to the back of her wrist. She licked it as she went to answer.

It was Fergal on an echoing line.

'Ah, you're back,' he said.

'From where?'

'From Belfast.'

'Oh – yes. I am.' She had forgotten she had even been

there. 'I just got in a short time ago. Where are you? In Italy or somewhere?'

'No. On the way from the airport. Just back from Milan. I can be with you in half an hour.'

Fergal. Her problems with him had gone from her mind. She should really tell him she wanted to be on her own but at the same time she felt the need of some company, some sort of comfort, which he would be happy to provide.

But she would draw the line at sex; that had to stop.

'Yes, all right,' she said.

'I'll take you up to my place,' he suggested. 'I bet your house is freezing.'

He was right. It was cold in here. With the rain had come a drop in temperature. The fire was too draughty to light and she had been too preoccupied to switch the heating on.

He was there in twenty-five minutes. She called the duty officer at the department and said that she would be on her mobile for most of the evening, which probably meant all of it, she knew.

'You don't look very happy,' Mulryne said as he drove. 'What's wrong?'

'Sorry. Got a lot on my plate at the moment.'

'Which leads me nicely to the next question – are you hungry?'

She was not but she was happy enough to sit in his big warm kitchen with a bottle of red wine while he went to the fridge, cut several thick slices of cold beef, smeared them generously with horseradish and made a towering sandwich for himself.

'Sure you won't have one?'

She shook her head and poured herself another glass of wine.

'So what's the big problem,' he wondered. 'Anything you can share?'

'Not really, no.'

Too right. I don't want to get you killed as well.

'State secrets?'

'Something like that, yes.'

Instead, they talked about his day. In between bites of sandwich he told her about his trip to Milan and about some new business ventures he was thinking of getting into. She made polite noises of interest every now and then but in reality she did not take in any of it because in her mind there was distress that not even the wine could ease.

Mulryne opened another bottle and asked her if she had seen anything of her father lately.

'No,' she said. 'I haven't.' She felt a surge of guilt at how hard she had been on him. 'I should call him when—' She paused.

'When what?'

'Oh, I don't know. Whenever.' She drank some more wine. She was getting drunk. Time to get out of here and go to bed before she let anything slip. She stood and pushed her chair back noisily.

'You're nice, Fergal, and I could sit here talking to you all night but I'm tired and I want to go to bed, okay?' She gave him a look that she hoped was stern. 'To sleep.'

He laughed gently. 'Whatever you want.' He kissed her on the cheek as she passed him and made her way towards the stairs.

She woke at two am with a raging thirst and a headache burning above her eyebrows. She had paracetamol in her handbag but she needed a glass of water badly.

She slipped gently out of the bed so that she would not wake Fergal but when she turned and looked back she saw that he was not there. She had not felt him getting up but then she realised that it was that which must have woken her, in spite of the sedative power of the alcohol.

There was a robe behind the door but she did not bother with it. She walked quietly along the darkened landing, heading for the stairs and the kitchen. The carpet was deep and warm and slightly ticklish under her bare feet.

At the top of the stairs she paused. There was a voice. In a room right beside her, Fergal was talking to someone.

She listened and heard something unfamiliar in his tone. He was keeping his voice low but she could hear a rasp in it, like anger being kept under control.

No one else was speaking. He was on the phone. At this time of night?

She stepped nearer to the door where the words were clearer.

'This is bad,' Mulryne said. 'How the fuck could he have missed her? When did he discover she wasn't there?'

Emma felt a chill run over her naked body. There was a silence. The other person must be speaking.

'What if they don't turn up?'

A pause.

'What, bluff it?'

He listened for a long time and then seemed convinced. 'Well, yes, that's true. I suppose you're right.'

Another pause. 'No, she won't try anything stupid, I'm

sure of that, and she won't know we're not in a position to deal with Mrs Forrest. But, Jesus, this is getting messy. What about the trace?'

There was another short silence while the other voice spoke once more.

'Good. Let's see what the fuck it's all about. Christ almighty, we don't need any of this.'

The phone beeped as he rang off.

God – he had finished.

She had to get back to the bedroom before he saw her. She took off down the corridor, moving as lightly as she could, and just as she was closing the bedroom door behind her, she heard the other door opening.

Had he seen her?

She slipped into bed, feeling numbingly cold. She gritted her teeth fiercely and tried not to shiver.

She could sense the door being eased gently open and then she felt the bed sag as Mulryne got in beside her. She lay with her back to him, eyes clenched shut, hoping she sounded as if she were breathing normally in sleep but her heart was beating so hard she could almost hear it.

'God, you're like ice,' he murmured. 'Let me warm you up.'

He snuggled up tight and she could feel the whole length of his body against her. His breath was on the nape of her neck and his arm was across her, a hand cupping her breast. She felt his genitals against her buttocks and his feet spreading their heat into hers.

She lay still and tense and afraid in the darkness and used all of her willpower to stop herself being sick.

Chapter Forty-One

At five forty-five, as Mulryne snored and a grey light began to suggest itself in the room, Emma slipped out of bed again, gathered her clothes and crept to the bathroom.

She was parched and hungover and still fearful but she was fired with a new determination. She had lain awake, her skin creeping with revulsion at Mulryne's touch with its clammy night sweat, and she had endured spasms of disbelief, then self-loathing and finally an anger that she could barely contain.

She turned on the cold tap and stuck her mouth underneath it. She gulped eagerly until the thirst had abated for the moment, then she looked at herself in the mirror.

Water was dripping from lips that looked bruised. Her eyes were red and raw and there was a sickly darkness in the skin around them. Remorse, rage and a bottle and a half of red wine had produced devastating effects.

She stared at herself, facing the bitter truth.

It was as if pages kept turning, each one revealing a further example of how much she had let herself be taken in. She shuddered with disgust. They had used her in every way possible. Even her body had been violated.

It was Goulding who had introduced her to Mulryne. She had been alone and unattached, an ambitious woman hungry to go places, and, calculatingly, she had seen him as a suitable person with whom to have a relationship. She had been taken in by his warm, easy-going charm, she had been flattered by his attentions, impressed by his wealth and influence, and she had figured that an association with him would further secure her own position.

You stupid bitch.

All the time he had been a plant, placed strategically in her life and in her bed, if not ultimately in her heart. That, at least, was something.

Mulryne, in turn, had suggested she use George Levy to look after her financial affairs. God knows what explosive devices lay hidden there, to be detonated when they saw fit, bringing ruin and disgrace.

It was Levy who had fed her all that stuff about Marcus Kelly's investigations that she had used in the *Dail*. It had not cost her a thought to ruin the life of a member of the Opposition, a man she did not even know. But that paled into insignificance when she thought of the murders – brutal killings that had guaranteed her advancement, slaughter carried out in her name.

She took her mobile phone from her handbag and called the duty officer at her department, asking them to send her car to Mulryne's address straight away. Ted had picked her up here a couple of times before and she had wondered what he thought in his discreet silence. Whatever happened, this would be the last time he would come for her at this house.

It took him forty-five minutes to get there during which, thankfully, Mulryne did not stir and she was able to repair some of the damage of the night. She did not want Ted to see her looking a mess. It was not just vanity but the need for her to present a public face that had the appearance of normality.

They drove first to her own house where she changed into a skirt and jacket. There was an important meeting in the diary for this morning, followed by a whole afternoon of routines with her staff and then Cabinet tonight.

Christ, how was she going to manage this, without a moment to herself?

Somehow she had to find Kate and talk to her father. He would know what to do. If Leslie and Mulryne did not know where Kate was, then they could not threaten her. And if she could track her down first, then maybe there was a chance of making sure they were hidden out of harm's way.

Ted seemed to be taking a scenic route to avoid the worst traffic bottlenecks. They were on the coast road, heading towards the city. It was raining again, a thick drizzle that the wind carried like a cloak across the wet sand.

As she took in her surroundings, she realised that she was near her father's apartment. She took the mobile out of her bag again and dialled his number, not expecting him to answer and not knowing what she would do if he did. It was desperation.

Nothing. There was just the sound of his voice on the machine. She hung up.

God where was he?

★ ★ ★

Gallagher's guilt kept watch with him as he prayed that history would not repeat itself.

He and Barrett Greeley sat in a vacant office on a third storey in South William Street, drinking coffee that was like tar and eating granary bagels from the health food shop on the ground floor. A sign outside their window said that the office was to let. They sat back a little, in shadow, glancing down through the rain at a lifeless building across the way.

It might be a long day. The caffeine hit from the coffee was badly needed, especially by Gallagher and his hangover. It had been a tough night, without sleep, and the stress of it had drained them.

Kate had not given her consent to her son's involvement in what they were doing. It was more a case that she had caved in, crumbling under Paul's insistence and their promises that everything would be all right.

But there could be no guarantees. No one knew that better than he did. Once again, he was putting someone's life at risk. A boy this time, just a kid, not a couple of trained agents.

Technically, the operation was under Greeley's command but Gallagher felt that he and he alone held the responsibility, that he and he alone had inspired Paul's involvement. And now he was letting him get in even deeper.

He wondered how Kate was. She would not have slept much, if at all, and she would have heard Paul leave this morning with Inspector Dolan, who had come to the house after installing Foucaud safely at the Shelbourne.

428

Greeley had called the Assistant Commissioner last night. What they were planning required authorisation which only he could give and so Greeley had gone to see him at his home. Gallagher had waited in the car while Greeley explained to his senior officer that he had good information from a reliable source that if they put a certain building in South William Street under surveillance there was a very good chance they would catch the suspect in the Temple Bar murder case.

He did not tell him any more than that and as discreetly as he could, he also suggested that the matter should be kept on a need-to-know basis. The Assistant Commissioner liked being on the inside track and he had agreed. Then, with the go-ahead negotiated successfully, Greeley put his stake-out team together.

The next move was to get access to the magazine offices, then find a spot from which to watch. They had selected this place as the best possible vantage point. A couple of officers had roused a flustered estate agent to get the keys, warning him that this was a matter of great secrecy and that there would be dire consequences if he opened his mouth and told anybody about it.

At three am the DJ who owned *Dave* had just got back from a gig and he and his wife were hardly in bed when two officers dropped in on them, too. Then they paid a visit to a bleary Max. There would be new staff in his office today. He and his team would find they had extra help.

There were now about two dozen involved in the operation one way or another. Too many, Gallagher worried. Were they good? Could they be trusted?

Whoever came for Paul, alias *Dave*, would come to find out what he knew and then kill him. He could not let that happen. Yet sitting here in this room, relying on people he did not know, he felt powerless to stop it.

They were not alone in the office, nor was it at all as empty as it had been several hours ago. One wall was taken up with surveillance equipment. Two men with headphones sat at a set of monitors. On the screens were several angles of a darkened office, relayed to them by cameras which had been installed and concealed with remarkable speed.

He had to grant them that; the technicians seemed to know what they were doing. But the sight of the monitors brought the past back to him.

The ghosts of Gaines and Dobchek seemed to hover in the room.

Greeley gave him a glance and saw the tension in his face.

'I don't want anything to happen to him any more than you do,' he said. 'And I'm going to make bloody sure that nothing does. But we both know it's the only way to get these bastards.'

'You've only got your job to lose,' Gallagher reminded him. 'It's his life.'

Emma's personal assistant was an effete young man called Charles Hearne who fussed over her constantly. Yesterday he had been complaining of a bad head cold and today he had phoned in sick.

She had not read any of the papers for this morning's meeting and now he was not here to give her a briefing.

Very inconvenient. It would be a difficult session, too, with the Attorney General and a team of legal advisers, to thrash out a new policy on the granting of bail. Normally, she would have relished getting her teeth into something so important but not this morning.

The meeting was due to begin at nine thirty. She tried to scan the documents as quickly as she could. It was no use. Her mind would not stay on the subject.

When the Attorney General and the others came in, she greeted them with a forced warmth. They got down to business quickly and she willed herself to concentrate but her contributions were vague and often confusing. Several times she saw people looking at her and she realised they were waiting for an answer to a question she had not heard.

When coffee came at eleven, she flew out of the room, oblivious to the irritated frowns round the table, and shut herself in Hearne's empty office with a telephone book. She did not know Kate Forrest's number but she knew the name of her travel agency. She looked it up and dialled.

'I'm sorry,' a woman's voice said. 'I'm afraid Mrs Forrest hasn't come in yet. We're expecting her any moment, I hope.'

To Emma she sounded surprised, as if it was an unusual occurrence for Kate not to have arrived by this time.

She went back to the meeting, walking in on an awkward silence from the men around the table, and knew that they had been talking about her. The proceedings resumed but after a while she stood up abruptly.

'Look,' she said, 'I'm sorry. This is pointless. There's no

use going on. You've probably observed that I'm not feeling myself this morning.' She touched her brow. 'A bit of a virus or something, I'm afraid. Really – I'm wasting your time. Might we reschedule?'

They looked at her curiously, then stood and shuffled their papers and told her they quite understood. They no longer felt insulted by her odd behaviour. It was all perfectly clear. She was just a woman, women were prone to women's – things – and they felt comfortable with that because it restored their feeling of male superiority.

Emma saw the patronising looks but she did not care. They could think what they liked.

When they had gone, she got the telephone book again and shut the door. What was the name of the magazine where Kate Forrest's son hung out? Kate had talked about it in conversation that night at Mulryne's house, saying she was worried about him being there so much.

Something to do with rave music – *Dave*, that was it.

In the book she found the number and the address. It was in South William Street, not that far away. Maybe someone there would have an inkling where Paul was. If not, she was finished. She would have used up her last idea.

'Hello,' a male voice said when she dialled. She could hear music thumping in the background.

'Oh, hello. I wonder if you could help me. I'm trying to track down a young man called Paul Forrest who works with you sometimes. Is there any chance anyone there might know where I could find him?'

"Sorry,' the voice said. 'It's a bit mental here. I'm going to have to put you on hold. Do you mind?'

'Well, actually—' she began and then she found herself listening to some techno thing being pumped down the line.

She waited for a couple of minutes and she was about to hang up when the voice came back.

'I'm really sorry,' he said. 'Who did you say you were looking for – Paul Forrest?'

'Yes.'

'He's here. Do you want to talk to him?'

She froze and then rang off abruptly without giving an answer.

He was there? She looked at her watch. Just after twelve. Had he skipped school?

Whatever – he might know where his mother and her father were. She had to talk to him but not on the phone. How could she do that? How could she get down there to see him?

She went to the window and looked out at the Green. The people had deserted it and left it to the mercy of the rain. There were just one or two passing through under umbrellas.

She could not simply walk out of this place and down to South William Street. When she was here, at work in her office, she could do nothing without telling her staff what she was up to and without Ted, her loyal minder, tagging along.

But *was* he loyal? That was the question. Were any of them? The girls in the outer office, for instance? Or had Leslie planted them, too?

God, she was going mad. The seeds of doubt had been established firmly by everything that had happened to her in the past twelve hours. There was no one she could trust except those people she could not reach.

There had to be a way.

She turned from the window. She felt warm, flushed with the stress. She took her jacket off and walked to the closet to hang it up.

Her sports bag was inside on the floor.

She stared at it as if she had just seen it for the first time and then she knew that she had not run out of ideas after all.

At *Dave*, Paul sat at his computer, logged into the chat room, and waited to see Gigolo's name appear. There were ten names down the side of the screen, some of them engaged in conversation, others, like himself, observing.

'But then the name might not appear at all,' he told Gallagher and Greeley, who were watching him on the monitors across the street.

The screens were no longer dim. Instead, they showed the workings of a busy office. Max was hyper-active. He still had a magazine to get out. He did not know what the hell was going on, but it looked bloody serious. He consoled himself with the knowledge that the conventional press, the newspapers he pretended to despise, would pay a fortune for the inside story once he was in a position to tell it.

Along with the hidden cameras there were several concealed microphones and Paul had been wired, too. There was a transmitter pad taped to the small of his back and a microphone like a tiny medallion on his chest.

'What does he mean?' Greeley asked.

'The guy might use another name,' Gallagher explained. 'He doesn't have to be Gigolo any more. He might be any one of these people in the chat room now. All he needs to do is make sure Paul's where he's supposed to be at one o'clock.'

The phone rang and Gallagher felt the tension tighten another notch.

A woman was asking about Paul Forrest.

The call was answered by one of Greeley's people and he kept the woman hanging on while they got the trace.

'Let him talk to her,' Greeley said.

But by the time he picked up the phone she had gone.

The call had brought a charge of excitement that crackled across the street. Something was happening at last.

Greeley's phone rang a few moments later.

'Thanks,' he said when he had listened. He looked up with an expression of regret.

'The call for Paul. It came from the Justice Department.'

'Emma?' Gallagher found it hard to believe.

Greeley nodded. 'Probably. It looks like it's started.'

Gallagher frowned. 'She asked for Paul by name?'

'Yes.'

'How would she know to do that?'

It was twelve thirty. Lunchtime. It should have been a sandwich with Hearne and a consultation about next week's diary but he was not here and now she was glad. It gave her the time she needed. She opened the door to the secretaries in the outer office.

'Get Ted and tell him he can take me down to the fitness club for an hour,' she said.

The club was in Great St George's Street, a rumbling one-way thoroughfare clogged with buses and lorries, and she could have walked there in ten minutes or so. The heavy traffic meant that Ted had her there in fifteen.

There was no parking directly outside because it would have meant blocking a lane and causing a jam so he dropped her at the door. He watched her duck under the awning and go in. Then he drove on, weaving through the side streets until he came out again at Fade Street, which was across the road and down a bit, and from where he would have a good view.

He got right up to the corner today, which was even better. Normally, there was a woman selling flowers just here but the rain had driven her under cover, to the Market Arcade a short distance away.

Inside the club building, Emma walked down the long narrow entrance hall with her sports bag in her hand. There were Herb Ritts photographs on the walls and she glanced at James Dean, alone and moody in a diner. Fish of many colours swam listlessly in their tanks and a receptionist was putting letters in envelopes while half watching MTV.

She looked up and smiled when she saw who it was. Emma tried to come here at least twice a week but in the days since her appointment she had not been at all.

'Miss Gallagher,' she said. 'Haven't seen you here for a while.'

'No, indeed. I've fallen by the wayside. Time to make up for it.'

She got a locker key and opened the door of the ladies' changing area just past reception. Beyond that was the main gym. She knew that at this time of day she was unlikely to be alone. There were three other women there, two in tee-shirts and lycra leggings, the third showered and dressed and zipping up her bag to go home. If they knew who she was, it did not show.

Emma undressed to her underwear then put on jogging trousers and a jacket with a hood. She folded her hair up under a baseball cap, took some change from her purse and stuck it in her pocket. She put everything else in the bag, unconcerned about how that would leave her elegant office clothes, and locked it away.

Most people came for a work-out or a game of squash but it was not unusual for someone to go for a run and then come back for a sauna or a shower.

One of the women looked at her. 'A bit damp for that sort of thing today,' she said.

'Miserable, isn't it? But I've got to keep up the miles.'

She laced up her running shoes and then spent a few moments stretching, touching her toes, feeling her calf muscles going taut and her back reacting to the strain. Then she opened the door and went back out into the hall. The receptionist was on the phone and did not pay any attention to her as she slipped past.

At the front door she paused and looked out. She could see Ted parked down there on the corner to her right. The traffic was thick but it was moving.

Somewhere further along, the lights changed to red and all movement stopped. The shadow of a huge container lorry darkened the doorway and she could no longer see across the street. She pulled her hood up over her cap, tied it tight at her throat, and ran out, turning left and away.

When Ted's view was restored, all he saw was the doorway, empty, as it had been before.

She needed to get to the other side. She dodged swiftly through the static traffic and was nearly across when a cyclist in a hurry almost claimed her. She saw him at the last moment and side-stepped like a bullfighter.

Her heart leaped.

Careful, damn it. Don't get yourself killed.

Slowing to a pace that would be less noticeable, she entered the big open Market Arcade, passing the flower seller looking unhappily out at the rain. No one bought flowers on a day like this.

She ran across the cobbles, past a stall selling memorabilia of Irish history, reproductions of momentous proclamations and prints of Michael Collins defiantly heroic in uniform. A Lebanese woman stood behind huge tubs of olives and dates and the scent of joss came from a stall selling third-world fabrics.

She was out of the arcade in seconds and into South William Street.

She stopped running and began to walk, looking at the numbers and finding that in some cases there were none at all.

A Volkswagen van bearing the name of a shopfitting company was right up on the pavement outside a building with boarded-up windows and she was forced to step out into the roadway. As she did, she looked across and saw a clothes shop with little office signs at the doorway beside it.

Dave – 2nd floor – one of them said.

She stood looking up at the windows and then went in.

From the inside the shopfitting van Frank Dolan gave them all the alert.

'Someone entering the building. A jogger, looks like. Got a hood up. Can't see the face but I'd say it's a woman.'

Gallagher looked down from the window but the figure had gone inside.

In the *Dave* office, it had gone quiet. Everyone seemed to be rooted to the spot for a moment, then they moved into position hurriedly. If the visitor tried anything, then four guns would come into play from four different angles.

One of them would belong to Detective Constable Nora Friel, a small, chunky young woman in a denim skirt which hung loose and covered the automatic holstered behind her back. Her hair was thick and untidy over the earpiece wire that ran up the back of her neck. She was only twenty-one but like the rest of Greeley's hand-picked team she was already a veteran of surveillance and undercover operations.

'Jesus, stick a CD on,' she said.

Someone crossed the room and pushed the play button. As the door opened and Emma walked in, a drum and bass track hit the room and they felt its impact on their skin like the shock waves of an explosion.

For a second Emma recoiled from it, too. The volume was so loud that no one seemed to notice she was there.

The place was a mess. There was no semblance of order, just sound equipment and posters and several desks strewn with papers and magazine. She wondered who she should speak to, which one of them was Paul Forrest.

There were a couple of computers. A boy in his teens

was sitting at one of them. He turned and glanced shyly at her, then looked away again.

'Excuse me,' she said. She had to raise her voice. She stepped forward and took her hood down, then she removed the cap. Her hair spilled out and she shook her head.

Across the street Gallagher breathed in sharply.

'It's Emma,' he whispered.

Pale beside him, Greeley watched the monitor.

'Turn that fucking volume down,' he muttered into a handset.

Paul was staring at Emma.

It was her.

Someone went to the CD player and the music dropped a few decibels.

'This is the *Dave* office, right?' she asked.

The boy nodded.

'I'm looking for Paul Forrest.'

'I'm – Paul Forrest,' he said, standing up.

Emma looked around the room. Everyone else appeared occupied. No one had recognised her. She moved closer to him.

Nora Friel shifted her position slightly and moved her hand behind her back.

'Do you know who I am?' Emma asked softly.

Paul nodded. He thought he had lost the ability to speak.

The woman looked agitated, very edgy.

'I've come to tell you that your mother's in danger,' she said. 'There are people looking for her and they mustn't find her. I've got to get a message to her and my father. I need to explain it all to you. But this isn't the place. Can you get away from here?'

He nodded again.

'Someone else coming into the building,' Dolan reported suddenly from the van, breaking the watchers' concentration. 'A man carrying something.'

Gallagher looked out of the window and saw a man in glasses and a raincoat with a bundle in his hand. The CD finished and there was a temporary silence. In the *Dave* office they could hear footsteps climbing the old wooden stairs.

'The Powerscourt Townhouse,' Emma said. 'Just up the street. The coffee shop on the ground floor. Can you be there in ten minutes?'

The footsteps went past to the floor above.

Paul found his voice. 'Yes,' he said.

The footsteps were coming back down. The door opened and a man walked in. A pair of trousers was folded in his hand.

'Excuse me,' Emma said and brushed him on her way out.

The man smiled at Paul. 'I'm sorry to bother you,' he said. 'The old guy on the floor above. The tailor. You don't happen to know if he's open again after lunch?'

'Sorry,' Paul said. 'No idea.'

'Thanks anyway,' the man said and left.

Dolan watched Emma come out of the building. She had her cap back on and the hood up. She walked towards the Powerscourt Townhouse. In a few seconds, the man came out, heading in the same direction, then turned a corner.

'Find out where he's going, someone,' Greeley said.

The Townhouse was an impressive structure which Lord Powerscourt had built in 1774 as his city dwelling. Now it was a shopping centre and it ran between South William Street and Clarendon Street. The elegant Georgian front had been maintained and restored but the interior had been scooped out to make way for bijou stores of all kinds and a big, open food court that could be viewed from every floor.

Some of the watchers were on their way there before Emma had reached the bottom of the stairs.

'What the hell's she doing?' Greeley wondered.

'It's not going to happen here,' Gallagher said. 'They want to take him somewhere and they've sent her because he'll follow her. They figure he knows who she is and he'll trust her. But—' he frowned. '— I still can't figure out how she knew about him.'

Greeley spoke to Paul. 'Do what she says. Follow her to the Townhouse. And don't worry – we'll have our people all over the place.'

'He's disappeared, sir,' a voice said.

'Who?'

'The man who came in. I think he's headed towards Grafton Street.'

'Fine. Leave it.'

'What about us?' Gallagher asked. The monitors would be of no use now. They could not see what was happening in the Townhouse.

'We wait here,' Greeley said.

'Jesus, this is unbearable.'

Greeley ordered a team to go to the Clarendon Street exit and a second group to the one in South William Street where a flight of broad steps led up to an entrance hall. Others, Frank Dolan among them, went inside the building and mingled.

The Mary Rose restaurant was on a slightly raised area on the ground floor. Although it was lunchtime not all its tables were occupied and Emma managed to find one on a corner. She kept her cap on. Behind her a bonsai stall displayed its miniature wares.

A waitress came and she ordered a coffee.

'We're doing lunches,' the waitress said.

'I'm waiting for someone,' Emma told her. 'I'll order when he gets here.'

On the floor just above her there was a deli. Dolan sat down at a table beside the ornate railings which ran along the edge and ordered a coffee and a corned beef sandwich. He never liked to miss an opportunity to eat.

Directly across from him, two of the team had taken up positions at a table in front of an antique gallery. Two others were on the floor above, studying the menus of an Italian restaurant. Dolan felt warm and bulky in his raincoat but he did not want to take it off. He had a microphone and transmitter in the inside pocket of his jacket and he had put on a shoulder holster because he found it easier to get at.

He hoped he would not have to. He sat closer to the railings. They would partially obscure him from anyone looking up.

'Everyone in place,' he said to Greeley and Gallagher waiting with blind faith down the street.

His order arrived and as he smeared mustard on the sandwich his ears picked up the song coming from the shopping centre's speakers. Pan pipes were cooing *Some-one To Watch Over Me*. He wondered if anyone else had noticed.

Paul walked in, looked around and saw Emma, then headed towards her table.

The sandwich would wait. 'The boy's here,' Dolan said.

Gallagher and Greeley heard the noise of the shopping centre and the snatched voices of people whom Paul passed by. They heard a rustle when he sat down and then Gallagher heard Emma speaking. At first it was not easy to pick up what she was saying but now there was more shuffling and the sound got clearer.

'Clever boy,' Gallagher whispered. 'He's moved closer.'

'I can't give you the whole story,' Emma was saying, 'but there's something very bad going on. I have to make contact with my father. Do you know where they are?'

Paul looked at her. Her eyes begged him to tell her. He was finding it hard to believe that she had come here to harm him.

'I'm not sure,' he said.

Dolan spoke suddenly. 'Something else here.'

A man was walking towards Emma and Paul. He wore glasses and a raincoat and he was smiling at them.

'Christ,' Dolan muttered, 'it's the guy who was looking for the tailor. Can everybody see him?'

He looked around and saw the eyes of the watchers fixed on what was happening below.

'I'm going down there,' Gallagher said.

Greeley put a hand on his arm. 'No, Tom, wait.'

The man sat down at the table with Emma and Paul. They looked startled and unsure.

'Well, now,' Parrish said. 'This is a surprise. When I walked into that office, I didn't expect to see you there, Miss Gallagher. I was looking for someone else entirely and I think you've helped me find him.' He looked at Paul. 'Much obliged. You've also made life a lot easier by getting him out of there without a fuss. But we can't sit around here. Let's go.'

'I'm not going anywhere with you,' Emma said.

Parrish looked disappointed. 'Well, I can shoot the boy here, if you like.'

His glance went beyond Emma's shoulder for a second. She turned and stared into the hard face of a man pretending to admire the bonsai trees.

'Two of them,' Dolan mumbled.

'Aw, shit,' Gallagher said.

Parrish stood. 'Up,' Humble whispered behind Emma. Slowly and nervously she and Paul rose.

'They're on the move,' Dolan said.

One of the Townhouse's security staff was wandering his way, doing the rounds. He was a burly, watchful man in a dark suit and he carried a radio receiver in his hand. As he passed Dolan, it cracked sharply and a voice said something loud and unintelligible.

'Ah, roger on that,' the security man said.

Down below they heard him and looked up. And then Parrish noticed a man at a table glance away quickly. But not quickly enough.

For just a second, he read the look.

He swung towards Paul. In the recognition and relief he saw in the boy's upward gaze he got his confirmation.

'Shit,' Dolan rasped. 'He's made me.'

It was happening all over again.

In his mind, Gallagher envisaged the hotel room, heard the sound of the shots and saw the bodies of Gaines and Dobchek.

'No!' he shouted.

He burst out of the office door, ran clattering down the stairs to the street and took off towards the Townhouse. He had no thought of what he was going to do or what he was going to find when he got there; just that he could not stay and wait.

In the shopping centre, Humble wheeled round, looking for other faces, and found them. Two men at a table above. A couple outside an Italian restaurant.

'Set-up,' Parrish hissed, pulling a Glock automatic from under his coat and pressing it into Emma's side. 'Move – move!'

They pushed her and Paul in front of them through shoppers browsing away their lunch break among the leather goods and the dried flowers and the silver ornaments with their Celtic designs. Dolan and the others stood and watched helplessly, unable to risk a shot into the crowd, and hoped the guardians at either door would get them when they came out.

Gallagher had reached the front of the building and was taking the steps two at a time. Greeley was a few yards behind him.

Dolan could not figure out where the gunmen were going. And then he saw to his dismay that there was a third door, a narrow side exit that led into Coppinger Row, which ran between the two other streets.

No one had remembered it was there. His eyes went to

the emergency exit sign that the gunmen must have seen.

Paul saw the situation at the same moment. Once out there, they could be away in seconds, down any one of a number of side streets, lost among the crowds.

He looked at Emma.

'Sorry,' he said, then hurled himself violently towards her.

He threw his arms around her body to provide what protection he could as they both fell hard across a black display stand of ethnic jewellery. The saleswoman sitting behind it was thrown backwards under the weight of the two tumbling figures and the collapsing wooden structure.

There were screams and a splintering crash as they hit the ground. Brooches, bangles and amulets fell like jangling rain across the cold stone floor.

Dolan stared in amazement. There was a second of shocked silence before the door out to Coppinger Row banged closed and he saw that the gunman with the glasses had gone.

People were shouting and running towards the commotion. Humble did not bother to conceal the gun in his hand as he headed for the stairs that would take him towards South William Street. He raised the weapon and fired two wild shots in Dolan's general direction. One ricocheted off a pillar and the other smashed a window.

The shots and the breaking glass caused the pandemonium that he intended.

He reached the top of the stairs and saw a tall man running straight towards him as if he were an obstacle to be swept out of the way.

He had seen the pictures. He knew who this was. He lifted his gun and aimed it.

Gallagher saw his death raise itself before him.

And then there was a shot.

Dolan's first bullet hit Humble between the shoulder blades and he stumbled forward as if he had been pushed. The second one was in the base of the skull and he fell dead at Gallagher's feet.

Chapter Forty-Two

Vinnie sat on his own in a room in a house at Howth to which he had been summoned to explain himself after the fuck-up at Ranelagh. How the hell did he know what had happened? She must have got out the back way or something.

'There's a lane at the rear. It leads to a kind of avenue running across. I didn't know it was there and anyway I can't be in two places at once.'

That is what he had told the man Schenk and the other two. He did not tell them about the half hour he had spent in the pub or the fact that he had fallen asleep in the car. All he told them was that he had sat and waited for a couple of hours and then when it was dark he had gone up to the house and had a look around but it was obvious there was nobody there.

Humble and Parrish had driven off a couple of hours ago and then Schenk had left him on his own in this room with the TV flickering in the corner.

'I might have something else for you to do,' he said, 'something which may make up for this disaster. Wait here for a while.'

For a nervous few minutes after he had been left by himself, Vinnie wondered if they were going to whack him. But the two hard men had gone and he did not think Schenk would try it. That was not his game. He was only a wee fellow, old too, and Vinnie could break his neck with a twist, but the guy made him shiver, whatever it was about him, and so Vinnie waited, fidgeting and unshaven, but doing what he was told.

Upstairs, Leslie stared out at the rain.

More than the weather was closing in.

When Humble and Parrish came back from Dublin they would take Dwyer away and kill him. He had served his purpose and it was pointless to have him hanging around any more. Yet as they had driven off he had been conscious that it was useful to have Dwyer here just at the moment.

In case something went wrong.

It was looking increasingly that way.

His mobile was on the windowsill beside him. It was silent now. A little while ago, Parrish had called with the startling news that Emma Gallagher had turned up in the magazine office where she had been talking to a teenage boy.

Damn it, she had not done what she was told. She was more obstinate than he would have believed.

But this boy . . .

Was it he who had started this business with the bank? Was he the person they wanted? If Emma Gallagher knew him was it possible that he was—

That he was the woman Forrest's son?

And if that was the case, then Tom Gallagher had to be involved, too.

Feeling alarm course through him, Leslie had instructed Parrish to take them both, her and the boy.

He had told them to call him every fifteen minutes.

The last call had been from Humble, a few hurried seconds. Emma Gallagher and the boy were in somewhere called the Powerscourt centre. They would get them out of there.

Leslie looked at his watch. Almost half an hour since that call. Something had happened.

He had better talk to Dwyer. He might indeed need him.

He went downstairs and opened the door of the sitting room. Dwyer was watching the lunchtime news. Leslie was tired of having to deal with him and wished there could be some other way. The man was an imbecile.

Vinnie jumped up as Leslie came in. 'Hey – big news flash there,' he said with a grin. 'Some sort of shooting at the Powerscourt Townhouse.'

Leslie made his decision.

'Let's go,' he said. 'You're taking me to the airport.'

They cordoned off the whole area around the Townhouse. The blockade paralysed the city.

In the entrance hall, Humble's body lay where it had fallen, a trail of blood startlingly red along black and white tiles.

Gallagher cradled Emma in his arms while they waited for the ambulances.

The woman who owned the jewellery stall was suffering from shock and a dislocated shoulder but Paul and Emma were unhurt, apart from a few cuts. Tomorrow there would be bruises, too, Gallagher thought, but at least there would be a tomorrow.

The horror of what he had done had drained the colour from Dolan's face. He stood with distant eyes and a cup of strong coffee which someone had handed him.

'I'll call the boy's mother,' Greeley said.

Emma looked up at her father, dazed and unable to understand how he came to be there.

So he explained. After that, she told him about Leslie and Goulding and Levy's house at Howth. As he listened, he felt some of the pain easing.

She was not one of them after all.

Suddenly, they looked at each other, registering a single thought.

The house at Howth. Was it possible Leslie was still there? Had the missing gunman been able to alert him?

Gallagher grabbed Greeley. 'Get us a car. We're going to Howth.'

They piled in, Gallagher, Emma, Greeley and a driver, and began to battle against the frozen tide of traffic. They mounted footpaths, drove across pedestrian zones, scattering passers-by, and took one-way streets the wrong way. But it was impossible.

'Christ, we're never going to get out of here,' Gallagher said.

Greeley took the handset and demanded to be patched through to the *Garda* station at Howth. He found a surprised sergeant on lunch duty and gave him the address of Levy's house.

'Get every car you can muster up there right away. Block every possible road out. Have you got that?'

'Well now, that's a bit of a tall order,' the sergeant said. 'I think I'd need to get clearance for—'

Emma leaned forward and grabbed the handset. 'Who am I speaking to?'

'Sergeant Declan Haire,' he said, responding without thinking and surprised to hear a woman's voice. He recovered himself. 'And who am I speaking to?'

'This is Emma Gallagher, the Minister for Justice. Now, Sergeant Haire, if you don't want to find yourself packing your bags for a new post in the arsehole of Mayo, I suggest you do what you're bloody well told.'

There was a second's silence while Haire took it in.

'Right away,' he said.

Greeley looked shocked.

She shrugged. 'Apparently that's the way to get things done.'

Gallagher looked out the window. They had escaped the log jam at last and he could see a signpost pointing them in the direction of Howth.

He had no great hopes of finding anyone when they got there.

Vinnie's car smelled rank and there was a mist of dust and old breath on the inside of the windscreen. Leslie, his overnight bag resting on his knee, felt contaminated just sitting in it.

'Why the airport? Where are you going?' Vinnie asked him as he drove.

'Something has cropped up in England and I need to attend to it. I've asked the others to meet us at the airport so that I can brief them. They'll explain later.'

'Why not explain now?' Vinnie wondered, surprising himself with his sudden cheek. But to hell with it. He was suspicious. Something had changed. He could see it in the man's face.

Leslie did not reply. Vinnie did not push it. He still had a vision of the big time they were offering but he was far from happy about any of this.

They reached the village of Howth. There were red lights at a crossroads and as they stopped, three police cars came at speed from nowhere, sirens shrieking, and roared up the road in the direction from which they had just come.

The lights changed and Vinnie drove on. He looked at Leslie with a question in his eyes.

'Nothing to do with us,' Leslie said. 'Just keep going. I don't want to miss my flight.'

Howth was not too far now, just another couple of miles. The radio had a message for Greeley.

'We're at the house, sir,' a voice said. 'There's no one here.'

'Damn!' Gallagher said. 'It was too much to hope for.'

'Had a word with one of the neighbours,' the voice went on. 'He saw a couple of people leaving a short time ago. A heavy-looking guy and an elderly man with a small bag. They drove away in a blue Mazda. We must have bloody well passed them on the road.'

Gallagher looked at Greeley. 'He's getting away.'

There was a junction ahead. A signpost showed a sign for Howth and Portmarnock and another one for the airport.

That was it.

'Head for the airport!' Gallagher shouted and they all lurched violently as the driver made the turn on two wheels.

Greeley picked up the handset again to set up a security block. Then he made another request.

'I want you to scan all flights going out in the next hour. See if there's anyone called Leslie or maybe Schenk booked on any of them. Quickly as you can. I know it's a long shot but you never know what might turn up.'

He turned and looked at the other two. Gallagher was holding Emma's hand. It was a hell of a way to have a reconciliation.

They reached the airport in twenty minutes, just as the vehicle checkpoint was being set up. There were eight cars ahead of them.

'Oh for Christ's sake,' Greeley said, 'I didn't mean them to stop us.'

The radio had another message.

'No one called Leslie. But there's a passenger Schenk booked on a flight to Birmingham. He's just checked in. It leaves in twelve minutes.'

'That's it!' Greeley shouted in triumph.

Their car was going nowhere so they scrambled out. Gallagher looked at his daughter in her jogging clothes. 'At least you're dressed for this,' he said.

They took off towards the terminal. Greeley had his ID in his hand and he flashed it at a young uniformed officer who was questioning someone in a car. Its driver was a red-haired man with a hang-dog look.

'What's this?' Greeley asked. The policeman had his notebook out and was writing something in it.

'His road tax is out of date, sir,' he said proudly.

'Ah for fuck's sake,' Greeley said and ran on.

Inside the terminal building, Gilbert Leslie and Vinnie Dwyer stood in the centre of the bustling departure concourse. Leslie had his bag and his boarding card for Birmingham in his hand.

Vinnie looked towards the glass entrance doors, then turned angrily.

'So where are they then?'

'They'll be here,' Leslie said, 'but I'm afraid I can't wait for them. My flight's being called. You stay where you are until they come.'

Vinnie had had enough. He snatched Leslie's bag and boarding card away from him.

'Ah well now, just hold on a minute,' he said. 'There's something fucking funny going on here. I'm tired of getting the runaround from you. When do I get my end of the deal? And what were all those police cars about? I want a fucking explanation.'

Leslie needed that bag. He looked around nervously. No one was paying any attention to them. People were streaming into the building, all of them in a hurry.

Among them was a young man in the outfit of a motorcycle messenger.

Dermot Davis had chosen today.

But as soon as he had done so, everything had started to go wrong.

First, there was yesterday's strange carry-on, with Vinnie going to Ranelagh and sitting outside somebody's house half the night. Then he had gone to a house at Howth. Dermot had sat in the bushes beneath a blanket of rain, watching until Vinnie and this man came out, got into the car and drove here to the airport.

He had had trouble finding somewhere handy to leave the bike in case he needed it in a hurry, which meant they had got inside the terminal ahead of him. He hoped he had not lost them.

At the doorway a couple of people waited in front of him while a uniformed security man waved an electronic wand over their cases.

He checked bags, Dermot saw, not people. A sash barrier alongside the door created a narrow channel towards where the guard stood and there was a long counter where doubtful baggage could be opened up and searched.

When it was his turn, Dermot put his helmet down on it with his gloves folded inside. He took off his satchel and held it out to be checked. The wand swept soundlessly over it and then the guard stepped to the side to let him past.

Dermot picked up his helmet and walked on.

He paused and gazed about.

He could not believe his eyes.

Christ, there they were. Standing about twenty yards away from him were the man with the grey hair and Vinnie Dwyer. Right in the middle of the concourse.

Vinnie was going somewhere. He had a travelling bag and a ticket in his hand.

Dermot swallowed. There were no choices left. It would have to be now. Whoever the other man was, he better not get in the way.

He slipped his hand into his helmet and clasped the small automatic hidden under the gloves. Then he began to walk as calmly as he could towards the two men.

Just a few feet behind him, the others arrived. Greeley flashed his badge at the security man and they swept past as if he did not exist.

'There!' Gallagher said and they stopped abruptly.

Gilbert Leslie.

He was not imagining it. Greeley was staring, too, rooted to the spot.

Emma broke the spell. 'Who's that with him?'

'Wouldn't you know,' Greeley said. 'Sean Donovan's right-hand man.'

Gallagher snapped out of it. He took in the situation. It looked like the two men were having an argument.

Leslie turned and saw him.

As he felt the chill of that stare, the anger of the years thudded in Gallagher's heart.

There was someone else now. Someone walking up behind Leslie's companion. A young man in motorcycle gear.

Leslie saw him too. His eyes darted to the hand taking the gun from the helmet. Instinctively, he raised his arm to cover his face and he swung his body to the side.

Vinnie turned to see what was happening.

He was frowning as the first shot hit him in the chest. As he staggered backwards, his feet giving way on the smooth floor, three more bullets followed. He fell back hard, clutching the bag, and as the life went out of his eyes he still did not understand.

There were screams of panic and people began to run

away. Leslie turned and dashed into the safety of the mounting confusion.

'Jesus Christ!' Greeley said, running towards where Vinnie lay. All around it was like a stampede.

The motorcyclist had disappeared.

Gallagher's eyes searched frantically for Gilbert Leslie.

And then above the sounds of chaos he heard a voice ringing loud and clear.

'This is the final call for passenger Schenk travelling British Midland to Birmingham. Please proceed immediately to gate A5. Passenger Schenk travelling to Birmingham, please proceed to gate A5. This flight is now closing.'

Gallagher grasped a woman in an Aer Lingus uniform.

'The departure gates. Which way?'

His grip was hurting her. She pointed across the concourse. Gallagher saw a sign with an arrow and ran towards it.

There was a security archway and people were lining up to go through. 'Excuse me,' he grunted and pushed a man out of his way.

He vaulted over a barrier alongside and he was off down the corridor before the security guards knew what was happening.

They began shouting.

'Hey, what are you doing?'

'Jesus, stop him!'

Alarm bells rang hysterically and red lights started to flash. Two of the guards sprinted after him, one of them calling on his radio for assistance.

Gallagher was surprised at his own pace but wondered

how long he could keep it up. He had to stay ahead. He had to get to Leslie.

Gate A5. Where was it?

He burst into a shopping area that was a duty-free Aladdin's cave. There were long rows of massive bottles of whiskey, tiers of designer perfume and cigarettes piled high in coloured cartons. He pushed his way between two women trying to decide which Guinness sweater to buy, the red one or the green, and left a stream of Italian invective in his wake.

Now the corridor split into two. Which way? There were directions on the wall ahead. The gate B area was to the left, gate A to the right.

Right.

It took him into another long corridor, this one with a glass wall. He could see the airport police speeding across the tarmac in open jeeps, heading in this direction. The commotion behind was growing louder and nearer but he did not turn to see. Passengers gliding in slow motion along a moving walkway stared in disbelief.

He was tiring. Someone was getting closer. Out of the corner of his eye he saw that a security guard was at his right shoulder, almost upon him, ready to dive and take him down.

He could not find the extra speed. He was finished.

'Leave him! He's with the police!' It was Greeley's voice, breathless, somewhere not far behind. The distance between him and his pursuer grew.

He passed gates one and two. Three, four. And there was five ahead with a British Midland attendant staring aghast at the mob running towards her.

Gallagher reached her first. He stopped, panting. He could hardly speak.

'Schenk,' he gasped. 'Schenk.'

'I'm sorry, Mr Schenk,' the attendant said firmly. 'We did try to page you but I'm afraid your flight has just left.'

Holding something to his chest, Gallagher stood at the big window in the viewing lounge with other people watching flights departing, imagining they could see friends and loved ones waving at them from the aircraft taxi-ing out there into the distance.

All around, the talk was of the shooting on the concourse.

Emma watched at his side.

It was a procession that never ended. From where he stood, he could see four planes, Aer Lingus, British Midland, American Airlines, Iberian Airways, lined up for take-off. More would be waiting to take their place. And so it went on, all day and all night.

Was Leslie out there on one of those planes, strapped securely into the seat he had booked under whatever name he had chosen?

Who was he today? Not Schenk, at any rate; that had been a security precaution, a false trail which they had followed enthusiastically and foolishly. What nationality was he? Where was he headed?

Gallagher turned away.

'This is a waste of time,' he said. 'He's long gone.'

The police searched the airport thoroughly but they found nothing that would give them a clue. Short of closing the airport down altogether, which is what Greeley wanted but did not get, there was nothing more they could do.

Vinnie Dwyer's killer had also disappeared without trace.

A gangland hit, broad daylight in the middle of the airport. A shoot-out in a shopping centre. Heads would roll and Greeley hoped his would not be one of them.

He looked at Emma standing with her arm around her father. She would have to resign. That would be the start of it.

Gallagher looked at the object he was holding, that he had found in Leslie's bag. It was a photograph in an ornate silver frame.

Emma peered at it. 'What's this?'

'Something he left behind,' he said. 'A memory.'

Chapter Forty-Three

No one's life was the same after that spring.

Emma made a statement, long and detailed, but even before she had finished it, the police had arrested Goulding in his office and Mulryne in his car, a suitcase in the boot. George Levy nearly made it but they got him at Dundalk, just before the border, when police boarded the train on which he was heading north, out of the jurisdiction.

With due deference to the dignity of the moment, Emma sent for fresh clothes from home and changed in the office she would use for the last time. Then she went to see the *Taoiseach* to hand in her resignation.

Others had been there before her, the *Garda* Commissioner among them, and she found the Prime Minister broken and beaten. When he held the Cabinet meeting that evening, it was not to discuss the bids for the airports but to announce that he was going to the President to tender his own resignation.

In the months that followed, Eamon Savage was elected leader of Democratic Nation and he led it to a predictable defeat in the subsequent General Election. But he is patient and he is biding his time, building the party back to respectability while he waits for what he believes will be an inevitable return to power.

The trial provided the biggest media circus Dublin had ever seen. Mulryne, Goulding and Levy were all charged with conspiracy and conspiracy to murder and all entered pleas of 'not guilty.'

As Gallagher suspected, the prosecution case was thin. It had been the Director of Public Prosecutions' view that charges should not be brought at all but political pressure from a new Government scenting blood had been impossible to withstand.

The evidence consisted chiefly of Emma's account of the confrontation with Leslie, Goulding and Levy in the house at Howth. There was nothing else. During the entire drama which had been played out at South William Street and the airport, none of the accused had been mentioned by name and nothing pointed to their involvement.

There were no incriminating documents, no peculiar bank accounts could be found and the only people who might have made useful witnesses were dead, including the man at the Townhouse. According to the FBI, he was a certain Harold Humble, a professional contract killer whose services were understood to be much in demand.

The defence lawyers were like hounds cornering a rabbit. They took Emma in their teeth and shook her viciously, without mercy.

She was jealous of Goulding, they said, a disloyal woman plotting the downfall of the man who had guided her career with such dedication.

She was a woman consumed by petty spite, bitter because Mulryne had decided to end their relationship, or so he had sworn in evidence, and she was desperate for revenge.

She was a woman who sought to destroy those who saw that she was vulnerable, they said, which was why she wanted George Levy to suffer. She had tried to persuade him to doctor her accounts so that she would evade tax liability. But he refused. At least, that is what he told the court.

Gallagher sat there helplessly, watching them destroy her.

The case collapsed and all three were freed. It was another sensation.

Within a year, Goulding had managed to drum up enough support to run for the Presidency, portraying himself as a statesman, decent and honest, someone who had devoted his life to the country, who had been wrongfully accused and then quite properly acquitted.

'God bless the good people of Ireland and the integrity of our wonderful justice system,' he told someone in an interview.

The good people of Ireland saw through him. His vote was the lowest of all four candidates. He retired from politics and moved to Sligo where he lives quietly and hopes that he will be forgotten.

'There is little chance of that,' Gallagher told Assistant Commissioner Barrett Greeley the last time they met for a drink. 'Being President would have given him somewhere to hide. But he no longer has the public eye to shield him.'

It is unlikely that Goulding sleeps much these nights.

Both George Levy and Fergal Mulryne left Ireland shortly after the trial and nothing was heard of either of them for a while. And then, about a month ago, Levy's body was found washed up on a beach in Mexico. So far there is still no sign of Mulryne.

In the United States, various federal agencies, the FBI among them, turned their attention to the Foundation Bank. On the evening before they were due to walk in through its doors, its President, a man called Heywood Corbett, went into the study at his home and apparently shot himself.

His private telephone extension, the police confirmed later, was 2740.

The Dhow Consortium disbanded. Some of its more prominent members issued statements saying how appalled they were that they had been used and that their reputation and respectability had been damaged by illegal activity on Corbett's part.

Hurll's share price took a dive for a short while. Now it is trading higher than ever before.

And at a precinct in Manhattan, the police scratched their heads for some time over the disappearance of a young man from an apartment crammed with thousands of dollars' worth of computer equipment. They never found him again.

Alan Warnock and Tom Gallagher wrote a book about it all and it became a best-seller, which helped Gallagher out of his financial hole.

But there was one piece of the story that they did not tell.

Because they did not know, nor do they now, how close Bruce Morrow's wife and children came to death.

Morrow is still the Chief Executive of Aer Rianta and Nicole has given up her part-time job to await the arrival of their third child. The privatisation issue has gone on the back burner and it is not high on the list of priorities of the new Government.

The airport business continues to grow and prosper. There is a new post in the lower management structure now, an executive in charge of security. It is an important role but Bruce Morrow knew just the man he was looking for.

Tom Gallagher was quite happy to accept.

Emma joined a firm of solicitors in north Dublin. It is not exciting work, mainly property and probate, but it is a new start. Her name is not on the door.

In the meantime, the old wounds are healing. She and her father see a lot of each other and they often meet Paul Forrest who is at University College and has a flat in Dublin with a couple of friends.

They do not see much of Kate. She spends her time shuttling between Dublin and Paris. Paul says she is talking about selling the business but keeping the house in Ranelagh when she and Philipe Foucaud get married.

Occasionally, Gallagher has regrets.

Frank Dolan never shot anyone again, nor was he ever able to reconcile himself with what he had to do that day. That was why he asked for a transfer back to Donegal and there he will probably see out the rest of his days as a policeman.

Sometimes he thinks of the dead girl, Sinead Patterson, and in a strange way he is glad that Gilbert Leslie was never caught. Her secrets, whatever they were, will stay buried with her.

At an inquest into Sean Donovan's death, the coroner

recorded an open verdict, often the case with unproven suicide or where the circumstances leave room for doubt.

No one was ever charged with the shooting of Marcus Kelly and Mr Justice Purcell and his driver. The killing of the drug dealer Dezo and his girl remain unsolved, too, as does the murder of Vinnie Dwyer.

The motorcycle messenger seemed to disappear into thin air.

He was not the only one.

Epilogue

The south of Spain is very hot this summer. In the villages on the slopes of the hills above Malaga, the sun is unremitting. But there are trees to provide shelter and it is in their cooling shadows that many of those who come to reside here have built their homes and their new lives of seclusion.

Far below, there is the Costa Del Sol, where the people with the yachts and the money and the gold chains pursue their pleasures, but in villages like this one life moves at a more delicate pace. Here anything unusual is noticed, even a breath of wind.

There is no breeze today as the man walks up the hill from the village and steps off the curving main road on to a narrow, almost concealed path that winds through the bushes towards his home, an apartment in a small block up there among the trees.

In a string bag he carries the things he has just bought at the market: olive oil, garlic, fresh tomatoes and peppers.

Signor Guillermo Vialli, a slightly built man of slowly advancing years, is a retired businessman from Naples and he has lived here for two years. The hair beneath his straw hat is silver and he has a grey moustache which makes him look very much like the picture on his Italian passport.

The hillside path provides him with the daily exercise he needs but sometimes, in the heat, he finds it too much. Near the top, he pauses. He turns to wipe his brow and looks down towards the village, which is ablaze under the sun. The colours of the geraniums and bougainvillaea seem impossibly vivid. From somewhere alongside him there is the scent of wild rosemary.

Something is moving in the village. There is a car pulling into the square, a car he has not seen before, a white car with a Barcelona plate. Apart from its unfamiliarity, something about the way it is driven, a little too urgently, alerts him.

It parks outside the bodega. Two men get out and stand beside it, while the third goes in. If he is looking for information he will not get it there. In the bodega they are wary of strangers.

The man comes out and when he does Signor Vialli has a clear view of his face.

He cannot see the eyes behind the dark glasses but he knows how cool and watchful they can be.

For a while the men sit at a shaded table and sip cool drinks while they eye the stillness of the village around them and wait. After half an hour and a last look round, they drive off.

Tomorrow they will return. Tomorrow when Parrish asks about the friend they are looking for, someone will know and will point up the hill to show them the way.

But tomorrow will be too late.